The Dragon's Fury

First published by Emily LK 2023

Copyright © 2023 by Emily L K

All rights reserved. No part of this publication may be reproduced, stored or transmitted in any form or by any means, electronic, mechanical, photocopying, recording, scanning, or otherwise without written permission from the publisher. It is illegal to copy this book, post it to a website, or distribute it by any other means without permission.

This novel is entirely a work of fiction. The names, characters and incidents portrayed in it are the work of the author's imagination. Any resemblance to actual persons, living or dead, events or localities is entirely coincidental.

Third edition

ISBN: 9798390441763

This book was professionally typeset on Reedsy. Find out more at reedsy.com

Prologue

The victor of war writes the histories, but what if the loss outweighs the triumph?

What if the victor doesn't feel like he's had a victory at all?

Writing the histories, however much we embellish them, will not bring back the dead.

- Rowan of the House of Auksas, Karalis of Tauta.

Chapter One

The rain had been falling relentlessly for almost four days, turning the ground underfoot to slush.

Any normal person would be indoors by the fire on a day like this, Cori reflected bitterly, not out frolicking in the mud.

Though frolicking was hardly the word to describe her dogged jog through the undergrowth. Her pants beneath her knees were caked in mud and even as she lept to avoid an overflowing stream, she slipped and landed hard on her backside, a pained breath hissing through her teeth.

"A bit further," Rowan urged from up ahead.

"I'll 'a bit further' you," Cori growled under her breath, using the back of her hand to wipe mud and water from her face. She pushed herself to her feet and, ignoring the pain in her side, glanced at the sky. The sun's position wasn't visible through the clouds but she willed darkness to hurry before resuming her uneven trot after Rowan.

Their time together after escaping Cadmus' palace and destroying Daiyu's mind with the Deathsong was short lived. Within hours they'd become aware of someone looking for them; Adro, Daniyl and the rest of the Sarkans House to be exact.

CHAPTER ONE

Unsure if they had enough magic left after their fight with Daiyu to know if they could face the others, they had decided to run. But they hadn't expected the others to be so persistent in their chase.

To add to the turmoil that the rain created, Rowan's hum crashed over Cori in angry waves. It was a tactic, she knew, to throw - and warn - the others off their trail and at first it had seemed to confuse them, but three days in, they were as close to catching them as ever.

Cori didn't bother to try to hide her own Hum. Not that she would have anyway; now that her barriers were finally down, there was no way she was putting them up again. She would have preferred to fight. Although she could feel their Hums almost constantly, none of the Sarkans House tried to speak to her.

"Enough," Rowan said finally, stopping beneath the boughs of an old fig tree that provided little shelter from the rain.

Cori slipped and slid into their temporary camp site and sank to the ground with a groan. Rowan sat down beside her, tugging her shirt up and placing his hand over the wound Daiyu had given her in their recent battle.

With their unrelenting pace, the healing Rowan had initially done on her wound was barely holding together. After their first day of running, Cori had vehemently objected to Rowan re-healing the wound. She was afraid of what he might see in her mind; how far into her past he might be inclined to delve.

"I won't *see* anything," he told her when she voiced her fears. "I can only perceive your thoughts and feelings, and only ones that you have at the time of healing."

Reluctantly, she had let him perform the healing song. She

needn't have worried so much; the song lulled her, easing her aching muscles and the pain that stabbed at her side. All she could think about was sleep.

Now, she lay in the rain, drawing air into her searing lungs, and welcomed Rowan's healing touch. She was beyond exhausted, her mind was still frayed from the use of the Deathsong that had been housed behind her barriers for over two hundred years, and neither she nor Rowan had recuperated their strength after their flight from Cadmus' palace.

"We should let them catch up," Cori said when she caught her breath. The pain in her side lessened but wasn't fully abated; Rowan didn't have the skills to fully heal her, just keep her in one piece.

Rowan snorted at her statement. "And then what?"

"We'll kill them." At this point, she was willing to risk a mental burn out rather than keep running.

He'd probably read the thought from her mind, connected as they were through the healing song. Still, he took a long moment to think about it. The healing song abruptly stopped, as did the angry radiating of his Hum.

"I don't want to kill them," he finally decided. Cori had expected that to be his answer.

"I don't think I can go on much longer," she admitted after a pause.

"I know."

He didn't offer an alternative, and she didn't ask for one. If he believed the best thing for them was to run, then she trusted that was all they could do. She placed her hand over his where it still rested on her midriff and closed her eyes.

CHAPTER ONE

* * *

Rowan woke her with a kiss.

"It's still dark," she groaned, though she let him pull her to her feet, muscles screaming in protest. Sleeping on the wet ground had left her shirt damp, and she shivered.

"They kept moving through the night," he informed her and he sounded as weary as she felt.

They stood for a long moment, facing each other. Cori despaired at the thought of yet another day on the run. She hoped their pursuers would give up soon.

"What would it take to... stop them?" Rowan asked, and she knew he'd been mulling on her suggestion from the night before.

"A simple strengthening song and I'd be able to take them on," she assured him.

He smiled tiredly. "Weave it then, but don't use it unless I say." He turned away but paused. "Please don't kill Adro," he requested and then they were off, setting a ground eating pace through the wet undergrowth. Within minutes, Cori was soaked through and muddy again.

Until now, they'd been heading southward along the edge of the Western Range. Today, Rowan set an easterly course. They ran without speaking until the grey sky lightened, heralding the arrival of dawn.

The rain eased as the day progressed but it made their path no less treacherous. The way was steep and slippery; even Rowan had trouble keeping his footing.

To take her mind off her aching body, Cori wove a strengthening spell. She revelled in the ability to use her Hum again, even though her magic was depleted from releasing the Deathsong.

It wasn't long before they heard the sounds of their pursuers crashing through the bush behind them. Cori glanced back to see flashes of coloured clothing through the trees. With a savage grin, she flexed her fingers, readying herself, and increased her pace to catch up to Rowan. When she was beside him, he pointed ahead to where the trees were thinning. He was leading them to open ground.

"Rowan!" Adro hollered from behind. They were almost upon them.

Cori burst from the trees first. She kept running with Rowan right behind. The moment Adro was free of the trees, Rowan stopped and spun on the spot. Not expecting him to halt, Adro almost collided with him. Rowan grabbed the front of Adro's shirt and yanked him forward.

"What do you want?" He hissed.

"whoa!" Cori skidded back between the two men, placing a hand on each of their chests to pry them apart. Rowan might have a superior skill when it came to swordsmanship, but she doubted he'd be able to beat Adro in a physical fight.

Adro didn't respond, and Cori realised that he was speaking to Rowan via the Hum. A moment later the first of the Sarkans appeared from the trees, Daniyl at their head. Rowan watched them over Adro's shoulder but he didn't move. Cori stayed where she was between the two of them.

"You want me to *what?*" Rowan said in surprise. His hand tightened on Adro's shirt and Cori increased the pressure on their chests; a warning to keep things civil.

"Lead us," Adro clarified, "to finish Daiyu, like you said."

"Guide us," Daniyl corrected as he reached them. "The Dijem don't have leaders." he bent double, hands on knees, to recover his breath.

"You were quick to replace Jarrah, Daniyl," Rowan said with a mere glance at the other man. It was then that Cori noticed the freshly inked dragon scales on Daniyl's fingertips. The sight of them was unnerving. She didn't like the idea of Daniyl having any capacity of authority. Just looking at him made her skin crawl.

"In any case," Rowan continued before Daniyl could explain himself, "Daiyu is defeated. Cori and I have seen to it already." He let go of Adro's shirt with a shove and turned away, ignoring Daniyl's disbelieving mutters. Adro made to follow Rowan but Cori stopped him.

"Don't," she warned. She shot Daniyl a filthy look before following Rowan.

"What about Cadmus?" Adro called after them. "Did you defeat him too?"

Rowan stopped short. "No," he replied without turning around.

That Cadmus was Rowan's father was common knowledge after Melita's outburst a few weeks ago, but the matter of Rowan and Cori's loyalty was still in question as far as the other Dijem were concerned.

"Then let us help you kill him. That's still what you want, isn't it?"

Rowan didn't speak for a long moment.

"We need them," Cori urged softly. Her heart thumped unevenly at the possibilities of Adro's suggestion.

"To waste time with ridiculous House politics? To have to discuss and vote on every single move?" Rowan started to walk away again. "No, we don't need them."

Cori waited until they were out of earshot of the others

before grabbing Rowan's arm and turning him back to face her.

"You wouldn't have to concern yourself with House politics if you put yourself above them."

"You want me to make myself Karalis?" He scowled. "Put myself on the throne the way Cadmus did?"

"You wouldn't be crowning yourself," Cori reasoned. "The realm put you on the throne fifteen hundred years ago. Legitimately, it's yours."

"If we're delving into legalities," he hissed, grabbing the front of her shirt, much the way he had with Adro. "Then the throne is actually yours; you held it after I did, why don't you lead them?"

Cori smacked his hand away but took hold of his shirt to stop him leaving. She yanked him forward so that their noses almost touched. "They don't want me, they want you. We need them, and we need an army. We will not beat Cadmus just the two of us - he's thwarted us twice already. *We* need you."

The fight left Rowan, his furious expression replaced with worry, self doubt.

"I don't know how to lead them. I can't manipulate their minds the way I did with the Hiram."

"You won't need to," Cori told him softly, trying to keep the anticipation from her voice. "They *want* you to lead them. Just be yourself."

Rowan stared over her shoulder to where Adro and Daniyl waited. They seemed to be bickering about something, both gesturing with wild arms in opposite directions. Rowan's bottom lip caught between his teeth in a gesture of indecisiveness. Cori waited.

CHAPTER ONE

"Can I have some time to think about it?" He asked finally.

"Of course," she conceded, though she couldn't help feeling prematurely triumphant. She let go of his shirt, and he walked away from her. She watched him for a moment before turning and trudging back to the others. She remembered belatedly that last she'd seen these people, they'd accused her of being in leagues with Cadmus. She was thankful she had the strengthening spell ready.

"He's thinking about it," she told Adro when he opened his mouth to ask.

"What does he have to think about?" Daniyl whined. "There's only two of you in the House, surely it's a simple yes or no to come back to the table." Cori and Adro simply stared at him.

Over the next hour, the rest of the Sarkans House trickled out of the forest. Adro filled Cori in on what had been happening after she and Rowan had left the others. Starch had fled Tuluyan when Daiyu had attacked and hadn't been seen or heard from since. The House of Uaine had also decided that a war against Cadmus was futile and went their separate ways. Adro had then waited for the Sarkans to vote on a course of action. They'd elected Daniyl as their elder, but the majority had also voted to seek Rowan's help in finishing the war, much to Daniyl's displeasure.

"When we went back to bury the dead, I got your pack from under your bed," Adro told her in a quiet voice when she noticed that the horses - including her grey mare and Rowan's dapple colt - had been brought along. Adro retrieved her pack from a saddlebag and gave it to her. She opened it up, relieved to see, along with the clothes that had been shoved in there, Orin's book still within.

"Thank you," she told him earnestly. She was grateful Adro was by her side; the rest of the Sarkans House still served her with distrustful glances.

"What's that noise?" Daniyl asked suddenly, wrinkling up his nose as if he'd smelt something bad. He, Myce and Melita were standing closer to Cori than she'd realised. She suddenly had several Hums brush over her mind - all sounding similar except for Adro's, which had its own nuances.

"It's Cori's Hum," Melita said with a smile - she'd felt Cori's magic before. "She's raised her barriers." Cori didn't return the other woman's smile. In her mind, Melita was a traitor for revealing Rowan's secret about his father.

"Why does it sound so… different?" Daniyl queried rudely. Adro scowled at him and before Cori had the chance to defend herself he said, "shove off, Daniyl. I think it sounds nice," he added kindly to Cori. She blushed.

"There he is!" Someone exclaimed and Cori looked away from their makeshift camp to see Rowan striding back through the drizzling rain. She ran to meet him.

"Well?" She asked breathlessly when she reached him. She wanted his answer before the others caught up.

"You'll do as I say at all times," he told her, somewhat awkwardly, and she could tell he was trying to fit back into a role he hadn't been in for a long time. Her stomach tightened at what that meant. "You cannot show me defiance, especially in front of the others."

"When do I ever show defiance?" She scoffed. Rowan raised an eyebrow at her. "Fine," she muttered. "No defiance."

"You'll join us then?" Myce asked as Adro and the Sarkans caught up. They formed a semi-circle as Rowan nodded to

CHAPTER ONE

Myce.

"Good. Let's vote on the next course of action," Daniyl said authoritatively, rubbing his freshly tattooed hands together. Cori could tell that he was attempting to take charge of the situation. "I propose -"

"No," Rowan cut him off with a ringing tone. "No voting. I will hear your advice if it's warranted but from this moment on the Houses are abolished and my word as the Karalis is law."

Chapter Two

The response to Rowan's declaration from the Sarkans was mixed but Cori could tell by those who clapped and cheered who supported Rowan over Daniyl as their leader. Even Melita, who Cori had always considered to be a staunch supporter of her own House, smiled a little at Rowan's words.

"Karalis?" Daniyl spluttered. He held up his hands to show the elder tattoos. "The Dijem don't have a ruler for a reason!"

"Those reasons are no longer valid," Adro told Daniyl sharply. "All the elders who know anything about Cadmus are either dead or have abandoned the cause. Rowan knows what he's doing so you need to let him."

Rowan put a hand on Adro's shoulder to calm him. To Daniyl he said, "I'm only agreeing to do this until Cadmus is dead, after which point you can re-establish your House if that's what you're so inclined to do. I-" he stopped, noticing someone at the front of the crowd that surrounded him. Cori followed his gaze, and with a groan of disbelief, she saw Jonothan standing there.

Jonothan was a child of no more than thirteen years and was the rare offspring of two Dijem parents. Parents who were not currently with him.

CHAPTER TWO

"What is he doing here?" Rowan demanded.

"Oh, he wanted to join the fight. I agreed that he could come along," Daniyl said with a dismissive wave. Jonothan stepped forward proudly, as if expecting praise for his bravery, but Rowan paid him no heed, instead rounding furiously on Daniyl.

"He wanted to come along? You brought a boy to a war you daft prick! And what did his parents say? Please tell me his parents know that he's here."

Daniyl's uncomfortable silence was all the answer Rowan needed.

"I want to be here!" Jonothan piped up indignantly.

"What you want is irrelevant," Rowan retorted. "I don't need children underfoot when starting a war!"

Jonothan stepped back, looking crestfallen, but Rowan had already turned to continue berating Daniyl.

"He's in your care until we can find someone from Uaine to take him back. If he gets hurt in any way so help me..." He didn't finish the sentence but the threat was implied. Cori hoped Rowan would ask her to carry out any punishment Daniyl had coming. No more was said after that and the matter of Jonothan was put to rest.

Rowan moved towards the makeshift camp and Adro and the Sarkans fell in around him. Everyone was speaking at once, vying for his attention.

Cori watched, fascinated, as a hierarchy was established. He chose them with his body language. Full attention was given to Adro when he spoke, as was Myce and an older woman that Cori had occasionally seen with Jarrah at the keep. Daniyl's words were tolerated, and Melita was given the cold shoulder. Clearly Rowan had not forgotten nor forgiven her betrayal of his lineage.

As she watched the group walk away, she remembered, somewhat wryly, her short stint as Karaliene and how she'd had to fight the whole way to the top of her own pecking order. With only a few words Rowan had established himself as their ruler, even if he despised being there.

What are you doing? His voice penetrated her thoughts, and she realised how far she had fallen behind. She hurried to catch up in time to hear Adro say, "we'll need a base if we're going to build an army."

"What about the keep at Tuluyan?" The older woman suggested.

"Most of it has been destroyed. We would have to rebuild," someone else said.

"Rebuilding will take time and resources that we don't have."

"What about basing ourselves in the city? Tengah isn't far north of here."

"Hearth's loyalties are with Cadmus," Cori spoke up. She hadn't meant to; at this stage she'd just wanted to listen. Rowan, however, indicated that she should continue. "We would have to fight for Tengah and there isn't enough of us."

"Where would you suggest then?" Daniyl asked her condescendingly. Oh, she hated him. She didn't care where she fell in Rowan's hierarchy but it would have to be above Daniyl.

"Lautan," she said. "It was the estate of the Karalis before, it should be again."

"We would have to fight for Lautan too," Adro pointed out.

"Lautan is held by rogues and scoundrels, an easier fight than any other city." Rowan pondered for a moment then nodded. "Yes, we'll go to Lautan."

"We may not have to fight," Cori added hesitantly. The strange look Rowan gave her was not without reason; she wasn't normally one to suggest a peaceful route. She wished they wouldn't stare at her. She was particularly nervous about what she was about to disclose. "I... may still have the land titles for the Auksas estates."

Most looked confused. Some shrugged, muttering to their neighbours. None of them, bar Adro and Rowan, had ever connected her with the brief war that had taken place five hundred years ago. Rowan's look was one of disbelief.

Why would you still have those? He asked through the Hum.

Just in case, she said, a little bashful. She didn't want to confess that they'd been held in safekeeping for a situation exactly like this.

Well, where are they?
Balforde, in Shaw.

***

It took more than a few hours for everyone to get themselves prepared for the trip. Those from the Sarkans House were not used to such quick decisions being made.

Cori didn't mind so much. She relished the opportunity to sit quietly by the fire for a few hours to rest her aching body. If only the rain would stop so she could dry out properly.

Nobody paid her any attention, intent as they were on the plans to resurrect the throne. She watched them bustle about her and wondered where Daiyu was at that moment.

Rowan had told her they'd broken the dragon's mind when they'd unleashed the Deathsong on her. She could only assume that it had been a similar thing that had happened to Rowan's mind when they had battled the green dragon all those years ago.

She had trouble believing that the expansive mind of the dragon could be broken. She remembered the way Daiyu had sung to her when she had been under the dragon's control at Cadmus's palace. The exact songs were a foggy memory, and she couldn't think of a reason why the dragon would sing to her when they were supposed to be enemies. Cadmus had told her and Rowan about the Dragon Magic and she guessed that that was what Daiyu had been attempting to teach her. Why though? Cori couldn't help but feel like it was a trap set by Cadmus.

She wondered where Daiyu was now. Did the dragon still lay where she had fallen, or had she managed to find her way back to Cadmus? What would he do with a dragon who could no longer provide him with near-limitless power? Cori hoped he would look after her.

She sat up straight, heart thumping unevenly; where had that thought come from?

A short sword thunked on the ground beside her and she looked up to find Rowan standing over her.

Their eyes met. Rowan's were a dull honey colour - a sign of his depleted magic - and she guessed that hers must be similar. It was wonderful to openly use her Hum but it would be even better when she was back to her full strength.

Rowan's expression was sombre as he surveyed her and she could tell he was still second guessing his decision.

"Sit down," she offered, shifting a little and patting the log beside her. He glanced back to the others to see that they were all preoccupied with sorting and packing saddlebags before sitting down beside her. He let out a heavy sigh and closed his eyes.

"I don't want to do this," he said in a low voice. Cori squeezed his leg.

"I know. It's the right thing to do though."

He nodded then scrubbed his hands over his face.

"A good night's sleep wouldn't go astray," he muttered. Cori had to agree.

Someone called Rowan's name, and he stood up, carefully schooling his expression as he did. Once more he was looking down on her.

"Stay close," he requested before returning to the others.

Cori watched him go and had the thought that she should get up and help, but the ache in her legs and the sharp pain in her half-healed wound stayed her. She would help later.

* * *

The farmland they rode through was familiar to Cori and she knew they weren't far from Balforde.

Although she hadn't been to the township in several hundred years, she was anxious about returning. She hoped that the Coffee House was still in operation and, more importantly, that it still functioned as a safe house. Her safe house.

Rowan rode at the head of their column, as he had for the past week of their travels. On one side of him was Adro, on the other was Daniyl.

Daniyl, since accepting that Rowan was now the Karalis, had not left his side. He still asserted his authority as leader of the Sarkans and Rowan allowed it, to an extent. They needed the Sarkans on side and therefore they needed Daniyl.

It hadn't stopped Rowan confiding in Cori late one night that if the opportunity to quietly dispose of Daniyl ever arose, he would take it. Since he'd said so, Cori had been fantasising about the different ways in which she could kill Daniyl without anyone finding out.

She rode back from the three men. So far she'd avoided getting involved in any of their planning and discussion - Rowan would ask if he wanted her advice - but she stayed close enough to hear most of what was happening. Right now, Adro and Daniyl were arguing about where they thought they might be able to find Cadmus. It was an argument that many in their entourage had been having and nobody had any great suggestions.

Kill me, Rowan begged. She smiled at his back and sent him a mental touch of sympathy. She could only imagine how tedious it must be for him.

The houses scattered through the farms were slowly getting closer together and the dirt road evened out, becoming wider and then paved. People in the town stopped to stare at the procession of one hundred Dijem coming down the main street.

They stopped when they reached the town square, an area lined with market stalls and cafes and centred around a trickling fountain.

"Cori," Rowan called as he dismounted from Mischief. Cori led her grey mare over to him just as a young lad came running from the stables behind a nearby inn.

"Water and food for your horses, sir?" He gasped as he reached Rowan.

"How much?" Rowan asked. The lad looked up the line of

CHAPTER TWO

Dijem still entering the town, pretending to count the horses. Cori doubted he knew enough numbers to get them all.

"Four gold coins for the lot," the boy said. It was an ambitious amount but Rowan didn't hesitate to reach into his pocket and withdraw the funds. He dropped them into the lad's hand. The boy stared at them in disbelief before running back towards the stables yelling "Pa! Pa!"

"Let's go," Rowan said to Cori. While Daniyl and Adro were distracted, she led Rowan across the square to the Coffee House.

The establishment was without doubt still the most popular place in town, with patrons lounging on the front verandah, and strolling through the rose garden at the side of the building.

Cori pushed open the front door and, stomach fluttering, made her way through the tables to the bar.

There was a woman there with long dark hair and when she turned to greet Cori and Rowan, Cori felt as though a knife had been driven through her heart, opening old wounds. All these generations and Saasha's gene was still strong in her descendants.

"Wow," Rowan said under his breath and Cori knew he noticed the same thing.

"Hello there," the woman said in a breathy voice. She set her cleaning cloth aside and gave them her full attention. "My name is Bel. What can I get for you today?"

"Bel," Cori said slowly, trying not to choke on her words. Her fists clenched and unclenched atop the bar, nails biting into her palms with each movement. "What a beautiful name. My mother's name was Bel."

Bel's eyes darted between Cori and Rowan. Her hand

fluttered over her heart, and her eyes widened.

"Oh my," she gasped. She looked as if she might faint. "Never in my lifetime did I think... Ailey, Ailey come quick!" Bel suddenly took off and disappeared into a back room.

"Well that was helpful," Cori muttered. She avoided the stares of the patrons as they looked for the source of the commotion.

Rowan didn't respond to her and when she looked sideways at him she found him staring, wide eyed and lips parted, at the wall above the bar. She followed his gaze to the sword mounted there. Its pommel was golden and wrought in the shape of a dragon's head. Black gem eyes glittered. It was a sword for a king. Before she could stop him, Rowan climbed up on the bar top and lifted the sword from its brackets. He hefted it in his right hand and admired the gleaming blade.

"I can't believe you kept this," he said in awe.

"It was Saasha who organised it all," Cori said awkwardly. People were really staring now. "If it had been left up to me, I probably would have burned the lot of it."

Rowan turned the sword in his hand, letting the light glint off the blade.

"I think I might have picked the wrong sister," he joked. Cori smacked his leg.

"Get down."

"Karaliene." Bel had returned with another woman - presumably Ailey. "It's a pleasure to meet you." She bowed low, and Cori groaned.

"Please don't do that."

Ailey ignored her, instead making a broad sweeping motion with her arm. "Please, follow me!"

Cori and Rowan, still holding his sword, followed her

CHAPTER TWO

around the bar and into the back room. A hatch in the floor was opened, revealing a staircase. Ailey gestured that Cori and Rowan should go on without them.

"We'll bring you some coffee," Bel called after them.

The room they entered was like a small library. The walls were adorned with bookshelves, intersected here and there by windows near the ceiling. A stone table, tall enough to stand at, was in the middle of the room and atop it sat a wooden chest.

Cori started around the walls, running her fingers over the spines of the books as she went. Some of the older ones were from Rowan's library in Lautan. Most though were ones she'd sent here throughout her travels for safe keeping. Not that she had ever been back here to check that they'd even arrived.

"Saasha really did all this?" Rowan asked from the table where he'd opened the chest and pulled from within a stack of yellowed parchment.

"I'd never realised the extent of her efforts but yes, she organised this. She told me, when last I saw her, not to worry about my affairs because she had put them in order. My affairs. As if I was the one who would perish, not she." Cori stopped and pressed her hands to her face, finding it difficult to breathe. It was all too much to be back in this place that she'd spent so long running from. A space her sister had created for her that she'd rejected.

"I was a rubbish sister," she whispered and her throat tightened painfully.

"You were not," Rowan assured her. He moved around the table and pulled her into an embrace. "Look, she left this for you." He held up a worn slip of parchment to read. Cori took it. She could almost smell the flowery soap that Saasha had always used in her hair.

My sister, my friend, my Karaliene.

I love you and I'm proud of you. I know you will find the happiness you deserve.

- Saasha.

"Oh," Cori choked back a sob and clutched the note to her chest. She squeezed her eyes closed, willing time to reverse so she could see her sister just one last time. Rowan kissed her hair and wrapped his arms tightly around her. She clung to him; the last person alive to know her childhood, to know how desperately she wanted her family back, even just for a moment.

"Come on, Little One, let's find what we need."

They moved together to the table. Rowan stood close, his arm a comforting weight on her shoulders as she began sorting through the rest of the parchment from the chest. Some were official documents such as the land titles and Rowan's original declaration as Karalis - both the carefully preserved originals as well as copies - but most were missives between Saasha, Antoni, Orin and other heads of states. Most discussed her whereabouts, her action in the wars she had created, the factions she had fought.

After her friends had died, the missives continued between Saasha's daughter-descendants and other interested parties. They continued to discuss her whereabouts - mostly by tracing the origins of the books she sent. After a time they began to refer to themselves as the Karaliene's Coterie. One of them had even dedicated his life to tracking her down. It sounded as if he'd gotten very close to finding her before letters from him abruptly ceased. They'd intended to entice her back to the throne.

As she read each missive, she set it aside, and Rowan picked it up. His eyes were wide, unable to hide his fascination with the Karaliene's Coterie.

"They adored you," he observed as they finished the last of the letters.

"They adored the idea of me," she corrected him bitterly. She stacked the letters up and placed them back in the chest. Their praise of her only made her feel her failings all the more keenly.

"Why do you doubt yourself so much?" Rowan leaned against the table and looked her in the eye. She felt her cheeks heat with embarrassment but she held his gaze.

"They wanted me to be something that I couldn't be. I was good at killing people. I wasn't good at leading people, not like you were."

Rowan snorted derisively. "You compare yourself to me? Why?"

Cori shrugged. "You make it seem so easy. You never have trouble making tough decisions."

"Just because I make decisions doesn't mean they're the right ones." He sighed and looked down. "It doesn't mean I don't dwell on the wrong ones, or lie awake at night knowing that the decisions I make affect people other than myself."

Cori watched him. She'd never seen him so doubtful of himself and she didn't know if it was because he revealed more of himself to her now than he had before or if she knew the signs to look for because she so often experienced the feeling herself.

The sound of footsteps on the stairs halted their conversation and Bel appeared a moment later with two mugs in hand.

"Sorry," she said in her breathy voice. "I forgot to offer you some food as well. Are you hungry? I can have the kitchens prepare something for you?"

"That would be very kind," Rowan said, accepting the mug of coffee from her. "We'll also need food enough for a hundred to get us to Lautan. That won't be a drain on your resources?"

"Of course not! It's been a good harvest this year." Bel handed the second mug to Cori before stepping back and staring at her in awe. "I truly cannot believe my luck. Twenty generations and you simply walk into my Coffee House!"

Cori didn't know what to say. She was torn between the guilt of not returning to Saasha's descendants earlier and wishing she'd not come back at all. Seeing how much Bel looked like Saasha also stirred up the old feelings of loneliness that she'd felt all those years ago when her sister had died. She glanced at Rowan to find him trying not to laugh at Bel's theatrics. When he noticed the expression on Cori's face, however, he instantly sobered.

"Bel," he said to divert the woman's attention away from Cori, "is the Karaliene's coterie still in operation?"

Bel nodded to Rowan, "yes it is," then she frowned. "Who are you?"

Cori couldn't help the laughter that burst from her lips. Perhaps Bel had inherited her tendency for silly questions. Rowan merely smiled.

"Just a servant of the Karaliene, as you yourself are," he said and Cori's laughter turned to a scowl. "I'd like to send them a letter and see if they might come to our aid."

"Of course. I have no doubt that they'll be delighted to be

of assistance. I'll get you a pen and some paper." Bel retreated up the stairs once more.

"Don't worry," Rowan said when Cori continued to glower at him. "I'll sign the letters with my own name."

"And Bel?" She prompted.

"And I'll set Bel straight. Really, would it be so bad to be the Karaliene again?"

Cori maintained a stony silence. Rowan sighed and drummed his fingers on the table.

"I've been thinking about how to deal with Cadmus," he finally changed the subject, "and I think we need to find out more about that spell that Jarrah used on those kids. I can only think that it's a song reserved for elders to deal out punishment."

"Cadmus told me that it was the Old Magic," Cori said.

"You two talked a lot then?" Rowan asked lightly. He didn't quite meet her eye and she could tell he was uneasy. Until now, they hadn't spoken about their captivity in Cadmus' palace.

"I wouldn't say there was a mutual enjoyment about it. He talked, I listened. Sometimes I managed to get a threat or two in."

Rowan's lips quirked, consoled by her words. "What did he say about the spell?"

"Nothing helpful. Well, he said he wouldn't tell me about it, he only said that Jarrah had retained some of the Old Magic and used it to kill those young Dijem."

"They belonged to Cadmus then."

"He used them. They didn't belong to him," Cori said, more tartly than she intended. She didn't want to think that Cat, the quirky and all-too-innocent girl she had befriended in the kitchens, had intentionally worked for Cadmus.

"Sorry," Rowan said, following her line of thought.

"It's all right. You weren't being malicious." Cori sighed and rubbed her hand over her eyes. "There might be something here." She waved back towards the bookshelves. "These books are from all over. Maybe the Dijem from the south wrote something down."

"No harm in looking." Rowan moved to the closest bookshelf and pulled a tome down. For the next few hours they combed through book after book for any information that might help them in the defeat of Cadmus. There were books on sword skills, recipes, natural healing remedies for nomad travellers and even one or two on the finer arts of Hiram magic. There were only a few on the Dijem and those that outlined any songs or spells were even more limited. The eventual arrival of Adro, Daniyl, Myce and Melita interrupted their progress.

"We've been looking for you for hours!" Daniyl said as they entered the room. Cori knew that Rowan had already spoken to Adro via the Hum so Daniyl's inability to locate them didn't bother her.

"What are you doing down here?" Melita asked. Her tone was polite, well aware that she was still out of favour with Rowan.

"Looking for a way to defeat Cadmus," Rowan explained. He didn't look at Melita, instead his eyes followed Daniyl as he moved around the room. "Daiyu might be out of the equation, but I don't doubt that Cadmus would have reserves full of her magic."

"What about a Deathsong?" Myce asked. Both Cori and Rowan blanched.

"Too long to create," Rowan said weakly. "We need something else."

"We'll help you look then." Daniyl pulled a book from the shelf and flipped it open. Cori felt entirely uneasy about Daniyl knowing about this room and it seemed Rowan did too by the way he continued to watch the other man with narrowed eyes. Cori looked back down at the book she had open on the table before her. She flipped through a few pages and skimmed the words.

The Hum requires a regular release to cleanse the mind of negative energies and rebuild positive energies. After the release, the user will experience heightened clarity, and an increased magical capacity.

Be warned: if a user delays between regular releases, or has an overcharged emotional experience, they may lose control during the release, resulting in mental damage or mental burnout. It is recommended that in these circumstances, a user releases with another Hum user present to anchor them and draw them back to reality before damage can be done.

Cori tapped the page with her finger then slowly closed the book. That was interesting. She'd never considered that Hum Intoxication, the relinquish of control of one's Hum, might serve a purpose. It was something she would need to think about, but she didn't want to draw the other's attention to it.

Chapter Three

"Find anything interesting?" Daniyl asked. It took every ounce of self control Cori had not to jump. She hadn't realised how close he'd sidled up to her.

"Piss off," she told him irritably. He sneered at her but moved away.

Let's go, she told Rowan. He snapped his book shut.

"Let's go," he said aloud to the others.

Cori looked down at the book still under her hands. The title was faded beyond comprehension but she decided to take it with her; it might contain other interesting snippets about the Hum.

Cori was the last to leave the room, and she met Ailey at the top of the stairs. Ailey was fairer than Bel, but still had Saasha's sharp cheekbones and intelligent eyes. She could even pick out mannerisms that her own mother had possessed, such as the small reassuring smile that played constantly at her lips, or the way she folded her hands neatly before her while she waited for Cori to speak.

"That blonde man," Cori pointed to Daniyl where he was taking a seat with Myce and Melita in the cafe. "If he ever tries to come back here, stop him at whatever cost."

To her credit, Ailey nodded, eyes blazing fiercely. Then

CHAPTER THREE

she suddenly smirked.

"You better go and save your Karalis from Bel," she said coyly.

"Worked it out, did she?" Cori muttered. She left the back room while Ailey closed up the hidden library and leaned on the bar in the cafe. She spotted Rowan and Bel by the door. Bel was berating him, her expression hard and a finger pointing accusingly at his chest. Rowan was letting her speak and Cori read the word 'liar' on her lips more than once. When Bel was done, Rowan placed a hand on her arm and began speaking earnestly. Cori couldn't see his lips, but she could imagine the tale he was spinning to cover his earlier untruths.

"So is what they say true? You're not the Karaliene any more?" Ailey appeared at her side and leaned on the bar as well. She looked to be around the same age as Cori - in human years at least - and the frank stare she gave Cori reminded her of Saasha. She realised that Ailey may be the true Coterie member, not Bel.

"I was only ever a caretaker in his place, and a poor one at that," Cori said truthfully with a gesture at Rowan. "I denounced any claim to the throne before my sister, Saasha died. Surely she passed that down the line with all the other information?"

"She did," Ailey admitted reluctantly, "but we didn't want to believe that you'd forsaken the realm to the false Karalis." There was a sense of betrayal in Ailey's words that surprised Cori. Did they really feel so strongly about the Karaliene?

"I haven't forsaken the realm to Cadmus," Cori told her, "I'm just not who you want me to be. There is a Karalis in Tauta again, one more deserving of your worship than I."

Even as she said the words, she remembered Citlali the stargazing prophet saying them to her. Had he meant them about Rowan all along? She also remembered, with a sinking feeling, that there was a second death waiting out there somewhere for her. A shiver of fear ran down her spine. Citlali was dead now. She would get no more information from him.

"If you insist," Ailey muttered, bringing Cori back to the matter at hand.

"You'll come with us to Lautan?" She asked, a gesture of apology. Ailey's eyes widened.

"Me?"

"The Karalis has written a letter for the other Coterie members and asked them to meet us at Lautan. I'm sure you don't want to miss something so monumental."

Ailey grinned, her eyes shining, and Cori's apparent betrayal forgotten. "Yes! I'd love to come!"

* * *

"Is that all?" Rowan looked wearily at the size of the entourage as it headed out of Balforde. Adro was leading the column of Dijem, Hiram, humans and carriages, much to Daniyl's dismay. As word had spread through town that the Karalis was there, the true Karalis, men and women had come forward to pledge themselves to him and join the fight. Rowan had been reluctant to accept at first, but they had informed him that Hearth had been invading Shaw's borders for years under the orders of the Cadmus, who they referred to as the false Karalis. They wanted to fight back. Rowan agreed.

CHAPTER THREE

"There is one more thing," Ailey said. Cori and Rowan turned to where she stood beside her sister, Bel. She was dressed for travel in brown leather pants and a grey tunic.

"We want to offer you our energy," she gestured towards their eyes. "We can tell that you're depleted."

Rowan's eyebrows shot up, and Cori smiled.

"Honestly," he said, "If Saasha were alive, I would kiss her. She truly thought of everything."

Cori smacked his arm.

"Yes, we'd be grateful for that," she told Bel and Ailey.

Cori wove the song first, and Rowan joined his Hum to hers. In her mind, the small white flame that was the human life force flared brilliantly. Energy filled her, as if someone had opened her up to pour a jug of sweet water into her body. She was instantly revitalised, like waking from a good night's sleep.

"What a strange sensation," Bel observed as the song faded. Ailey couldn't keep the smile from her face.

"Your eyes!" She exclaimed.

Cori turned to look at Rowan. His eyes, previously a dull amber colour, now flashed their normal golden hue.

"How do I look?" She asked him.

He smiled and cupped her cheek with his hand.

"Beautiful, as always," he told her and kissed her.

Bel and Ailey giggled at the gesture and Cori waved a hand irritably at them.

Rowan broke the kiss slowly. His eyes twinkled as he smiled at her, and she realised that it had been some time since she'd seen him enjoy a carefree moment.

"Time for us to go," Ailey said finally. She held out the reins of Cori's grey mare before mounting a shaggy bay stallion.

Rowan mounted mischief who pranced, eager to follow the other horses. Rowan stilled him with a hand to the neck.

"You'll write?" Bel asked Ailey as Cori mounted her mare.

"Of course. I'll tell you all about my adventures!" Ailey replied. Her cheery tone seemed to bring tears to Bel's eyes.

"Mama would be so proud of you," Bel choked. Ailey rolled her eyes.

"I'm sure she would have wished it were you going. All you Bels and that first-born daughter business."

"Time to go," Cori said lightly before Bel could respond. She could sense an argument coming. Bel closed her mouth, touched Ailey's hand, then stepped back and waved them off. The three of them urged their horses forward to join the end of the column as it made its way out of Balforde.

"What happens when we get to Lautan?" Ailey asked. Her voice was low, as if she were only just now realising the gravity of her decision to leave her home.

"We can only hope that the locals will let us in with the papers we have," Rowan told her. "I hope it doesn't come to a fight."

Ailey paled at his words, but Cori supposed she needed to hear the truth.

"Ailey!" A woman called in greeting as a man further up the line, leading two horses, called out to Rowan.

"Karalis, a word if you will?"

"We'll meet up later," Cori told Ailey with a wave before following Rowan.

The man that had called them turned out to be the Stablemaster who'd fed and watered their horses in Balforde. He asked Rowan several questions about horse lodgings in Lautan and complimented him on what a well-bred horse

CHAPTER THREE

Mischief was.

Someone else called for Rowan's attention then and they spent the entire day riding up the column talking to their fellow travellers, or the Karalis' new subjects, Cori mused.

None of them prostrated or bowed, as they had in the old days, and Rowan did not expect them to. He stopped for everyone who wanted to speak to him, and he answered all of their questions politely and with a smile.

They asked Cori questions too, some of which she answered awkwardly. Others she spoke with a brutal honesty that left the asker cringing.

I suppose this would have been my life as your heir? She queried Rowan in the afternoon as they helped right a carriage full of grain sacks that had tipped over. Cori had wanted to use her magic - she was itching to test it out now that her magic levels had been restored. Rowan expressly forbade it. Instead, the two of them, along with twelve other men and women, heaved the carriage upright with brute strength.

Mostly you would do this while I stayed in the palace drinking wine and reclining on silk pillows, he replied.

I've never been good at this small talk, she warned, *I could ruin some sensitive diplomatic souls.*

You'll pick it up.

I'd much rather the wine and pillows, thanks.

We can swap if you like, he suggested, his tone far too serious for Cori's liking. Sensing a trap, she didn't reply, instead saying aloud, "help me with this." Together they hefted a sack of grain back into the carriage. When it was finally moving again, they went back to their horses.

For a time they rode alongside some of the Dijem. At

the back of the pack, slumped in his saddle and looking miserable, was Jonothan. While Rowan chatted to the Dijem he knew, Cori reined in her mare and dropped back to ride beside the boy. She could hear small songs and spells being woven but, because most of the Dijem's Hums sounded the same, it took a few moments to be sure it was his.

"You should be more careful expending your energy."

Jonothan scowled at her and hunched further in his saddle. Cori couldn't help but smirk at his attitude.

"I'm serious," she said earnestly. "You don't want to suddenly turn Dijem at this age, do you? I bet you don't even have hair on your balls yet."

His green-gold eyes - a mark that his transformation had begun - flicked uncertainly to hers. The songs abruptly stopped.

"Not the adventure you had hoped?" She mused.

"No," he replied eventually, sounding close to tears. Or it could have just been his adolescent voice, it was hard to tell. Rowan suddenly dropped back to ride on Jonothan's other side.

"Jonothan," he greeted.

Jonothan scowled at him before losing his bravado and muttering "Karalis," in return.

"Has Daniyl been ensuring you get enough to eat?" Rowan queried. Cori already knew the answer; Daniyl had barely left Rowan's side in his quest for relevance. She was sure he'd all but forgotten about the boy in his care.

"I've been getting what I can," Jonothan admitted.

"And your magic? Has anyone been continuing your lessons?"

"I've been working on them myself."

CHAPTER THREE

Rowan pondered the boy's words for a moment.

"Come to my tent tonight," he said finally. "I'll teach you until Acacia comes to get you. Cori is right. You need to be careful using your magic from now on."

Jonothan seemed to struggle with the proposition, then he sat up straight deciding that getting lessons from the Karalis himself would be exciting. "Thank you!"

Rowan nodded, then met Cori's eye. "It's probably time for us to find Adro."

* * *

By the time they reached the head of the column, Adro had found an open field and had ordered camp to be set up for the night. A large circular tent was pitched at the centre of the camp and once Cori and Rowan had greeted Adro, the three of them retired there.

"I sent Daniyl ahead to scout," Adro said as they entered the tent, "I hope you don't mind."

"Not at all," Rowan responded. "I wish I'd thought of it myself."

Adro chuckled. "He really is insufferable."

The interior of the tent was furnished with a square table and assortment of chairs. A large cot covered in furs was to one side behind a privacy screen, and a second smaller table held a washbasin and cloth. The flaps and one side of the tent had been raised to let in air and light, but candles were ready on the table for when it got dark. Rowan sat down at the table and let out a heavy sigh.

"I'm sure I should call in one of the Balforde folk to find out more about the Hearth-Shaw border wars, but I don't think I can be civil to one more person."

"Don't worry about it," Cori said. She went to the washbasin and splashed water on her face. "I can tell you about the border wars. I started them."

She dried her face and turned around in time to see Rowan and Adro exchange a glance.

"Well, I suppose that shouldn't surprise me," Adro muttered. He looked somewhat uneasy and Cori hoped he wasn't losing his nerve - there was a lot worse to come than her war stories.

"Four hundred and fifty years ago, small factions began popping up in Hearth. I'm sure they had a name for themselves, but I never found out what it was. They were simply an anti-Dijem group." Cori leaned back on the table with the washbasin. "Anyway, I asked Shaw to assist me in pushing them back from the border. We were, of course, victorious. I left the army at the border and continued up through Hearth, wiping them out as I went. I executed the Head of State as an example. Hearth's loyalties had been in question since the Advisor's war." She lifted her hands and inspected her fingernails. She knew that Rowan would know some of her story from the books he'd been reading about her, but she was still hesitant to watch his and Adro's reactions to her own retelling.

"I went north and fought them off Resso's border, then returned to Tengah and killed another Head. Things got a little messy after that, and I was advised to leave. So I left Shaw to hold the borders and travelled south. I know a few Dijem were caught and killed, and that the factions spread to other states, but I never considered that the whole thing might be Cadmus' orchestration."

CHAPTER THREE

She finally looked up at the two men. Rowan gave her a small encouraging smile, but Adro was frowning at her.

"When you say you left the army behind and went on alone," he began slowly, "how did you wipe out the factions by yourself?"

Cori glanced at Rowan, who turned to Adro.

"Cori can use Hiram magic," he explained to his friend.

Adro's frown deepened. "Daniyl said as much. He said those kids he found could use it as well."

"I didn't know any of them before we met Daniyl in Tengah," Cori said, answering his unspoken question as to whether Cadmus had sent her as well. Adro rubbed a hand over his face.

"Even so," he continued, "Hiram magic alone isn't all that formidable. How did you do it?"

Cori looked to Rowan once more. *Should I show him?* She asked.

Might as well, he replied.

Get the walls please, she requested.

Rowan stood and moved to the edge of the tent. He fiddled with the bindings to release the flaps of canvas. They rolled down, enclosing them in near darkness. Rowan turned back to face the centre of the tent, but he didn't return to the table. Adro's eyes flicked between them apprehensively.

Cori flexed her fingers and reached out. Her ghost hands found Adro's chest, and she applied pressure.

"Can you feel that?" She asked. He nodded.

She suddenly clenched her hands, and applying her Hum to strengthen herself, pushed upwards. The front of Adro's shirt bunched as if she'd grabbed the material and he shot up in the air.

"Hey, Cori!" He shouted in alarm. His hands scrabbled at his chest and his legs kicked the air fruitlessly.

"It took me a while to perfect this one," Cori explained proudly. Hands still raised to keep Adro in the air, she walked towards him, as did Rowan. "For a long time I kept ripping the shirt off before I could get the person in the air."

"Very impressive," Rowan said, amused. The two of them looked up at Adro.

"I agree," he huffed as he struggled. "Very impressive. Can I come down now?"

"I'm sure I don't need to ask you to keep this to yourself," Rowan said lightly. Threateningly.

"Tell people that Cori can string me to the ceiling by my collar? I'd rather throw myself on my sword than suffer the embarrassment."

Cori lowered Adro slowly back to the floor until he was standing before her. She smoothed his shirt out for him while he ran a shaking hand through his mass of black ringlets.

"Your Hum changed when you did that," he observed.

"Huh," Cori replied. She glanced at Rowan who nodded in agreement with Adro, however what he said next finished the conversation.

"Jonothan is here."

No sooner had he said the words, then there was a timid "hello?" at the flaps of the tent.

"Come in," Rowan said, and Jonothan stepped inside. He paused, looking nervously between the three adults. "Sit down," Rowan offered, pulling a chair back. The boy came forward.

"Should we go for a wander?" Adro asked Cori. She

nodded, though she would have liked to stay and watch Jonothan's lesson. She was curious to see if Rowan would teach him the same way he had taught her.

"Don't go far," Rowan cautioned them as he took a seat across from Jonothan. "Daniyl is on his way back."

Cori followed Adro from the tent and they set off across the field where tents were being pitched and fires being lit. The atmosphere was jovial - people were excited to be part of the resurrection of the throne. For most of them, the human and Hiram anyway, the Karalis was the stuff of legends.

"I've been meaning to talk to you alone," Adro said as they paused for an escaped pair of goats to be herded past.

"If it has anything to do with me working for Cadmus, I don't want to hear it," she warned. She was sick to death of the mistrust the other Dijem afforded her. Adro blinked, then threw back his head and laughed loudly.

"All I wanted to know was what we are to Rowan," he chortled.

"Oh," Cori considered his question.

"You knew him last time," Adro elaborated. "I thought you'd know a bit about how he prefers to present his court."

"I suppose we would be his Advisors," she said, though she wasn't sure how she felt about the title considering her sour relationship with the last Advisor who had worked for Rowan.

"You wouldn't call yourself Karaliene?"

"Call me that again and I'll hang you up by your undergarments," she growled. "I don't care who's watching."

"All right, all right," Adro held his hands up in surrender, but he grinned at her nonetheless. Cori supposed that he must have heard the Balforde folk talking about her.

"Karaliene!" A man called. She turned and snarled at him as Adro wiped a forearm across his mouth to contain his laughter. The man faltered, but didn't stop until he was before her.

"I wondered if yourself and the Karalis would like some dinner brought to you."

"That would be kind," she was sorry that she'd snarled at him, "but I am not the Karaliene. I'm the second Advisor."

The man frowned at her. "Who is the first?"

She jabbed a thumb at Adro, who puffed out his chest and flexed his biceps.

"Would you like your meal at the Karalis' tent as well?" The man asked. Adro clapped the man on the shoulder.

"Make my portion a double."

"And bring a fourth meal. There's a boy dining with the Karalis tonight."

The man nodded and hurried back the way he had come.

"Should we have organised food for Daniyl?" Adro asked as they headed back through the camp.

"Daniyl can go rot for all I care," Cori muttered.

"You really don't like him, do you?"

Cori recalled the incident at the back of the tavern, remembered how Daniyl had put his cold hands on her and demanded she kiss him.

"No," she said quietly, suppressing a shiver, "I really don't."

They made their way back to the Karalis' tent, stopped occasionally by those who recognised her as either the Karaliene or the Karalis' travelling companion. They saw Ailey, and the woman seemed to be in higher spirits than she had that morning, now that she'd found a cluster of friends to travel with. Finally, with darkness settled around them,

CHAPTER THREE

they reached the tent opening.

Rowan and Jonothan still sat at the table. The boy had his back to them, and Rowan held up a hand to halt them.

"Tell me who stands first in the entryway," he asked the boy. Cori felt Jonothan's Hum briefly touch hers, sounding similar to the Hums of all other Dijem who meditated, except for a slight nuance that made him individual.

"Cori," he said confidently.

"Lady Cori," Rowan corrected. Cori glanced back at Adro behind her to see him shrug. It seemed the boy was being educated in court decency as well as the Hum magic.

"Now tell me how far apart they are standing."

Once more she felt Jonothan's Hum reach out. She remembered this lesson in gaining one's bearings with the magic. She wondered if Jonothan saw other living beings as sparks of light as she did.

"Two feet perhaps," he said hesitantly. "No, four feet. No, there is a third person."

Cori glanced back again to see Daniyl behind Adro. She quickly entered the tent so she wouldn't have to stand too close to him. Adro followed her, and Daniyl followed him. The latter stood tall, his chest puffed out as if he were about to say something important, then he noticed Jonothan.

"What are you doing here?" He asked the boy incredulously.

"The Karalis is giving me lessons," Jonothan said proudly. Daniyl glanced, open-mouthed, between Jonothan and Rowan. He looked uncomfortable, as if he suddenly realised he'd been neglecting the boy.

"There are Hearthian soldiers three valleys from here," Daniyl said abruptly, as if ignoring Jonothan might make him disappear. "We should send soldiers out immediately to deal with them!"

"Daniyl," Rowan warned. Cori noticed Jonothan perk up to listen intently to Daniyl. "Jonothan, give us a moment, please."

Jonothan stood and went to the entrance of the tent, his feet dragging. When he was out of earshot, Rowan sighed. He seemed to deliberate on whether to berate Daniyl for speaking out of turn. Finally he said, "tell me what you saw."

"Soldiers in Hearthian garb, three valleys from here. They were stopping to set camp when we spied them."

"How many?"

"between fifty and one hundred that we could see."

"And which direction are they headed?"

Daniyl had to think on that for a moment. "North," he said finally, then added quickly "We should go and fight them, before they become aware of us!"

Rowan stood slowly, tapping his fingertips on the tabletop.

"Cori?" He asked, "What do you think?"

"I think," she said, trying to contain her enthusiasm. An army to fight! How exciting! And what a perfect opportunity to expend some of her energy. "That we should go and kill them, lest they discover us and tail us to Lautan."

"Adro?" Rowan asked next. His face betrayed nothing of what he thought of Cori's words. She couldn't help but feel a little disgruntled by that.

Adro was slow to answer. "I don't think we should fight." He said eventually. "They aren't aware of us and if they keep moving north, and us east, then it is highly unlikely that we'll cross paths. It seems like an unnecessary waste of life on our part to seek them out."

CHAPTER THREE

"I agree with Adro," Rowan declared after a few moments of consideration.

"You do?" Adro said in surprise as Daniyl shouted, "What?"

No defiance, Cori received the mental message before she could speak. She snapped her mouth shut.

"I agree with Adro," Rowan repeated. "We'll move cautiously, but we won't engage them for the moment." He stared at Daniyl, daring him to disagree again. Daniyl muttered something under his breath and left the tent.

* * *

"Do you understand why I agreed with Adro?" Rowan asked later that evening when only he and Cori were left in the tent.

"Because he was right?" She pulled her tunic off, dusty with the day's travel, and tossed it aside. She unstrapped her brassiere and sighed contentedly. Her entire tenure as Karaliene had been filled with people advising her not to fight. She was used to being warned against conflict. This time though, she'd have to heed the word of the Karalis rather than heading off to kill the soldiers anyway.

"Not necessarily. I want Adro to know that I value his advice. I don't want him to be afraid to be the voice of reason."

"So I was right?"

Rowan sighed. He pulled off his own shirt and continued to the washbasin. "Not necessarily," he repeated after he'd washed his face. "I don't know what the right course of action is. I just hope this one brings the least harm." He moved to her then and wrapped his arms around her waist.

"How do you feel?" He asked with a soft smile. "Since the Deathsong has been released?"

Cori put her hands on his arms and pondered his words. Since she had released the Deathsong upon Daiyu, they had not had a moment's peace. They'd run from the Sarkans and then travelled swiftly to Balforde with them. Only now did she truly assess herself. She realised that she no longer experienced the extreme highs and lows that had plagued her for centuries. Her emotions were her own, no longer food for the song. She was confident in her decisions and at ease with herself. She felt hopeful for the future. And, above this assessment, she realised that Rowan asked because he'd come to this realisation in himself once his own Deathsong had been expelled.

"I feed good." She returned his smile. His arms tightened around her, and he dipped his head to give her a quick kiss.

"I can tell," he whispered. "You look positively radiant." He kissed her again and pulled her towards the fur-covered cot.

* * *

Their travels the following day were uneventful and, although they were aware of a potential attack on their flank, they made good ground. Daniyl continued to sulk over Rowan's decision, and for the first time since Rowan had declared himself Karalis, he did not seek to ride by his side.

That evening Rowan invited some of the Balforde folk to his tent. The Stablemaster was there, and a smithy, a tavern owner and a few wealthy farmers. They seemed a mixed bunch, but they would be the foundations of raising Lautan and the estates back to its former glory.

CHAPTER THREE

"Where's Daniyl?" Adro asked late into the evening. Their guests were still there, but the conversations had become more social as they plied themselves with drink.

"And Jonothan," Rowan said suddenly. Cori stood and stretched.

"I'll go have a look around for them," she offered. "No doubt Daniyl is sulking and is withholding Jonothan from you." At Rowan's nod, she left the tent, pausing only to strap her short sword to her belt.

There was still movement in the camp, but it was slow as everyone prepared themselves for bed. Cori wove through the tents at a wandering pace. Most of the Dijem camped together, and that was where she was headed. When she reached their tents though, she found them empty, not even a fire lit in the spaces between them. She stopped and turned in a slow circle. Where were they?

From the darkness at the edge of the camp she heard shouting and the rolling thunder of hoofbeats. She lifted her hands, preparing for an attack, and squinted into the darkness. Balforde folk who also heard the commotion gathered around.

"Stay behind me," she warned those who got too close. The shouts amplified as a handful of horses galloped into the firelight. She pulled on her strengthening song.

It was only that she recognised one of the red-headed twins, Myce, among them that she stayed her hand. They were splattered in blood. About half looked injured. Myce pulled his horse up before Cori, though she didn't think he really saw her. He had a burden across his saddle and as he tried to dismount, it fell to the ground. A few of the people around her let out screams and shouts, and Cori was sure her heart tried to leap up her throat.

Void of normal colour, right arm mangled and mostly severed at the elbow, was the small body of Jonothan.

Chapter Four

Cori dropped to her knees beside Jonothan. She could tell he was still alive by the way his blood pumped feebly from the wound that had previously been an arm. Someone, most likely Myce by the amount of blood down his front, had tried to staunch the blood flow with a clump of material.

"Get the Karalis!" Someone yelled from the surrounding mayhem.

Rowan, she called out.

I'm coming, he replied.

Cori leaned over Jonothan and pressed her hands over the blood-soaked bandage on his arm, using the full weight of her body to staunch the flow. Her body's natural inclination to panic rose, tightening her throat and chest. She pushed all emotions from herself. Now was not the time.

Rowan appeared beside her and let out a wordless cry of horror. He dropped to the ground, his hands hovering over the boy. His Hum was already forming the notes of the healing song.

"Where is Melita?" Rowan begged. "I don't know how to heal this!"

Cori looked up at Myce who was still standing dumbstruck

by his horse. She reached out with her Hum, beyond the camp. She found other Hums, all in various states of fury and panic. She couldn't tell them apart, couldn't find Melita. She cursed the Sarkans and their meditation practice.

"Myce," she demanded, and he jumped. "Where is your sister? The Karalis needs her."

For a too long moment, Myce stared at her and she thought she would have to get up and hit him, but then he remounted his horse and wheeled it away, shouting "I'll find her!"

"There won't be time," Rowan muttered. "He's going to bleed out."

"If we take the arm off, can you seal the wound at least?" Cori asked him, thinking of the times he'd healed the surfaces of her wounds. He blanched but nodded.

"Adro," she said, looking around to find him hovering behind them. "I need you to hold his arm straight. Rowan, you apply pressure." She lifted her hands, and Rowan's quickly replaced them. She drew her sword.

"Is this really all we can do?" Adro asked faintly.

"It is," Rowan responded with more strength in his voice now.

Adro gingerly lifted the two bits of Jonothan's arm and held it straight. Chunks of flesh and bone hung from it. Cori pushed aside the sick feeling that rose within her; she'd seen worse. She'd dealt worse. She touched the edge of her blade to the remaining sliver of Jonothan's arm and, with a clean stroke that spoke of no hesitation, she severed his forearm from his body.

Jonothan groaned but didn't rouse. Blood spurted from the new wound, and Rowan clapped his hand over it. Cori heard the healing song flare anew and as she watched, skin slowly regenerated from the outside in. It crept over the wound at an agonising pace.

Galloping hoofbeats announced the return of Myce, and Cori was relieved to see Melita with him. The woman seemed to have her wits about her as she slid off the back of the horse. Hands shaking, she dropped down beside Rowan.

"Show me," she requested faintly. Rowan lifted his hands, and Melita quickly inspected the wound. She wove her own healing song. Cori sheathed her sword and watched them work. The healing moved quicker now that Melita was here.

Occasionally Melita would mutter instructions to Rowan such as, "slow down and push the bone shards out first," and "cauterise the veins before you build the skin." Once, Rowan looked up at Cori and said, "find a human for Melita, She's running out of energy." Cori looked around, only then realising the size of the crowd that had gathered.

There were some other Dijem who'd been injured and were receiving aid from the Balforde folk. Others were catching horses and directing those who were still trickling into camp. She wondered briefly where Daniyl was and hoped he was dead; no doubt he'd led the other Dijem into a foray with the Hearthians they'd been trying to pass by unnoticed. She spotted Ailey watching the healing with a pale face. Cori waved her over.

"The redhead needs some energy," she told Ailey in a low tone. "Can you offer some?"

Ailey nodded and hurried to crouch beside Melita. She whispered urgently in her ear, and Melita's healing song was momentarily replaced by one to receive energy from Ailey.

It seemed like hours, but finally Rowan sat back and wiped the sweat from his brow. Melita wiped the blood from

Jonothan's arm to reveal a clean stump with no scarring, as if he'd been born without the lower limb. Cori's eyebrows rose, impressed. She wasn't the only one; a murmur of surprise rippled through those who watched on.

"He still may not survive," Melita said in a low voice to Rowan. Cori barely heard the words. "He's lost so much blood." Rowan simply nodded.

It was at that moment that Daniyl made his return. He galloped into the camp with a handful of others around him, scattering those who had already arrived.

"Rowan!" Daniyl called wildly, his eyes wide and his front splattered with blood. He spotted Rowan still crouched by Jonothan's prone body and wheeled his horse towards him. "Some of them got away! We have to go out after them!"

Daniyl dismounted and in one fluid movement, Rowan rose to his feet and punched the Sarkans leader in the face. Cori heard the satisfying crunch of his nose breaking.

"Owh, what was that for?" Daniyl cried as he hit the ground. He clamped his hands over his face, but Cori could see blood seeping through his fingers. She moved forward to stand by Rowan's left shoulder. She was peripherally aware of Adro mirroring her on their Karalis' right.

"You disobeyed me," Rowan said, and his voice was like thunder. The crowd that had gathered about them whispered and more than a handful of them moved a few steps back. "Not only did you go against my order to not engage the Hearthians, but you failed to protect Jonothan."

For the first time, Daniyl noticed the boy on the ground behind them. Melita was still beside him, but she watched Daniyl fearfully.

"Oh," said Daniyl and his face paled. "But there's still

CHAPTER FOUR

Hearthians out there. Perhaps twenty of them. We have to stop them getting back to-"

Rowan's Hum blasted Daniyl back into the dirt. The Sarkans elder gasped for breath as the Karalis bore down on him. Cori knew the feeling of Rowan taking control of one's mind all too well.

"Adro," Rowan's voice was deadly, "Get my sword."

"Ro-Karalis," Adro said as a few other Dijem shouted in dismay, "is that necessary?"

"Adro," Rowan warned.

"Please, Rowan!" It was the older woman from Sarkans. She pushed through the bystanders and crouched protectively behind Daniyl. Her hands gripped his shoulders. "Show some mercy!"

Rowan glared down at them and his fury rolled off him in cold waves. "Cori," he said quietly. She placed a hand on the hilt of her sword, ready to pass it to him when he asked. Adro shot her a pleading look, which she ignored. She wouldn't deny the Karalis this execution.

If Daniyl had been fearful before, he now looked petrified. Cori smiled coldly at him, taking immense satisfaction in the fact that he knew she would never show him mercy.

"Finish what Daniyl started," Rowan told her. It wasn't the order she had expected, but she would heed it. Before them, Daniyl wet himself with relief, but Rowan wasn't done with him yet.

"Daniyl, you, and everyone who followed you tonight are banished from my realm. If I see any of you again, there will be consequences." He pointed at Daniyl. "If I see you again, I will kill you. Cori," he added, indicating that she should go to her task. She stepped forward and crouched before Daniyl.

She first met the older woman's eyes, then the watery gold eyes of the despicable man before her.

"You better run fast," she warned him with a smile, "because if you're still nearby when I've finished cleaning up after you, I will come and find you myself." She didn't wait to see his reaction, instead she straightened and strode from the camp.

Once she was clear of the firelight, she broke into a jog, following the churned up tracks that the Sarkans had made on their hasty return to camp. She pushed the incidents that had happened in the camp from her mind and tried to focus on the task ahead. Daniyl had said approximately twenty had gotten away. She assumed they would head north towards the border.

She came across a riderless horse making its way back to camp and she commandeered it and turned it around, pushing it to a canter.

It was perhaps half an hour before she came across the site of the battle. The grass had been flattened to dirt, and blood and bodies were strewn across the ground. Already Cori could hear wild animals setting to work on the dead. She rode past a few Dijem bodies as well and felt renewed hatred for Daniyl and the fact that he had left his own dead here.

It was difficult to see in the dark and the stench of blood spooked her mount, but by riding the perimeter of the trampled ground, she found tracks leading away. They were on foot, she noted. Good. Hopefully they hadn't gotten far.

She followed the tracks at a trot for only twenty minutes before she heard voices and saw flickering firelight under a stand of trees. She reined in her horse and dismounted. Leaving it with its reins over its head, she stalked towards the Hearthian camp. She flexed her fingers at her side and wove a strengthening song.

She was a hunter stalking her prey. She was strong, powerful. This was what she had been born to do. A smile curled the corners of her lips, and the ground rumbled beneath her. *The ground rumbled beneath her?* She paused; that was new. She stood still for a moment, but she couldn't feel anything more. Perhaps she'd imagined it. She resumed her hunt.

As she neared the camp, the voices became audible. They spoke in low tones; there was no hint of celebration that often happened at the end of a battle.

"We have to get word to the Karalis and the Captain that we've been attacked," one man said. Cori spotted him poking the fire with a stick. He looked to be quite young.

"In the morning, boy," an older man replied. His arm was wrapped in a bloody bandage and his face was pinched with pain. "We won't get far in the dark."

"But them Gold Eyes might come back."

"I doubt that. We got them as good as they got us. They weren't battle ready."

"I heard their leader - the blonde one say he would send his true Karalis after us," another soldier piped up; a woman this time. All the soldiers looked towards the older man and Cori assumed he was their captain. She paused, unseen, at the edge of the firelight and waited to see what he would say.

"A bluff, I'm sure," he said in a disgruntled tone, not sounding sure at all. "You know as well as I that Cadmus is the only Karalis in Tauta. It's him we serve. Those Gold Eyes were rogues, and in any case," he added, suddenly seeming more sure of himself. Cori crept forward to stand at the edge of the group of soldiers. "If this other Karalis is so formidable, don't you think he would have led the charge?"

A murmur went through the soldiers and Cori nodded along.

"I agree," she said and those closest to her startled, some turning and some reaching for weapons.

"Who are you?" the captain demanded, drawing his sword and raising his other hand defensively. Hiram, then.

Cori pointed to herself, looking around at them with wide eyes, but also making sure she had enough space. More than half the soldiers had drawn their swords. She counted over twenty men and women there; not the biggest army she had taken on alone. Not the smallest either.

"Who, me?" She asked innocently, then she smiled. "The Karalis sent me."

"Which Karalis?" The woman from before called out. Cori's smile widened.

"Does it matter? Neither is your friend." She noticed a burly man with a grey flecked beard had sidled close to the captain and was whispering urgently to him.

"Going to share?" Cori asked him politely. He straightened and stared at her. She could see fear in his eyes.

"You are the Karaliene of Crushed Skulls," he said matter-of-factly. Cori didn't think her grin could possibly get any wider. This was a time when she delighted in being recognised; not when men pandered to her, but instead ran in fear of her.

"My reputation precedes me."

Many of the younger soldiers seemed confused, but the older ones who had been told stories by their parents and grandparents looked as if they'd seen a ghost.

"Run!" the captain roared. He flicked his hand at her and

CHAPTER FOUR

she felt the force of his magic touch her. She took one step back and brought her hands together. The captain's head exploded into a fine red mist.

If his orders hadn't roused his soldiers, her actions did. Shouts of alarm overrode the thunder of feet as they tried to escape her. She swung her arm, sending those on her left high in the air, then those on her right. They all returned to earth with fatal thunks. A brave soul rushed her with his sword, and she gave him a quick death.

She broke bones and snapped necks. She flung bodies like sacks of flour and tore limbs from torsos. She did it all without taking a step and without allowing a single person to leave the circle of firelight. Except one.

The air was red with blood as Cori picked her way across the chaos of corpses to where the man with the grey-flecked beard was trying to crawl away. She put her foot on his back and he lay flat, letting out a strangled sob.

"A moment, please," she told him. Fighting done, she was aware of a Hum waiting at the edge of her mind. She was surprised to find it was Adro. His reach wasn't strong - something she'd have to speak to him about - so she sent her magic towards him to strengthen the connection.

Everything all right? He asked.
Almost done, she replied. *How is Jonothan?*
Still alive. She could hear a hint of worry in his voice.
What's wrong?
It's Rowan. I don't think he's all right.
Where is he?
Here, with Jonothan and I.

Cori reached out and touched Rowan's mind. He sent back a feeling of acknowledgement, but that was all. He had some

55

inner barriers up, but she could feel the tendrils of the storm brewing behind them.

I'll be back shortly, she told Adro before returning to the matter at hand.

She used her foot to turn the man over. He stared up at her with angry grey eyes.

"You're a monster!" He spat at her.

"Yes," she agreed. She watched him for a moment while she decided what to do. She reached out with her mind and was pleased to find that he had some Hiram magic.

What is your name?

"Ahsyn," he said aloud in an automatic tone.

Where is Cadmus, Ahsyn?

Small flashes came back to her. A black dragon circling above Tengah before flying east. Orders being given by his captain. Nothing else though; he'd never personally laid eyes on Cadmus.

She drew her sword, and Ahsyn closed his eyes, panting. She inspected her blade. It still had the blood from Jonothan's amputation on it. Her old mentor, Shanti, would not have been impressed.

She pressed the sword tip to Ahsyn's thigh and drew it across the skin, deep enough to cut the muscle but not deep enough to kill him - it would slow him down. He roared in pain.

"Just do it quickly, woman!" He yelled at her. She squatted down beside him.

"Don't worry, I'm done."

His eyes snapped open to meet hers. He was still fearful, but now he allowed himself to feel hope.

"Go to Cadmus, or whoever's running Tengah, and tell

them about tonight," she paused, "then tell them I'm coming for them." She pressed two fingers to her lips, then transferred the kiss to his forehead.

"A kiss for good luck," she told him.

"Your kisses are never for good luck," he said warily. She laughed.

"I like you, Ahsyn. Live a long life and tell your grandbabies stories about me." She straightened then and headed back the way she had come. She looked back once to see Ahsyn sitting up and watching her. She raised a hand in farewell, then set off at a run in search of the horse. She needed to get back to Rowan.

Chapter Five

It was as she rode back past the battlefield that she remembered her promise to Daniyl.

She reined in her mount, who stood pawing and snorting beneath her, and reached out with her Hum. She saw the world as flares of light around her; small and harmonious songs that was the surrounding nature. Pricks like starlight were the humans back in the camp and brighter flames that signified those with Hiram magic. The brightest lights of all were those of the Dijem and she found a mass of them to the north-west, moving fast. She couldn't tell Daniyl from the rest, so she let her Hum blanket the lot of them. She felt their collective fear, felt them increase their pace. She smiled, withdrew her Hum and kicked the horse forward.

The camp was subdued compared to the state she'd left it in. She rode through at a trot and those who were still awake stared at her. She dismounted outside to the Karalis' tent and approached the fire where she found Adro. Beside him on a low cot was Jonothan. Cori paused over the boy and looked down at him. His skin still lacked colour, but he was breathing normally. A blanket covered him to his chin and if Cori hadn't known better, she would think he was just sleeping.

"Has he woken yet?" she asked Adro. He shook his head, staring at her. She sighed. "Where's Rowan?"

He jammed his thumb in the direction of the tent. When she stepped that way, however, he stopped her.

"Cori," he warned, and his voice was hoarse. "Before you go in there, I think you should wash your skin."

She glanced down at her arms to find them coated in an even layer of sticky blood.

"Give me the waterskin," she requested, and Adro tossed it to her. She poured water on her arms and scrubbed them, then did the same to her face and neck. She wasn't entirely clean by the end of her wash, but it was better than before. There was nothing she could do about her clothes, however; they were ruined. She held her arms wide and Adro nodded his approval.

She moved to the entrance of the tent and pushed back the flap. The tent was as it had been several hours earlier when they'd been dining with the Balforde representatives. Cups and plates sat discarded on the table, left in everyone's rush to get to the scene with the Sarkans.

Rowan was at the side of the tent near the cot they shared. He was crouched down, rummaging through her pack. When she stepped inside, he glanced over his shoulder at her.

"Where is your rum?" He asked. His voice was deceptively calm.

"I don't have any."

His head dropped in a moment of defeat, then he rose and turned to face her. Even from across the tent she could see the beads of perspiration on his forehead and, with a sinking feeling, she saw that he was staring through her, not at her. He took a shuddering breath.

"I can't stop it," he said, lifting a hand to his head. His fingers fisted in his hair, and he gave it a tug.

"Let go, then," she replied, taking a few steps towards him. He shook his head, a few jerky movements.

"It's been too long. I might kill someone." That gave Cori pause. Did he mean Adro, sitting outside, whose mind wasn't as strong as his? Or the Hiram in the camp who she knew were susceptible to a mental blowout such as Rowan was about to have? Or was he possibly talking about himself?

"I can fix this," she said, thinking of the passage she'd read in the book in Balforde about releasing the Hum. She hadn't perused the book further, but she recalled what it had said about anchoring a person fallen into Hum intoxication. Could she anchor Rowan? She took his arm. "Come on, let's get away from the camp."

She used her sword to slice the material at the back of the tent and pulled Rowan through. They stole away into the night, arm in arm, as if they were out for a stroll. Cori led Rowan out of the camp and towards the south. She didn't want to accidentally come across the battlefield again. They walked until Rowan was staggering. She glanced back the way they'd come, but couldn't see the lights of the camp anymore. This would have to be far enough.

She let go of Rowan and he dropped to his knees. She reached for his mind with hers, hoping she could create an anchor as his barriers came down. She readied herself.

"All right, let go," she instructed. He didn't need telling twice. His Hum exploded, shattering his barriers and expanding to consume the still night.

CHAPTER FIVE

If Cori thought their years apart had closed the gap between their magical capabilities, then she was woefully wrong. The force of Rowan's Hum blasted her off her feet. She landed hard on her back, and lay there, dazed for a moment. Then she reached out again.

Fighting through Rowan's magic was like walking through raining glass. Every note sliced through her, making her gasp. But she was nothing if not stubborn. She pushed on until she could twine her Hum with his. She dug her mental heels in and hung on for dear life.

Perhaps some part of him realised what she was doing, for she felt the maelstrom around her ease. The fury and pain lessened. There was a flicker of curiosity.

Time was undefined, as was always the case when one was lost in a Hum intoxication, but Cori was aware of the transition from the maelstrom to a gentle floating sensation. She still held tight to her connection with Rowan, but now that she perceived that the danger had passed, she allowed herself to follow him as he reached across the realm.

The touch of his Hum on all living things was feather light and indiscernible. He didn't seek anyone or anything in particular. After her fight to hang on, Cori felt the lilting notes of his renewed mind like a caress. She didn't want this to stop. When his reach waned, she took the reins and pulled him onwards. Her reach was greater than his and she let her magic run until the land ended and the beings they touched were foreign and fearsome.

Enough. Rowan's voice was a gentle whisper in her mind. She withdrew immediately and opened her eyes. The stars spun above her for a dizzying moment while she gained her bearings.

She was still laying on her back, and Rowan was sitting beside her. He watched her curiously, as if he'd never seen her before.

"Where did you learn that?" He asked in wonder. "Never have I been able to maintain such a sense of self. It was like you-"

"Anchored you?" Cori sat up with a groan. She felt as if she'd been belted all over. She wasn't sure if it was the beating she'd just received from Rowan's Hum or from her earlier escapades with the Hearthians. "I read it in a book."

Rowan quirked an eyebrow at her and she sighed. "Yes, I learn things from books too. How do you feel? The book said you should experience heightened mental clarity and increased magical capacity."

"Yes," Rowan said slowly, "that's exactly how I feel."

He flopped back on the ground, his head pillowed on his arms, and looked up to the stars. Cori followed suit. They lay in companionable silence for a long time. Cori felt her eyes drooping towards sleep. It had been a long night.

"I thought it was the Deathsong that used to make me react this way, but it seems not." He turned his head to look at her, and she did the same. "Do you think there's something wrong with me?"

"Of course not," Cori chided, though she was taken aback. She was still not used to the way he'd been second guessing himself lately. "I've told you before that this is how you cope. It's probably a very natural way to react to trauma."

"Why do you cope so well?" He jutted his chin at her. "Look at you, you're covered in blood and you return as if it's nothing, to stop me losing my mind. How do you make it seem so easy?"

"I lack empathy," she admitted awkwardly, not meeting his eye. "It's not traumatic if I enjoy it."

Rowan made a small noise in the back of his throat and looked away.

"I'm sorry," he said eventually, "for sending you to do that."

"What?" she was surprised. "Didn't you just hear me say I enjoyed it?"

"Yes, but it was reckless on my behalf, sending you on your own. It could have been dangerous."

"I wouldn't have done it if I was in danger."

"Really?" His brow rose sceptically. She said nothing. He was probably right; she would have died before relinquishing the fight.

Rowan sighed heavily and stood up.

"Do you think you can stand yet?" He held out his hand for her. She took it, not realising how badly she was shaking until she was on her feet.

"I might cope well in a crisis, but it catches up to me eventually," she muttered. Rowan put his arm across her shoulder and hugged her tight to his side.

"Come on, Little One," he coaxed her and together they started the long walk back to camp.

"Well, I suppose the debate of which of us is stronger ended tonight," she said to him.

"There was a debate?" He queried, a smile touching his lips.

"You never wondered?"

"No. I know I'm stronger than you."

"Smart arse," she muttered. He laughed and hugged her tighter.

***

Everyone was well and truly abed as they ghosted between the tents. When they reached their own, they re-entered via the slit Cori had made in the back.

She immediately began peeling off her bloody clothes and Rowan helped her, tugging her shirt over her head and untying her brasserie.

"Shouldn't you go to Jonothan?" She asked as he next filled the washbasin.

"You first," he replied. Together they methodically scrubbed the blood from her skin until she was pristine. When he made her stand in a tub so he could pour water over her hair, he frowned.

"It's still pink," he told her after the third jug of water.

"It'll take a few days to come out," she informed him. She bundled her hair in her hands and squeezed the water out. Rowan handed her a towel, then went to her pack to select some clothes for her. When he returned, he also had the title-less book.

"This is the book?" He asked, and she nodded. He handed her the clothes and tucked the book under his arm.

Cori dressed slowly, really feeling the fatigue in her muscles now. She did feel much better for being clean, though.

"Will you go to bed?" Rowan asked as she wove her hair into a knot on top of her head and secured it with a leather thong.

"No, I'll come with you to see Jonothan first."

***

CHAPTER FIVE

Adro was still sitting by the fire, his eyes heavy. When he saw Rowan and Cori approaching, he lurched to his feet.

"Thank you," Rowan said, "for staying with him. Why don't you go and get some sleep?"

Adro nodded and turned towards his own tent, pitched across the fire.

"Oh, and Adro?" Rowan added before the other man could push through the flaps of the tent.

"Yeah?" Adro called back.

"Next time I ask you to get my sword, you get it."

For a tense moment the two men stared at each other, then Adro said, "Yes, Karalis" and entered the tent.

Rowan sighed and knelt down beside Jonothan. Cori knew it was difficult for him to berate his friend. The three of them would have to sit down the following day to discuss the fact they'd also lost half their army that night. She sat by the fire and drew her knees to her chest. The sky was lightening - dawn was not far away.

When Rowan finished checking over Jonothan, he moved to her side and tucked her under his arm. He opened the book so they could read together. She didn't even get through the first page before falling asleep.

She woke when Rowan shifted beside her. She opened her eyes and blinked. It felt as if someone had thrown sand in them. The sun was against the horizon, and around them the camp was stirring. Adro was up again, sitting across the fire from them. Cori tilted her head to look up at Rowan, but his attention was on Jonothan. The boy was stirring. He groaned, and she sat up so Rowan could get free of her.

"Water," Jonothan gasped. Rowan held a waterskin to his lips. The boy took two swallows before turning his head away. He didn't open his eyes, but...

"I can hear his Hum," Cori whispered.

"Yes," Rowan agreed, leaning over the boy to look at his face. "He's not ready to wake yet, though." He sat back, opening the book back to his place.

"Do you want to sleep?" Cori asked him. He'd been awake all night.

"Increased mental clarity," he reminded her.

"Cori," Adro drew her attention. He pointed away from the fire. "I think those two women want you."

Cori looked to see Ailey and another woman hovering nearby. Cori got to her feet, stifling the groan that threatened to defend her overused body. She went to Ailey, who greeted her and gestured to the woman beside her.

"This is Harmony. She wishes to have an audience with the Karalis."

Cori looked at Harmony. She was young, with black hair tied in a tail that fell all the way to her backside. She wore strange clothes full of pockets that tinkled when she moved.

"It would need to be life or death to see the Karalis today," she told them heavily.

"Please, Karaliene," Harmony begged in a lilting voice. Cori scowled but ignored the misuse of her name. "I'm a herbalist. I thought the boy might need some healing tea this morning."

"Didn't you see last night? He was healed."

"Yes, but," Harmony seemed nervous. Cori wondered if the herbalist may have seen her ride back into camp after her massacre. Had that only been a few hours ago? "He still lost an arm. That's quite a blow for a boy his age. I have wort which is helpful for a depressed mind. Ginger root will assist with blood regeneration and -"

CHAPTER FIVE

"All right." Cori pinched the bridge of her nose. She could feel a headache coming on. "All right." She led Ailey and Harmony back to the fire.

"Rowan," she said and Rowan looked up, closing the book as he did. "This is Harmony, she has some herbs for Jonothan."

"Yes, Karalis, Sir," Harmony said before Rowan could speak. She launched into her list of teas and more, speaking of ghost limbs and young male hormones.

Rowan listened to all she said, then replied with "Thank you, Harmony. Jonothan still sleeps, but when he wakes, I would appreciate you tending to him. In fact, take one of these tents for yourself so you're close by when he wakes."

"Yes Sir." Harmony and Ailey bowed at the waist then hurried away to collect their things. Rowan looked at Cori then.

"Are you all right?" He asked.

"Positively haggard," she replied truthfully. She looked at Adro then, before Rowan could tell her to go to bed. "How's your stomach?" She asked him.

"Fine, why?" He narrowed his eyes at her and she waved him to his feet.

"We have a battlefield to clean up."

* * *

They didn't pack up the camp that day. Cori, Adro and any of the Balforde folk willing to help, went down to the battlefield from the night before and spent most of the day digging a large grave. Cori's headache pounded within her skull, but she needed to work to keep her mind occupied.

From what thoughts, she wasn't sure. She didn't feel any remorse for her actions the night before, but perhaps that was it; perhaps her lack of guilt that had been her armour the past five hundred years had now caught up to bother her. How could she be any sort of decent person if she felt no empathy towards others? Rowan had said nothing to her admission the previous night. Did he agree?

"Here, this one," Adro said, swatting flies away from his face. Cori stooped to lift the legs of the dead Hearthian while Adro collected his head. Together they heaved the body to lie with the others at the edge of the grave. Adro wiped the sweat from his brow and Cori followed him to the next body, this time a Dijem woman.

"Just like the Last Fight," Adro muttered as they collected the woman up.

"Just like any war," Cori corrected him.

It was as they were heaving this body to the grave that Rowan arrived. He brought with him more people from the camp to relieve those who'd been digging the grave all morning. Cori and Adro were not dismissed.

Rowan surveyed the dead with a blank expression before letting out a string of expletives under his breath. Cori was sure she heard Daniyl's name among them.

"Where are the rest?" He asked Cori suddenly.

"What?" She feigned confusion while her stomach sank. She'd deliberately not mentioned the second, smaller battlefield.

"The rest," he repeated, staring at her. "You didn't do any of this." He waved a hand at the dead before them. Cori stared back at him, then reluctantly pointed towards the north.

"There's more?" Adro said in disbelief.

CHAPTER FIVE

"Come on," Rowan told the two of them. "Let's go get them."

The three of them took a horse and cart up the track Cori had followed the night before. Why Rowan was so insistent that they collect these bodies, Cori didn't know. Did he want to witness her carnage?

"We could have just left them to the animals," she muttered as they neared the site.

"Everyone deserves a grave," Rowan told her. She didn't remind him of the Nomad Islanders they had left in an orchard five hundred years ago. They came to the campsite and stopped.

"Far out, Cori," Adro said on an exhaled breath.

The grass was red with blood and it formed a near-perfect radius around the dead fire. Within the circle were the bodies and limbs that were her victims. She put her hands on her hips and glanced at Rowan. His expression was unreadable, but when he met her eye, she couldn't help smirking.

"Not a bad job, if I do say so myself." she declared. Rowan gave a small shake of his head and unlatched the back of the cart.

* * *

Legs are heavy, Cori thought as she dragged one across the ground. The sun beat down on her, and the stench of spilt bowels and decaying flesh filled her nostrils. The flies were unbearable.

"Twenty-three," Rowan said as she loaded the limb on top of the other bodies.

Adro let out a low whistle. "Remind me not to catch you

in a foul mood," he told Cori.

"There were twenty-four," she replied to Rowan, ignoring Adro.

"One got away?" He guessed.

"Of course not. I let him go." She thought of Ahsyn and hoped he was travelling well. "Actually, I gave him a message for Cadmus."

"I hope it was a good one," Rowan muttered as he pulled a canvas over the top of the cart.

"Are we done now?" Cori said. Her head was throbbing violently, and she'd had enough. "We surely could have left these ones here. I feel like you're punishing me."

Rowan glanced first at Adro, then at her. "You're not being punished," he explained, "I asked you to do this. It was my word that meant the death of these people. The least I can do is witness them and give them a final resting place."

Cori hadn't expected him to express remorse over a battlefield he hadn't even fought on. Adro was nodding along with Rowan's words, as if he understood them. And perhaps he did. He and Rowan had been comrades in the Last Fight. They probably understood each other better than Cori did. The moment reminded her of the ones she had often shared with Orin. Granted, they'd always got drunk post battle, not tortured themselves with grave digging duties.

"Don't try to share the guilt," Cori said, more harshly than she intended. "It won't come to any good."

"It's good to share it, Cori," Adro told her gently. "Fighters on both sides have to grieve."

"Yes," Rowan said, tying down one side of the canvas and moving to the other. "And like you said, it will catch up with you, eventually."

CHAPTER FIVE

Cori flung her hands up in defeat and went around to the front of the cart. If they wanted to share guilt, they could clean up the last few parts. She was spent.

* * *

They returned to the grave to find the other dead had already been laid in it. The Balforde folk murmured at the fresh cartload of corpses. Many of them looked at her, no doubt remembering her return to camp the night before. She avoided their gazes as she helped unload the cart, and once the grave was full, she took up a shovel to fill it.

The sun was getting low when she finally rode back into camp. Her skull screamed in protest at her continued activity. Still, she went through the motions of the evening, bathing and dining before taking up a vigil at Jonothan's bedside for a time.

The boy woke up part way to midnight, and she watched his anguish bloom as he discovered his missing limb. Rowan spoke to him in quiet, earnest words. Jonothan's gaze was averted from the Karalis' and tears streaked his face. Cori felt awkward; like an intruder at a funeral, but she stayed by the fire until Jonothan finally nodded at Rowan's words and the Karalis asked Harmony to move the boy to a tent and brew a tea to assist him back to sleep.

They watched the boy go, then Rowan held out his hand to pull Cori to her feet. She took it gratefully, and together they finally ended a very long day.

Chapter Six

Cori had stood on this hillside once before, looking down at the seaside town of Lautan. She'd led an army then, as she did now, but then she'd been a broken and grieving girl. Now, Rowan was at her side, a warm, living man and her Karalis. This was how she should have returned to fight the Advisor all those years ago.

Lautan was different too. The town, once a thriving port and marketplace, was now heavily fortified and, from what Cori understood, was under the governance of thugs and scoundrels. No ships sat in the bay and the once magnificent palace was crumbling and dark upon its cliffside perch.

"The gates are closed," Adro observed.

"Not surprising with a hundred unknown people bearing down on the town," Rowan replied. He scratched his chin thoughtfully, then clicked his horse forward. "Might as well get it over with."

They approached the gate at a sedate pace. No weapons were drawn, but everyone in the Karalis' party had one.

"Hey there!" a man called down from the parapets atop the gate and the party stopped. "What do you want?"

Cori, Rowan and Adro glanced at each other. Cori motioned that Adro should take the lead. Adro rode for-

CHAPTER SIX

ward a few paces, and the man atop the gate lifted a bow threateningly.

"Hey there," Adro returned the greeting in a clear, carrying voice. "The Karalis has come to reclaim his throne!"

The man's weapon lowered a little in surprise. He surveyed them for a long moment.

"Reclaim, you say?" He sounded curious now. "You're not that new Karalis who sends his dragon down on us?"

"He's the true Karalis!" The Stablemaster yelled, backed by calls of approval from his peers.

The man leaned back over the parapet and yelled to those below. The gate creaked open, and they came face to face with a small army.

Most were men, though there were a few women among them. They wore mismatched pieces of leather armour and carried weapons that ranged from well made - and no doubt stolen - swords to knives more suited to a butchery.

As they rode towards the gate, Rowan drew his sword and lay it across his lap. Its golden pommel flashed in the sunlight, a quiet threat that the citizens of Lautan best heed him or reap the consequences. Cori wanted to smile. All eyes were on the Karalis' sword, but if push came to shove, she would be the one dealing the blows.

"Karalis, you say?" Another man stepped from among Lautan's defence. Cori stared. Did she know him? He seemed familiar...

"Yes, That's correct." Rowan dismounted from Mischief. Cori and Adro followed suit to flank him.

"An, you want the throne, you say?"

"Indeed."

The two men stopped a few feet from each other. The

Lautan man looked from Rowan to Adro and then to Cori. She suddenly recognised him; the leader of the three thugs whom she had beat up in an alley over a year ago. He frowned at her.

"Do I know you?"

"Erm," she looked away, scuffing her boot in the dirt. At the edge of her vision she saw Rowan turn his head to look at her and felt his querying touch on her mind.

"Han, That's the bitch who broke my nose!" One of the other men from that night charged from the crowd. There was no mistaking him. His nose was bent at quite an angle.

"Doesn't look that bad," Cori offered with a shrug. Rowan sent her a feeling of exasperation. The man with the broken nose roared and rushed at her. She raised her hands, ready to break his nose again.

Rowan put his sword before her, the flat side of the blade against her chest to caution her to stillness. Han, Lautan's leader, had the good sense to fling his arm out in a similar movement to stop his friend.

"Wait, Olav," Han ordered roughly. "Revenge in good time."

"We would prefer to return to the palace peacefully, but we will take it by force if you oppose me," Rowan told Han in a warning tone. He lowered his sword from Cori's chest. Han stared at him, sucking the inside of his cheek thoughtfully.

"What's in it for us?" He asked eventually. His hand remained on Olav's chest. The latter glowered at Cori, his fists bunched at his side.

"What do you want?"

Han and Olav glanced at each other, then Han looked over his shoulder at the army behind him. A few men nodded at him.

CHAPTER SIX

"One thousand gold coins," Han requested.

"Done," Rowan replied immediately. Cori tried not to gape along with everyone else. Rowan always had money on him, but how on earth did he have that much? He continued, "and further to that, if anyone has any skills that I can use, either in fighting or domestic, I will pay them a wage."

A murmur rippled through Lautan's army. Han couldn't hide his look of surprise. "Work for you, you say?"

"Yes."

"How do we even know you're the real Karalis? How do we know that you won't send your beasty down on us once we let you in?"

Cori was sure Rowan had to hide a sigh of frustration. "You have my money, is that not enough?"

"We have morals too, yeh know," Olav spoke up angrily. He shot a filthy look at Cori. "We still want what's best for Lautan."

"I have the original titles to the land, if you want to see them."

"I dunno, could be forged," Han drawled. Cori decided that he was being deliberately hesitant. She wondered if, after hearing how quickly Rowan agreed to the purse, he might request more money.

"Put him on the throne," she suggested. Whispers of shock flowed through both armies this time. Han gave her a brutish grin.

"Well, that would be a quick way to find out. I like your thinking, girly."

"What does putting me on the throne mean?" Rowan asked at the same time as saying in Cori's mind, *what are you up to?*

You'll see, she replied.

"The Karaliene who used to haunt these parts," Han explained, the grin still on his face, "put a curse on the throne, didn't she? Said no one but the true Karalis could sit upon it, yeh? Never even sat on it herself, I heard, and any man who thinks himself bold enough to try is crushed to his horrid death."

During Han's tale, Rowan had turned to stare at Cori. She wished he wouldn't; clearly Han hadn't worked out her true identity yet.

A bit dramatic, don't you think?

This is as much Arasy's doing as it is mine, she countered.

"All right, I'll sit on the throne," Rowan said.

Han finally stepped aside with a mocking bow, and the army behind him parted.

"Lead the way then, Karalis."

* * *

Rowan rode mischief up the cliff road. The Balforde folk followed, and the Lautan army - and any others who came out of their dwellings to discover the happenings - brought up the rear.

The procession followed the old road that led to the front of the palace and the throne room. There were enough people there that they could shift a few of the fallen stone pillars to create an opening for everyone to enter through.

The passage of over three hundred people into the throne room lifted the dust from the floor to swirl in eddies in the sunlight that streamed through the gaps in the crumbling arches.

The spectators spoke in hushed tones that echoed eerily

CHAPTER SIX

through the hall. Rowan, Cori and Adro stood below the dais. Rowan had his eyes on the throne and Cori could feel a gentle song in his Hum. She wondered what he was saying to Arasy, the white wood throne that was carved from a dragon soul tree into the likeness of a great beast.

Jonothan pushed through the crowd with his one good arm to get to Rowan's side. Since waking from his healing sleep, he'd not strayed far from the Karalis. Harmony, the boy's appointed carer, was always in sight too.

"It won't really crush you, will it?" He asked in a frightful whisper. "That's what all these people are saying, that the throne kills everyone who sits on it." Rowan briefly touched the boy's shoulder but didn't respond.

"Come here, Jonothan," Adro said, taking the boy's arm and pulling him to his side. Jonothan looked even younger beside Adro's hulking figure.

"On with it then, Karalis," Han said from where he stood nearby with Olav and a few other cronies. He had a smug look on his face, confident that Rowan would become another victim of the curse.

Rowan nodded, then turned to Cori. He handed her his sword and gave her a small wink. She could have laughed. Now who was being dramatic?

Silence descended on the hall as Rowan climbed the steps to the throne. He briefly brushed his hand over the carved dragon head, then turned around and sat down.

There was a collective intake of breath, and for a moment nothing happened. Then the dragon's tail twitched, and the wood came alive. Before he could move, the tail coiled around Rowan's forearm, pinning it to the arm of the chair.

There was a mixture of noise around them, from the

horrified shrieks of the Balforde folk to the sighs of disappointment from those who lived in Lautan. Jonothan let out a strangled sob and Adro hushed him.

Cori kept her eyes on Rowan, trying not to roll them. He looked to Han, who had already turned to joke with his cronies. He waited until Han met his eye, then he reached for Arasy's tail with his free hand. Slowly, and as the room fell silent again, he unwound the wooden tail as easily as if it had been rope.

The smug smile fell from Han's face. The leader gaped, white-faced, at Rowan and then looked back towards the crowded room.

"The Karalis," he said hoarsely, waving a wild hand towards the dais. "Our holy Karalis!"

Like a wave on the ocean, the people in the throne room sank to the floor in deference. Beside Cori, Adro and Jonothan went down on one knee. She alone remained standing, knowing exactly how Rowan felt about this sort of prostrating. She turned her gaze back to him to find him watching her.

Here we are again, she mused.

Here we are again, he agreed grimly.

***

Han proved to be an effective leader of the Lautan community, using equal methods of coaxing and intimidation to get things done. Olav was his right-hand man. Thuggish and stupid, Olav cracked his knuckles and growled at anyone who got too close.

Han took charge of the situation immediately; ordering

his men to help the Balforde folk bring the supply carriages to the palace. He requested anyone who worked in the town taverns to prepare food until the palace kitchens could be restored and asked for anyone who could, to spare some furniture.

Rowan let Han go, watching the man work the room into a frenzy from the throne. Cori climbed the stairs of the dais. She stopped close to the throne, standing a little to the side but still facing it. She reached out a hand to touch the smooth wood of the dragon's head.

Karaliene, Arasy greeted her. *We have completed a circle.*

More like a wonky oblong, she replied. *But yes, we've come all the way back around.*

"What do you think?" Rowan asked in a low voice, his eyes still on the room.

"About Han? He seems resourceful and knows he needs to make himself indispensable to you."

"I like him."

"Not so much his friends though. Too unrefined to work this close to you."

Rowan looked at her, his eyebrows rising mockingly. "A bit rich of you to speak of refinement."

"Ha," Cori laughed sarcastically. Rowan stood.

"Come with me." He gave a wave to Adro, indicating that he would be back in a moment, then led her behind the throne to an old stone door. It had once formed part of the wall, hidden by a mural that had depicted a war scene with Daiyu. Now, the mural was all but gone, leaving the outline of the door visible. Rowan pushed against it, and it swung open smoothly, considering its age. Rowan stood aside to let her enter before him, then he pulled the door closed behind them.

Cracks in the walls provided just enough light for Cori to see that they were in a long passageway. It was too wide to be a secret passage, but too narrow to be a hallway. It was simply a personal route used by the Karalis when he wanted to avoid the main thoroughfares of the palace.

The moment the door closed, Rowan took her by the shoulders and pushed her against the wall. His lips found hers, and his hands went to her waist. Cori locked her fingers behind his neck and returned his kiss, grinning at his sudden cravings.

She said nothing when he broke away; simply happy to see him smile. She knew it was a genuine one reserved just for her, and it made her heart beat faster.

"Surely you didn't just bring me back here to fondle me," she teased. He squeezed her hip, the other hand rising to brush across her face. His gaze was heavy, molten, but he smiled again.

"Mostly. But there's something else we have to do. Follow me."

He led her through the passageway and into the hallway of his suites. One side of the double doors had come off its hinges and once more, Cori preceded Rowan into the room. They wandered the receiving room for a few moments, each of them lost in thought.

Cori remembered the days they'd spent here in her youth, when Rowan had become her first true friend and they had shared in the secret of being the only two Dijem in the realm. She had, naively, felt like they'd been invincible.

She watched Rowan walk to each doorway. First the bathroom where the pool had been drained, and the panoramic windows smashed. Next was the study, with only rotting shelves to adorn it. He then went to the spiral staircase that led up to the bedroom. He gave the railings a shake. They seemed sound.

He turned from the stairs and took several measured paces back towards the centre of the room. Crouching down, he pressed his hands against the stone floor. Cori couldn't see how this patch of floor was different to any other and was appropriately surprised when a large portion of it sank down with a rumble and slid into a side compartment. Rowan jumped down into a space about as tall as his chest. Cori moved forward and looked into it.

Well, here was the answer to Rowan's wealth. Gold coins - hundreds of thousands of them - were stacked in neat piles on little shelves carved into the stone walls. And that wasn't all. There were also piles of gold bars - Cori didn't even want to guess their individual value - and chests of precious gems and stones. Cori cleared her throat as Rowan started counting coins into a bag.

"This would have gone a long way to keep the realm afloat," she said, thinking of how Antoni had always been requesting more money from her. She'd always found some for her Advisor - mostly by raiding Orin's coffers - but it hadn't been this much.

"I left plenty of money in the coffers," Rowan responded.

"It wasn't enough."

Rowan smiled up at her. "You were never good at your estate management lessons but it's nice that you cared. Here," he flicked a single coin up to her. "Buy yourself something nice." She scowled as she caught the coin, but put it in her pocket nonetheless. Rowan was right about one thing; she was hopeless with money.

Rowan set the bulging sack of coins on the lip of the secret vault and heaved himself up after it. Cori didn't see how he did it, but the stone floor slid out of its compartment and back into place.

They went back to the throne room, this time by the main door. Those closest were surprised to find them suddenly among the crowd, but it quickly turned to jubilation to have the Karalis there. Rowan made directly towards the dais where Han was now conversing with Adro.

"Your coins," Rowan said, handing the bag of coins to Han.

Han opened the top of the bag and peered in. He paled considerably. Olav, looking over Han's shoulder, let out a low whistle. There was enough money there for everyone in Lautan to have a gold coin and more. Cori hoped that if Han decided not to share, he at least had the smart sense to hide the money lest he get his throat slit in his sleep.

"K-Karalis, I-" Han stammered.

"I said I would give it to you," Rowan cut him off. "As I also said I would pay anyone willing to come and work for me. There are domestic duties, but the palace needs to be restored. I have carpenters among those who came from Balforde, but I need a mason."

"Ah well, I'm your man then," Han said, still staring into the bag. "I am a stone master by trade. Even have myself a pair of apprentices."

"It's settled then," Rowan declared. "Let's get to work."

The rest of the day was spent in a flurry of activity. Most of the Lautan citizens went back to town. Rowan told the Balforde folk that there were plenty of rooms on the second floor if they wished to reside in the palace. Some stayed, but most sought lodgings in town where they could sleep in proper beds. The Stablemaster took some men with him to clear the old stables and to erect temporary fencing for the horses. Some took it upon themselves to sweep out the throne room, and others delivered basic furniture from town.

A long table was placed in the throne room and builders' plans laid out on it by Han and the carpentry master from Balforde. Rowan directed them as to which rooms needed restoring first. The kitchens and stables were a high priority, as was the throne room. Han insisted that the Karalis' suites be done in haste too. On dark, cooks from town arrived with hot food, and all work ceased.

Cori sat on the steps of the dais, a roast lamb sandwich in hand, watching the men and women sharing the meal flock around the table and Rowan. Adro came and sat beside her with his own food.

"It's like they've been waiting for him," Cori observed, waving a hand at the busyness around them. Adro nodded in agreement, then said something that Cori hadn't even considered until that moment, but immediately knew it to be true, not just for the people here to see their Karalis, but for her too.

"The realm has hope again."

Chapter Seven

Cori's mind raced across the realm, the pinpricks of life flashing past in a blur.

Higher, Rowan instructed.

She lifted her Hum, imagining herself among the clouds.

Higher again.

How can you find anything from so far away?

Trust your magic.

Cori lifted even higher. The stars and flares of life became almost indistinguishable from each other. Still, she seemed to be able to tell where in the realm she was.

Now, Rowan said.

She abruptly stopped her climb. For a moment she was suspended somewhere above the Nomad Islands, then she fell. It was exhilarating to feel such an expanse of space around her. It was her universe. She owned it.

Rowan was with her, falling faster than she. Cori increased her speed, racing after him. The life forces below flared into sharp relief as they fell closer. Cori picked a Dijem from among them, far brighter than the others. It was towards this light that Rowan sped. He stopped at the very last moment, before the other Dijem could sense him, and flung his Hum skyward again. Cori turned and rocketed after him.

CHAPTER SEVEN

They went so high this time that the world below vanished completely. Rowan caught hold of her, wrapping her Hum in his.

Time to go back, he told her.

No, more, she begged. She loved this freedom; it was intoxicating. She wanted to hurtle across the realm forever, get lost in this weightlessness, surrender to the madness. He indulged her, pulling her down in another free fall. Laughter bubbled within her as they fell. Faster and faster they went until they were all that existed. And then they slammed back into their bodies.

Cori opened her eyes, and the world reeled in sharp clarity around her. She breathed hard, as if she'd physically been racing. She didn't want to stop. The cliff was close by, with the ocean below. She could jump just to feel the rush one more time.

She shook her head, coming back to herself better. They were laying on their backs in the cliff side garden beyond the Karalis' suite. Rowan had finished the title-less book about energy release and had suggested they try it.

The waves crashed against the cliffs below. No, Cori wouldn't jump, that would be stupid. And in any case, Rowan would have stopped her. He had played her anchor and wasn't close to intoxication like her. Exhilaration still rushed through her though, setting her heart thundering and her skin tingling. Although it was night, even colours seemed brighter. This must be the increased mental clarity. She wanted the feeling to stay. She looked to the side and knew how she could get the fix she wanted.

She rolled towards Rowan, throwing her leg over his waist to straddle him, then she leaned down and kissed him. Her hands crept beneath his shirt to steal the warmth of his skin. He laughed against her lips at her urgency, but once more that night he indulged her.

They'd been at the palace for a few weeks now, and the return of the Karalis breathed new life into Lautan. The streets bustled with purpose as the workmen restoring the palace came to and fro. True to his word, Rowan hired most who came for a job. The kitchens were restored and a handful of cooks now lived there. The Stablemaster took on a few lads from the town as hands, and others who didn't have a trade made themselves available to clean and serve. They called themselves servants, which made Cori uncomfortable, but the people seemed to take pride in the title.

Cori herself helped wherever she could. Some days would find her in the stables with the horses. Others she would drop by the kitchens to see if they needed anything. Sometimes she went to town with the purse of the estate to settle invoices for materials used at the palace. It all felt so surreal to be doing menial tasks when Cadmus was out there and a war with him was imminent.

They discussed the war sometimes. Rowan appointed two captains; Ether, who was a cousin of the Head of Shaw and had fought in some border wars against Hearth and Han, who knew everything about everyone and hadn't gotten to the top spot in Lautan without his considerable fighting skills.

In meetings with the captains, they discussed recruitment, weapon procurement and strategies. Han, surprisingly, had information on a potential lead to Cadmus. Not quite a year ago he'd been approached by a Hearthian man who had offered him a purse of gold to fight for the Karalis. Han had wisely declined, but the man had said if he changed his mind, Han could find him in a town called Hammat on Hearth's border. Daiyu had come and instilled some fear into Lautan after that, but Han had remained resolute in his decision.

Late at night, once everyone had retired, Rowan, Cori and Adro would seek each other out to talk about how they would kill Cadmus when the time came.

The first night they met, Cori was shocked to see Jonothan tailing after Rowan. Adro had been too, for he voiced his concern.

"The boy's a bit young for this sort of talk, isn't he?"

"Perhaps," Rowan had replied as he'd steered Jonothan towards a seat. "But maybe if he hears what actually goes on in wars then he may think twice about rushing into the next one."

It was a chiding and Jonothan had hung his head, appropriately contrite. Cori thought losing half an arm was deterrent enough, but she didn't say so. And that was how Jonothan joined their circle.

One evening, close to a month after they'd returned to Lautan, Cori found herself in Adro's office. He'd taken up residence in the old Advisor's suite beside that of the Karalis. The front room of the suite was an office and was partway through being restored. The walls had a fresh coat of white paint, and a fine dark wood desk had been placed in the centre of the room. The only thing left to do was lay fresh carpet.

"But this one is cheaper, why not accept it?"

"Because that smithy doesn't have the steel available yet. See here? They want a retainer. By the time the steel gets to port, we'll be paying double."

Cori squinted at the numbers, not seeing at all what Adro was talking about. They had been looking at proposals from smiths for the provisioning of weapons for their soldiers. She was perched on the corner of the desk while Adro sorted through the paper before him. He set the proposal they'd just read in a rejected pile.

"How do you know all this?"

"Starch has a few merchant vessels." Adro marked a few notes on a slip of parchment before pulling the next proposal towards him. "He taught me to do the books. I also have a few holdings in the far south myself. They keep me with a steady income. Most Dijem I know have some assets, don't you?"

Cori made a noncommittal sound in the back of her throat. She had always lived in the moment, expecting to die any day, and had never considered that she should make long-term contingency plans.

The door to the office opened, and Rowan and Jonothan entered. Rowan placed four beers on the table and gifted Cori a kiss on the cheek.

"How are you faring?"

"Well," replied Adro. "There are a few bogus proposals but a few very good ones too. See, this smithy gets his iron from the Dodici mines." Rowan scanned the proposal and nodded appreciatively.

"What about you?" Adro asked, selecting one of the beers and pulling the cork from it. He handed it to Cori, then uncorked his own. "How was your day?"

"Well enough. The stables are finally complete, but Olav got into a brawl with one of the carpenters. That took a while to smooth over." Rowan handed the third beer to Jonothan, who pulled the cork with his teeth.

"Han needs to get rid of Olav," Cori muttered. Han was civil to her in the presence of the Karalis, but she knew both he and Olav were still out to pay her back for the beating she'd once dealt them.

"I've spoken to him but he insists that Olav is too good a mason to let go."

"You're the Karalis. Order it."

"That's not the relationship I want to have with my workers, Cori."

Cori sipped her beer. "I'll deal with Olav if you like."

Rowan laughed. "There's a reason I won't have you about when I'm dealing with the masons."

They sat quietly for a time, each unwinding from another long day.

"Cadmus then?" Adro said finally, beginning their evening ritual of discussing their nemesis. Cori saw Rowan visibly deflate and wondered if they should give the topic a rest for that night. It wasn't like they ever got far. They discussed ways to kill Cadmus. Daiyu was defeated but her master's mind was still strong and he wouldn't succumb to the usual songs. A Deathsong would take too long to sing to maturity, even if the three adults wove it. Killing him in combat was so far the best option, but they wanted more in case that failed. They always circled back to the strange song that Jarrah had used to kill the rogue Dijem.

"I have an idea," Jonothan said timidly. Until then, he'd endured these meetings in relative silence. Cori and Adro were quiet, but Rowan gave him an encouraging smile.

"Go on, then."

"Well, if Jarrah knew the song, then maybe the other elders knew the song too."

"Yes, we know that to be a likelihood, given Starch was always present at the killings," Rowan replied.

"Well, what if we ask them?"

"I would if I could, but so far I haven't been able to contact Acacia, even to get you home and Starch fled after the battle at the keep."

"Daniyl -"

"-Is not an elder," Rowan finished harshly. "I guarantee he would not have known the song."

"We could look for the others," Jonothan added after a moment.

"He might be right," Cori agreed slowly. "We haven't thought of a single other option."

Rowan spread his fingers wide, palms up in helplessness. "Who can I spare? I'm tied to this place. I need you and Adro here too."

"I-" began Jonothan. Rowan held up a finger to silence him.

"Don't even suggest it."

"It would have to be me," Adro said heavily. "I'd be the only one who could coax it out of Starch-"

"I'm sure I could coax it out of him," Cori cut in.

"-Without killing him," Adro finished.

They sat quietly for a time before Rowan rubbed his temples and sighed. "I'll have to think on it."

* * *

The Hen clucked nervously, perhaps sensing its fate to come.

CHAPTER SEVEN

Cori put the bird on the chopping block. Pinning its body under her knee, she stretched its neck and lifted the hatchet. A swift chop and the bird was silenced. She set the carcass aside to drain and reached for the next hen.

"Here you are."

Cori glanced up to see Rowan striding towards her from the palace. She did a double take and rocked back from her task, grinning at him.

"Well, don't you look like you're set to ruffle some feathers."

He paused before her, straightening his pressed white shirt. She saw rubies flashing at the cuffs, an effective contrast to his deep blue pants. His hair was brushed and tied neatly, and he'd shaved. He raised an eyebrow at her and looked pointedly at the birds, both dead and alive, surrounding her.

"Must I point out the irony of your words?"

Cori let go of the bird she was about to slaughter and stood.

"Why are you so dressed up?"

Rowan smiled. "The Karaliene's Coterie has arrived."

"Oh. You're going to meet them?"

"You'll come with me."

She grinned and held up her hands, sticky with blood and feathers. "Like this?"

"They would most likely recognise you like this, considering the stories," Rowan said dryly, stepping back to stay out of her reach, "but no, Han has organised some nice clothes for you too."

"Han?"

"He knows a tailor, or, no doubt, has bullied one into assisting."

"Well then, I best get dressed."

Cori entered the throne room not half an hour later. She

was scrubbed clean of chicken blood and had tidied her hair into a neat braid. She wore loose cotton pants that, when she stood still, looked like a skirt. They were blue, though several shades lighter than Rowan's, and were matched to a white blouse.

Rowan sat on Arasy, leaning forward to chat to Adro, who lounged on the top step. Jonothan was there too, standing quietly by the throne. Both he and Adro were wearing colours the same as Cori, and she realised that they'd been dressed as Advisors to the throne.

Cori reached them as Han and Ether entered the room. They were both dressed in bold colours of deep blue and red. Captain uniforms. Cori was quietly impressed by Han's work - the six of them looked like a true court now.

"They're about to enter," Ether informed them. Rowan straightened, and Adro stood. As the first Advisor, he took his place on the left of the throne and Cori stood beside him. Jonothan stood to the right of the throne and a few steps back - the place of a page who may need to rush quickly to the whims of his Karalis. Han and Ether stood side by side below the dais and to one side.

"They're your coterie," Adro said to Cori in a worried tone, "don't you think you should stand beside the throne?"

"Oh, don't worry," Rowan said dryly before Cori could respond. "She can distance herself as much as she wants, they'll find her."

Cori scowled but was cut short of replying by movement at the end of the hall. Five people entered the room, including Ailey. They walked in a tight group, equally awed and overwhelmed by the size of the room.

Cori glanced aside to her peers and found Rowan watching

her rather than their guests. His look was calculating, and their eyes met for a moment before he looked away. No one on the dais spoke, but the coterie whispered to each other, and it sounded like a wind blowing through the partly repaired arches. They were three quarters of the way up the hall when one of the men in the group stopped dead, causing the others to stumble in their pace.

"It's her!" The man said excitedly, pointing at Cori with one hand and clutching at Ailey's arm with the other. "You were right! It's her!" The man was a tall, weedy fellow with strange spectacles on his face that magnified his eyes. He dropped to both knees and raised both arms to the ceiling. "Never in my lifetime did I think I'd see this day!"

"Why do I end up with the fanatics?" Cori groaned under her breath. Adro snorted with laughter. Rowan kept a straight face, but only just.

"My lady Karaliene," the man continued, "my name is Evdox and I am eternally in your service."

There was a long pause in which Cori realised Rowan and Adro were looking at her, waiting for her to respond. She bit back a sigh.

"It isn't me that requires your service," Cori finally spoke. She gestured to Rowan with an open palm. "The Karalis requested your presence."

"This is the Karalis?" A second woman in the group asked sceptically.

"Hush, Bharti," Ailey urged, "It's really him." But the group had worked itself into a state.

"But you killed the Karalis," a second man said. He had a stoic posture and might have been a soldier. "You ripped him apart and fed him to the spirit trees in the north."

"That's not how she killed him," the third man, an orange haired fellow with wide blue eyes, countered. His round face made him look younger than he probably was. "She killed him in a sword fight that lasted two days and a night. She gave his head to the state of Resso and that's why they followed her to war."

Adro threw up his arms and turned away. "I can't. I'm done."

Rowan stared at the two men, his eyebrows lifting higher and higher with each statement. Jonothan looked at Cori, his mouth slightly ajar. Below the dais, Ether and Han muttered to each other, perhaps deciding if they should intervene. Cori looked to the arched stone ceiling. Why her?

"I'm sorry, Cori," Ailey said. "I tried to warn them."

Bharti sucked in a breath. "You use her true name?"

"Yes," Cori said before they could go any further. "And I would prefer that the rest of you did as well. Now, please present yourself to the Karalis."

The group exchanged looks, and two of the men continued their bickering in whispers, but finally they collected themselves and moved forward. Ailey bowed first.

"My Karalis, I am Ailey of Shaw, executor of the Karaliene's trust."

"Karalis, sir," the second woman stepped forward, hand over her heart, "I am Bharti of Resso, emissary of the Karaliene, appointed to the task of recruiting followers to our lady."

The orange haired man was next. He declared himself as Kenneth of Hale, also an emissary dedicated to keeping tales of the Karaliene alive and recruiting followers. Cori could only wonder what sort of following she had after hearing

CHAPTER SEVEN

their versions of how she'd apparently murdered Rowan.

Evdox was next. He was a scholar from Dodici who had often travelled to Balforde to read the texts Cori had sent there for safekeeping. He proudly declared that he had read every book in the library. Rowan's interest was predictably piqued.

The last person to step forward was the soldier.

"I am Eamoyn. I was a soldier who discovered the Coterie when I went searching for my missing brother, who had also been a member. He vanished while tracking the Karaliene through Dodici."

"Eamoyn is a Hearthian name," Rowan observed, leaning forward. Cori felt tension spring to the room as Han and Ether put their hands on their weapons. She noted that Eamoyn had neglected to announce his origin, and she wondered if he had done so on purpose. She flexed her fingers, ready to fight if she had to. Eamoyn inclined his head.

"Yes, I am Hearthian and yes, I fought for the false Karalis. I am not proud to admit it, Karalis," he added quickly when Rowan looked as if he might speak. "Few are proud to admit it but the false Karalis has Hearth under a spell and has done so for centuries. There is no way to defy him."

"There are many ways to defy him." Rowan sat back in the throne and considered Eamoyn. "Do you serve the Karaliene now or are you merely using the Coterie to escape Cadmus?"

"I serve the Karaliene," he said, his eyes flicking to Cori's then back to the throne. "And as an extension of that, I serve you also, Karalis."

Cori reached out with her Hum and was pleased to find that Eamoyn was Hiram.

Are you telling the truth? She demanded. His eyes glazed over and she felt an affirmative feeling.

Do you know where Cadmus is? This time the feeling was negative, though he had thoughts of seeing Daiyu circling Tengah, much the same memory she had felt from Ahsyn. She withdrew her Hum to find Rowan watching her, waiting for her verdict.

"I believe him," she shrugged. Rowan nodded and stood.

"Thank you all for coming when I asked. I admit I didn't know what to expect but your credentials are rather unique and already I can see uses for them in my court. Would you consider staying?"

Cori already knew what they would say, but she was pleased when they all looked at one another then responded to Rowan with a resounding "Yes."

* * *

Rowan had had a rough day, Cori could tell. Usually in front of others he maintained his calm, almost indifferent, demeanour. But that day his frustrations were seeping through.

It started in the morning, when one of the ovens caught light, burning half the kitchen down before it was brought under control. Half a dozen kitchen hands had been badly burned and Rowan had spent most of the morning with them, helping Harmony apply salves.

He was moody after that and Cori should have spoken to him; she knew the suffering of others was a trigger for him and that he'd need time to collect his thoughts. No sooner was he finished in the kitchen though, then the Stablemaster called on him to inform him that a temperamental stallion had escaped his stall and attacked and killed a good broodmare.

It was something that was sometimes unavoidable when dealing with livestock but Rowan, who took pleasure in his stud, took it to heart. He ordered the stallion killed as well. Cori hadn't been there when he'd received that news, otherwise she definitely would have removed him from the situation. When Rowan began ordering killings, he was close to going into a cold fury.

The final straw was Cori herself.

She met with both Rowan and Adro late in the afternoon for a drink and meal. Rowan, in a heavy voice, told Adro that he would have to seek out Starch.

"I see no other option," he said. "And the longer we delay in finding this song, the more time we are giving Cadmus. Do you think you can find him?"

Adro nodded slowly. "I couldn't be certain which of his haunts he may have gone to, but I would wager that he's at Wolfman's Peak. It would be the easiest place to flee Tauta on one of his boats if he needed to." Adro took a bottle of wine from the table and poured each of them a glass. He held his up as a salute. "Don't worry, mate, I know this is necessary. We haven't been able to think of any other way."

They managed only a sip when there was a commotion outside the room they were in. Rowan sank back into his chair, perhaps hoping it would pass them by. Cori stood and went to the door, poking her head out to see what was happening.

"- Last straw, Han! I am sick of him bullying my lads!"

"It's part and parcel of being an apprentice to cop a bit

from their elders."

"Not when he's beating them black and blue!" They reached the door and Cori opened it wider.

"Is the Karalis in there?" The Carpentry Master demanded.

"We don't need to bother him with this," Han retaliated.

"Let them in, Cori," Rowan said tiredly from behind her. She stepped back, letting the two men enter. She followed them back to the table and stood beside Han.

"Karalis," the Carpentry Master began with a bow at the waist before jabbing a finger at Han. "His man, Olav, has been beating my lads again. Young Rogan was so blue he couldn't get his work done today."

"Han," Rowan said, rubbing his face, "we've spoken about Olav before. You said you'd pull him into line."

"And I will, sir. Honestly, the boy isn't that bad."

"I beg to differ," Cori muttered under her breath. She had seen some of Olav's victims around the palace.

"Hey there, girly," Han warned her, "mind your business, yeh?"

"Han, Olav has to go," Rowan said bluntly.

"But sir -"

"Han, I've given him too many chances."

"Sir, I really must insist that -"

Cori's anger flared, both at Han's dismissal of her and his defiance of Rowan. She picked up a cheese knife from the platter on the table.

"The Karalis said he has to go," she reiterated and Han turned on her.

His thuggish side broke through. He snarled at her and swung his arm. It would have resulted in a backhand across her face had she not swayed out of reach and raised the

CHAPTER SEVEN

cheese knife. With uncanny precision, she stabbed the knife through his hand while it was still mid-swing, driving the blade down and pinning it to the tabletop.

Both Adro and the Carpentry Master yelped in surprise. Rowan jumped up in shock, his chair falling back. Han stared white-faced at his hand, then let out a long, low howl.

Rowan swore. "Cori, what have you done!"

"He deserved it," she retorted.

"Out," he said, covering his face with his hands. Suddenly he picked up his wineglass and flung it against the wall. "Get out!" He roared over the shattering of glass.

The Carpentry Master and Adro fled. Cori turned on her heels and stormed from the room after them. She slammed the door so hard the frame cracked.

Rage consumed her as she stalked through the palace, flinging her hands to crack the wall or smash a window every few corridors. Her anger was hot though, and with no one to take it out on, it eventually cooled.

Then she felt a little remorseful; she probably shouldn't have stabbed Han, but he'd treated her disparagingly since they'd arrived. She knew he and Olav had intended to get her back for the beating she'd given them in the ally. She was just getting in first.

She found herself at the Karalis' suite and entered. She would apologise to Rowan; he hadn't deserved to get stuck in the middle of this. He wasn't in the suite, though she hadn't expected him to be there. He was probably still tending to Han's injury. She decided to wait. He'd been angry; no doubt he'd seek her out to rage at her.

She waited hours. Darkness fell, and she worried. She reached out with her Hum and found a wall of cold fury waiting for her. She hastily withdrew and decided to give him more time. What ifs leached at her; had she gone too far? What if Rowan stayed mad at her?

Jonothan was the one who eventually came for her. He entered the room timidly, his fingers plucking at the pinned sleeve of his missing arm. Perhaps he'd been warned that she might be in a mood.

"The Karalis has asked to see you in the throne room," he blurted and fled before she could ask why. Worry knotted in her stomach, but she went to find Rowan.

He sat on his throne and watched her approach with a stoic expression. Official business, then. Cori moved quickly down the room, the sound of her footsteps on stone the only thing to penetrate the tense silence. She stopped before the dais and resisted the urge to bow mockingly.

"Karalis," she did say quite dryly to boost her bravado. He surveyed her for a long moment.

"I need you to go with Adro to find Starch," he told her finally, his voice curiously flat.

Cori experienced a few things at once. First, a sinking sensation in the pit of her stomach as her mind processed his words, then a cold dread that washed over her as she realised what he was telling her and finally, a crippling fear seized her as she considered the implications. This had been the final straw for him. Her fear that her violent tendencies would drive him away, had come to fruition. He was sending her away.

Chapter Eight

"You're sending me away," her voice was hoarse, and she couldn't stop the shaking that had started in her hands. His brow knitted. "Is it because of Han? Because I can fix it. Please." She hated that she begged, but she needed him in her life. She couldn't just walk away. The fear of being alone, like she had been for five hundred years, was a sharp knife in her gut and she pressed a hand to her chest, an attempt to stop the hole growing.

"I'm not sending you away because of Han," Rowan said, and she heard surprise in his voice. She looked at him and saw his eyes wide. He stood and took the steps of the dais in two bounds, landing before her. He put his hands on her arms, feeling her shaking. "I would never send you away from me if there wasn't a need."

"Why then?" She whispered. The relief was intense, but the fear of what could have been was still there. And he had still asked her to go.

"Because," he explained, just as quietly, "I know you will come back. I need that song, *we* need that song and I cannot guarantee that once Adro is reunited with Starch, that he'll return."

His reason was logical, but she didn't like it. "Can I say

no?"

He hugged her then, as tight as he could. "Of course you can say no. I want you to say no, but the Karalis needs this of you." Cori pressed her face against his chest and clenched his shirt in her fists. He smelled of his day's work; horses and comfrey.

"Why would you think I'd send you away for something as silly as an argument with Han?" He demanded, almost furiously.

"It's only a matter of time." The relief made her weak now. "There will be a moment when you realise who I really am and you won't want me around anymore."

Rowan drew back and tilted her chin so their eyes met. "I know who you really are, Cori," he said fiercely, "and we may argue or disagree, but there will never be a time when I don't want you at my side. You are my forever. I mean it."

"So you're not mad about Han?"

"Not at all," he asserted. "It was messy to clean up, true, but don't think I didn't see that he was going to hit you first. If he had, I would have been quicker to kill him than you were to stab him."

Warmth spread through her. So many years fending for herself, it was still a pleasant surprise when his protective side showed.

"You were so angry, though."

"I've had a bad day and knowing that I had to ask you and Adro to do this didn't help."

"Will I have to kill Adro if he doesn't come back?" She asked eventually. She would do it if she had to, but she liked Adro and didn't relish the thought of having to be his executioner. Rowan gave a small laugh.

CHAPTER EIGHT

"No, please don't kill Adro. If he wants to remain with Starch, then I won't begrudge him that. Just make sure you come back alive."

"I'll do my best," she muttered. "When do we leave?"

"As soon as possible, unfortunately."

* * *

"You can still say no." Rowan told her.

She was mounted on Mischief - Rowan had insisted that she ride his stallion - and he stood at the horse's side, his hand on her leg.

"You know I can't."

"You can," he insisted. He looked up at her, worried. No longer behind his Karalis mask, his doubts about his decision showed.

To the side, Adro sat upon a bay gelding, twisted to check the straps of his saddle pack. What he thought of Cori accompanying him, he didn't say, but she was sure the topic would arise once they were alone.

"Are you sure you'll be all right?" She asked Rowan. She knew she had to do this task, but the thought of leaving him still felt wrong.

"We'll be back in a month," Adro told them both. "If the travelling is good, we'll be at Wolfman's Peak within a fortnight."

Cori didn't look away from Rowan. She could feel the anxiety radiating from him. "Will you be all right?" She repeated.

"I'll be fine," he told her, though he couldn't even muster a smile, before looking at Adro. "Don't let her get hurt."

"I wouldn't dream of returning to face you if I did," Adro replied dryly. Rowan's gaze returned to Cori.

"Try not to kill too many people."

"I'll try," she smiled at him, then nudged Mischief forward. "You better let us go."

Rowan finally released her leg and stood by the stable door as she and Adro rode down the drive. She turned once to look over her shoulder, and Rowan raised a hand in farewell before he was lost from sight as they descended the cliff road.

As they rode through Lautan, Cori tried to get a hold of her emotions. Adro, correctly interpreting that she didn't want to talk, stayed quiet. They gained the gate, and Cori kicked Mischief to a canter. The dapple stallion covered the ground with a smooth stride that Adro's bay had to race to meet.

She felt a small touch on her mind, but she didn't reach back for it lest she never let go. The three of them had agreed that Cori would contact Rowan after a fortnight and that it was not safe to do so otherwise. The reach required to communicate such a distance may alert Cadmus to the fact they were separated.

They gained the hill that provided a vantage point over Lautan and paused, looking back.

"Do you think he'll be all right?" Adro asked, a hint of worry in his tone.

"He managed for a thousand years without us, I'm sure he'll handle a month."

Adro rubbed his brow. "You make us sound so dispensable." He turned his horse back to the road and Cori followed.

"We are in the greater scheme of things."

They rode at a ground eating trot after that, making good

time along the road from Lautan. Eventually they joined a coastal highway that would lead them north and slowed to a walk to let the horses rest.

"So, you're going to kill me?" Adro asked after a time. Cori wasn't surprised that he'd come to that conclusion, but was that he raised it.

"You seem so calm about it," she replied. He stared ahead, his mouth working.

"It was bound to happen."

Cori felt her stomach twist. Was she so psychotic that Adro simply assumed that she'd kill him one day? Or was his faith in Rowan waning, and he expected his Karalis to order the blow.

"Every time push comes to shove," she explained, "Rowan has always explicitly told me to spare you. Every time."

"But you still ask the question?"

"Of course I do, it's my job. It doesn't mean that I want to, however."

Adro was thoughtfully quiet for a time. Finally he asked, "so why did he send you?"

"He doesn't think you'll come back."

Adro snorted but didn't reply. They resumed their trot, and for a time the conversation ceased.

They passed through a few farmsteads throughout the day, and by evening they reached the first town. It wasn't as big as Lautan, but it had a few taverns to choose from. Adro pointed out one that was brightly lit and had an accompanying stable. They paid the Stablemaster a handful of silver coins to take Mischief and the bay - whose name was Morro - and entered the bar.

"Could we book two rooms for the night, and dinner,

please," Adro asked the woman behind the bar. She narrowed her eyes at the two of them, distrusting their golden eyes. Adro held up a gold coin - more than rooms and meals were worth - and the woman took it.

"Take a seat," she gestured out past them. "Your rooms will be ready after your meal."

They picked a table in the corner, out of the way but close to the fire. Cori went to sit at it while Adro got their beers. She considered the room. Some of the patrons stared at her, looking away hastily when they saw her glance at them, but most were occupied with their drinks or meals. There was no music playing, but a man was setting up his drum and getting ready for the evening entertainment. Adro arrived at the table and set their mugs down.

"I'm just going to the outhouse," he told her. "I'll be back in a moment."

She nodded and watched him leave out the back. No sooner was he gone then three men came to her table with their drinks and sat down.

"Hullo there, love," one of them said with a wide smile. "Not from around these parts, eh?"

He was a handsome man. Young and cocky. Cori would wager that he'd weaselled his way into most of the beds of the young women in his town. Obviously hers was his next conquest. She forced a smile back at him. She'd dealt with his type before. More often than not it would end in a fight, but she figured that if she waited for Adro to come back, they would probably clear off with little trouble.

"No, I'm not. I'm just passing through."

He jutted his chin to her drink. "It's a nice night, eh? Why don't we drink to it?"

CHAPTER EIGHT

Cori reached slowly for her drink, looking at the other two men to see if there was a trap. They weren't looking at her, rather talking to each other across the table.

Suddenly Adro was there. He slammed his hand down on top of Cori's glass and the three men jumped in their seats. Adro jabbed a finger at one of the two men who hadn't spoken to her.

"What did you put in her drink?"

Cori tilted her head to look into the beer through the glass. She could just see the remnants of powder dissolving on the bottom. She pushed her chair back and stood, pushing away the wild combination of fury and fear that bloomed in her chest. Assholes.

"Awh man, it wasn't me!" The man groaned, lifting his hands in surrender. Adro grabbed him by the front of the shirt, lifting him bodily from his chair. The other two men jumped to their feet.

"Hey there!" the woman behind the bar called out. "No fighting in the bar!"

"Outside, then," Adro growled. He dragged the man he already had hold of towards the door.

"After you," Cori said to the handsome one. He stared at her, wide eyed, then rushed after Adro and his friend, Cori and the third man close behind. There was a deafening clatter of cutlery and scraping of chairs as the rest of the patrons followed.

Adro dragged the man, who was now hollering for help, into the street. The tavern patrons circled around, yelling and cheering. Adro shoved the man forward and raised his fists. The man staggered a few steps, then turned. He looked around wildly for a way out. When he found none, he lifted his own fists tentatively.

Adro's first punch landed square in the man's stomach. His second cracked his jaw.

"Are you going to help your friend?" Cori asked the handsome man who was standing beside her.

"Erm, it would be unfair if I joined in," he excused himself weakly.

"Not if I join in too."

Cori aimed a punch at his pretty face, putting a bit of magic behind the swing. The handsome man jolted away from her and into the circle. She followed him in, kicking at his side. He went to the ground with an oomph.

They were easy pickings, the two of them, and Cori could only take pleasure in the fight from knowing that these thugs would hopefully not prey on any more unsuspecting women.

She punched the man twice more in the face, hoping to disfigure him and make him a little less desirable, before she let him find his feet and stagger away. The crowd parted to let him free. Cori turned to find Adro had finished his fight too. His victim had not been as fortunate as hers and was lying in a bloody, groaning heap at his feet.

"Where's the third one?" Adro said with a heaving breath. Cori glanced back to the crowd in time to see the third man pushing through the people and making a break for it down the street. She laughed.

"He's long gone."

Adro reached down and pulled the man he had beaten to his feet. "You've learned your lesson?" he asked. "No more preying on the ladies."

The man groaned through bloody lips, but nodded. Adro gestured to the crowd. "Can someone come help this fellow home?"

No one moved for a long moment, and Cori knew no one wanted to be associated with the man. Finally, a woman stepped forward.

"He's my brother," she sighed, embarrassed. "I'll take him home to Pa."

Adro helped the man's arm around his sister's shoulder, then watched the two of them limp away. Now that the fight was over, the crowd moved back into the tavern. Adro and Cori were left alone in the quiet, dark street.

"You all right?" He asked her.

"Yes. You?"

He inspected his knuckles. "A bit bruised, but none of the blood is mine." Cori looked at her own hands and decided the same.

"Do you think we'll be allowed back in the tavern?"

"We better be. We paid triple the price for those rooms."

They went back inside. A few people cheered and clapped them back to their table. The bar woman came over and set their meals down.

"Thanks for taking it outside," she said. "Most don't."

"No problem," Adro said, pulling his plate towards him. He tucked straight into his meal.

Cori looked at her own, not feeling much of an appetite.

"Not a great start to the trip," she muttered. "Rowan wouldn't be impressed."

"Hey now," Adro said, patting her hand on top of the table. "This was their fault, not yours. And no one got killed. I'm sure Rowan would be impressed by your restraint."

She smiled. Adro was right. And no doubt if Rowan had been here, he probably would have been out fighting in the street too.

Still, that night she lay on the bed in her room and didn't sleep. Old habits kept her on edge, expecting the men to come back for her.

Fear of being attacked wasn't the only thing that kept her up. It had been months since she'd slept alone, and she hadn't realised until now how comfortable she had become sleeping beside someone else each night. She missed Rowan.

Chapter Nine

"We can go back to Lautan," Adro said the moment he saw Cori's haggard appearance the following morning.

"If one sleepless night was enough to fail this task, I wouldn't have come to begin with. And if last night was anything to go by, I don't think this trip will be an easy one."

Adro tightened Morro's girth. "I still can't believe the nerve of those pricks."

"Clearly a usual game of theirs." Cori lifted her pack and tied it to the back of her saddle.

"Well, hopefully they'll think better of it next time."

They left the town at sunrise before anyone was about. The highway they followed veered inland.

"You know, I've never asked you how you met Rowan," Adro said when they stopped for lunch.

"He hasn't told you?" Cori selected some bread and cheese from her pack and handed half to Adro.

"He said it was your story to tell."

Cori chewed her lip thoughtfully as she sliced her cheese with a paring knife. She wondered if Rowan declined to tell Adro their story because he thought she might be ashamed of where she had come from. Was she?

No, she decided. To be ashamed of her upbringing would mean she was ashamed of her mother, of Saasha, and of all the servants who had helped raise her.

"I was a servant in his palace," she said eventually. Although she wasn't ashamed, she braced herself, expecting Adro to laugh, to taunt her the way the Hiram nobles had.

"As a cook?" He asked curiously.

"How did you know?"

"You're a good one," he smiled, popping a bit of cheese in his mouth. "Back at the keep when you would help Cat, I could tell you'd had some training."

Cat. Her quirky, upbeat friend who had been a hopeless and horrid cook had ended up as a pawn of Cadmus and an eventual casualty of the war.

"What sort of Karalis was he back then?"

She thought of all the things Rowan had been; cold, frightening and unforgiving on the outside but warm, kind and generous when it had only been her around. She tried to think of something he had been in both his personalities. "He was... reticent."

"Even to you?"

"Yes. Sometimes. But not intentionally, I think."

"He's good at being in charge, but he doesn't seem to like it much," Adro surmised.

"It's not a very desirable job once you do it," Cori muttered. She finished her bread and stood.

"You're the only other person who would know." Adro smiled and stood as well.

* * *

CHAPTER NINE

That night they left the highway on dark and found a sheltering stand of trees to camp under. Adro made a fire while Cori cut up some of the fresher food they'd brought with them.

"So what about you?" Cori asked, continuing their conversation from earlier. "How did you start out in life?"

"I was the seventh of eleven sons," he said with a fond smile. "I think my Ma kept having babies because she wanted a girl. In any case, it was enough lads that my Da could man his fishing boat entirely within the family. We weren't poor, but we all had to work to keep it that way. Thanks," he accepted the food Cori handed him.

"You told me once that your father sold you to Starch. Don't you hate him for that?"

Adro shrugged. "I was almost a man grown. We were taking our ship on its first voyage north to Dodici and Starch found us and bought passage with us. Ginto was what we called Dijem down there. They were thought of as prophets, but now I know it's just an uncanny ability to lie through one's teeth," Adro laughed and Cori nodded along. She'd once been to the south and called 'Ginto'. They'd treated her reverently. Adro continued.

"Well, Starch gave me the absolute shivers. Every time I turned around, I would find him watching me. Once I even thought I heard his voice in my head."

"I know the feeling," Cori muttered and this time it was Adro's turn to nod in agreement.

"Aye, I can imagine how intense Rowan would have been. Anyway, we reached Dodici and Starch handed Da a sack of gold, told me I was going with him and that was the last I saw of my family." Adro was quiet for a moment as he poked the fire. Cori picked at her food, not liking the feeling that discussions of family brought up in her.

"Starch explained what I was as we travelled. At the borders of Dodici and Shaw, we met up with the rest of Starch's House. There were ten of them; all sailors or sea maidens of some sort. My training was rushed as we continued north and into the Last Fight. A bit over a decade later I was turned full Dijem during the final stand against Cadmus and Daiyu."

"The same time as Rowan."

"Yes, the same time as Rowan."

"Do you find it interesting that we were never asked if we wanted to be Dijem? I'd never thought about it before hearing your story. But…" she trailed off and Adro looked up, his warm gold eyes meeting hers.

"You feel Rowan forced you into this?"

It was Cori's turn to take up a stick and poke the fire. "I don't feel like he forced me, but he never asked if it was what I wanted. I guess being born knowing that you're going to live forever like he was, it didn't even cross his mind that I might not."

"Would you go back and change it if you could?"

"I don't know. Sometimes I wish I could, and other times I couldn't imagine my life any other way. Would you?"

"I think I feel the same way as you."

They sat quietly for a time, only the crackling of the fire penetrating the silence between them.

"So," Adro said finally, his voice once more cheery, "if you had to choose between cake or rum every day for the rest of your life, what would it be?"

"Rum," Cori laughed, "Hands down. Do you prefer fist

fights or sword fights?"

"Fist fights. I've never lost."

Their game carried them through that night and the next two on the road. By the fifth day they were due to come across their next town. They weren't expecting the town to come to them.

"Can you see that?" Cori asked, squinting up the road. Adro stood up in his stirrups, using his hand to shield his eyes against the midday sun.

"People. Lots of them."

"Weapons or no?"

Adro looked at her. "Is that a joke?"

Cori drew her sword and laid it across her lap. As they neared the group, she pulled Mischief to the side of the road and Adro fell in behind her.

The group contained about fifty people and they trudged wearily, paying little heed to Cori and Adro. As they passed, Cori noticed that they were dirty, covered in ash and blood.

"What happened to you?" Cori asked, reining Mischief in. Some of them glanced at her, but no one spoke.

"Stop," Adro said, dismounting from Morro. "We can help you!"

Those nearest him flinched away, but a few children finally stopped.

"They burned our homes," one of them said miserably.

"Who did?"

"A gold eyes like you," a man spat, pulling one of the children away. Cori and Adro glanced at each other.

Not Cadmus, surely? Cori queried.

Maybe one of his creations?

"You don't need to fear us," Adro said aloud, "we won't hurt you."

"Won't you?" The man countered.

"Adro, give them some coins. All of you, go to Lautan and ask for the Karalis. He will help you."

"And how do we know this isn't a trap? It was apparently the Karalis' men who burned our homes for not joining him," a woman piped up.

"He is the true Karalis," Adro explained. The people looked in two minds; some hopeful, most still distrustful. Cori leaned forward in her saddle.

"Tell him," she said, not quite believing the words that were about to come out of her mouth, "that the Karaliene sent you."

Expressions changed at that. The older people in the group exchanged glances.

"Oh, aye, we could travel under your name, Karaliene," the first man who'd spoken said. He didn't smile - he'd seen too much tragedy that day - but he looked relieved.

"Take the coins," Cori said, and Adro held them out to the man who took them and put them in his pants pocket. "Go straight to Lautan and to the palace. I promise you'll be safe there."

"How did you know that would work?" Adro asked as they watched the stragglers walk away.

Cori shrugged awkwardly. "When I used to hunt down the Hearthian armies, I often chased them out of towns and villages. I got a bit of a reputation and I guess it's still around."

"A handy reputation," Adro muttered, though he seemed impressed. "Why doesn't Rowan have the same one?"

"When you kill as indiscriminately as I do, people tend to talk. Rowan was impressively frightening when you were before him, but he was not a horrible person, and only horrible people seem to outlast history." She urged Mischief forward, back onto the road. Adro urged Morro alongside.

"You're not a horrible person," he told her. "I don't know why you talk about yourself that way."

"Should we go and look at the town?" Cori asked, changing the subject away from herself. "See if we can't find this Dijem?"

* * *

They left the horses tied to trees and approached the town on foot. Smoke still billowed from many of the gutted buildings, and a few had flames flickering within. Cori searched nervously with her Hum, at the same time being ready to slam her barriers up if she needed. She'd never fought another Dijem, and she wasn't sure what to expect.

"I really don't know if we should do this," Adro said in a low voice. His sword was in hand, already raised defensively. "Perhaps we should just circle around the town."

"If we don't kill them now, we'll only have to fight them later in the war."

Cori paused at the cornerstone of a house. She could hear voices. She peered around the corner, being careful to keep her body out of sight. There was a group of men there, standing in the middle of the road, talking to each other. She reached out with her Hum. Two were Hiram, two were human. There was no Dijem there.

She held up her fingers to Adro, indicating that there were four of them. He nodded and gestured that she should go first.

She stepped into the open and flicked her hands at the men, flinging two of them high and back. A shout came from behind them and she turned her head to see several more men racing towards them from side streets, swords drawn.

"Cori," Adro groaned before raising his sword to meet the first attacker. Two quick parries and his sword was in the man's chest. Cori pushed at one man while slicing at another. She could feel forces hitting her from the back. The closer the two men got, the stronger the pushes became until she staggered forward with each one.

She tried to turn towards them and flung her magic back at them. To her horror, they ducked low, sliding along the ground. She pushed again, but they swerved aside, preempting her move, before shoving their own magic back at her. These men had been taught how to fight her.

In all her years, she'd met very few who could defend against her. Some brave souls had tried to fight her, but most, when they saw the level of her magic, would run. For the first time in her fighting life, she felt fear.

She managed to stab her sword through a close soldier's neck. She let go of the hilt as the man fell back and turned fully to the two still racing towards her. She put the full force of her strengthening song behind her and shoved with all her might. One of them ducked aside again. The other fool tried to counter with his own magic. He was thrown so high and far that he vanished from sight.

Adro staggered into her as more Hiram soldiers appeared around the side of the building. She pulled her sword from the dead man's neck and lunged at the last of the two who'd been attacking her. He pushed with his magic, but she

CHAPTER NINE

ploughed through it, slashing first at his legs and then at his middle. He cried out and fell back.

She didn't have time to finish the kill - he would die shortly anyway - as she turned back to the scrum Adro was in. She felt his Hum flash and a Hiram close by suddenly sagged to his knees, his eyes glazed. Adro took off his head.

Cori reached out as another man shoved at her.

No, she ordered, and his eyes glazed. He stopped, and she gutted him.

"Grab her!" Someone shouted. A few closed in behind her, but she couldn't turn away from those in front. Desperately, she stabbed forward and reached back with one hand. She was glad to hear unison cries of pain both before and behind her. But it wasn't enough; they caught hold of her arms, pinning her hands down so she couldn't use them.

No! She screamed with her Hum. Some of the men around stopped. Adro killed two of them. Those holding her, though, were all human and unaffected. They forced her to the ground, using their body weight to hold her. Adro roared, staggering backwards as another Hiram man advanced on him. He pivoted through his stagger, punching one of those holding Cori down. She got one hand free and blasted two of the men away from her. More replaced them and caught hold of her arm again. She struggled beneath them, the dirt of the road grazing her back.

Beside her, Adro was overwhelmed. He slashed and dodged, but men were jumping at him, trying to get him to the ground as well. It was clear they wanted her alive as they could have stabbed her by now, but if she didn't do something, they might kill Adro. Even as she struggled, she saw him disappear beneath his attackers.

STOP! She roared with her Hum. Every Hiram there finally froze. She twisted her wrists so her palms faced upwards and, using just the movement of her fingers, she pushed her captors away, shooting them up into the sky.

She scrambled to her feet, taking up Adro's sword, which had fallen from his hands. It was heavy. Using two hands, she swung it at one of the humans over Adro. She cleaved him almost in two. The sword stuck in the man and she let it go, using the last of her strengthening song to blast two more men away and rip the arms off the last.

The street was finally silent, save for the breathing of the Hiram who still stood frozen by her order. Blood stained the dirt road, and dust swirled in the air. Adro lay flat on his back, his eyes closed. She crawled towards him.

Chapter Ten

"Please don't be dead!" She begged.

"I'm not dead," Adro groaned.

Cori sighed with relief. "Thank goodness, Rowan would have killed me if you were."

Adro's eyes snapped open. "Rowan would have killed you?" He said incredulously, then lunged at her, his hands grappling for her throat. "I'm going to kill you for -" he broke off with another groan, flopping back to the ground. Cori laughed and patted his chest.

"Are you hurt? I can't see any blood."

"Just my head," he lifted his hand to cover his eyes, "I need to meditate."

"What?" Cori asked, confused. Then she realised what he was saying. He was about to fall into Hum intoxication. "No," she told him quickly. "Don't meditate. It's better to let it go."

"You sound like Rowan. I told him I can't do it. I'm not as strong as you two are."

"You can be!" Cori said excitedly. Adro lowered his hand to glare at her. "Please Adro, stop this meditating nonsense. It was just a mechanism for the elders to keep the Dijem cowed."

"It's hard," Adro's voice was wavering, his words punctured by long pauses, "to go against what you've known your whole life and to do something you were told would kill you."

"It won't kill you. I'll help you. Come on," she took his hand and pulled him to a sitting position, "let's get somewhere safer than here."

Adro groaned to his feet and looked around. "Shouldn't we bury them?"

"Graves are Rowan's thing, I'm quite happy for them to rot here."

"And them?" Adro nodded to the Hiram still frozen in place. There were four of them.

"Look away," Cori suggested, collecting her sword from where it had fallen. Adro had the good sense to avert his eyes as she quickly dispatched the four men. It would be no good having them come around and follow them north, or to go back to Cadmus and tell him what had happened.

"There was no Dijem here," Adro said lightly, and Cori could tell he was close to losing it. She handed him his sword then took his arm, leading him back to where they'd left the horses.

"No," Cori replied. The lack of Dijem concerned her too. The town's folk had said there had been one here, so that person couldn't be far away.

"Will it hurt?" Adro changed the topic as they reached their mounts. Cori took the reins of both horses and led them, and Adro, further away from the road.

"Maybe a little to start," Cori said truthfully, "but then it becomes pleasant. When it becomes too much fun, that's when you know you're becoming intoxicated. I'll pull you back at that point."

CHAPTER TEN

They came by a stream that was probably the town's main water supply. She let Adro go where he sagged to the ground, his head in his hands. She quickly unsaddled the horses and turned them free to graze along the stream bank.

"All right," Cori said purposefully, sitting down beside Adro. She reached out with her Hum to his. He flinched away at first, but she waited patiently. Finally he reached back towards her and she threaded the notes of her Hum through his, holding on tight. *Let go,* she offered, and he did.

Energy release with Adro was not the same intimate experience she shared with Rowan. She kept a respectful distance, holding onto Adro with only as much magic as she needed. She didn't lead him, sure that he would not appreciate the way she hurtled across the realm, but she followed.

Having never fallen into Hum intoxication before, she could tell the explosion of magic in his mind was painful; he was used to being contained, and it strained him to do otherwise, but after a time the floating sensation overtook the blast and Adro let his magic reach out, sensing the life all around them.

His reach was not great, having meditated for so long, and it wasn't long before Cori was gently calling him back.

Just a bit further, he pleaded.

No, she replied firmly. Rowan often let her go beyond her bounds, but she wasn't confident she could get Adro back safely, the way Rowan could with her. She gave a firm tug on the threads that connected them and, being stronger than Adro as she was, he had no option but to follow.

She opened her eyes and watched Adro as he opened his. He stared ahead for a while, pupils dilated.

"Is it always so colourful?" He wondered, his eyes suddenly darting around. Cori laughed.

"Yes. That's the increased clarity. You could probably fight quite efficiently with your Hum if you needed to now."

"I bet," he said in wonder. Then he turned to her. "Thank you," he said earnestly. "I knew I needed to do that to be any use in this war, but I admit I was anxious."

"It's no problem," Cori said, then stood. After the rush of the battle they'd been in and the urgency to get Adro to a safe place, she could now keenly feel the pain of her body.

"Cori!" Adro said in alarm. She heard him get to his feet behind her. "You're bleeding!"

"Oh," she twisted to look over her shoulder, wincing at the movement. "It's just a graze."

"It's ripped your shirt from your back." He took hold of her shoulder and peered at the graze. "It looks like there's gravel in it."

She sighed. "It won't kill me."

"It might. You better let me clean it."

Cori considered arguing, but decided against it. Adro was probably right, and they didn't need the delay that a septic wound would cause later. She agreed and went to the stream.

She pulled off her shirt - the back was well and truly ruined - and dropped it on the ground. Her brassiere was still intact. While she'd undressed, Adro had gone to his pack and withdrawn a bandage and some salve.

"Did Rowan make you pack those?" she asked curiously as Adro placed the salve beside her and dipped the bandage into the stream.

"Yes," he chortled. "He said you might need them. Actually, he said it was a certainty that you would."

CHAPTER TEN

Cori snorted derisively, then yelped as Adro squeezed water onto the graze.

"It goes down your whole side, but most of it isn't too bad. What's this?" he poked at one of the silver scars that crossed her side to her back.

"Long story," Cori muttered, "but I've been in more dragon fights than I care to admit to."

"You're a strange Little One," Adro said. He used his fingernails to pull something from Cori's back. She hissed. He held it up for her to see; a thin shard of stone about the length of her thumb.

"Why does everyone call me Little One?" she asked, trying to distract herself from the pain as Adro extracted more gravel. "Rowan calls me that, the dragons called me that, even Cadmus said it once."

"The dragons called you that?" He seemed impressed. "Little One is a term of endearment, originating from the dragons themselves and meaning something along the lines of fierce, or brave. I've only ever heard that the dragons call their young that."

"Hmm," Cori said. One hand went subconsciously to her side to trace the newest scar that crossed over the other three. Adro squeezed more water over her back then wiped the blood and water from her skin.

"I think it's clean," he said uncertainly. Cori nodded, however, happy to be done. She went to Mischief's saddle and pulled a fresh shirt from her pack. She hadn't brought many, and she hoped she wouldn't run out.

"It's getting late," Adro said, looking towards the sun where it hung low on the horizon. "Should we camp here?"

"I'd rather keep moving," she replied. "And get as much

distance between us and that town as possible."

***

The town that they'd had their battle was one in which they were supposed to restock their supplies. By the time they reached the next settlement four days later, they were completely out of food.

They rode into Rikdom, the capital city of Hale, after dark. Being a large city, the streets were lit with lamps and people were still out and about, travelling home from work or dining at restaurants.

"Let's just find the closest Inn," Cori said as they rode down the main street. People turned to stare at them and Cori kept her gaze downcast, hoping that they were just looking at their fine mounts rather than their gold eyes. She was exhausted and hungry, and she wanted a bath.

"There's one up there." Adro pointed to the next intersection.

They left their horses in the stable and paid for two rooms and meals. Cori went straight to her room, a stuffy, windowless box with a floral adorned bed. She was happy to find a steaming wash basin waiting for her, and she stripped off her dusty travelling clothes as quickly as she could.

The warm water felt good on her skin, though she was gentle while washing her graze. When she finished, she dressed in clean clothes and braided her hair. She considered falling straight into bed, but decided she better have a meal in case she didn't get breakfast the following morning.

She found Adro downstairs, already in the dining room with two glasses of wine before him.

CHAPTER TEN

"The meals are coming," he informed her as she sat down. She pulled her glass of wine towards her and took a large gulp. "Red or white wine?" he resumed their game from the road.

"Tonight, any wine. If you had to give up meat or vegetables for the rest of your life, which would it be?"

"Vegetables." Adro made an expression of mock horror. "How would a man like me survive without meat?"

Their meals arrived, and they abandoned their game while they ate with a famish that was almost unseemly. Once they had finished, a waitress brought them some complimentary coffee, and they lounged back in their chairs, finally full.

"Summer or winter?" Cori asked, sipping her hot drink.

"Summer. I hate the cold. Do you -" Adro stopped, staring at the door. Cori glanced towards it and did a double take.

A woman had just stepped inside. Her clothes were dusty from travel, and she had dried blood on her hands. They weren't the reason the woman had drawn Cori and Adro's attention though. As the woman scanned the room, both Cori and Adro hastily averted their gazes, hoping that the woman didn't notice that the three of them shared the same eye colour. She was a Dijem.

"Should I reach out?" Cori asked in a low tone, her heart thumping. The woman's bloodied hands surely marked her as the Dijem who'd ransacked the last town. Adro seemed to deliberate for a long time before shaking his head.

"We shouldn't fight her. We should run."

After her blunder of dragging Adro into their last battle, Cori was willing to heed his words this time. She glanced towards the woman to see if they could sneak away, and met her eye.

The two of them stared at each other for a long moment, then the woman's lips curled in a snarl and her hands flicked up, slamming an empty table towards Cori and Adro with Hiram magic. Cori's own hands came up in defence and the table shattered in the air. The other patrons in the room screamed and ducked for cover. Adro jumped to his feet, his Hum flaring out towards the woman. Cori followed his lead in time to feel the woman's barriers snap up. She jumped towards them, her hands outstretched. Cori flung her hot coffee towards her and dived out of her chair.

The woman cried out as the hot liquid splashed over her face and chest. She landed hard where Cori had just been sitting. Cori reached out, intending to grab her, when the woman's barriers shot open and a forceful song hit Cori's mind, attempting to take control. It was Cori's turn to put her barriers up, which meant she could no longer use her Hiram magic at its full strength. She reached out and shoved at the woman anyway, forcing her into the table she and Adro had been sitting at. Adro reached across, grabbing the woman by the back of the shirt and lifting her into the air. The woman snarled and shoved at Adro with her magic, forcing him back. He lost his grip on her.

The woman landed in a crouch as Cori scrabbled to her feet. "Get her hands!" She yelled to Adro. She then saw the woman reach into her shirt and withdraw a dagger. She turned low, slashing at Adro. Adro jumped back, but not before the woman sliced the dagger across his leg. Cori let her barriers drop away to feel Adro attacking the woman, each furiously trying to take control of the other's mind.

Cori wove the song that would help her gain control of the woman's mind, but she was sluggish; she'd never fought

CHAPTER TEN

another Dijem, had never had a mind to mind battle. She flung the song at the woman who quickly snapped up her barriers again, but not before Cori caught the sound of her Hum. It reminded her of Cat; a Hum created and moulded by Cadmus.

Cori shoved hard with her magic, sending the table slamming into the back of the woman. Adro pounced forward, taking advantage of the woman's momentary confusion and throwing himself bodily over her, pinning her to the ground. Cori jumped forward too, grabbing the woman's arm that held the dagger so she couldn't stab Adro.

"Get into her mind!" Adro grunted. Cori didn't know how, so she slammed her Hum against the woman's barriers. She did it over and over until the woman cried out, squirming beneath Adro. Adro joined his Hum to Cori's and in one final push, they forced their way into the woman's mind. Four words were waiting for them, *Cadmus sends his regards*, and then there was nothing.

Cori thought the woman might have put her barriers up again before she realised that she'd stopped moving beneath Adro. He sat back, and Cori stared down at the woman's dark eyes.

"She burned out," Adro whispered. Cori suddenly felt sick. Had she and Adro done that? Or had the woman done it to herself to stop them getting to her mind? Cori rocked back on her heels, looking around the silent and empty dining room, the dead Dijem woman between them.

Now what?

Chapter Eleven

She'd survived her first Dijem fight, but not by any real skill of her own. If Adro hadn't been there to assist her, she wasn't certain the outcome would be the same. As it was, a dead woman now lay on the floor between them in the trashed and deserted dining room.

"What do we do?" Cori asked dully, oddly deflated after killing the woman. She didn't feel the same sense of satisfaction at killing her own kind as she did when she hunted Hiram.

"We need to leave," Adro responded, though he didn't move from where he was crouched on the other side of the woman. Blood dripped from the slice on his leg, but it didn't seem deep.

"Hey there, Gold Eyes!" a shout came from outside in the street. "You are surrounded. Come out and surrender yourselves!"

Adro turned wide eyed towards the door. "This is not happening, is it?"

Cori bowed her head and sighed. "It's my fault, I attract this sort of attention like a curse."

"You don't say." Adro lurched to his feet. "Do we have time to get the packs?"

CHAPTER ELEVEN

"Come out! Or we'll come in to get you!"

"Yes." Cori stood as well and started weaving a new strengthening song. "They're only town guards. I'll deal with them while you get our things."

Adro considered her for a long moment. The way he calculated her words reminded her of Rowan.

"No," he said eventually. "Hale is not our enemy. We don't want them to join Hearth against us."

"Then what do we do?" Cori held her hands palm up, fingers splayed. She had nothing. "If they come in here, we'll have to fight, and personally, I'd prefer the space of the street for that."

"Would your Karaliene trick work?"

"My *what?*"

"Tell them who you are, like you did with those townspeople, they might remember you too."

Cori deliberated, her eyes on the door as Adro headed for the stairs. She'd rarely been through Rikdom, and she thought it more likely that Hale would remember her for the noblemen she'd killed in the Advisor's war rather than any good she'd done in the state.

"What do I say to them?" She called out. Adro paused halfway up the stairs.

"Just tell them who you are and try to keep them calm."

"Easier said than done," Cori muttered. She strode to the door, palms sweating, and wrenched it open, just as a guard was reaching for the handle on the other side. The two of them stared at each other, then the guard pointed his sword at her. She lifted her hands in surrender and stepped forward. The guard took several steps back to join the ranks of his fellows.

"You're under arrest," the captain said. He was the only one without his sword drawn, though his hand hovered near the hilt.

"What if I told you," she began in a choked voice. She cleared her throat, "that I'm the Karaliene?"

"I wouldn't believe you," the captain responded smoothly.

Cori took a few more steps forward. "What would I need to do to convince you?"

As she moved, the guards tensed, but the captain withdrew his hand from his sword hilt. His gaze was not on her face, but on her still raised hands. Well, at least he knew where the danger was, even if he claimed not to believe her. He crossed his arms. "If you were the Karaliene, then the stories dictate that you would attack first, and talk later."

"I've been practising restraint." Adro appeared behind her, their packs over his shoulder and their swords in each of his hands. Some of the closer guards yelped in alarm and raised their swords higher. Cori ignored them. She knew it was just a natural reaction for men to feel threatened by Adro's hulking size. She was glad to have him there.

Say something, she pleaded. *I'm ruining it.*

Adro handed her the swords and stepped forward. He clasped his hands before him and smiled at the captain. "We're here as emissaries of the Karalis and would like to speak to your Head of State."

Cori's eyebrows shot up. "We would?" she said. Adro waved her to silence.

The captain frowned, glancing between them. "And how do I know this isn't a ploy so she can get in and kill the Head?"

"So you do believe me!" Cori said. Adro once more flapped a silencing hand at her, but the captain faced her squarely.

CHAPTER ELEVEN

She had to admit, she quite liked his austere attitude.

"Of course. No one else would dare lay claim to that title if they weren't prepared to fight for it. But," his gaze flicked back to Adro, "you mentioned the Karalis. I presume this is the one who has taken up residence in Lautan?"

"The very one. He would be very amicable to an alliance with Hale."

The captain considered them for a time, then nodded. He turned aside and gave an order to one of his men. The guard and a few others left the ranks and headed up the street at a jog.

"Come on, then," the captain said. Cori started down the steps towards him, but Adro jerked a thumb back towards the inn.

"There's a dead woman in there. You may want to move her before the inn patrons return."

The captain shook his head as he waved some of his men to the task. "Bloody Gold Eyes."

* * *

The stone manor was well lit when they arrived. The residence of the Head of Hale was a lavish building set on a hill that overlooked the town and had distant ocean views. well-kept gardens surrounded the manor and although it was dark, a few courtly people were out strolling in them.

Cori and Adro were marched right to the front door, where the guards of the manor took charge of them.

"You better give me those," the captain said to Cori, gesturing to the two swords she still held. She handed them over without complaint - she fought better without a sword in any case - before following the guards inside.

The inside of the manor was a stark contrast to its outside. The walls were mostly bare, save for the occasional modest tapestry. The floor was polished timber with no carpets. Nooks that should have held plants and vases were empty. They were led through the manor, seeing no one, until they reached a glass atrium that had magnificent views of the city below.

Waiting for them there was a man who looked no older than forty at a stretch. He had black, dishevelled hair and his clothes seemed to match. He had been staring at the view, a steaming pot of tea beside him, but when the guards ushered them into the room, he stood and turned gracefully to face them.

"Dristan of Hale," Adro greeted with an incline of his head. Cori did the same.

Dristan returned the nod, then gestured them into the room. "Be welcome," he said, looking first to Cori. "You are the Karaliene? It is a pleasure to have you at the manor."

"I only used that title to stop myself being killed by your men," Cori replied. "These days, I'm the second Advisor to the Karalis."

"I see." Dristan smiled charmingly before turning to Adro. "I'm sorry, sir, I don't know your name as you seem to know mine." He extended his hand.

"Adro," Adro introduced himself, accepting Dristan's hand. "First Advisor to the Karalis."

"Ah yes, I received a letter from you, informing me of the Karalis' return to Tauta. Please, sit."

The three of them sat at the table and Dristan poured each of them a cup of tea.

CHAPTER ELEVEN

"So, you're here to follow up on your letter?"

"Truthfully," Adro began, "we're just passing through, but had an altercation at a local inn which resulted in your town guard being called down upon us. I will take this opportunity, however, to discuss an alliance."

Dristan looked between them for a long moment, his fingers drumming on the table. "Admittedly," he said finally, "Hale is not the powerhouse it once was. The state has been slow to recover from the Advisor's war, particularly with Hearthian armies pillaging our borders ever since. I'm not sure what I can offer you, but I am willing to discuss this alliance if it means Hale will once more fall under the protection of the throne."

Adro smiled. "Good. Perhaps you can have someone bring us some parchment and we can discuss the details."

Dristan motioned to the guard at the door. "Please send for pens and parchment, and some refreshments."

"Yes, my lord." The guard bowed and left.

"Firstly," Dristan began, "I think it would be best if you tell me what you would need of me, to ensure I can deliver before I commit."

"Mostly we need soldiers," Adro explained. The paper arrived, and he began jotting down notes. "We will provide supplies and pay their wages, but they should have their own weapons, armour and horses. We need a mix of both human and Hiram - loyal and trustworthy, of course. We've noticed, travelling through your state, that Hearthians are already burning some of your smaller towns. You need to secure your borders so that Hearth cannot use Hale as a thoroughfare to Lautan."

"My towns are being burned?" Dristan said in surprise.

Cori, who had been staring quietly out the window while Adro negotiated, raised an eyebrow at the Head of State.

"For someone whose state has apparently been humbled by war, your head seems very high in the clouds."

"Cori," Adro warned quietly.

"No, she's right. I've been... preoccupied the last few months. I should have paid more attention." Dristan drained his tea and poured himself another cup. "Which brings me to my side of the deal. To seal this alliance, I want you both to attend my wedding in three days' time."

Attend his wedding? Cori said to Adro incredulously. *I don't think we can spare three days.*

We might have to. If we can secure Hale's army, at least the trip will be worth something if we cannot find Starch.

"That's all you want?" Adro asked carefully. "In exchange for your support in the war, we attend your wedding?"

"Yes, that's all."

"Who are you marrying?" Cori asked. Dristan raised his eyebrows.

"A strange question. My intended's name is Samyla."

"It's strange of you to ask us to attend, but I think I know why now. Samyla is Hearthian, isn't she?"

Dristan stared down at his tea, twisting the cup on its saucer, looking very uncomfortable.

"Is she intending to kill us? Or are we supposed to kill her?"

"Neither!" Dristan cried, jumping to his feet. "You've come to the wrong conclusion, my lady!"

"Well then you better explain quickly otherwise we'll kill you and put a more amicable Head in your place."

Dristan blanched. Adro sighed, but he didn't refute her

CHAPTER ELEVEN

words.

"Samyla is the daughter of Fentyn who is the younger brother of Brentyn, the Head of Hearth. Me marrying outside of Hale is apparently blasphemous enough, but to marry a noblewoman of Hearth without the Head's blessing means that I fear for her life on our wedding day."

"You think someone will assassinate her?" Adro queried. He placed his pen down and leaned back in his chair.

"I'm certain of it, and who better to protect her than the Karaliene?"

"If she's in so much danger, why not just send her back to her family?" Cori asked. The whole situation was making her uncomfortable.

Dristan gripped the back of his chair, his demeanour suddenly haggard. "Because we love each other."

Cori had no answer. She knew very well what it was like to have a love that others disapproved of, though her and Rowan's relationship was not political like Dristan and Samyla's was.

What do you think? Cori asked Adro. He was quiet for a long moment.

This could be dangerous for us. We don't know what sort of assassins Hearth might send.

We have the element of surprise, though. They would hardly expect two Dijem to be attending the wedding.

Adro was quiet again, and Cori let him think. Politically, he was more well versed to decide than she. Finally he said, *I think we should contact Rowan.*

Cori's stomach lurched. They weren't supposed to contact him for a few more days yet, so to reach out to him early... Well, she wouldn't be saying no.

All right.

"Will you give us a few minutes to discuss it?" Adro asked of Dristan. Though the Head of Hale must have been wondering why they'd been sitting in silence for so long, he nodded. Cori and Adro stood and left the Atrium via a door set in the glass that led them to the garden.

There was a fresh ocean breeze in the air and Cori sucked it in through her mouth. Her heartbeat quickened and her stomach fluttered nervously. Adro reached out to her with his Hum, twining a few strands with hers so he could come with her. She took a final deep breath and reached out.

Rowan was there instantly, his Hum catching hers and strengthening their connection.

Cori? What's wrong? His voice was faint, a result of trying to speak over such a distance, Cori guessed.

Nothing bad, she reassured him. *We just need to ask you a question.*

Rowan?

Adro. Rowan paused, then, sounding impressed, *you've stopped meditating.*

Cori didn't give me much of an option. Listen, we have a little situation with the Head of Hale.

Cori listened as Adro told Rowan of their predicament. She savoured the connection she had with Rowan, even if she had to share it with Adro.

Cori, do you think you can handle it? Rowan asked when Adro had finished explaining.

Yes, I think so.

Then do it. But if it appears that the situation is not controllable, leave them to their fate and get out of there.

Rowan, if I agree to protect this woman, then I'll be doing it

CHAPTER ELEVEN

with my life. I won't walk away.

Adro, Rowan pressed the order on the first Advisor instead. *If it becomes too much, get the both of you out. Hale is a sweet deal, but not at your expense. Understand?*

Yes, Rowan. Adro withdrew after that, leaving Cori and Rowan alone.

They were both quiet for a long moment, simply letting their minds connect.

Still contact me at the fortnight mark, Rowan said eventually. Cori sent him a feeling of acknowledgement. *Are you all right?* He asked softly.

I don't want to let go, she whispered.

Neither do I.

They hung on for one more moment and then Cori withdrew. She opened her eyes to the lights of Rikdom twinkling below. Adro put his hand on her back.

"Take a minute," he suggested. She did, attempting to get her breathing under control. She dashed a single tear from her eye.

"Let's tell Dristan," she said when she was sure her voice wouldn't waver. They returned to the Atrium to find Dristan pacing nervously. He stopped when he saw them, hands clasped behind his back.

"We've decided to stay for your wedding," Cori told him. The relief on his face was palpable. He sagged into his chair.

"Oh, thank goodness. She's going to live."

"You'll need to sign on it," Adro warned. "Protecting your bride in exchange for your army."

Dristan seemed suddenly hesitant. Cori spoke for him.

"He'll sign," she said, and Dristan looked up at her. "Because I'm sure Hale recalls what happened last time they defied the throne."

"Yes," agreed Dristan weakly, "of course I'll sign." He stood again, gesturing to the guard at the door. "None of our big suites are prepared yet, but I'm sure you will be comfortable in our guest rooms. Hank will show you up there."

"Actually," Cori interrupted, "I'd like to meet Samyla."

Chapter Twelve

Cori followed Dristan through the dark corridors of the manor, their footsteps echoing faintly on the stone floor. Finally, he paused by a door on the right and rapped lightly on it. A muffled voice came from within and Dristan entered.

The room was dark save for faint moonlight that spilled through the window and across the bed. From beneath the covers, a woman sat up, rubbing her eyes.

"Dris?" Her voice was airy, like many noblewomen. "What's the matter?"

"Shh, nothing Sammie, my love," he moved over to her bed, sitting on the side and taking her hands in his. Samyla looked at him with sleep confused eyes, then glanced at Cori.

"Who is she?"

"She is going to save us, Sammie!" Dristan said excitedly. Cori rolled her eyes and remained in the doorway, her arms crossed. She surveyed Samyla frankly.

The woman looked as if she had only just escaped childhood, with wide eyes and pouting lips. Her light hair fell in soft waves around her face and her hands were dainty in their grip on Dristan's. Yes, Cori could see why Dristan would fall for this doll.

"Samyla," Cori said before Dristan thought to introduce her. "Your fiance has asked me to protect you on your wedding day. I wanted to know, do you think you would know any of the assassins when you see them?"

Samyla shook her head. Some hidden piece of jewellery tinkled prettily. "All I know is that if it's someone my father sent, they will try to kill Dris. If it's someone my uncle sent, they will try to kill me."

"Assassins on all fronts then," Cori muttered.

"Will you really be able to stop them?" Samyla asked. Hope lit her eyes, making them, if possible, even rounder. Beside her, Dristan couldn't stop smiling.

"I will, or die trying," Cori replied, remembering as the words left her lips, the promise Adro had made to Rowan.

"We're really going to be all right!" Samyla threw her arms around Dristan, kissing him deeply. Cori backed out of the room, resentful of their passion. She left them there, returning to the atrium where she asked Hank to show her to her room.

That night, as she lay on the too soft bed, she thought of Rowan and their brief exchange. She wondered if he were laying in bed too, thinking of her as she was thinking of him. It took every bit of restraint she had to not reach out again to find him. With a heavy sigh, she rolled to her side and willed sleep to come.

***

Wedding preparations had the manor of Hale in a right state for the next few days. People came and went, delivering food, decorations, furniture and gifts. Cori tried to keep

CHAPTER TWELVE

track of them all, wondering if perhaps one of them might be an assassin, but it was hard to watch everyone at once.

She'd never hunted an assassin before, and she wasn't sure what she was supposed to look for. Always, her prey had been soldiers in uniform.

When she realised her attempts at picking potential assassins from crowds of workers was futile, she began instead to shadow Samyla. She quickly noticed that those who lived at the manor - servants and lesser noblemen and women alike - were utterly infatuated with the woman. Samyla moved with an enviable grace and she gave any who spoke to her her fullest attention.

"I can see why they'd want to assassinate her," Cori said to Adro when they met on the afternoon before the wedding. "She's insufferable." The atrium had too many people passing through, so they'd opted to sit out in the garden at a wrought iron round table among the roses. The weather was fair, and insects buzzed contentedly around the flowers. The wedding would shape up nicely. If no one was killed.

"She's quite lovely, actually," Adro replied without looking up from the parchment he was reading. Adro had been in his element whilst they'd been residing in the manor. He'd met with many dignitaries and nobles, negotiating and sealing deals.

Cori snorted. "I should've guessed that you'd fall head over heels like the rest."

Adro finally looked up. He regarded her over the top of the parchment with a frank look. "I haven't fallen in love with her. I merely see her for the friendly person she is. Have you even tried talking to her?"

Cori paused. "I don't think she likes me much. She doesn't

have much to say when I talk to her."

"Have you considered that perhaps she's intimidated by you?"

"By me?" Cori laughed. "She's a proper noble born woman, not to mention beautiful. Why would she be intimidated by me?"

Adro set his parchment aside, giving her his full attention.

"Because you're the Karaliene. I know you dislike the title, and I know that you've done more fighting than politics, but you are technically the highest ranking woman in the realm."

Cori sat back. It had never even crossed her mind that the beautiful Samyla might be in awe of her. She rubbed a hand over her face. "This wedding cannot come fast enough," she muttered.

"Indeed," agreed Adro, resuming his perusal of the parchment. Cori stood and stretched, deciding that she best check in on her charge one last time.

* * *

The atrium had been transformed into a magnificent display of white ribbons and flowers. Chairs were arranged in a semi-circle, facing the view of Rikdom and the farmlands and ocean beyond. Guests flitted about the room, glasses of sparkling wine in hand as they mingled with their peers.

Cori stood in the outer room of a suite on the lower floor of the manor, staring at herself in a mirror. She wore a red, figure hugging gown with a flared skirt. She'd been caught by surprise when the dress had been delivered to her room the night before. She hadn't even considered that she should dress up for the occasion. Of course, the dress had presented a problem that its maker probably hadn't considered; how would Cori fight, if she needed to, in something so restrictive? She'd stayed up most of the night, altering the gown herself, until the skirt could easily be torn away to reveal the leggings she wore underneath. She'd had to cut her leggings at the knees, lest her ankles show beneath the skirt. She lamented another piece of clothing ruined.

She turned to the side, admiring the curves the dress created on her figure. It had been a long time since she'd dressed in something so beautiful. She wished Rowan was there to see it; it was definitely a look he would appreciate. She leaned forward to the mirror, first touching her hair, loose and wavy down her back, then inspecting the black lines she'd painted carefully around her eyes. The door opened behind her, and Adro stepped inside.

She straightened, and he gave a low whistle. "Looking lovely there, Second Advisor," he said.

"You don't look so bad yourself, First Advisor," she replied with a smile. Adro wore black trousers and a deep green vest over a white shirt.

"Dresses or pants?" he asked with a grin. Cori laughed and hitched her skirt so he could see the leggings beneath.

"Both!"

Adro laughed too, a great booming sound that echoed around the room. "Well, I better get out in the crowd. There are a few Hearthian nobles there, and I'd like to pick their minds." He tapped his temple, winked, then left the room. Cori turned back to the mirror as another door - one leading to a bedroom - opened.

Samyla stepped into the room in her white wedding dress. It was an old style ball gown with a fitted torso that accentuated the breasts and a flouncing, puffy skirt. Cori had never liked this particular style, but of course Samyla suited it perfectly.

"You look beautiful," Cori told her truthfully.

"Oh, thank you, Karaliene," Samyla replied in her breathy voice as she smoothed her hands down her front.

"Cori," Cori corrected.

"Pardon?"

"It's my name. I'd prefer you use it to my title."

"Oh," Samyla paused. "Of course, Cori. If you prefer."

"I do."

The bride-to-be flushed then gasped, as if she suddenly remembered something. "I have a gift for you!"

"Oh, you don't need…" Cori trailed off as Samyla went back to the bedroom. She returned with a small, flat box. Cori took it and carefully lifted the lid. Inside, nestled on a silken pillow, was a dagger. She lifted the blade, and Samyla took the box away.

"Do you like it?" She asked with wide eyes and flushed cheeks.

"It's very… pretty," Cori said. She held the dagger on her palm, inspecting the large pink gemstone set in the hilt. A lady's weapon.

"I'm glad you like it," Samyla gushed. "My Mama gave it to me. She said I would need to protect myself here in Hale, but you are protecting me so I think you should have it instead."

"Thank you," Cori said. She took the lace sheath Samyla offered, then put the dagger down her dress between her breasts.

A light tap sounded at the door, and Cori tensed. She knew, from the only other two weddings she'd ever attended, that family and close friends would now call on the bride to offer their well wishes.

The first person was undoubtedly Samyla's mother. She was an older woman, soft about the middle, but she had the same wide eyes and full lips as her daughter.

"Mama!" Samyla cried, rushing forward and throwing herself into her mother's arms.

Cori ignored the exchange - it was unlikely Samyla's mother would be the one to kill her - and focused instead on a second woman who had entered the room. She was as old as Samyla's mother, and seemed like the homely type. She smiled at the exchange between mother and daughter, but her hands twisted nervously together.

Samyla and her mother broke apart, and the bride smiled warmly at the second woman. "Tonyla, I'm so glad you could come!"

"Me too, child." She stepped with jerky legs towards the girl. Cori glided forward to intercept them.

"No," she warned the woman. Tonyla's eyes glazed momentarily, almost too quick for Cori to notice. Who was Tonyla being controlled by? Surely Cadmus wouldn't have any interest in the wedding of Dristan and Samyla. One of his other Dijem might though, and for Tonyla to be controlled, it would mean the Dijem had to be close.

Keep alert, she told Adro. *I think there could be another Dijem around.*

Adro sent her a feeling of assent, and she returned to the matter at hand.

"Cori?" Samyla said in confusion. "What's the matter?"

Tonyla's eyes glazed again and her hand shot out towards the bride's throat. Her movement was faster than a woman of her age should be capable of, but Cori had quick reflexes. She smacked Tonyla's hand away forcefully, even as Samyla and her mother screamed. Cori grabbed Tonyla by the throat. The old woman paid her no heed, all her energy going towards trying to get the girl.

"Get in the other room!" Cori ordered Samyla and her mother. Both sobbing, they backed towards the bedroom. Cori reached out to Tonyla's mind with her Hum.

She'd once had the painful experience of having Cadmus and Rowan fight for control of her mind, but she couldn't even find this woman's magic. There was just a blankness. Cori growled in frustration. She really needed to learn how to fight other Dijem. Her strengthening song flared and she snapped Tonyla's neck.

The woman crumpled to the ground, and Cori let out an exasperated sigh. She glanced towards the bedroom door, but Samyla and her mother had disappeared within. Sighing again, she stooped to grasp Tonyla's legs and, cursing under her breath, she dragged the body to the couch and shoved it behind. She straightened and glanced at herself in the mirror. She smoothed her hair and straightened her dress, then went to the bedroom door.

"Is Tonyla all right?" Samyla asked weakly when she saw Cori. She was clutching her mother.

"She's fine," Cori lied. "Come on, it's time for you to marry." Cori knew it was common decency to have more guests visit the bride, but she didn't know if she could deal with them as cleanly as she had Tonyla. And there was not much space behind the couch.

Samyla straightened and walked timidly towards Cori. Her mother followed with a dark look. She didn't believe Cori

CHAPTER TWELVE

for an instant.

Under the glowering stare of Samyla's mother, Cori ushered the bride into the hallway. Samyla composed herself, an excited smile blooming on her face. Cori had to give it to her, the girl knew how to perform under pressure. They reached the door to the atrium where the buzz of many guests in conversation sounded from within. Cori pointed to the door, indicating that Samyla's mother should go in.

"I'm going in too," Cori told Samyla. "If anyone comes while you're out here - and I don't care who it is - you scream, all right?"

"Yes, Cori," Samyla responded. "Thank you!"

Cori eyed the hallway once more before opening the door and stepping into the throng of people waiting within. Some of them looked at her, whispering curiously to their companions. She ignored them; most people who'd been hanging around the manor the past few days knew the Advisors to the Karalis were in residence.

She spotted Adro near the windows and wended through the crowd towards him. She passed Dristan as she went and she nodded to him, indicating that they could begin. The celebrant called for attention, and Adro moved towards her.

"Anything?" Adro asked quietly as they took their place at the far end of the first row.

"A friend of Samyla's mother, Dijem controlled." Cori scanned the room, looking for the same nervous movements she had seen in Tonyla. "I left her behind a couch. Remind me to fetch her later before some servant finds her."

"That man there," Adro pointed along their row to a handsome, dark-haired man, "is Fentyn, Samyla's father."

"Has he been talking to anyone strange?"

"Not that I can tell, but why would he talk to his assassins in public?"

Cori shrugged, then reached out to Fentyn with her mind. Human. No good.

She resumed her scanning of the room as the guests fell silent, their attention moving to the celebrant.

"Welcome, friends and family of Dristan and Samyla. Our groom and his bride are thrilled to have you here. And they wish to welcome two very special guests, the Advisor to the Karalis," the celebrant inclined his head to Adro who returned the gesture. "And the Karaliene."

Cori could have killed the man. Behind her she heard a murmur rise, and she forced herself to turn to watch the guests fall to their knees. Pushing aside her distaste for the gesture, she noted those who did it reluctantly and marked them as Hearthians.

This is strange, Adro said. She was glad to see that he had stayed on his feet.

Tell me about it.

The assassins may be swayed against action, now that they know you're here.

We can only hope. Cori turned back to the celebrant, and Dristan as the guests returned to their feet. Music played, and the doors at the end of the atrium opened. Samyla entered to collective 'oh's' and 'ah's'. Cori wasn't watching the bride walk to her future husband though. She'd noticed a glint of silver in the hands of a man standing at the edge of the aisle Samyla was walking down. Cori slid through the crowd, ignoring the stares some gave her. She felt Adro following closely behind. She reached for the man's mind, but couldn't pick it from the masses. She had to hurry.

CHAPTER TWELVE

She shoved through the last line of people and grasped the man's wrist with an inhumane strength, just as he tried to lift his dagger.

"Easy there," Cori warned softly. The man glanced at her fearfully. She stood, holding him by the wrist, until Samyla had passed, then she quickly reached up and snapped the man's neck with her other hand. Adro, standing behind the man, caught him as he fell. Most of the guests were focused on Samyla, but one or two muttered in surprise as the man collapsed.

"I'll get him some water," Adro muttered to those watching and dragged the man away through the crowd. None of them had seen Cori kill him. She turned back to the proceedings. Samyla had finished her walk and now stood opposite Dristan, her hands clasped in his and tears streaking her face. Cori drifted towards them. It seemed that the assassins so far were trying to complete their mission before the two were wed, so she had to keep an eye out.

Her heart pounded in her chest, despite her cool demeanour. She was suddenly anxious that she might miss someone. She needn't have been so concerned; Adro got the next one. She watched the quick scuffle at the edge of the group before Adro hauled him bodily from the atrium.

Need help? Cori asked, though she knew she couldn't really leave the room. Adro was quiet for a long moment before he replied.

It's done. I'm fine. A moment later he reentered the atrium.

"You may kiss your bride!" The celebrant declared. Cori started. So focused on the crowd, she had missed the whole ceremony. Dristan took Samyla in his arms, swept her low, and kissed her. The guests cheered heartily, throwing handfuls of rose petals in the air and Cori clapped along with them. She noticed Samyla's father Fentyn did not look impressed.

"Now for the party," Adro said, sidling alongside her. Cori groaned.

"I'm not cut out for this sneaking business," she complained. "Can't I just throw the lot of them through the windows and be done with it?"

Adro chucked and clapped her on the shoulder. "You need a drink."

* * *

Cori was tense through the entire party. It proved twice as difficult to watch people as they mingled with other guests. Servants were now also wending through the crowd, serving food and drinks, and to top it off, as the guests drank, their behaviour became erratic and it was difficult to spot someone who might act strange due to a compulsion.

"Here." Adro sat down beside her, handing her a nip of rum. Cori thanked him, taking a sip and turning her eyes back to Samyla. The bride was slowly circling the room on the arm of her husband. They greeted their guests, thanking them for coming to the wedding. Samyla was positively glowing and her eyes barely strayed from Dristan.

"Have you ever been in love, Adro?" Cori asked suddenly. Adro sipped his drink slowly.

"Yes, once," he admitted. His throat worked and Cori knew it hadn't ended well. She was about to apologise for her question when she noticed a surge of movement, a group of people who parted the crowd as they made a beeline for the newlyweds.

"Come on," she said, downing the last of her rum in one gulp and lurching to her feet. She ripped the skirt from her dress and cast it aside. "The assassins are done. Now they've sent soldiers."

Chapter Thirteen

Cori darted forward before Adro had even stood. She drew the dagger Samyla had given her from between her breasts. The soldiers - there were six of them that she could see - were so intent on the newlywed couple that Cori was able to plunge the dagger into the chest of one of them without resistance. The man's cry turned into a gurgling moan as Cori shoved him away with her shoulder, wrenching the dagger free as she did.

Three of the soldiers rounded on her, but two continued towards Dristan and Samyla. From the corner of her eye, Cori saw Dristan push Samyla behind him and draw a hunting knife from within his jacket. Cori shoved at a female soldier, being careful not to use too much magic; she didn't want to accidentally blow up the room and kill the guests instead. The woman staggered back several steps, but righted herself quickly. She reached to her shoulder, drawing a sword over it. With a roar, she slashed at Cori.

Cori dropped beneath the swing, her knees hitting the floor. Around her, guests screamed and chaos ensued as they tried to flee the room. From her lowered position, she saw Dristan fighting against two soldiers. Beyond him, Fentyn had taken hold of his daughter's arm and was trying to pull

CHAPTER THIRTEEN

her away.

Adro, get Samyla, Cori said urgently. She felt a flash of Adro's Hum as he immobilised a soldier, took his sword and stabbed him.

On it, he confirmed.

Cori felt the woman's sword whoosh past again and she rolled to the side, then to her feet.

"Karaliene," The woman said, her brown eyes boring furiously into Cori's, "I've been looking for you." She drew a long knife from her belt.

"I don't think we've met," Cori replied, jumping back from another swing. The dual blades were making it difficult to get close. She pushed at the woman again, but the soldier sidestepped the blow.

"My name is Llyna," she growled, stalking towards Cori, both sword and knife whirring so fast that Cori could barely see them, "and you killed my husband."

Oh great, Cori thought dryly. She whirled away from Llyna for a moment, slashing at one of the men fighting Dristan. She managed a deep cut across his shoulder before she had to duck under Llyna's blade again. "Sorry, I can't recall which one he was."

"It was only a few months ago! You massacred them all!"

"Oh, them." Cori's apathy briefly broke Llyna from her hysteria, and Cori lifted her hand and pushed. Llyna staggered back and Cori followed through with her dagger, aiming for Llyna's throat. The other woman recovered too quickly, and Cori only managed to slice her upper chest before she had to fall back. "Look," she tried to reason as she backed away. She could see Adro in battle with Fentyn. "It wasn't personal, you know how war is. I buried them, if that's some consolation for you."

"It's not!" Llyna screamed. her sword hit Cori's shoulder, slicing down over her collarbone. Burning pain bloomed along the path of the blade, but she could still use her arm. Hopefully it wasn't serious. She slammed back into a table, groping behind her with her free hand and found a glass of wine. She lifted it, downing the contents, then smashed the top on the edge of the table. Still holding the stem, she surged forward between Llyna's blades and plunged both her dagger and the wineglass stem into the woman's abdomen. Llyna's eyes widened and she choked up a mouthful of blood that splattered over Cori's arms.

"There was a reason your husband died at my hands," Cori hissed as Llyna fell back, her swords clattering to the floor, "and you should have learned from his errors not to cross me."

Cori pulled her dagger free as Llyna convulsed on the floor. She turned to see Dristan stab the second soldier he'd been duelling. Cori darted forward towards the fight between Adro and Fentyn. Dristan turned at the same time that Adro knocked Fentyn's sword aside. Three blades plunged into the bride's father, and Fentyn died instantly, propped upright by the weapons in his torso, suspended between Adro, Cori and Dristan. The room was deafeningly silent, then Samyla screamed.

"Sammie!" Dristan let go of his knife and Fentyn sagged away, off Adro's sword and Cori's dagger. Dristan ran to his bride, catching her in his arms. "Look away, my love!"

"Do you think it's done?" Cori asked with a heaving chest. She stared down at Fentyn, watching his blood pool on the floor around her feet.

CHAPTER THIRTEEN

"I hope so," Adro replied tiredly. He nodded towards the slice on Cori's shoulder. "Does that hurt?"

"Yes," she admitted, looking down at it. Her shoulder wound oozed thick rivulets of blood, and it blended into the top of her red dress. She could feel the wound pull when she lifted her arm, which made her think she could have injured some of the muscle.

"I think the night is done," Dristan said aloud to the room. Guests, where they'd cowered back against the walls during the fighting, now stirred and moved forward. Some of the Hearthian men went to their fallen countrymen. Hank, Dristan's guard, burst into the room, cradling a bloodied arm.

"Sir, we were attacked!" He said as he reached Dristan. His tone was almost guilty. "We couldn't stop these ones getting through!"

Dristan put his hand on Hank's good shoulder. "You did your best," he told the guard. "Fortunately for us, the Karaliene and Adro were here to stop the soldiers doing any real damage." He turned back to his wife, pulling her into the circle of his arms. Samyla was sobbing.

"Here," Adro handed Cori a cloth napkin. She took it and pressed it against her wound, wincing.

"I think I'll need stitches," she muttered. Adro nodded, but neither of them moved. They watched the room as the guests slowly left, and the bodies were carried away. Finally, only the two of them and the newlyweds were left.

"Sorry, Samyla, about your father," Adro said heavily. Samyla didn't respond, except to cry harder into Dristan's chest.

"You two should go to your rooms," Cori suggested.

Dristan nodded. He took Samyla by the shoulders and steered her towards the door.

"Hale's army better be good," Adro muttered when they were alone in the trashed and blood splattered room. "Here, let me look at your shoulder."

* * *

"Thank you again," Dristan said earnestly, shaking Adro's hand. "We would no doubt be dead if it weren't for the both of you."

"As long as you deliver your end of the bargain, no thanks are needed," Cori told him. It was early morning the day after the wedding. A cool fog hung over Rikdom, making the hill that the manor was perched upon seem as if it were floating on a cloud.

"You needn't fear that, Karaliene," Dristan told her. "I intend to deliver the army and fight with it."

Cori nodded and moved to Mischief's side. She rubbed her hand down the stallion's neck, and he turned to nuzzle her.

"Samyla sent her apologies for not coming down to see you off," Dristan continued. "She is rather… distraught after last night."

"Understandable," Adro said. He was already mounted on Morro. Cori seized a fistful of Mischief's mane with her good arm and heaved herself into the saddle. Her shoulder throbbed, but the twenty stitches Adro had put in it the night before held.

"Time permitting, we may call on you on our way back through," Adro said. Dristan nodded and stepped aside.

CHAPTER THIRTEEN

"Farewell. Safe travels," he bid them.

Cori and Adro rode slowly through Rikdom, the clop of their horse's hooves muted in the fog. They saw no one on the streets until they reached the northern gate. A figure loomed in the fog and Cori put her hand on the hilt of her sword, but as they drew close, she realised it was the captain of the town guard. She hadn't seen him since he'd taken them from the inn to the manor three days prior. He stepped forward, but not into their path. As they passed, he inclined his head respectfully. Cori returned the gesture before she'd even realised what she was doing.

Rowan was rubbing off on her, she decided as they pressed their mounts to a faster pace and left the city behind. They didn't stop for lunch; they'd already delayed too long in Rikdom, but they slowed their horses and ate in their saddles.

"We never found that Dijem last night," Cori said. After Tonyla's death, she had almost forgotten that someone had been controlling the woman. Adro was quiet for a time.

"These Dijem worry me," he said eventually. "They aren't young like those that came to Tuluyah with us. That one we fought was mature, and had learned to use her Hum."

"She didn't seem to know how to connect it to her Hiram magic, though," Cori observed. That at least was the same as Cat and her peers. They had used both magics in separation of each other.

"Maybe Cadmus didn't want them to be that strong. Imagine a whole army of you getting about."

Cori shot him a scathing look. She didn't voice the fact that she had taught herself how to combine the magics. Either Cadmus' Dijem were dense or something else was stopping them from using their Hiram magic at their full potential.

"What's that?" Adro said suddenly, pointing up the road. They were entering a stretch of the highway that wound through a wooded area of the state. Sprawled on the ground beneath a tree was the body of an older man. Cori drew her sword, but Adro put out a hand to stop her. "I'll look," he said. "If you do any more fighting, you'll rip those stitches."

So Cori stayed obediently on Mischief while Adro moved cautiously towards the body. He crouched down beside it, flipping the man onto his back. "Hasn't been dead long," he observed. "A few hours at most."

"I don't see any blood," Cori said. She scanned the surrounding woodland, almost expecting an ambush. Adro pushed one of the man's eyelids open and sucked in a breath.

"Dijem," he said. "Burned out."

Cori looked back to the body. A sickening feeling - much the same as she had felt when they'd killed the Dijem woman - settled over her. Was he the one who'd been controlling Tonyla the previous night? "No other signs of fight?" she asked quietly.

"None." Adro sat back, looking perplexed. "That woman burned out quickly too. It's like they don't have a sufficient store of magic, but that seems contradictory to someone who has Hiram magic and doesn't meditate."

"Maybe they do meditate," Cori hazarded a guess. "They do all sound fairly similar."

Adro looked up at her and shrugged. "Then how would they use Hiram magic? I don't know. Cadmus is far older than any of us. Maybe he knows how to manipulate the magics."

Once more Cori said nothing. She remembered Cadmus telling her and Rowan that he could no longer use Old Magic because he had meditated. If he could make it so that his creations could do it, wouldn't he have worked out how to get the other half of his magic back for himself?

She watched Adro take the legs of the man and drag him off the road into the trees. He came back quickly and mounted Morro.

They continued on their way in silence. Cori tossed her lunch aside, no longer able to stomach it. It was strange, the sick feeling that had taken hold of her, and she wasn't sure how to deal with it. She'd killed more people than she could count and it had never bothered her, yet a Dijem laying on the side of the road - one she hadn't even had a hand in killing - had stirred up emotions she hadn't even known could exist for someone's death.

To take her mind off the man, she kept her eyes on the trees in case there were Hearthians waiting to ambush them. The woodland stretched on and on. By dark, they hadn't reached the end of them and they started looking for a space big enough to camp in. Quite suddenly, Adro reined in his horse.

"Did you hear that?" he hissed.

"No, what was it?" Cori asked, glancing around wearily.

"A Hum."

Cori quickly reached out with her mind instead. She felt nothing.

"Wait," Adro told her. She did, for what seemed like an eternity. Then suddenly she heard it; a lapse in someone's barriers.

"Wait!" Adro said again. But Cori had already dived off her horse and made a break for the woods. She dodged through the trees, Adro right behind her. She didn't know what she was expecting, or what she would do when she caught the person, but if it was one of Cadmus' proteges, then she wanted answers.

She heard a stick snap and whispers before she saw who it was. Realising there was more than one, she jerked to a stop and Adro ran into her.

There's more than one, she told him, pushing him back.

I know. I would have told you that if you'd waited.

There was nothing for it now, though. She set off again, this time at a creeping pace. They climbed a small rise and looked down the other side. Crouched there, doing quite a good job of hiding so many people, was the House of Uaine.

"Acacia?" Cori said in disbelief. The elder's head snapped up, and she stared at Cori and Adro, open-mouthed.

"Adro!" Shaan jumped up first and ran up the hill to them. The other Uaines rose wearily. Cori belatedly remembered that the Uaines had left the Sarkans when they all still thought Cori was working with Cadmus. She felt a few curious touches on her mind, and she readied her barriers in case they decided to attack.

Shaan reached the top of the crest they stood on and hugged Adro. She then turned and looked curiously at Cori.

"I can feel your Hum," she said.

"Yes," Cori replied awkwardly. "Weird, isn't it?"

Shaan shrugged. "It's different, but not in a bad way."

"Where's Rowan?" Acacia asked suddenly. Cori and Adro glanced at each other.

Have they been living under a rock?

Be nice, Cori.

"He's returned to Lautan and the throne," Adro explained. Cori watched the Uaines for their reactions. Shaan smiled

CHAPTER THIRTEEN

knowingly. Acacia held her expression, though she seemed to pale a little. The others murmured to each other.

"And the Sarkans?" Shaan asked. "Are they at Lautan too?"

Cori and Adro exchanged another look. Her turn to break the news. She looked at Acacia. "Are Jonothan's parents here?"

* * *

Cori stared into the fire, listening to the conversations around her. As usual in large groups, she found herself at the outer. Across the fire, Adro sat with Shaan and a few others, telling them about their travels so far. Cori didn't fail to notice that he left out most details about their fights against the Hearthians.

"Hello Cori," Acacia greeted quietly and Cori shifted so the elder could sit down beside her. Acacia listened to the conversation across the fire for a moment before speaking. "You haven't mentioned yet why you and Adro are travelling alone."

"We're looking for Starch," Cori explained. She met Acacia's eye. She knew she would have to ask the elder about the song, but she wasn't sure how to broach the subject. Might as well get it over with. "Do you remember when I was detained by Jarrah and Starch at Tuluyah?"

Acacia blanched. "How could I forget? It was very out of character for Jarrah."

Cori didn't think so, but she didn't voice her opinion. Instead, she continued. "Well, before they caught me, they killed Cat. They used a... song, that wasn't really a song. It was like a blast of magic, but also a draining of energy. Do you know the one I mean?"

Acacia stared at her, and Cori knew the elder was deciding whether to trust her. "Is it true what they said that day?" Acacia asked. "That you can use Hiram magic?"

"Yes," Cori admitted. "I would have thought you'd know something about Old Magic, considering you're an elder. I can use it because I've never meditated, not because of Cadmus like everyone thought."

"I'm a young elder," Acacia said. "I was never taught all the old secrets."

"But you were taught that song?" Cori asked, hopeful. Acacia shook her head sadly.

"I've heard stories about it, but I don't know how to use it."

Cori looked back towards the fire, pushing away her disappointment.

"Does Rowan really think he can beat Cadmus? His father?"

"Yes," Cori said firmly, ignoring the second part of Acacia's comment. "I'm sure he can defeat him. We could use your help, however. Cadmus' armies are large and well trained; too many for only three Dijem to fight."

It was Acacia's turn to stare into the flames. Across the fire, Shaan looked to her elder. "We should help them, Acacia," she urged, and the rest of the Uaines fell silent to listen. The two women looked at each other with a look that spoke of many arguments on this matter.

"It's only the right thing to do," someone else spoke up.

"And we have to get our boy back," Jonothan's mother said. Her eyes were still red from crying after Cori had delivered the news of her son.

Acacia looked among her people. "Shall we vote on it?"

CHAPTER THIRTEEN

Cori started. She had expected Acacia to simply say no, or at least put up some resistance. But undoubtedly the elder knew what her House truly wanted. This must be the true function of an elder, Cori decided, to be a facilitator rather than a dictator to the group's needs.

One by one the hands of the Uaines rose in the air. Cori stood excitedly, as did Adro and Shaan. There was no need to count the votes, they were unanimous.

Acacia stood as well and held her hand out to Cori. She gave her a weary smile. "It seems, Cori, that you have the House of Uaine as your allies once more."

Chapter Fourteen

They parted ways with the Uaines the following morning. Cori and Adro continued north while Acacia and her fellow Dijem started their journey south to Lautan.

Cori felt jubilant as they rode. Even if they didn't find Starch, they had now secured Hale's army and the magical force that was the Uaines. It was beginning to feel like they had a chance, that the realm was getting behind Rowan and it was no longer just a vendetta. Her check in with Rowan was due that evening too.

The day seemed to crawl and Cori almost wished they'd come across some Hearthians. The fighting would have taken her mind off the evening. Eventually they stopped though, at the other end of the woodlands in a hilly field.

They turned the horses out and made a fire. Adro insisted on checking her stitches, which she sat through impatiently. Then he told her he was going to find a stream nearby and have a wash.

Cori knew this was his cue to give her privacy to reach out to Rowan. She watched him walk away towards the west before she stood and turned to the east. She climbed a small hill and sat on the top of it, facing the south. A cold breeze

CHAPTER FOURTEEN

lifted her hair from her face - the start of winter - and she took a deep breath. Her Hum fanned out, gently covering the realm, but directed towards the south and Lautan. Rowan met her halfway, catching her Hum in a gentle embrace.

Hello, he said softly.

Hello, she replied. For a long moment they didn't speak, rather sat quietly in each other's company.

Finally Rowan asked, *how was the wedding?*

Romantic and bloody, she told him. He laughed.

Only you could use those two words in the same sentence.

It served our purpose. Hale is behind us.

I never doubted that you could get it done. What did you wear?

A dress, she wished she could show him a mental picture. *It was red. You would have liked it.*

You could bring it back and show me, he teased.

Afraid not. It got destroyed. You know how I am with clothes.

Indeed. He was amused.

Well, well. What do we have here? A third voice joined them, settling smoothly into their conversation. Cadmus. Rowan vanished, as they had agreed if their conversation was interrupted, but Cori hesitated.

You're a long way from your man, Cori, Cadmus said to her, sounding delighted to have found her. Her Hum was spread wide, so she hoped he wouldn't be able to pinpoint her actual location, but she tried to follow his Hum to discover his whereabouts. He laughed. *Silly girl, you won't find me.*

Are you afraid of what we'll do to you when we do? She retorted.

After what you did to my dragon, you're the ones who should be concerned. His tone was conversational, but Cori could hear the hint of thunder beneath it. Before she could respond,

Rowan returned. He didn't speak, instead he flung his Hum over them, saturating them with his magic. Cori was instantly disorientated. She could no longer feel Cadmus, and she could barely feel herself. It was like being held in the vastness of a dragon's mind.

Then Adro's Hum was there. *Come back!* He told her urgently. She followed him, albeit reluctantly. She knew neither he nor Rowan would be impressed that she'd stayed and talked to Cadmus, but they had to find out where he was somehow; the people he was sending after them had so far led to dead ends.

She fell out of Rowan's spell and opened her eyes. She still sat where she was on the hill, arms wrapped around her knees, and for a moment she stared to the south, willing herself not to reach out again, even to make sure Rowan was all right.

"Cori," Adro came staggering up the hill, panting and dripping wet. He had a fish clutched to his bare chest. "Are you mad?"

Cori didn't answer; it would have been affirmative, anyway. "Dinner?" she asked lightly, her tone implying that she didn't want to speak of what had just happened. Something must have shown in her eyes because Adro didn't push the subject. Cori stood and together they walked back to their camp.

They worked in silence; Cori built up the fire and sliced some root vegetables while Adro gutted the fish. His brow was knitted, and she knew he would soon say something to her, despite her earlier non-verbal warning not to. When he did, though, it was not what she'd expected.

"Did you find out where he was?" Cori continued to watch him for a moment. There was no malice in his voice, rather

CHAPTER FOURTEEN

he seemed resigned. He didn't look up from his task.

"No," she admitted. "His magic was too well spread."

Adro nodded, as if confirming some suspicion. He moved the fish to a flat rock that had been heating at the edge of the fire.

"Rowan called me," he told her, answering her unasked question as to how he knew to reach out to her in Rowan's diversion. "He said *'get Cori,'* then was gone. That... whatever that thing was that he did to separate the link between you and Cadmus... I've never felt anything like it."

"I have." Cori slid some rounds of potato onto the rock beside the fish. "Daiyu did it to Rowan and I once. It was a bit different. Her mind was far more... vast, but I think he used the same concept."

Adro shook his head in amazement. "I knew he was strong, but I've never really appreciated it until tonight. He launched an attack from Lautan. I've never even heard of such a feat."

Cori pushed the food around the rock so it received even heat. She had seen bursts of Rowan's strength in the past, but she too had perhaps not appreciated the extent of his power. Rowan would have a solid understanding of his own capabilities, and he had often voiced his concerns at facing his father, so how strong did that make Cadmus? The exuberance she had felt earlier in the day at the chance she thought they had in this war evaporated. She suddenly felt insignificant under the might of the two Karalises at war with each other.

They didn't talk much while they ate and once done, Cori went straight to her bedroll. She stared up to the stars for a long time while Adro tidied their camp and went to his own bed. She was just drifting towards sleep when she felt a touch on her mind. She jerked, sure it was Cadmus, but relaxed when she realised it was Rowan. He didn't speak, rather just pressed against her Hum for a moment before withdrawing. She knew he was just reassuring himself that she was all right and letting her know the same for him. Her tension melted away, and she slept.

* * *

"I think you should put your barriers up."

Cori started and looked at Adro, her surprise quickly turning to suspicion. He held up his hands in surrender. "I promise I'm not turning on you, but we aren't far from Wolfman's peak and if Starch hears that you're with me, he will escape faster than we can get there." She couldn't deny the logic of his words.

Although she had spent the greater part of three hundred years with her barriers in place, putting them up now left her feeling naked and vulnerable. With her barriers up, her Hiram magic was restricted to the level of her own physical strength, which wasn't great. She was a good swordswoman, but Adro was also adept with a blade and if he got her close enough to Starch, well, the elder was in possession of that killing song.

It took every bit of willpower she had to keep her barriers up as they rode the last hour to Wolfman's peak. She watched Adro very carefully for any signs of betrayal. Sensing her mistrust, he tried to play their game of this or that, but Cori could barely concentrate on the options he was giving her.

They reached the river that separated Hale from Resso and turned to follow it east. Cori felt Adro's Hum, muted by her

CHAPTER FOURTEEN

barriers, reach out and she almost drew her sword to kill him.

"I'm just letting Starch know I'm coming," he said calmly, though he eyed her hand on her hilt warily.

The river widened as it reached the ocean and fell away in a canyon as they climbed towards the peak. Atop it, Cori could make out a stone cabin, and beside that was a stand of white trees.

"There are dragon soul trees," she said in surprise.

"Yes, there are a few around Tauta, though most are at Hen Goeden. Before Starch built his cabin here, men used to come and jump to their deaths, driven mad by the trees."

They reached the cabin and dismounted. Starch came to the door, a look of relief on his face. Until he saw Cori. He paled and looked at Adro. "What have you done?"

* * *

The kitchen of the cabin had a lovely view of the ocean below. Cori had let her barriers down the moment Starch had seen her and now, sitting at the small square dining table, she could hear the insistent whispers of the dragon souls outside.

She watched Starch wearily, not wanting him to get too close, though the elder seemed to want to keep his distance from her as well.

"I can't believe you, Adro, throwing your lot in with her," Starch raged. "I taught you better! You know how dangerous she is! You saw her call Cadmus' beast down on us! She killed Jarrah!"

Both Cori and Adro were silent through Starch's tirade. Adro winced at each accusation against her, but Cori gave them no weight.

"Do you know why they outlawed the Old Magic?" Starch continued. "Because the Hiram side of the magic made people violent and uncontrollable. Tell me you haven't seen it, boy? Tell me you haven't seen her slaughter people as easy as cattle and not bat an eyelid. Any sane person shows compassion and empathy. Yet I would wager she kills without reason!"

Cori almost nodded in agreement with Starch. It made her uncomfortable how close his definition of her was. Cadmus had lamented the loss of the Old Magic, yet was he not as unforgiving as she?

"No," Adro said firmly, stopping Starch in his tracks. "Cori is not those things. Yes, I've seen her kill people, and yes, her methods leave me feeling ill sometimes, but I have never seen her kill without reason and without a cause. I've watched her avenge the innocent and defend those who cannot defend themselves. I've watched her do her duty for this realm, and she's done it alone so that others don't have to bear that burden. So yes, Starch, she can be violent, but you are wrong on every other count."

Starch had turned his eyes on Cori during Adro's response, and she had trouble keeping a straight face. She hadn't expected him to defend her, and she'd never considered herself in the light Adro's words cast her in. Warmth spread through her, reddening her cheeks.

"I know you don't want to believe me," Adro continued heavily and Starch looked back to him, his eyes still smouldering with anger. "All we want is the song, and then we'll go."

"The song?" Starch said in surprise. He once more looked

at Cori. "You want me to give her *the song?*" he gave a barking laugh. "Over my dead body."

"It's for the Karalis," Cori finally spoke. Despite Adro's glowing endorsements, she had the urge to throw Starch through the window into the ocean and be done with him. Over his dead body indeed.

"Cadmus? I think you'll find your master knows the song already, girl,"

"She means Rowan," Adro corrected. Starch was finally speechless. He looked between the two of them.

"The boy's put himself back on the throne, eh?" Starch looked disturbed. He watched Cori warily for a moment, his fingertips drumming on the kitchen counter, before turning to Adro. In a low tone he said, "there's something I should tell you about Rowan, boy."

"We know that Cadmus is his father," Adro said tiredly. He was leaning against the kitchen bench, seeming too large for the room. His face showed no hint of how he might be feeling at being reunited with his elder, though Cori thought Starch's conduct left a lot to be desired.

"And still you ally yourself with them?"

Adro nodded. Starch shook his head sadly. "I won't be giving you that song, boy."

"Then we won't be leaving until you do."

* * *

The cabin had three other rooms; a bathroom and two bedrooms. Starch didn't invite them to stay, nor did he tell them to leave.

Cori and Adro took up residence in the second bedroom,

and for five days they tried to encourage Starch to give them the information they needed. Cori barely spoke, knowing that anything she said seemed to make Starch more resolved not to give them the song. Instead, she watched Adro gently try to coax it out of him.

Cori itched to go. It had already been almost a month since they'd left Lautan and every day that they had to spend with Starch was one day longer that she was away from Rowan.

She was also dreadfully tired. Starch didn't seem to sleep often, preferring to stay up well into the night smoking his herbs, and Cori found herself unable to sleep while he was awake, lest he try to do away with her in some way. Adro sat up with him some nights, trying to reason with him and telling him of what had befallen them since they had all escaped Tuluyah.

It was on their third night there that Starch tried to convince Adro to stay with him. Cori had expected it, and she listened tensely to their conversation from the other room.

"My boat is here, we could go south by the Nomad Isles then down onto your homelands for a time. This war is not for us, boy, leave it to Rowan and Cadmus to sort out their differences."

Adro stayed quiet for so long that Cori drew the dagger Samyla had given her from her belt. If Adro stayed with Starch, she would probably have to fight her way out. She would avoid killing Adro, but she would take Starch down if she could; they would just have to find another way to destroy Cadmus.

"No, I don't think so," Adro decided and Cori exhaled the breath she'd been holding. "You may think this war isn't ours, but it is. We are more powerful than the other races and it's our duty to protect them from our own."

"They're just using you, boy."

"Are they? Like you used me? Tell me, Starch, what was the purpose of taking me from my family if not to be another body in the Last Fight?"

Starch snorted. "Still holding onto that? I love you like a son, you know that."

"And I love you, Starch, but you lost me when you left me at Tuluyah. I'm Rowan's man now." Both men were quiet for a moment. "You can join us, Starch, help us finish the fight."

"No, boy," Starch sighed and drew on his pipe. "This war is not mine to fight anymore."

* * *

On their fifth night there, Cori found herself outside the cabin, watching the dragon soul trees. She'd come out here many times over the past week, both to escape the tenseness inside the cabin, but also because she was drawn by their whispers. She knew what they really wanted was to leech away her sense of self and throw her over the cliffs, so she'd so far avoided touching them, but that night she moved closer than she had before, looking up into their glowing white boughs. These trees were older than those at the edge of Hen Goeden that she'd once talked to the many times she'd wanted to cross the forest to find Rowan. Younglings were easy to withstand. She wondered if these would present more of a challenge. She lifted her hand.

Footsteps crunched across the grass behind her, and she turned her head to find Starch approaching. He was up later than usual - part of the reason she was outside. She lowered her hand slowly, but remained facing the trees. Out across the ocean, Lightning flashed, followed by a roll of thunder; a winter storm approaching.

Starched stopped several feet from her and lit his pipe.

"What do you get out of this war, Cori?" he asked, exhaling smoke as he spoke. Cori wasn't expecting that question, and she had to think about it.

"It's my inheritance," she explained, "As past wars have been yours and future wars will belong to the Dijem of that time. I have personal reasons for wanting Cadmus dead, and they are different to Rowan's, and different to those who fought him in the Last Fight. What do I get out of the war? Nothing but a dead man, if I can manage it, and that's enough for me."

Starch watched her without expression, smoke curling in tendrils from his nostrils. A fork of lightning split the sky, throwing the creases of his sun-hardened skin into sharp relief. "You're not the good samaritan Adro would have me believe, are you?"

Cori shook her head. "I haven't done the things you accuse me of, but I also feel no remorse for the people I kill so no, I don't believe I'm a good person."

"And yet you surround yourself with those who are."

"Perhaps I'm trying to be better."

A blast of wind hit them, howling up the canyon, and the first few drops of rain came with it. At the edge of her mind, Cori could feel the dragon souls trying to lure her closer. She finally turned to face Starch fully. Tendrils of her hair escaped her braid and whipped about her face. "Why does it bother you so much, to give me the song?"

CHAPTER FOURTEEN

"Giving a killer another weapon just doesn't seem right to me."

"And yet you seemed to have no problem using it on those kids at Tuluyah."

Starch looked uncomfortable. He lowered his pipe and scratched his beard. "You're right there, girl. At the time, killing them seemed the best course of action but I've had time to think on it since, and I, quite frankly, wish I had never learned the damn song to begin with." He shook his head, suddenly agitated. "I'm going to regret this," he muttered under his breath before turning to face Cori fully. "Get Adro up, I'll teach you the damn song."

Cori froze for only a moment, sure she'd misheard him, then she started back to the cabin.

"Cori?" The elder made her pause. "Just promise me you'll only use it on Cadmus."

The three of them gathered around the dining table as the storm hit. Wind raged across the cliffs, rattling the windows, and rain pounded down upon the roof. Starch began his lesson.

"This song is one of the Old Magic songs and seemingly survived the split of the two magics. It requires two people, one to perform the song and the other to act as a vessel for the victim's energy. The song itself is not difficult, it's merely an extension of the song that we use to receive energy from a human."

"That song takes time," Cori interjected. "When I saw you use this one, it was almost instantaneous."

Starch nodded. "The song should already be woven, and the partners connected so that all that needs to happen is for the vessel to touch the victim."

That made sense to Cori. She often had her strengthening songs already woven and ready to use with her Hiram magic. She suddenly wondered if there were other songs that complimented both magics. She made a mental note to mention it to Rowan; he would be able to find them if there were.

"The song, then?" Adro spoke up. His hair stuck up at all angles and his expression was still slack from being woken, but his eyes were bright.

"Yes, yes," Starch muttered. He hesitated a moment before reaching out to both of them. He Hummed the song twice only, but Cori could tell the similarities to the other song used to collect energy from humans.

They stayed up the rest of the night, which only had a few hours left, and Starch told them more about the song. The following morning, as the storm abated and a weak dawn broke through the rain clouds, Cori and Adro prepared to leave.

"Are you sure you won't join us?" Adro asked as they saddled the horses. Starch sat on the steps of the cabin with his pipe. "Uaine are meeting us in Lautan, it would be good to have your expertise too."

"No, boy," Starch said gruffly. "I said I was done with wars and I mean it. Seek me out when you're done though. I have a lot to make up for, I think."

Adro hugged his elder and Cori and Starch begrudgingly exchanged a handshake and then they were on their way.

Cori was awash with relief. After five tense days with Starch, they had what they needed and were finally ready to return to Lautan and Rowan.

Chapter Fifteen

It rained on and off in the few days it took to reach the woodlands. Winter had truly set in and Cori and Adro spent each night huddled back to back in a futile attempt to share warmth and blankets.

"I hate the cold," Adro said, and not for the first time, as they entered the woodlands. Cori agreed wholeheartedly. Even the fur coat Rowan had given her the year prior didn't fully keep the cold out.

"At least we're headed south," Cori reassured him. "Lautan has mild winters."

"It would be even better to go to my homeland. They don't have winter at all."

The trees of the woodlands provided some measure of shelter from the rain and wind. It also provided cover for the ambush waiting for them.

Cori heard a branch crack to her left and she only just managed to draw her sword when a dozen men broke free of the trees, rushing towards her. She employed her strengthening song and shoved at them, sending a handful back and impaling one on a branch. Mischief reared beneath her, striking a man down and scattering two others. She heard Adro curse and glanced behind her to see they were being flanked on both sides.

"Shit," she hissed, grasping the reins to keep her seat. All she wanted to do was get back to Rowan. Could these Hearthians not back off for just a few weeks? She slid from the saddle as Mischief lunged forward, teeth snapping at a soldier's face. Cori had only a second to wonder when Rowan had had time to teach the stallion warhorse tricks before six soldiers were on her. She shoved three away as hard as she could and whirled to stab a fourth. Blood sprayed over her fur coat, and she swore again. She heard Adro yelling and turned to see him fighting against five soldiers.

"Barriers!" he roared at her, bringing his sword in a downward chop that almost cleaved a woman in two. Cori got her barriers up just as she felt a Hum slam against them. The other mind battered her barriers relentlessly, not allowing her any space to lower them.

She slashed at the fifth man, forcing him back, before she transferred her sword to her right hand and stabbed the sixth soldier. The man jerked in surprise, and Cori kicked him off the end of her sword. She whirled back towards the last soldier, noticing as she did that more were coming through the trees. The Dijem attacking her mind didn't relent. She slashed her sword across the last solider's face before diving forward to meet the next wave of opponents.

The first thing she noticed was that these new soldiers had glazed eyes. She scanned the trees again, hoping to catch sight of the Dijem. There had to be more than one; even she wouldn't be able to control that many soldiers and attack someone's barriers.

"Cori!" she whirled quickly to see that Adro had dispatched his opponents and was pointing to the trees on his side of

CHAPTER FIFTEEN

the road. Through them, she could see someone standing, watching.

One of her own opponents got close enough to grab her arm. She put her hand up, shoving him back a few steps, but he held on, pulling her with him. With a burst of pain, she felt the stitches in her shoulder tear. She cried out as the man kept pulling her with him, opening her wound further. She swung her sword around and sliced off his arm.

She shook free of the limb's grasp as the man screamed, then she sliced his throat. She put the fist that held her sword to her shoulder and saw it come away sticky and red. Mischief squealed nearby then plunged into the soldiers coming towards her, kicking and biting. Cori staggered back from them and turned away.

The Dijem still attacked her barriers, though it was more of a nuisance than anything; Cori was too strong for them to have a chance of breaking through. She saw Adro running through the trees and she took off after him, switching her sword to her other hand so she could clutch her shoulder.

After the noise of the skirmish they'd just been in, the woodlands were oddly muted. They crashed through the undergrowth and Cori could see three figures running ahead of them. She dropped her sword and instead pulled out her dagger.

"Come on," she growled, her eyes on the figure at the back. They darted between two trees and Cori flung the dagger. It spun through the air, landing with a thunk in the person's back. They cried out as they dropped to the ground. Cori felt the attack on her barriers vanish, and she dropped them. She reached out with both her hands, ignoring the tearing pain of her shoulder, and made dual grasping motions. The final two figures jerked to a stop and Adro crashed into one, tackling them to the ground.

"No, no!" Cori heard him say as she stopped beside him. "Burned out," he told her, releasing the man he was holding. She looked to the final figure who'd fallen to the ground after Cori had grabbed them. It was a woman, and her eyes were dark and staring. There was no other mark on her.

Despite their fight and run, Cori felt suddenly chilled. "Let's get out of here," she said. She retrieved her dagger from the first Dijem she'd felled, and they left the three bodies and trudged back towards the road.

"Why do they keep dying like that?" She demanded of no one in particular, collecting her sword as they went back past it.

Adro shook his head. His breathing was laboured, and she noticed his hand kept straying to his chest.

"What happened?" She asked in alarm. With her own injury, she hadn't even thought to check if Adro was all right.

"Broken rib, I think." He winced. They reached the road to find their two horses standing beside a handful of Hearthian soldiers. Cori raised her sword, but each of them lifted their hands in surrender.

"Please," one of them begged. "I don't even know how I got here."

* * *

Adro's side was swollen and mottled purple by the time Cori got a chance to look at it. They'd sent the confused soldiers on to Rikdom to deal with them there. Most of them couldn't remember even leaving their families, and when Cori and

Adro had picked their minds, their stories seemed to be true.

Adro had then stitched Cori's wound back together. The fighting had made it worse, and she had to use her bloodied shirt as a sling to keep her arm close to her body and her shoulder immobile. Finally, it had been Adro's turn. She pressed her fingers to his ribs, and he hissed.

"I can't feel any bone poking up. Maybe it's just cracked?"

Adro nodded, his face pinched and white. "Just bind it," he told her.

"That attack was deliberately for us," she said as she wound their last bandage around his massive torso.

"Cadmus probably had a guess at where we were," Adro surmised dully. Cori felt a stab of guilt. That was her fault. "We just need to get to Rikdom quickly," he continued, "and perhaps get some soldiers from Dristan to escort us the rest of the way."

Cori didn't respond as she tied off the bandage. She didn't like the idea of travelling with a retinue. They would slow them down.

"I mean it, Cori," Adro said, following her train of thought. "We were lucky today, but as you said, that ambush was specifically for us and Cadmus doesn't seem to have a shortage of Dijem to send after us. They're learning to fight us and don't think I haven't noticed your handicap when it comes to fighting our own kind; you're out of your depth."

Cori sat back in a crouch, her fingers lifting to brush the wound on her shoulder. "You're right," she admitted. "I can't fight them. I've never had to before."

Adro shook his head once more. He lurched to his feet, clutching his side, then held out a hand to help her up. "It's not your fault you haven't had to face one in the past. We'll need to teach you; Rowan is particularly skilled at getting inside people's heads. But first we need to get back to Lautan alive, and that means getting there with help." He gave her a tired smile. "That was a good throw of your dagger back there. I should have realised that you had good aim with projectiles as well."

"It's a similar aim as my Hiram magic," Cori explained as they mounted their horses. She had already checked Mischief over, but the stallion was surprisingly free of injuries. She held her hands up to show Adro. "The magic follows a trajectory directly from my hands so if someone dodges, I miss. The same with throwing a dagger."

Adro pointed to a rock further up. "Show me?"

She pushed gently, and the rock rolled away from them, then she made a pulling motion and the rock paused before coming back in their direction. Morro snorted nervously as the rock rolled between the two horses.

"It's quite an impressive skill when you get past the horrors of watching men being flung ten feet in the air."

"I thought that *was* the impressive part."

* * *

The town guard was waiting for them at the gates of Rikdom. They were escorted straight to the manor where both Dristan and Samyla were there to greet them.

"You look as if you've seen better days," Dristan said as the two Dijem slid from their saddles.

"All part of the job," Adro replied heavily. Cori watched him from the corner of her eye. Since their escape from the ambush a few days prior, he'd not been his lighthearted self.

CHAPTER FIFTEEN

Of course, his broken rib was giving him grief.

"Will you be staying long?" Samyla asked in her pretty voice. She wore a pink, flowing gown, and her hair was dressed with winter flowers. Cori felt at once awed and jealous by the other woman's beauty.

"Only a night, then we must continue on," she replied. She climbed the steps, Adro beside her, and Samyla took her hands and squeezed them.

"Come," she urged. "I think a nice soak would do you a world of wonders."

They were shown to their rooms, this time impressive suits that in the old days had been reserved for the Karalis and his court. Samyla and some of her maids accompanied Cori, and she allowed herself to be bathed and her hair washed and dressed.

"Dristan and I will come to Lautan in a few weeks," Samyla told Cori as a healer carefully changed the bandage on Cori's shoulder. "I'm so excited. In the books I've read about the Karalis' last rule, he threw some magnificent parties. Did you ever go to them? Were they as fun as the books say?"

Cori allowed a maid to help her into a soft blue dress, similar to the one Samyla wore, and remembered back to the only ball she'd ever attended as a guest, the one where Rowan had declared her his heir before the realm. "They're something all right," she muttered. She looked down at the dress. It wasn't as fitted as she was used to, but it was comfortable.

The two women descended to the lower floor of the manor and met Dristan, Adro and the captain of the town guard in the Atrium. A table had been set for them to dine together.

"Karaliene," the captain bowed to her. "We haven't formally

been introduced. My name is Alastar."

"Adro was just telling me you'd like some soldiers to travel to Lautan with you," Dristan said as the five of them sat down. Servants appeared and placed plates of roast beef and vegetables before them. One went around the table, pouring wine.

"Yes," Cori agreed. "We ran into a bit of trouble coming back south and thought it best that we boost our numbers for the rest of the trip."

"Myself and two others will accompany you, Karaliene," Alastar offered. and Dristan nodded.

"Alastar is the best I've got and he will see you through safely."

"I don't think you'll run into trouble," Samyla spoke up. "Dris has sent his army to secure the borders."

Dristan nodded again. "Ten mounted contingents to secure the border and drive the Hearthians back. When the Karalis needs them, they'll regroup and be ready."

"I heartily hope there's no more trouble," Adro spoke up, "but it's better to be safe, I think."

"Of course. Now, enough of armies and battles. Let's enjoy this fine meal."

* * *

Yoku and Stalmond were the names of the woman and man Alastar had chosen to accompany them. Cori's fears of being slowed down by extra people were unfounded; the three soldiers rode and camped with an efficiency that had both Cori and Adro picking up their game.

They made good time and for almost eight days they saw

CHAPTER FIFTEEN

no signs of Hearthian soldiers, save for the pillaging and burning they'd seen on their way north. It was a day outside of the town they had first stopped in when starting their journey that they found a contingent of twenty Hearthians camped off the road.

They watched them for a time, trying to discern if there was a Dijem among them. They were a ragged bunch and Alastar thought they may have fled towards the coast, cut off from Hearth by Hale's army. Cori had expected at least one of the others to suggest they just ride past, but none of them did. They all knew they would have to kill these men before they attacked the next settlement.

"Let me go first," Cori suggested. She and Adro had found no traces of Dijem; she could use her full strength unhindered. "If I look overwhelmed then jump in, but try to stay out of range."

"There are twenty of them, my lady," Yoku said hesitantly. "Are you sure that's wise?" Alastar and Stalmond looked similarly concerned. She didn't blame them; they'd been sent to protect her after all.

"Don't tear your stitches," Adro said by way of farewell. Cori grinned at him, then set off at a run towards the Hearthian camp.

She jumped into their midst, grasping the closest man by the shirt and flinging him directly upwards. The other nineteen soldiers watched the man rise, screaming, into the darkening sky. Then he dropped, hitting the ground with a heavy thud at Cori's feet.

"Who's next?" She asked, and the soldiers jumped from their logs and bedrolls, grasping for swords and axes. Cori flung them away without discrimination. She turned and ducked under the blade of a soldier who got too close, ploughing her fist into his stomach. She felt his organs burst under the impact. Twisting, she kicked the legs from beneath another before shoving him into the fire. She didn't tear limbs or explode heads; she was aware of the others still watching her and she didn't want to deal with their fear afterwards so she kept her fighting neat.

Several men rushed her at once, and with a great sweeping motion she threw them to the side. She also felt her wound open again. She hissed at the pain, looking down to see blood blooming through her shirt. Her last shirt.

Tore my stitches, she told Adro guiltily as she punched a woman, collapsing her skull. Adro seemed to take that as a cue for he and the three soldiers suddenly joined the fray, slashing and stabbing at those who tried to escape. The battle was over in minutes, just as rain began to fall.

"Why did you need us to accompany you?" Alastar queried as he, Yoku, and Stalman dragged the bodies to a pile by the fire. His face showed a mixture of admiration and disgust. It was a look she was used to.

"She was just showing off," Adro answered for her. He was rummaging through his pack for a needle and thread. "Generally speaking, her fighting skills during our trip left much to be desired."

"Ha," said Cori sarcastically. Adro smiled at her, letting her know he was joking. She sat on a log beside him, the shoulder of her shirt pulled down to expose her wound. The rain had soaked through her clothes and hair, leaving her chilled. Crumpled over the log on her other side was one of the soldiers she'd killed. As she waited for Adro, Yoku came and grasped the soldier by the boots and dragged him away.

CHAPTER FIFTEEN

"Hold still." Adro grasped her shoulder, plucking the last few stitches free before starting again. She gritted her teeth and closed her eyes. For the third time in less than a month she had twenty stitches sewn into her shoulder.

Cori?

Cori jumped at the voice in her head and Adro slipped with the needle, jabbing it into her skin.

Shaan?

I thought I felt you fighting. Is everything all right?

Yes, just a few Hearthians. Where are you?

Shaan paused. *Half an hour south of you, I think. Will you join us?*

Yes. We won't be long.

"Shaan?" Adro asked when Cori opened her eyes. She nodded.

"Yes. They're not far. We'll meet up with them for the night."

Adro finished her stitches, then the group finished cleaning up the Hearthian's campsite. They left the bodies in a pile and Alastar doused the fire before they went back to the road and their horses.

Finding the Uaines camp in the rain was welcoming. They'd strung canvases between several trees, which provided some dry ground. They also had several cook fires going, and they welcomed Cori and her group with a hearty energy.

They ate and drank and laughed. The mood of the Uaines, now they'd decided to join Rowan, was purposeful and boisterous, and rather infectious.

Alastar, Yoku and Stalman were awed to be surrounded by so many Dijem, but they were pulled into the ranks and offered all the courtesies that Cori and Adro were afforded.

"I'm going to contact Rowan," Cori said to the group she was sitting with as they neared midnight, "and let him know we'll be there tomorrow."

"Wait!" Acacia said as Cori made to stand. The elder glanced at Shaan. "We wanted to surprise Rowan. Will you give us a moment?"

Cori watched curiously as Acacia stood and called the attention of her House. "Barriers, everyone!"

Like a wave, Cori felt fifty Hums blink out of existence. She'd always wondered how large groups such as this went unnoticed, but it seemed Acacia had trained them well. The elder nodded to her and Cori turned and walked a little away from the camp and into the drizzling rain.

It only took a moment to reach Rowan now that they were so close to Lautan. His Hum was clear too, as if he were standing right beside her.

We'll be back in Lautan tomorrow, she told him.

Good. Was all he replied, but his voice projected warmth and eagerness.

They said nothing more, and Cori knew she would rather see him in person to tell him about their travels. She went to bed that night, almost unable to sleep due to anticipation. When she finally did though, her dreams were a disturbing recollection of her imprisonment in Cadmus' palace and Daiyu's attack of her when she'd released the Deathsong.

She was wretched when she woke the next morning and knew it was a mixture of her dreams and overdoing the wine with dinner the night before. Still, she was among the first to awaken and she roused Adro and her soldiers. "Let's go," she told them quietly.

CHAPTER FIFTEEN

Acacia found them while they were saddling their horses, her blond hair mussed from sleep. "We'll try to travel fast today," she said, "so hopefully we should only be a few hours behind you, or a night at the most."

Cori nodded and mounted Mischief. "Reach out to me when you're close by. I'll let Rowan know then."

The two women clasped hands briefly, then Cori turned her horse and kicked him to a canter, into the rain and towards the road. They were almost there.

Chapter Sixteen

They pushed their horses harder than they normally would, alternating between canter and trot. The drizzling rain was unrelenting, and time was undefinable under the blanket of grey clouds.

Despite their pace, they hadn't quite reached Lautan by dark. Cori ordered them on, much to the grumbling of the group. The rain soaked through their clothes to their skin, making them all shiver. Finally, well into the evening, they crested the rise over Lautan and looked down on the glittering lights of the town. Above it, set majestically on the cliffs, the palace blazed.

"We made it back alive," Adro said in amazement. Cori smiled at him and patted Mischief on the neck.

"Come on," she said. "I'm very ready for a bath."

"And some hot food," Adro added.

"And a warm bed," Yoku sighed.

The five of them nudged their horses forward and walked the last league to Lautan.

The streets were still busy despite the drizzling rain and Cori noticed immediately the changes that had happened since they'd last been there. The main road was now well lit with lamps, and many of the dingy bars had been

CHAPTER SIXTEEN

converted to restaurants with street-side dining. Taverns played cheerful music and the towns folk lining up to get in were dressed colourfully.

Riding through the town was like seeing the ghost of her childhood. The fashions had evolved with the times, as had the music, but people still sought their pleasures in much the same way.

They reached the cliff road and climbed it slowly, ensuring the horses were cooled and stretched from their long day. The Stablemaster and a few of his hands were waiting for them. Cori dismounted with a sigh. She was cold, her shoulder ached, but she'd made it back. She was almost as surprised as Adro had been that they'd managed the task alive. She pulled Mischief's saddle off and untied her packs as a stable hand started on wiping the stallion down with a cloth.

"Cori." Adro got her attention and nodded in the direction of the palace. She turned to see Rowan striding across the grounds towards the stables. Cori set her packs down and went to meet him. She saw the warm smile bloom on his face and couldn't help herself; she ran the last few steps and flung herself into his arms. He wrapped the folds of his coat around her and kissed the top of her head. She pressed her face against his chest, breathing him in and felt all her tension melting away.

"Where's my hug?" Adro appeared behind her and threw his arms around the both of them, sandwiching her in the middle. Rowan laughed, pulling his right arm free to slap Adro on the back. Cori noticed that his left arm stayed tight to her. She also noted how he winced ever so slightly. He said nothing, so neither did she, but she could tell he'd somehow injured his shoulder and the moment they were alone, she would find out how.

"I have a surprise for you," Rowan told them as they walked towards the palace. Servants had appeared to collect their packs and take Alastar, Yoku and Stalman to some guest rooms.

"I hope it's food," Adro said. His humour seemed to have returned now that they'd arrived safely back at the palace.

"There's food, but that's not the surprise." They entered the palace through the restored arches of the throne room. The room was well lit and bright tapestries had been hung along the far wall. The wall behind the throne had been scraped clean of its peeling mural, but nothing had replaced it yet.

Rowan led them from the throne room and through the corridors of the palace to one of the small receiving rooms. He stepped aside so that Cori and Adro could enter before him. The space was comfortably furnished with a square table and chairs, soft cream carpet and two plush armchairs. Cori noticed none of it though, her attention immediately claimed by the two people already there. Sitting side by side at the table, their appearance dishevelled and their expressions despondent, was Myce and Melita.

"Myce, Melita?" Adro said in amazement, brushing past Cori to hug each of the twins in turn. Cori didn't move as Rowan quietly closed the door behind them. "Where are the rest?"

Melita looked at Rowan with tear-stained cheeks. He nodded to her as he pushed Cori forward to sit at the table. He took a seat beside her, taking her hand under the table and lacing his fingers through hers. "Tell them."

CHAPTER SIXTEEN

Melita looked like she was struggling with her words before she burst into fresh tears. Myce touched her arm, his expression wooden, before facing Cori and Adro.

"Daniyl has taken the Sarkans to Cadmus."

Cori stared at him, stunned. Cadmus had gained a whole House of Dijem. Ones that had been privy to some of Rowan's plans. "We should have killed him," she whispered. Rowan squeezed her hand. Adro had turned even whiter than she. It had been his words that had spared Daniyl in the first place.

Two servants knocked on the door and entered, bearing trays of hot food. They placed them on the table and quickly left, sensing the tension in the room. Cori stared at the tendril of steam that rose from a bowl of soup and felt no appetite.

"How? When?" Adro asked in a cracked voice.

Melita calmed herself enough to speak. "After Rowan sent us away," she began, her voice accusatory. Cori snarled.

"After Rowan sent you away?" She hissed. She rose, intending to throw herself across the table at the other woman, but Rowan jerked her back into her seat. She wasn't done, however. "Your tone implies, Melita, that he was wrong to banish you, that your direct disobedience of his orders and your engagement of those Hearthian troops was acceptable. You should think yourself lucky that sending you away was all he did."

Melita threw Cori a sullen glare.

"She's right," Rowan said quietly and Melita looked away. "You cannot elect me as the Karalis and then pick and choose which of my orders are enforceable. Any of you could have come to me with Daniyl's plans, and yet you followed him rather than me. As a result, Jonothan was almost killed, and Cori had to finish what you'd started, which I didn't appreciate having to ask her to do."

Melita stared at the table, red faced with shame. Rowan stood and unloaded the bowls of soup from their trays, placing one in front of each of the others. "Eat," he commanded. "You've all travelled a long way today." he sat back down, dipping a bit of bread in Cori's soup and popping it in his mouth. Adro slowly lifted his spoon and dipped it into his bowl. Cori and Myce followed suit. Melita continued her story.

"After Rowan sent us away," she said again, this time contrite, "we went back to Tuluyah. It wasn't the same without Jarrah though. Daniyl was so angry all the time. We voted on whether to go to Cadmus, but he bullied the majority into it."

"At least tell me you now know where Cadmus is," Cori asked dryly. Melita shook her head, her cheeks flushing pink again.

"We went to Tengah to seek him out, but Myce and I left in the night. We couldn't... Jarrah would never have forgiven us for giving ourselves to Cadmus."

"They may not have found him yet," Cori mused. "I could go and look for them and kill Daniyl. It might snap the others out of their stupidity, otherwise I could kill the lot."

"No," said Rowan and Adro in unison. Myce and Melita looked shocked. Adro, almost finished his soup, gave her a meaningful look; she would be useless against that many Dijem.

"Please let us stay, Rowan," Melita whispered. Myce set his spoon down and put his arm over his sister's shoulder. He

CHAPTER SIXTEEN

watched Rowan, his expression reserved. Rowan shook his head slowly.

"I won't turn you out, but I hope next time you'll listen to me."

"Of course," Myce said firmly. "We won't doubt you again."

* * *

"This changes things," Adro muttered as he, Rowan and Cori headed towards their suites.

"It does," Rowan agreed. "But it's late. Let's talk about it tomorrow."

Adro nodded, bid them goodnight and entered the Advisor's suite. Cori and Rowan continued to their own rooms. She was exhausted, her clothes still damp, and her wound throbbed. Still, she stopped Rowan before he could open the door.

"Are you going to tell me what happened to your shoulder?"

"Noticed that, did you?"

"Were you going to tell me?"

"Yes. Come inside first." He reached past her, pushing the door open with his right hand.

The renovations on the suite had been finished. Cream coloured carpet covered the floor and a few armchairs and a couch were set around a low table. To one side was a taller table with six chairs surrounding it. One chair at the table was slightly skewed, and she noticed a deep scratch in the wood over one corner.

Rowan closed the door and shrugged out of his coat. He started on the buttons of his shirt with his right hand, and Cori turned to help him.

"Last night," he began in a calm voice that set Cori on edge, "someone tried to assassinate me."

She stopped, a chill descending on her that had nothing to do with her damp clothes. He undid the last two buttons, wincing as he pulled the shirt off. His shoulder was swollen and bruised. "I dislocated my shoulder trying to dispatch him. I had to force the joints back together myself."

"Who-" mouth suddenly dry, she swallowed and tried again. "Do you know who it was?"

He shook his head as he attempted to pull his shirt back on. Cori helped him. "I thought you might though," he said and led her through the receiving room and out to the cliff-side garden.

At the edge of the cliff lay a dead man, head slightly askew atop a broken neck. Cori crouched beside him, imagining Rowan fighting him off with a dislocated shoulder. She felt sick at the thought of him almost being killed.

You were almost killed multiple times in the last few weeks, she told herself sternly. He trusted that you could protect yourself. You need to trust the same of him.

"Why would you think I'd know him?" She asked. The body was stiff and blue.

"I thought there might be a chance you saw him in your travels."

"I killed every-" she trailed off as she pushed the man's eyelids open. His eyes were glassy, but she could see the veins of gold through brown. "He was turning into a Dijem?"

"Seems that way."

"And he didn't burn out?"

Rowan frowned. "Why would he? He didn't use any magic. I couldn't get in his head though. It was like a blank space."

CHAPTER SIXTEEN

"Every Dijem we fought burned out before we could catch them and get in their heads."

Rowan's frown deepened. He reached down and pulled Cori to her feet before placing his boot on the man's side and rolling him off the edge of the cliff. They watched him fall, his descent obscured by the rush of the waves below. "Come on," Rowan pulled her back towards the palace. "I bet you'd appreciate a bath."

"Why are you so calm about all of this? This man attacking you? The Sarkans going to Cadmus?" She demanded as he steered her towards the bathroom.

"Because you're back, and for the moment, the rest doesn't matter."

The bathroom had been restored too, with white tiles surrounding the sunken pool and great panes of glass fitted in the window frames. A sink was set into the benches, and a bouquet of wildflowers stood in a vase beside it. The pool itself was full and tendrils of steam rose from it, wafting the scent of lavender through the room.

Cori felt out of place in her travel worn and blood-stained clothes. Well, there was only one way to fix that. She stripped out of them.

"From the wedding," she said when she noticed Rowan looking curiously at the wound on her shoulder.

"That was over three weeks ago. It should be more healed than that."

Cori shrugged, pulling her hair from its binding so it tumbled down her back. "I tore it open once or twice." Rowan shook his head with a smile, and she turned to the pool. "When I was your page, I always wanted to swim in this bath." She sat down at the edge, dipping her feet in to find a bench beneath the surface that also acted as a step. The water was deliciously warm, and she stepped off the bench into the water with a sigh.

"You could have asked," Rowan said. He moved to the sink and rummaged in a draw beneath it. "I would have let you."

Cori moved towards the middle of the pool where the water reached her chin. "That would have been unseemly. Imagine what people would have said; that you were taking advantage of me, corrupting my innocence."

Rowan snorted. He placed a small knife and a cloth by the pool, then undressed. "The other two statements I will give you, but you've never been innocent, Cori." He slid into the pool and Cori moved back towards him, eyeing the knife warily.

"What's that for?"

He smiled, wiggling the small blade between his fingers. "I'm going to take your stitches out."

He made her sit on the lip of the pool while he plucked her stitches out one at a time and placed them on the cloth. She sat through it with her eyes closed, a grimace on her face at each tug.

"Come here," he said finally, pulling her back into the pool. He sat on the bench and positioned her between his legs, her back against his chest. He placed his hand against her chest and she lay her head back, anticipating the calming effect of the healing song. She marvelled at the times she'd shied away from his healing touch. Now she couldn't remember why she'd made such silly excuses.

The song started and Cori instantly felt a horrible tug in the sliced muscles under her skin. She jerked forward with a gasp of pain. Rowan stopped the song, though he didn't

CHAPTER SIXTEEN

remove his hand. "Sorry," he said, "I'd forgotten that you've never been conscious for a proper healing."

"It's supposed to hurt?"

"It's the nature of a body that's rapidly repairing itself. You need to let me finish."

She sat back again and submitted to the sharp discomfort. "Why don't you tell me about your trip?" He suggested, and she knew he was trying to take her mind off the pain. She told him about the wedding and the strange Dijem they'd fought, and she recounted their week with Starch. Fortunately, the pain only seemed to last ten minutes at most. Eventually she felt the pain fade away to be replaced by the calmness that she was more accustomed to when he used the healing song on her.

Glancing down at her shoulder, she found a pink puckered scar where the wound had been. She rolled her shoulder experimentally, only feeling a little tightness. "You're getting better at this."

"You prove a very willing subject to practise on."

She lay back against him, letting the scented water wash around her. Now that she was warm, fed and healed, she was drowsy. He cradled her for a time, occasionally leaning down to kiss her face or lips, his fingers running delicious trails up and down her side. It wasn't until she was almost asleep that he roused her to get out of the bath.

It must have been past midnight, she surmised as they dried off and headed for the bedroom. The rain fell heavier now, splattering the great window that overlooked the ocean. Winter furs had already been spread over the bed and Cori slid between the sheets with a contented sigh.

Rowan extinguished the lamps before climbing into the

bed as well and pulling her close. "I love you," he whispered, and she held him tighter. Renewed relief at being back with him washed over her once more.

She was almost asleep when she felt a touch in her mind. Beside her, Rowan sat up.

"Was that Acacia?" He asked incredulously.

He didn't miss a thing. Cori sat up too, smiling. "I almost forgot," she said. "I have a surprise for you too."

She reached out with her mind towards Acacia, and Rowan followed. Like a sea of stars lighting up the sky, the Uaines lowered their barriers to reveal themselves. Cori could feel Rowan's surprised grip on her arm.

Cadmus may have gained himself a House, Cori thought fiercely, but they now had a Dijem army too. And the Uaines had always been stronger than the Sarkans.

Chapter Seventeen

The mattress dipped under someone's weight, and Cori woke with a start.

"Rowan," she gasped, her hand over her hammering heart. He raised an eyebrow at her, amused. "I thought you were going to kill me."

He frowned at that. "I think you better take a break from conflict for a while. It's making you paranoid."

She scrubbed her face with her hands, then threw back the covers and sat up. Despite her abrupt awakening, she had slept deeply. "What time is it?"

"Midday. I would have let you sleep longer but the Uaines have just arrived in Lautan, I thought you might like to greet them."

"Yes, I do." She yawned, then pulled her hair up into a knot, securing it with the leather thong that she kept around her wrist. Rowan took her hand.

"Come on, There's some breakfast downstairs."

She followed him down to the receiving room where a breakfast tray of fruit, toast and oats was the table. She sat down and Rowan sat across from her, watching as she buttered the toast. "Lost some weight, have I?" she asked, taking a stab at why there was so much food.

"A little."

"You're being very nice to me, why?"

Rowan laughed. "I thought I was always nice to you."

"You are," she tore the bit of toast in half. "But the bath, and now breakfast? It all seems extra special."

"I've asked you to do some pretty horrible things since I took the throne back and not once have you questioned me. I wish I could repay the favour somehow, I don't want to seem like I'm using you."

Cori eyed him as she ate her food. She once again wondered at his calmness and if there was something he wasn't telling her. Perhaps it was just that he'd come to terms with being the Karalis again, though she doubted that. She reached out and touched his mind tentatively. He smiled.

"Don't worry, I'm fine."

She sat back and picked up the other half of her toast. Maybe he was right, and she was becoming paranoid. Her time would be better spent enjoying his mood rather than analysing it. There was a knock on the door, and Adro let himself in. He was already dressed in his Advisor's uniform, his wild mane as tamed as he could manage.

"They've just arrived at the stables so they won't be long." He stopped when he saw Cori's breakfast tray, then looked at Rowan with an expression of mock hurt. "I thought I was special getting breakfast from you this morning. Seems any commoner gets to dine with the Karalis these days."

Cori snorted and threw the crust of her toast at him. He caught it and put it in his mouth with a grin. "Don't make me break another rib for you," she threatened. He waved her words away.

"Go for it, Rowan did a good job healing the first one. I

bet he could heal broken ribs all day."

"I'd rather not," Rowan said dryly, rising from his seat. "We just have to get dressed and then we'll meet you in the throne room."

"You took him breakfast?" Cori asked once Adro had left. She stood and followed Rowan back up to the bedroom.

"He's lost weight too," he joked as he pulled his Karalis finery out of the closet. Cori shook her head with a smile. She hoped this mood of his lasted. She was quite enjoying it.

They walked through the palace side by side and Cori marvelled at the changes that had happened while she'd been away. She'd noticed the completion of the renovations the night before, but now she could really study them in the light of day. The colour scheme was neutral and soft, completely opposite to the dark, rich tones of her childhood. Where there were splashes of colour, it was bright and bold.

The other thing she noticed was the amount of people in the corridors. When she had left, the palace had buzzed with tradesmen and townspeople who had appointed themselves as servants. Now, the servants who hurried past them were dressed in white uniforms and the tradesmen had been replaced with noblemen and women who strolled about in pairs, wearing courtly clothes.

Through the windows she saw that a building had been erected where the School of Auksas had once stood. Outside it, she was a contingent of soldiers working through drills in the mud. Things were certainly moving quickly now.

* * *

The Uaines were wet from the rain, but each of them stood

tall and proud as they entered the throne room. They flowed like a current through the arches, moving with purpose towards the dais and looking every bit war ready as Cori could have hoped.

Rowan smiled from his place upon the throne, and Cori wondered if he noticed the same things as she. On the other side of the throne, Jonothan stood in his page livery, looking as if he might burst with pride at his courtly position. He struggled to keep a straight face as the members of his House swarmed forward towards the throne. Rowan leaned towards him and said something that Cori couldn't hear. Jonothan's face finally split into a grin, and he raced down the steps just as his parents came to the fore of the group.

"Jonothan!" His mother cried. The boy fell into her arms and his father embraced the both of them. Rowan rose and descended the stairs of the dais to meet Acacia. He embraced her despite her wet clothes.

"Thank you," he said earnestly, "for coming back."

"This was what my House wanted," Acacia smiled, "who am I to deny them?"

"Well, it's a choice I'm very grateful for."

At that moment, Myce and Melita entered the throne room via the doors at the back. They looked timid, walking among the Uaines, but they were greeted warmly by those who knew them and smiles soon rose to their lips.

"I thought the Sarkans had been banished?" Acacia said. Her tone was hard; she hadn't appreciated Jonothan's injury in the slightest and Cori knew she blamed the Sarkans as a whole, not just Daniyl.

"The rest have gone to Cadmus," Rowan said in a low tone so that only Acacia could hear. "Myce and Melita left them

CHAPTER SEVENTEEN

to come and tell me."

Acacia looked troubled by the news, though not surprised. "Daniyl always was a snake. I could never understand what Jarrah saw in him."

Rowan shrugged his agreement. "It doesn't matter now. I wanted to greet you, but I'm sure you would welcome food and rest. The rooms in the palace are fast filling up but the barracks are comfortable and there is space for all of you."

"Seems fitting considering we're now your army. Yes, rest would be very welcome at this point."

Rowan waved forward some servants who had been waiting against the wall and gave them orders to make the Uaines comfortable in the barracks. Slowly the Dijem filed out of the room after the servants, chatting excitedly among themselves.

Rowan turned back to Adro and Cori, who still stood steadfastly by the throne. He held his arms wide and grinned them both. "You two may have saved us in this war."

Adro and Cori glanced at each other. "Good job, First Advisor," she murmured.

He grinned. "Couldn't have done it without you, Second Advisor."

* * *

Rowan's court moved with purpose now. Everyone at the palace had their duties, and they went about them with a prideful air. The noblemen and women that Cori saw around were mostly dignitaries of Shaw, whose Head had visited the Karalis in the past month. Many of his accompanying lords and ladies had stayed on at the palace for a time, probably intending to elevate their social status. When she had called out that this practice in a time of war was stupid, Rowan had explained that the nobles was where they got money from to fund the war, as well as trained soldiers and supplies.

Even Cori's own Coterie had found their places among the nobles, servants and soldiers.

Ailey had fallen into the role of Administrator, answering and sending missives as well as delegating tasks and managing the servants while Adro and Cori had been absent. Bharti and Kenneth had been sent out to the realm to spread the word that the Karalis had taken up residence in Lautan and to send any who might want to serve the throne back. They also directed many refugees to the seaside palace, many of whose towns had been burned and pillaged like the townspeople Cori and Adro had sent on.

Eamoyn had been appointed the title of captain alongside Han and Ether and spent his days in the barracks training new soldiers. Evdox had landed his dream role, though he seemed to have no official title. He spent his days studying books that Rowan gave him, learning everything from ancient histories to long forgotten Dijem magics. When he wasn't reading, he was with Rowan and they would discuss philosophies or he was providing advice based on his research.

Cori alone seemed to be out of place in this new, thriving court. She knew it was a matter of giving herself time to adjust; she had always felt displaced when reentering society after she'd done extensive fighting, but a few weeks after her return, even the Uaines seemed more comfortable about the palace and Lautan than she.

One night, three weeks after she'd returned, she dreamed

of dragon scales. Her dreams had been fairly disrupted lately, but this dream was strange. The scales, a bluish-black hue, glistened in her mind as if they moved beside a candle flame. There was nothing more to the dream; she didn't see the dragon in full or hear it speak to her, but she could feel its infernal heat, and its reptile stench filled her nostrils. She awoke with a start, disorientated.

"Bad dream?" Rowan asked sleepily from beside her. He reached out a hand to her, but she sat up, out of his grasp.

"Yes," she replied. "Go back to sleep, I'm just going to go for a walk."

"I'll come with you." For a moment he was still, then he pushed back the covers and swung his legs over the edge of the bed. They dressed in silence, then left the suite. Cori led the way through the dark palace. Most were abed, save a few servants. They went to the public gardens via the kitchen and Rowan stepped up beside her, resting his arm across her shoulders.

"Are you all right?" He asked as they strolled through the gardens towards the barracks. "You haven't seemed yourself lately."

"Being back here just seems so surreal. I don't really know where I fit."

"You fit right here," he pulled her tight against his side and kissed her temple.

"I know that but, I don't know, I just feel out of place."

They walked by the barracks, nodding to the soldiers who stood guard outside it. "As much as I loathe to say it," Rowan told her, "your place will come when the fighting starts and I think you'll find you fit better than most."

That was true. "Any idea when that will happen?"

He shrugged. "You know as much as I. We have no idea where Cadmus is and I don't particularly like the idea of taking the army out until we have more of a plan."

"Maybe he'll come to us."

"Maybe."

They stopped by a wilder part of the garden, a space that hadn't been forced to conform like the rest, and they turned to face each other. Cori reached up to lock her hands behind Rowan's neck, thumb grazing along his hairline. "Thank you for walking with me," she told him. "I feel better now."

"Good," he said with a sly smile. "Because the next stop would have been the taverns to see if a pub brawl would cheer you up."

"Actually, that doesn't seem like such a bad idea," she pretended to contemplate it. Rowan dipped his head and kissed her before she could say anything further. A branch snapped in the trees behind them and they both tensed, pulling apart only slightly.

"Wait," Cori whispered. She carefully lowered one hand from Rowan's neck and reached for the pink-gemmed dagger that she now kept on her belt. She pulled it slowly from its sheath, her eyes still locked with Rowan's. Another rustle sounded, and she whirled, flinging the dagger. It thudded into a tree, right beside Adro's head.

Adro froze, staring at it. Cori took several steps towards him, her hands raised. "What are you doing out here?"

"I - You meant to miss, right?"

"What are you doing?" She demanded more forcefully. Another branch snapped, and a figure pushed out of the shrubs beside Adro.

"Shaan?" Cori said incredulously. Behind her, Rowan

burst out laughing.

"Oh, hello, Cori," Shaan said innocently. Both she and Adro studiously avoided looking at each other. A grin curled Cori's lips. Shaan and Adro slowly smiled too. Then Rowan's laughter abruptly stopped.

Cori twisted to see a man had grasped him from behind, his arms around Rowan's neck and a dagger in hand. Cori's own hand automatically went to her empty sheath as Shaan and Adro cried out in alarm.

Rowan's hands were on the man's arms, trembling with the strength it took to hold the dagger away from his throat.

"Cadmus sends his-" the man began in a low voice but Rowan cut him short, lurching forward and flipping the man over his shoulder. The man hit the ground on his back and Cori dove forward, landing on his chest and pinning his arms to the ground. She felt Shaan and Adro land across the man's legs.

"He's about to burn out!" Cori said, watching the golden colour fade quickly from the man's eyes. He didn't look afraid, only stunned.

"Knock him out!" Adro roared from behind her. She let go of the man's arms and grasped his head. With a forceful jerk, she smashed it back against the ground, knocking him out cold.

"Cori." Rowan's tone was nothing like she'd heard before, trembling, panicked. A rush of cold fear slid down her spine before she'd even looked towards him.

He was down on one knee, his hands hovering by his thigh. Buried to its hilt in his leg was the assassin's dagger.

Chapter Eighteen

Cori stared at the darkness through the window, her palms resting flat on the sill. Her reflection stared back at her, flickering as the lamplight did. She paid it no attention, instead her mind raced. Cadmus was behind the assassins - they were using his signature greeting - but who was controlling them? Thinking back to the attack, it had moved so quickly, but she remembered the flare of Rowan's Hum as he'd tried to take control of the man's mind, remembered her own instinctive reaching and finding only blankness.

Whoever was controlling these Dijem must be close, surely Cadmus couldn't control them from such a distance. Or maybe he could; he was strong, was he strong enough to have such a full control over his Dijem? It seemed unlikely, though. When he and Rowan had fought for control of her mind, Rowan had been on par with his father in strength. Surely he could wrest control of a Dijem who was standing right behind him.

Maybe Cadmus was closer than they thought. She dismissed this idea almost immediately; she and Adro had fought a few Hiram on their travels who had untouchable minds. Unless Cadmus happened to travel at the same time and to the same places they had, it was unlikely it was him.

Rowan cried out behind her, before letting loose a string of expletives.

"Don't speak to her like that!" Myce said angrily. Cori turned from the window to watch.

Rowan lay on his back on the table. They'd brought him to an empty receiving room on the lower level of the palace. Adro had then detained the assassin in another room while Shaan had gone to wake Melita and Myce.

"I have to get the knife out." Melita's voice shook, and her face was pale. "I can't heal you until -"

"Then just bloody do it!" Rowan roared.

"I - It's so deep!" She put her hand over the dagger again, and once more Rowan cried out.

"I'll do it," Cori said. She moved towards the table and put her hand on Rowan's chest. She met his eye and there she saw pain, fear and defiance. Sweat beaded across his brow, licks of dark hair plastered to his skin. His hands were fisted at his sides, but he lifted one to grasp her wrist against his chest, holding it like a lifeline.

Whatever you don't want her to see, hide it.

It hurts. I can't concentrate.

You have to, she told him forcefully, trying to ignore the pain behind his words and the gut wrenching feeling it brought upon her. *You can. Use your barriers, only give her the access she needs.*

She held his gaze until he finally nodded then she turned to Melita. "Are you ready? There will be a lot of blood when I pull the dagger free."

Melita perhaps took something from Cori's hard expression, for she straightened, a determined look coming to her eyes. "Myce," she said, waving her brother forward. "Get the cloth ready."

Cori looked once more to Rowan and hoped he could see the apology in her eyes. In one swift movement, she grasped the hilt of the dagger and wrenched it free.

His cry cracked through her chest, echoing around the room and his blood, crimson and gleaming in the lamplight, spilled from the wound, coating his leg, splattering across Cori's shirt.

Her breath came in short pants and her vision narrowed as his life flowed from him. An assassin had done this. Cadmus had done this. To the Karalis. To Rowan. She would kill him for this alone, for trying to take away everything she loved in this world.

Then Myce had the wad of cloth pressed against the wound to stifle the bloodflow, and Melita's hands were either side of it. The healing song flowed from her to Rowan.

Cori tore her eyes away and back to Rowan's face. He still held her wrist against his chest, and she pressed down harder with her fingertips, giving him the pressure he craved.

He was hurting. The pain had tears brimming in his golden eyes. The muscles in his neck were taunt and his teeth clenched so hard they might crack. But he didn't cry out again, and he didn't fall unconscious. Cori stayed there, watching him until the healing was done.

* * *

Cori sat at the edge of the bed and watched Rowan sleep. His breathing was slow and even, although his expression still looked troubled. She sighed and pulled the blankets up

CHAPTER EIGHTEEN

over his shoulders before quietly leaving the room.

The healing had taken far longer than she'd expected, but she'd remained at Rowan's side until the pain had subsided from his features and relief had slackened them.

She'd also watched Melita, aware that the woman was limited in her strength and that the healing would take a lot from her. The red head's eyes had slowly grown darker as the healing went on, but Cori knew she couldn't call a human to give her energy. No one could know the Karalis had been attacked that night. Myce also kept a close eye on his sister, but he didn't insist that she stop, so Cori said nothing.

Blood eventually stopped seeping from the wound, and then it slowly knitted back together until the skin was smooth and there was no sign that Rowan had been injured at all.

The experience had exhausted both the healer and patient. Cori had taken Rowan back to their suite while Myce had led Melita away.

She found Adro and Shaan in the throne room. Adro was sitting upon Arasy, but he stood as she approached. She waved him back down and sat beside Shaan on the top step.

"Rowan?" Adro asked.

"Sleeping," Cori replied. She drew her knees up and wrapped her arms around them. "The assassin?"

"Still out cold. I've forced some Grybas into him so that when he wakes, hopefully whoever was controlling him can't find him."

Cori dropped her head to the top of her knees. "Whoever is controlling them must be close, Adro."

"Them?" Shaan asked. "There's been more?"

"One other," Adro told her before sliding from the throne

to sit on Cori's other side.

Her hands trembled as she wrapped them around her legs and a lump formed in her throat. Now that the danger had passed, it was all she could think about. What if the assassin's dagger hadn't hit Rowan's thigh? What if it had slipped further up, into his chest or neck? What if the assassin had used his Hiram magic to force the blade to Rowan's throat? They were lucky he'd been compelled to deliver his message first. She felt Adro's hand on her back.

"I couldn't protect him," she whispered, hands tightening around her legs. "I was right there and I couldn't do anything."

"I was there too, Cori." She could hear the failure in his voice as well.

"He's the Karalis for a reason," Shaan told them both. "If he can't handle these situations on his own, who can?"

* * *

Cori watched the man giggling and wondered how he'd come to be an assassin. He'd woken in the early hours of the morning, and Adro's idea of giving him Grybas to dampen his Hum and stop him burning out seemed to have worked. Unfortunately, the man was as high as a dragon in the clouds.

"What's your name?" Cori asked again. The man turned his head slowly from one side to the other, and Cori knew he was seeing colours streak across his vision. She gripped the edge of the table she sat on and forced away her frustration. She wanted to just kill the man and be done with it, but she had to try and get information if she could; he was the first of Cadmus' Dijem they'd caught before they burned out.

CHAPTER EIGHTEEN

She reached out with her Hum and found only a muteness. It was different to the blankness of one who was being controlled. This was an effect of the Grybas. She growled in frustration, and the man mimicked her before laughing.

"Any luck?" Adro stepped into the room, closing the door behind him.

"None," she sighed.

"Why don't you go and get some sleep. I'll watch him for a while. Maybe if we let the Grybas wear off a little, he'll be more lucid." She didn't want to sleep, but she also didn't want to sit and look at the assassin any longer. She thanked Adro and left the room.

She didn't go back to the Karalis' suites, however. Instead, she went to the throne room, leaving the palace through the arches. The sun wasn't far from rising, and its first rays lit the horizon as she made her way down the cliff road.

Already, workers were on the streets of Lautan. Shopkeepers were opening their fronts, and merchants were collecting stock at the ports. Soldiers also patrolled the streets in small contingents.

She walked past them all, looking at nothing and yet taking in everything. Sometimes she'd let her Hum float across the people around her, looking for blank spaces that might indicate an infiltrator. She knew the controller would be Dijem, but she didn't have high hopes of finding that person. If she'd botched an assassination such as the one the night before, she'd be pretty quick to leave town too.

She made it to the gates and stopped, looking down the road that led away from Lautan. The guards there greeted her and she nodded back to them.

"My Lady."

"Han."

The captain stepped up beside her. She'd spoken to Han a few times since she'd returned from her trip north. He'd apologised to her for his outburst, and she'd apologised for stabbing him. Since then he had been nothing but cordial towards her.

His hand came to his face now to scratch his chin, and she saw the puckered red scar from the stab wound on the back of it. He wore his blue and red captain's uniform and looked sharp for the early hour. Probably because he's had a full night's sleep, Cori thought dully.

"Anything in particular bringing you to town this early, my lady?"

She considered him for a moment. He was the unofficial leader of Lautan. If anyone had seen someone out of place in the town, he would have.

"Have you noticed anyone suspicious around lately?"

He continued to scratch his chin and pondered her question. "It's hard to tell, my lady, with all these new recruits and refugees flooding the town, you see, but particularly suspicious? No, I haven't noticed anyone acting untoward."

"What about Dijem?"

"Sorry to say, my lady, but those Gold Eyes that came a few weeks ago, well I can't tell them apart."

Cori didn't blame him, even she didn't know all the Uaines personally. Could it be one of them?

"Thank you, Han."

"Anything else I can assist with, my lady?"

"Not today." She turned from the gate and headed back to the palace.

She went straight back to the room where the assassin was

CHAPTER EIGHTEEN

being kept and found Adro hovering outside it.

"Is he comprehensive yet?" She asked.

"He's dead," Adro wrung his hands nervously. "Rowan killed him."

"Ro-" Cori pushed past Adro and into the room. The assassin was there, slumped against the wall in a pool of blood, his own dagger rammed into his neck. She stepped backwards, closing the door.

"I didn't know what to do, Cori," Adro said apologetically. "He had that look in his eyes, like he doesn't know who you are. After Daniyl, I didn't know if I should stop him… Would you have stopped him?"

"I don't know," she murmured. Would she have stopped him? Perhaps for his own sanity; he'd never coped well with killing. She would have killed the assassin eventually, though she would have liked to speak to him first. She pinched the bridge of her nose. It had been a long night, and she didn't think she could deal with any more right then. She lifted her hand and used her magic to shift the locks in the door. "We'll deal with the body tonight," she told Adro. "Right now, I need to go to bed."

* * *

Rowan's mood in the week following the second assassination attempt was nothing less than foul. Cori didn't broach the subject with him, though she definitely preferred the calm, humorous demeanour he'd held before. She also kept watch on his mental state, but he didn't show any signs of blowing out, and she guessed that their regular energy releases had helped with that.

She knew she should talk to him, but she found herself preoccupied with trying to find out who the controller of the assassin was. Her attention had turned to the Dijem she knew; Myce and Melita had arrived in time to tell them that the Sarkans had gone to Cadmus. Perhaps they hadn't run away, but had been sent. The Uaines they had found near Rikdom where they had fought the other blank-minded Hiram. They'd also agreed to join Rowan's cause without much argument.

"Are you listening?"

"Sorry?" She was leaning on the fence of the sparring ring, watching soldiers fight against the Dijem from Uaine. She'd just finished sparring with Adro and the two of them stood side by side, dripping with sweat. Adro had a nick on his collarbone where she'd beat him in the game of First Blood.

"You need to talk to Rowan about his attitude. An advance retinue arrived from Rikdom yesterday, Dristan and Samyla will be here tonight and there's going to be a welcome party."

As much as she'd been distracted with her manhunt, she had noticed how nervous the residents of the palace had become around Rowan. He wasn't outwardly hostile, but he prowled around the palace, his anger barely concealed beneath his Karalis mask, which was intimidating in itself. Perhaps it was a facet of the Karalis that Cori took for granted; she'd seen that side of him many times when growing up in his palace, but she now realised that his old friends, the soldiers and the staff had never seen him this way.

"I don't know what to say to him," she admitted. She watched Jonothan and his father walking slowly through some defensive stances. "It's not nice to be almost killed, do

CHAPTER EIGHTEEN

you really blame him?"

"Perhaps it's not the fact that someone tried to kill him, perhaps it's *who* sent the assassin that's the problem. It does things to a man when he knows his father wants him dead."

"You think Cadmus is the problem?"

"On a deep level, yes."

Cori hadn't considered that possibility before. She didn't understand fathers. She hadn't had one growing up and hadn't felt lacking because of it. But she'd felt the sense of abandonment when Adro talked about his father, even after so many years. Could Rowan be feeling the same way?

"All right, I'll tell him to behave tonight." She handed Adro her sword and went in search of her Karalis.

She found him in the garden by their suite, standing at the edge of the cliff.

"Come here," he said when he heard the door close behind her. She went to his side, and he put a hand on the small of her back before pointing out towards the sea. "Look."

Cori spotted it almost immediately; a black dragon circling high over the water. She tried to stagger back, but Rowan held her firm.

"Daiyu," she breathed. Her heart thudded and her hand strayed to her side. She remembered vividly how the dragon had attacked her from the inside out. "Is she here to kill us?"

"I don't think so. I couldn't find any trace of a Hum, I think she's still damaged from our fight."

As they watched, Daiyu dove towards the water, disappearing below the surface before bursting upwards again, leaving a shower of glistening droplets in her wake. There was something large and grey in her mouth. She gulped down her prey before resuming her circling. They watched her as she slowly moved further from the coast until she was no more than a speck against the sky.

"You came to find me?" Rowan asked.

"Yes." Cori remembered the reason she'd come. "Dristan and Samyla will be here tonight. There's going to be a party and you need an attitude adjustment."

He raised an eyebrow at her. "Do I?"

"A bit more smiling, a little less scowling."

His lips quirked at the corners, and she saw some warmth in his eyes. Not that he'd acted horribly towards her over the past week, but he had been dispirited. "I promise I'll behave."

"Rowan," she said slowly, "about your mood, is it because of Cadmus?"

"Who else would it be about?"

"Is it because he's your father?"

The light vanished from his eyes and his hand dropped from her back. "He lost the right to that title when he killed my mother. Don't bring it up again, Cori."

She watched him walk away from her and knew that Adro had probably hit the nail on the head with his theory. In any case, she would need more than words to cheer Rowan up for the party that night.

Chapter Nineteen

Cori stood outside the dressmaker's store, looking at the wares through the window. She had walked past this store a few times in the last week while she'd been hunting for infiltrators. The dresses within were of a Dodici trend, rather than the more conservative Tauta fashion, which was just what she was after.

She watched a couple inside make a purchase and exit the store before she pushed open the door and entered.

"One moment," the dressmaker glanced at her from his workbench before doing a double take. "My Lady Advisor!" He greeted in surprise. "How can I be of assistance today?"

"You may have heard that there's a party at the palace tonight," she said, walking past a rack of dresses and brushing her fingers over the material.

"Oh yes. I have had a few customers, but the noble ladies seem intent on reviving the ballgowns of the old days, and I just don't stock such frivolous outfits." His nose wrinkled at the mere thought.

"I'd like you to dress me for the evening, if you will."

"Of course, Lady Advisor!" The dressmaker almost fell off his stool in his haste to collect his measuring tape. He ushered her towards a wooden box and had her stand upon it while he took her measurements. As he did, he muttered to himself. "Something to turn heads, I think. A nice bust, let's show that off. Black will draw out the gold of the eyes and that hair..." He paused behind her and tugged the thong that bound her hair so it fell down her back. "Long. It would look lovely over lace."

He had her try on three dresses, all black, and she decided on the third. It was form fitting with a single slit up one side that ended almost at her hip. The front was cut in a V shape to show off the roundness of her breasts and the back, from her neck to her waist, was a panel sheer lace.

The dressmaker wrapped the dress and took it to the counter. Cori was counting out the coins when she noticed a rack of small lace garments. She pulled out a black one and held it up.

"Ah," said the dressmaker coyly, noticing where her attention had strayed. "Just off the ship this week, our new sensual undergarments. Guaranteed to turn a man's eye should he be lucky enough to see beneath this lovely dress of yours."

Cori knew that already. She'd worn undergarments like this regularly when she had been in residence at the Court of the Twelve Kings of Dodici. She placed them on the counter and met the dressmaker's eye. His knowing smile slipped a little under her gaze. "I'm sure I can count on your discretion," she told him. He nodded quickly.

"Of course, Lady Advisor."

* * *

Dristan, Samyla and their retinue of Hale nobles arrived in the early afternoon. True to his word, Rowan kept his

CHAPTER NINETEEN

attitude in check and greeted the Head of Hale and his wife graciously. Cori, standing by Adro, was sure she was the only one who noticed the tense set of his shoulders, a sign that his genteel performance was just for show. Dristan greeted Cori next, and this seemed to shift Rowan's mood slightly.

"Lady Karaliene." He bowed at the waist as Samyla curtsied. "I hope your onward trip from Rikdom was pleasant."

"We travelled smoothly enough," Cori replied with an incline of her head. The couple turned to Adro next, and the First Advisor descended the steps to shake Dristan's hand. Cori noticed Rowan watching her from the throne and knew he wondered at her unfazed acceptance of Dristan using her other title. She didn't blame him, she wondered at it herself. Could it be that she was growing accustomed to the role? Dristan and Samyla's earnest use of it certainly made it easier. She gave him a small smile which seemed to startle him from his musings. A moment later he returned it.

"Cori," Samyla greeted when the formalities were over. Servants had arrived and were beginning to lead the nobles away. With so many guests, the palace was full to bursting point. "May I still call you Cori?"

"Of course," Cori said warmly. As always, she was struck by both Samyla's beauty and her flawless decorum. Samyla looked around them with an awestruck expression.

"It's more magnificent than I ever imagined," she exclaimed, a hand fluttering over her breast. Cori laughed.

"I'm glad you like it. We're having a party tonight, just for you."

Samyla looked back to her with a lovely smile and grasped both Cori's hands in her own. "Oh Cori, you must help me choose a dress!"

***

Cori could hear the noise of the revelry before she'd even entered the hallway to the throne room. She'd had Samyla help with her hair, and it was brushed high and back before tumbling down in undefined curls. She had also painted black along her eyelids, and Samyla had suggested she stick some small gold flakes to the corners of her eyes for effect. "Fierce," was how Samyla had described her and in her black dress, Cori felt it. She nodded to the servants at the door before entering.

The room was full to capacity with hundreds of Dijem, nobles and the senior officers of Dristan and Rowan's armies mingling together. Servants wended through the people, bearing trays of food and drink. Some of the guests spilled out into the gardens where Cori could hear musicians playing.

She accepted a glass of wine from a servant and moved further into the room. She saw Rowan in conversation with Alastar and Han, but his eyes were already on her, hooded, hungry, tracking her movements through the guests. She turned her back on him with a small smile to herself. He could stew in his mood a little longer.

"You look lovely, Cori," Melita said, appearing at Cori's side.

"As do you." The red-haired woman was stunning in a deep green gown that flared about her feet.

"I was wondering if I could speak to you privately for a moment?"

Sounds ominous. She followed Melita to a small alcove near the dais. Melita turned to her, but not before casting a furtive look over the crowd. "I've been meaning to speak to you since… since last week."

"Since the attack?" Cori said it for her.

"Yes. Well, I just wanted to let you know that while I was healing Rowan… You know how healing works, right? The healer can access the thoughts and feelings of the patient?"

"I'm aware, yes."

"Well, many thoughts usually filter through a person's mind. Most of them so fast and done unconsciously that the person doesn't really notice them. A healer gets a sense of all these thoughts though."

"Your point?" Cori wasn't sure where this was going, but the unconscious thoughts had given her pause. Rowan had told her he could only see the thoughts she had at that moment in time. Did she have other thoughts that she wasn't aware of that he had been privy to?

"Well, when I was healing Rowan, he didn't think of you."

"He was in pain, thinking of me was hardly a priority."

"No, I mean there was no trace of you in his mind at all. I know the two of you are close, I would expect that there would be some thoughts or feelings filtering through, but there was absolutely nothing. It's like you didn't exist in his head."

Jealous, was Cori's first thought. Melita was telling her this to make her jealous. She knew the other woman harboured some feelings for Rowan, but she'd always been respectful enough to keep them to herself, especially once it became apparent that Cori and Rowan were in a relationship. Why would she try to make Cori jealous now? Melita watched her curiously, and Cori kept her expression schooled.

"I hope you understand that having the privilege of healing

the Karalis means that you should show discretion for his thoughts, or lack thereof," Cori said slowly, pinning Melita with a look much as she had given the dressmaker earlier. "Sharing his knowledge with the wrong person could prove disastrous for this realm."

"I -" Melita looked appropriately ashamed. "I understand, of course. I'd never tell anyone else. I just thought you should know."

"Hello, ladies," Shaan stepped into their alcove. She looked lovely in a silvery gown. Cori took a moment to marvel at how well dressed all the Dijem were. Normally she only saw them in shirts and pants, much as she herself wore day to day. "What gossip has got you hiding out over here?"

"I was just telling Cori that I thought the Head of Hale's wife is pregnant," Melita said without skipping a beat.

She is good, Cori thought, turning quickly to scan the crowd for Samyla. She was by Dristan's side and was wearing a red dress made of floating chiffon material. Cori wondered if what Melita said was actual gossip or if she had made it up on the spot. Samyla's outfit was suspiciously formless.

"Excuse me," Cori said, holding up her wine glass. "I need a refill."

She left the two women there and headed back into the crowd. She spotted Rowan again, this time with Acacia. He still watched her from the corner of his eye, and she wondered at what Melita had said. The fact that she was absent from his mind didn't overly worry her; she had told him to hide what he needed to, she just hadn't expected it to be her. She was curious as to why.

She turned away again, and with a swish of her hips that she knew would drive him mad, she signalled a servant for

CHAPTER NINETEEN

more wine.

***

The hour was late, and many of the guests had retired. A long table and benches had been brought to the throne room for those who wanted to continue on to sit at.

Cori tipped the bottle of rum over her glass and watched the last of the liquor dribble out. She'd run dry, and by the state of her companions, they had too. She threw the last of her drink back and put her glass down. She was very drunk.

Near the head of the table, Adro told an Ol' Bodee tale that had those around him in fits of laughter. "And then he took the goat and told the priestess to… to… I can't. I can't finish it." Dristan, sitting across from him, snorted beer from his nose.

Rowan sat between them at the head of the table. He didn't laugh at the joke. Instead, he watched Cori, golden eyes smouldering. She'd led him on long enough, it seemed. She rose and stepped away from the bench, giving her excuses to Shaan as she went. She walked to the door, pausing there to glance back. Rowan had pushed back his chair and stood to follow her. Good.

She went to their suites, the Karalis trailing behind her, and climbed the stairs to the bedroom. In the closet she found a bottle of rum she'd stored there earlier and she pulled the cork and took a swig before setting it aside. Rowan arrived and closed the door, leaning back against it and watching her. She slid her hands under the straps of her dress and peeled it down her body, letting it pool at her feet and revealing the black lace undergarments. She picked up the bottle of rum and took a long swallow. Rowan pushed off the door and stalked towards her.

She stopped him with a hand on his chest before he could touch her and a low growl rumbled up his throat. With a gentle push, she guided him backwards until the back of his legs hit the side of the bed. He sank down, and she moved between his knees and pulled his shirt over his head. She lifted the bottle and pressed it to his lips. He took a deep swallow before she lowered it to her side again. His hands slid up the back of her thighs to cup her buttocks.

"You're perfect," he murmured, pulling her forward to kiss her stomach, first above her navel and then below.

"Don't say that," Cori took another gulp of rum, "you know it isn't true."

"It is." His lips whispered across her skin, over the silver scars on her side. "You are the most perfect creature to ever walk this earth."

"Have I brought the Karalis to his knees?" She pondered with a sly grin. She pressed her fingers through his hair, musing it, before fisting it in her hand and tugging his head back. His eyes, whirling and just a little feral, met hers.

"I would drive this entire realm to its knees and make them worship you if you so desired it."

She dipped her head, letting him feel her smile on his lips before she released the hold on his hair. He once more pressed his face against the planes of her stomach and tendrils of heat curled low in her abdomen. He thumbed the edge of her lace panties as the tip of his tongue grazed her skin.

"You are going to sit on my face and I'm going to devour you," he murmured.

CHAPTER NINETEEN

Cori chuckled, though heat flooded down to her core.

"And what if you suffocate?" She lifted the bottle back to her lips.

"It would be a worthy way to die."

She felt a small, querying touch on her mind from Adro, but Rowan settled his barriers around both of them, blocking out the Dijem still partying below.

"Melita told me tonight that you hid me while she was healing you."

"Because you're mine," he said against her stomach, his lips resuming their trail of fire across her skin. "And no one else gets to know about us."

Cori lifted the bottle to his lips again. He drank deeply and then she kissed him, feeling the burn of the alcohol pass between them. He pulled her into his lap, hands sliding down the length of her thighs as they settled each side of his hips.

"Ahem." They hadn't even noticed the door open, nor Adro step into the room.

"I'm busy," Rowan growled, his breath curling over her collarbone as he pressed a kiss to the top of her breast, catching the skin lightly between his teeth.

Cori raked her fingers through his hair from the nape of his neck, resting her cheek against the top of his head as she raised an eyebrow at the Advisor filling out the doorway.

"I can see that," Adro grinned. "But there's something I think you should hear." He tapped his temple. Rowan reluctantly let down the barriers that had held them both. He quested out with his Hum, and Cori followed him. There were Dijem outside, about twenty of them, and ones they didn't know. Or so she thought.

"Oh," Rowan said in surprise. He stood quickly, and Cori

stumbled back to her feet, the rum bottle sloshing in her hand. Not even bothering with a shirt, he pushed past Adro and left the room.

"Thanks," Cori said dryly, taking a final drink before returning to her dress.

"I could always help," Adro joked. "Those look great on you, by the way."

Cori shot him a sideways glance as she pulled the dress back on. "I don't think Shaan would appreciate that."

Adro jammed a thumb over his shoulder. "I'll go get her, she can join us."

"Ha." Cori secured the straps over her shoulders and shoved past Adro to follow Rowan.

They were coming along the drive, a group of Dijem, all with light hair that glowed in the moonlight. Rowan stepped through the arches from the throne room, the last of the party-goers following him. Cori moved to stand beside him. She was drunk enough that she didn't really care who these newcomers were, though she knew she should. She watched Rowan shake the hand of an older man at their fore, watched a disturbance from the back of the group push through to the front, watched as a woman cried out "Rowan!" as she flung herself at him and kissed him.

Cori saw red.

Chapter Twenty

It was only Cori's slow reflexes in her drunken state that saved the other woman. That, and Adro's foresight to restrain one of her hands. Rowan pried himself free of the woman - too slowly, Cori thought - but he smiled at her.

"Sigrid, it's nice to see you."

Cori snarled, and Sigrid looked towards her. The woman was tall and exotic and looked like winter. Where Cori's hair was golden like the sun, Sigrid's was silvery like the moon. Even her gold Dijem eyes seemed cold, like ice. Jealousy, like she'd never felt before, punched her in the gut.

"This is the one you came back for?" Sigrid's accent was as foreign as her appearance, but her tone implied disbelief. The look Rowan gave Cori, however, as he turned to her at his side, was one that lit up his features. "Yes, she's the one."

"It's late," the older man who'd first greeted Rowan said. He was frowning at Sigrid. "And we've travelled a long way. Might we rest and talk in the morning?"

"Of course," Rowan told him, waving towards the throne room. "Come in, make yourself welcome."

Both parties moved towards the archways, mingling together and greeting each other. Cori wrenched her hand free of Adro and stalked away. She went back to the suites, her dress swishing around her legs.

She guessed, by their accents and their fair hair, that the new Dijem had come south from the Tundra. She didn't know what they were doing here, but she wished they'd stayed in their frozen wasteland.

Sigrid. Cori fumed just thinking of the woman, but she also felt a twang of insecurity knot in her stomach. She knew Rowan had had past lovers, as had she, and they'd sometimes talked about them. But this woman... Cori entered the bedroom and slammed the door so hard, the room shook. She retrieved the bottle of rum from the floor and tugged the cork out and took a long drink.

She'd expected all of Rowan's lovers to be dead, like hers. She hadn't expected one to be a Dijem. The thought made her sick to her stomach. She yanked her dress down and kicked it away, bitterly disappointed. She'd worn that for him.

The secret door at the other side of the room opened, and Rowan slid inside.

"Cori," he said apologetically.

"What was that?" She exploded. He moved towards her, his hands held up in surrender.

"They're the House of Valkoinen. I stayed with them for a few years in the Tundra. I honestly didn't know they were going to come here."

"That's not what I'm talking about," she said through gritted teeth. "That woman kissed you!"

To her disbelief, he grinned. "Are you jealous?"

"Have you slept with her?"

"I kissed her once."

She didn't care if he'd kissed her, and it wasn't the question

CHAPTER TWENTY

she'd asked. The way he continued to smile was infuriating. She flung the bottle of rum, and it smashed against the far wall, raining glass and liquor across the carpet. To his credit, he didn't even flinch.

"Have you slept with her?" She demanded. He stepped closer. His grin had faded, but he still seemed amused. She raised her hand to hit him, but he caught her by the wrist and tugged her forward. She braced her palms against his chest, unwilling to submit to the embrace.

"Put your barriers up," he suggested. "You're alarming people."

Only then did she realise that her Hum crashed outwards in angry waves. She'd been so furious she hadn't even noticed. She didn't do what he said, however. She met his gaze with a defiant stare. After a moment, his barriers settled around them both. Her Hum crashed against them and resounded back into her own head.

"No, I haven't slept with her. I've never been with a Dijem woman other than you." He tried to pull her closer, but still she resisted him.

"She seemed pretty familiar."

"I told you, I kissed her once. I probably shouldn't have because she thought it alluded to something more. I never set her straight because I knew I was leaving the Tundra and I didn't think I'd ever see her again."

"Coward."

"I know," he tugged her forward again and this time she let him, though she turned her face aside so he couldn't kiss her.

"You need to fix this," she told him. "If I see her try to kiss you again, I will smash her head through a wall."

"I believe you." His hands slid down her back and across the lace of her underwear. He bent to kiss the curve between her neck and shoulder. "I have to go back downstairs," he whispered. "Will you come with me?"

She shook her head, and hot tears slid down her cheeks. She didn't want him to see her cry, but the disappointment at having the night she'd planned for him ruined was a tight lump in her throat. He let go of her and tried to turn her chin to face him, but she kept her gaze studiously away. "I'll be back soon," he promised, then left through the hidden door.

Cori extinguished the lamp and crawled into bed. She curled in a ball, wrapping her arms about herself. Thankfully, the copious amounts of rum she'd drunk that night took her quickly to sleep.

She roused in the early hours of the morning when Rowan climbed into bed behind her. He wrapped his arms around her and hooked his leg over hers. "You are mine," he breathed against the nape of her neck, "and I am yours. Forever, I promise." She sank back into sleep.

When she woke, the sun was shining through the window, and Rowan was already gone. Cori sat up, shielding her eyes and feeling the pounding of her head. Her hangover didn't help her forget the events of the night before. She remembered the new Dijem, remembered Sigrid, and didn't want to go downstairs. She knew she had to though, or he'd come looking for her.

She dragged herself out of bed and rubbed her face. Her hands came away black with the makeup she'd worn the night before. For a moment she sat still to let her head stop spinning and noticed that Rowan had cleaned up the smashed rum bottle and had hung up her black dress. Finally, she forced herself up and to the bathroom to wash her face.

She found much of the court eating breakfast at the table that had been left in the throne room overnight. Rowan was at the head of the table and he smiled and waved her to the seat beside him. She sat down with Samyla and Dristan on her other side and the older man who had led the Valkionens across the table. In the light of day, she could see the elder tattoos that covered his hands and disappeared beneath his sleeves. He was old, but his hair, like many of the others he had travelled with, was silvery blonde.

"Cori, this is Bjarte," Rowan introduced her. "I stayed with his House for a few years before crossing back through Hen Goeden."

"Nice to meet you," Cori forced a smile and shook his hand across the table.

"I was just sharing my surprise with Rowan to find him in a palace," Bjarte told her in his strange accent. "He didn't tell us he was a Karalis."

"I wasn't when I was living with you," Rowan said. He made a motion to a servant who moved forward and poured a mug of coffee for Cori. She wrapped her hands around it and looked down the table. Some of Dristan's nobles were there, as well as Acacia and a handful of the Uaines. Adro and Shaan were absent, as was Melita. Myce was seated beside Evdox and Ailey and the three of them were in conversation with some of the Valkionens across from them. She also saw Sigrid further down the table. The woman was watching her curiously. Cori looked away and down to her coffee.

"Did you have a nice night, Cori?" Samyla asked beside her.

"I think I drank too much," she admitted, and Samyla gave

a pitying laugh. "And what about you? Did you enjoy your night?"

"Oh, it was wonderful! So many people and such pretty dresses. And the dancing! I'm afraid I retired quite early though, you see," Cori watched her hand move from the table to her stomach and marvelled that Melita had been right. The Sarkan might annoy her at times, but her gossip was accurate, "we're going to have a baby!"

"Oh Samyla," Cori smiled and squeezed her hand. "That's wonderful! And so quick! You didn't waste time."

"Oh, well," Samyla blushed, "you know how it is, I'm sure."

"- Dragon's flying south," Cori heard Bjarte say, and she quickly excused herself from Samyla's attention to listen. "That is why we came down. We could sense another war brewing and came to offer our aid to whatever forces might be rallying."

"How many?" Rowan asked.

"Three that we saw. Only younglings, perhaps only a few hundred years old. It was strange to us that they would leave their nests so soon."

Do you think Cadmus is using them? Cori asked Rowan.

I hope not. That puts us at quite a disadvantage.

Bjarte otherwise didn't seem concerned by the dragons, and Cori wondered what it would be like to live in the Tundra where dragons flying overhead were a regular occurrence. She looked down the table again. Sigrid was still watching her.

* * *

People came and went from the breakfast table, but when

CHAPTER TWENTY

Rowan finally stood, Cori took it as her cue to leave as well.

"What are your plans for today?" He asked her as they walked together from the throne room.

"I was going to go to town for a while," she replied. His dark mood of the past week seemed to have lifted. No, transferred to her, she decided. She wasn't feeling particularly social today. She thought she'd go to town, as she did most days, to see if she could find signs of anyone acting suspicious, and to get away from the buzz of the people who filled the palace now.

"You won't find anything," Rowan told her. They paused by the door to let a sorry-looking Melita pass by. Cori looked at him, lips pressed to a thin line. Of course he would have guessed why she'd been spending so much time in Lautan. He was probably right, she decided, looking back to the Dijem in the throne room. The infiltrator was probably in the palace already. "Why don't we go for a walk?" He suggested.

"Don't you have Karalis things to do?"

"They can wait until tomorrow, I think. My head is too sore for politics today."

She considered declining - she still harboured some anger for him for the night before - but she glanced back towards the breakfast table and Sigrid, who no longer watched her but was now talking to Melita, and decided that if she didn't go with Rowan, she was sure the other woman would be quick to find him.

"All right," she agreed. He gestured towards the archways and she preceded him into the public gardens. It was warm for a winter morning and many people were already out enjoying the weather. Cori and Rowan started down the drive towards the stables.

"You and Samyla seem quite friendly," he observed. "From what I've heard others say, they're quite jealous of her."

"Oh, I'm very jealous." Cori shoved her hands in her pockets. "She is more beautiful than any woman has a right to be, but she's just so... sincere. I can't help but like her."

Rowan nodded, and they lapsed into silence. They greeted the Stablemaster as they passed by, continuing on around the back of the kitchens and towards the barracks. They didn't talk about the night before, though the issue hung in the air between them. Cori didn't think she could broach the subject without it turning into an argument again.

A few soldiers were running through drills in the sparring ring, but many lounged on the grass, soaking up the sunshine. It seemed it was a lazy day for all at the palace. Some made to rise when they saw the Karalis, but Rowan waved them back down.

Behind the barracks, they found Jonothan with a leather ball. The boy was kicking it against a tree, running to retrieve it when he missed.

"Here," Rowan called and Jonothan kicked the ball to him. Rowan moved forward with it and kicked it towards the tree. He missed, and Jonothan laughed. "Give me another go," Rowan requested.

Cori sat down on the grass with her back against another tree and watched as the two of them took turns kicking the ball, which soon turned into a game of trying to steal the ball from each other.

Rowan would be a good father. The thought came on her unbidden as she watched them joke and wrestle with each other. She felt a simultaneous tightening in her stomach, something she hadn't felt since she had been with Dahl. She wrapped her arm across her middle and tried to force the sensation away. They were about to go to war, she scolded herself. Now was not the time to suddenly become maternal.

"Here you are." Adro appeared around the side of the barracks, a handful of people with him. Cori saw Sigrid among them. "I was wondering what important tasks you were getting up to."

"This is important," Rowan joked. He kicked the ball towards Adro, who kicked it at the tree. Some of the others who'd followed him found spots to lounge on the grass, but most of them moved towards the ball game and split into two teams. Samyla sat down beside Cori.

"Do you have a feeling," Cori asked, "what gender your baby will be?"

"A boy," Samyla said instantly. Her smile made her face glow, and she put her hand to her still flat stomach. It made Cori aware that her own arm was still wrapped around her middle. She forced it back to her side. "I'm sure it is, though Dris told me he would like a girl to dote on."

The game started and Jonothan claimed the ball first, kicking it past Rowan and Shaan only to have it stolen away by Dristan. Cori noticed that Sigrid was on Rowan's team. For a time they all played the game seriously, but banter eventually rose among the teams and Cori watched the way Sigrid found reasons to have physical contact with Rowan. As the game went on, she'd 'accidentally' bump into him, or brush against his arm when they passed each other. He ignored it mostly, glancing only once at Cori to gauge her reaction.

Ailey scored the first point against Jonothan's team. Her team cheered, and Sigrid used it as an excuse to quickly hug

Rowan. Cori almost wished the Valkionen would try to kiss him again so she could follow through with her promise and break the woman's skull against a stone wall.

"That woman is acting rather unbecoming towards the Karalis," Samyla said with a small frown.

"Yes," Cori agreed. Rowan darted away from Sigrid in pursuit of the ball. He scored a second point for their team before Adro grabbed him and wrestled him to the ground. Samyla hadn't finished with her disapproval.

"Has she been at court long? She's quite clearly taken leave of her senses, or at the very least forgotten her lessons in decorum. A woman shouldn't touch a lord so inappropriately in public, even in a casual situation such as this, unless he invites it." Samyla's frown deepened, and her lips puckered a little. "The Karalis doesn't seem like a man who would encourage such behaviour."

A shame he's too spineless to tell her otherwise, Cori thought. Still, Samyla's adherence to court manners was amusing and she took a moment to imagine Sigrid as an uneducated peasant.

A few soldiers arrived from the barracks and joined the game. Unfortunately for Jonothan's team, Rowan's continued to dominate.

"Cori!" Adro called. "Get in here and help!"

"Duty calls," Cori said to Samyla as she stood.

This would be too easy. She didn't even need to lift her hands to control the ball once Myce kicked it to her, the swinging movement of her arms as she ran disguised what she was doing. She followed the ball, nudging it imperceptibly out of range of those who tried to steal it from her. Within moments, she'd kicked it at the tree, scoring the team's first point.

Her team behind her roared in triumph. She scored twice more this way, then Jonothan scored a point, and Adro. Dristan scored another for the other team. Cori stole the ball from a soldier and kicked it towards their tree. Rowan ran to intercept her. She moved the ball slightly, expecting him to use his feet, but he let her step past him before he grabbed her from behind, pinning her arms to her side and lifting her bodily from the ground.

"Cheat," he whispered as she squirmed against him. She laughed as one of the soldiers from her own team rescued the ball.

"Use your magic," she told him. The soldier gave her a strange look where she was still suspended in Rowan's arms, then he caught onto her meaning and shoved his hand out. The ball flew through the air and smacked into the tree. The game suddenly changed as the other Hiram utilised their magic to control the ball. It zipped through the air, and the players surged around them.

"Are you going to let me go?" Cori asked. Although they didn't keep their relationship hidden anymore, they generally didn't display affection in public, so it surprised her when Rowan kissed her neck before setting her back on the ground. He turned away and took off after the ball.

Sigrid had watched the exchange, and Cori could only guess that Rowan's actions had been to warn the Valkoinen off him. Still a coward, Cori thought as she returned to the tree where Samyla still sat.

"How was that for unseemly?" Cori asked, sitting down beside the other woman. Samyla beamed at her.

"That was very sweet of him, Cori. Of course, decorum

dictates different rules for the Karaliene and her interactions with the Karalis."

Cori laughed and gave Samyla a playful nudge with her shoulder. "You read too many books, Samyla."

Chapter Twenty-One

Their day of respite was followed by the busiest week Cori had experienced since her return to Lautan. With so many in residence, Cori, Rowan and Adro's time was stretched to the limits. Cori was put in charge of organising the soldiers into functional contingents. Rowan didn't want to march his army in the traditional way, he wanted to use their men and women as efficiently as possible.

She worked from dawn until dusk with Han, Ether, Eamoyn and Alastar to sort the soldiers by strength and skill. She had to fight with many of them to get a good gauge of their abilities, and it left her sore and exhausted by the end of each day but she enjoyed working with the soldiers. They were easier to relate to than the nobles who stalked the palace corridors.

While she relished the task, she was also becoming increasingly worried about another potential assassination attempt against Rowan and the more she watched all the new Dijem freely wandering the palace, the more she knew she would have to confide in him her suspicions.

It was midmorning when he found her lying on her back on the floor of their receiving room.

"There you are," he stopped at her side, looking down on her. "I was looking for you at the barracks but they said you'd returned to the palace. Is everything all right?"

"I'm just thinking," she replied, peeking at him from beneath the arm that she'd thrown over her eyes, "of the right way to broach something with you."

"That sounds ominous."

"It's official business," she added. Rowan paused, then sat at the edge of the couch, his hands clasped between his knees.

"Should I call Adro?" He offered.

Should he? She didn't know how Adro would take her suggestion, but he was perhaps a neutral opinion who could remove the relationships from the situation. Either that or tell her she was acting as paranoid as she was starting to think she was.

"Yes, get Adro."

She felt Rowan's Hum reach out briefly, then he sat back on the couch, watching her with a small smile.

"Will you tell me about unconscious thoughts in healing?" She requested to take her mind off her proposal.

His sudden guilty expression told her that he'd intentionally kept this from her. "Unconscious thoughts are those that accompany the thought at the fore of the mind. They are usually related; the mind isn't so great that it can think on several different topics at once. For example, if I were to ask you a question while I was healing you, you would immediately consider several responses based on what you think my expectations are, what your past experiences have been and of course, the words you choose to respond with. You're probably consciously aware of three, maybe four, potential responses, but your mind is concocting many more just in case."

"Good," Cori replied.

"Good?" Rowan echoed in surprise. "You aren't mad that I kept this from you?"

"What's done is done, I suppose."

"How diplomatic of you."

The door opened, and Adro strode in. He had a stack of papers in his arms and he looked harried. He said nothing at being interrupted in his tasks, however. When the Karalis called, he knew to come.

"Cori has some official business she'd like to discuss," Rowan explained. Adro set his papers on the table and sat on the couch beside Rowan.

"Go on, then."

Cori stood and faced them both. Years of experience kept her hands still at her side, although she wanted to fiddle nervously with something. She took a breath.

"I think we need to check the minds of all the Dijem here. I see no other alternative than one of them is the controller. Their arrival at the same time an assassin attacks you doesn't feel like a coincidence. At the very least," she added, "if we find nothing, we'll be sure of their loyalty."

"Cori," Rowan began. "If this is about Si-"

"She's right," Adro cut in. Both Cori and Rowan looked at him in surprise.

"She is?" Rowan said at the same time Cori said "I am?"

"I've been coming to the same conclusion. Myce and Melita being the only ones to return when Daniyl joined Cadmus? The Valkoinens travelling all this way south just because they saw dragons? Even the Uaines being so far east when we know they prefer the north-west of the realm. I'll admit, it worries me."

Cori stared at her fellow Advisor. Was it possible that he was even more paranoid than she? She'd assumed that there was a single person among the many who was a traitor, but the way Adro spoke, he thought it could be the lot of them. If assassins didn't work, how many Dijem would it take to bring down someone as strong as Rowan? She felt cold just thinking about it.

"How would we do it though?" Adro continued. "We can't read fellow Dijem's minds the way we can the Hiram."

Cori looked to Rowan. "Unconscious thoughts," he said. "You want me to use the healing song on them."

"Start with Melita," Cori suggested. "If she's clear, she can help with the rest."

Rowan looked between them. "Do I get any say in this?"

"No," Cori and Adro said together. Rowan sat back on the couch with a sigh.

"Serves me right for having two Advisors," he muttered.

* * *

Rowan finally agreed that he would search the minds of the other Dijem currently living at the palace. He requested some time to think on how he would explain it, which Cori and Adro conceded.

It was only later that day, however, that Cori found herself in the throne room. Rowan had called her back from her soldiers and wanted to speak to her. Despite asking her to meet him here, he'd still not arrived.

Hello, Arasy, she greeted the throne, running her hand over the smooth wood of the dragon's head.

CHAPTER TWENTY-ONE

Karaliene, he responded. *We see little of each other.*

She smiled at his almost petulant tone. *I've been busy.*

Footsteps sounded behind her and she glanced over her shoulder, expecting Rowan, but instead finding Sigrid walking towards the throne. She turned to face the other woman.

Sit down, Arasy suggested. She slowly sank down onto the throne, realising belatedly that this was the first time she'd ever sat upon it. Arasy seemed pleased.

"I asked Rowan to meet me here," Sigrid said without greeting. "Where is he?"

"The Karalis," Cori corrected, "will be here momentarily, I'm sure." She knew now why Rowan had asked her here, and he was a coward for doing so.

"I'll wait, then."

Cori surveyed the other woman and, as she did every time she saw Sigrid, she felt her insecurities rising. Sigrid wasn't beautiful in the way Samyla was - not that Cori had ever met anyone who could match Samyla in looks - but she had a wildness about her that was mysterious and alluring. Cori had heard some of her soldiers talk about the Valkoinen Dijem; the silver-haired people turned heads.

She also knew that Rowan had kissed this woman once. While kissing didn't bother her in a general sense, and Rowan had told her it had happened in a moment of frailty for him, it *had* happened, so he must have found some sense of attraction for her.

Sigrid watched her with a cocked eyebrow, as if she knew how uncomfortable she made Cori. Cori didn't look away, however, and she drummed the dragon's head with her fingers. She wondered if she could snap Sigrid's neck and get rid of the body before Rowan arrived. Or, if she moved a little to her left, she'd be able to push the woman through the arches and possibly over the cliffs from here. Her aim was pretty good...

She heard stone grind against stone behind her, and a moment later Rowan appeared beside the throne. Cori knew the right thing to do would be to stand up and give the throne to the Karalis, but she wouldn't relinquish any power in front of Sigrid, so she stayed where she was. Arasy practically hummed at her defiance.

Rowan didn't ask for his throne, instead opting to lean against the side of it. "Sorry, Sigrid," he said, "you wanted to speak to me?"

"I would like to speak to you alone, Rowan, if I could," Sigrid replied without looking at Cori.

"Cori is my Advisor, whatever it is you need to discuss can be said here."

Sigrid seemed to think for a long moment. "My House and I," she began, "are very adept at fighting with our minds, but unfortunately we have not had much opportunity to learn weapons. We were hoping you could spare one of your captains to train us."

Liar. Oh, Cori had no doubt that they needed the training; she'd seen none of the Valkoinans at the sparring ring, but she guessed that this was something that Bjarte had intended to raise with Rowan, not Sigrid.

"Cori is in charge of our army and their training. She's also the best swordswoman we have; no one has beaten her, including myself. I'm sure, if she's willing, she'll be able to teach your House some basics."

Thanks, Cori told him dryly.

My pleasure. Seeing you on that throne is such a turn on, by

CHAPTER TWENTY-ONE

the way.

"I'll train you," Cori took fierce pleasure in Sigrid's poorly concealed disappointment. "Come to the sparring ring first thing tomorrow morning."

Sigrid hesitated a moment, looking once more towards Rowan.

"You can go," Cori dismissed her, receiving twin nudges of delight from both Rowan and Arasy. Sigrid finally turned and left the hall.

The moment the other woman was out of sight, Cori tried to rise. Rowan put his hand on her shoulder, forcing her back down. "Stay there," he said and moved to sit on the step of the dais. The moment his hand lifted, however, she scooted off the throne to sit beside him.

I don't bite, Arasy promised.

You do, Cori replied, then said to Rowan "you coward."

"You've been calling me that a lot lately."

"Why can't you just tell her to go jump off the cliffs? Now I'm stuck with her."

"She makes me nervous."

"What?" That surprised her.

"She's just so... insistent. I've dealt with infatuation before, but I think Sigrid has real feelings for me."

"You don't want to hurt her feelings?"

"I guess that could be it."

Cori met his eyes and forced him to hold her gaze. "You know you're hurting my feelings by leading her on, don't you?"

"Cori..."

"No, don't worry. I'm a big girl and can look after myself." She stood. "If all you needed was for me to be here to shield you so you don't have to fix this problem, then I'll be on my way."

Rowan grasped her hand and tugged her back down. "I actually wanted to speak to you too. After I've picked through everyone's mind to find your infiltrator, I'm going to tell the rest to stop meditating."

* * *

Cori couldn't deny that she was nervous as she watched the House of Valkoinen walk across the grass towards the sparring ring. Working with the soldiers was one thing - they were already well trained and simply needed to keep their skills fresh - but training people from scratch was something she'd never done before.

"Thank you, Cori," Bjarte said when they reached her, "for accepting us into your regime. I know you are very busy already and I hope that by training us, we will be of more use to you."

"It's not a problem, really," Cori replied awkwardly, shaking Bjarte's outstretched hand. "Come, let's get started."

She had them gather around and one of her soldiers handed them each a wooden sword. "Now who's held a sword before?" she asked and each of them raised their hands. "And who's killed with a sword before?" All their hands lowered, except for one man. She waved him forward. "What's your name?"

"Herleif," he replied. She nodded.

"Show me."

She allowed him to attack, blocking each of his blows with her own wooden sword before reversing their positions

CHAPTER TWENTY-ONE

and swinging the practice weapon at him. Herleif's defence wasn't as strong as his attack - she got a few hard slaps on his arms - but he had some skill. She paired him with one of her soldiers, then asked the rest of the Valkoinens to split into pairs.

"Sigrid," she called to the woman who hid at the back of the group. "You're with me." She watched the woman approach reluctantly. If Rowan wasn't going to warn her off properly, then Cori would.

She had Ether and a few other soldiers spread through the group to run them through some drills. She turned to Sigrid, her practice sword at her side. "Attack me."

She had to give credit to Sigrid; the woman tried to catch her off guard with a quick and determined swing of her sword. Cori stepped out of range. "Again."

She didn't even raise her own sword as she dodged each of Sigrid's blows. She could see the woman was getting frustrated, but she continued this way until Sigrid was dripping in sweat, then she attacked.

"Fight back," she said, darting forward to slap the flat side of her wooden sword against Sigrid's arm. "Again," she demanded, ducking under the wonky blow Sigrid tried to deal her and slapped her sword against her leg. "Again!"

She felt a sudden sharp stab against her mind as Sigrid attacked with her Hum. She slammed her barriers up and lashed out with her sword, smacking it hard over Sigrid's back. Sigrid fell to her knees, crying out in pain. The rest of the Valkoinens stopped their drills to watch. Cori slammed the wooden sword down, embedding it in the dirt so the hilt wobbled near Sigrid's head.

"Unless you're ready to fight for your life," Cori said angrily, "do not attack my mind again."

She turned to the others, who watched her wearily. "I'll see you all tomorrow."

Chapter Twenty-Two

"I just don't know what he sees in her."

Cori faltered outside the door of the dining room, hearing Sigrid's voice from within. When she'd been a child, guests at the palace had dined privately, but with so many in residence now, and so much work to be done, Rowan had converted one of the larger receiving rooms into a dining room where people could come and go at any time to get a bite to eat.

"She really came from nowhere," Melita replied to Sigrid. "She just showed up one day with Rowan, but there have been stories about her…"

Walk away, Cori told herself, come and eat later, you don't need to hear this. But she didn't move.

"She just seems rough around the edges and Rowan is so…" Sigrid trailed off, but Melita giggled.

"I know what you mean."

Cori knew too. Rowan was indescribable. She knew she should move on, but still she stood by the door, chest tight.

"Someone as powerful as he is needs -"

"Have either of you considered," a third voice cut in and Cori realised it was Shaan, "that perhaps you're underestimating her? You may like to put your heads in the sand over the matter, but you cannot deny that she is powerful, perhaps as, if not more, powerful than Rowan. Has it ever crossed your mind that Rowan might be the only thing standing between Cori and the rest of us and that one day, he might not be there? Then what? I for one would prefer her onside."

Sigrid snorted derisively but Melita was quiet; she'd seen glimpses of Cori's magic and had heard the stories. Cori herself didn't know what to make of Shaan's words. They were dramatic, but perhaps harboured some truth. She couldn't deny that she did sometimes rely on Rowan to still her hand. Shaan herself, Cori didn't know what to think of. She had considered the other woman one of her few friends in this place. It sounded, though, as if Shaan was only kind to her to avoid being killed by her. That hurt a little.

The women said no more and Cori steeled herself and stepped into the room. The three of them sat at the table closest to the door, and Cori didn't look at them as she made her way to the buffet. She spotted Samyla and some of her ladies dining there.

"Hello, Samyla," Cori said, leaning over the table for a bread roll. She didn't have time to sit down, so she tore the roll open and started adding chicken and salad to the middle.

"Hello, Cori!" Samyla replied with her usual lovely smile. "Has it been a busy day?"

"Honestly? I can't tell the days apart anymore."

"-Dragon migration," she heard Sigrid say in a carrying voice. "It's such a beautiful sight. When an elder dragon is ready to give back to the earth, it and its family fly south to Hen Goeden. It's family celebrates the life of their elder by shooting bursts of flames across the sky. Rowan and I watched them one night, it was truly magical."

CHAPTER TWENTY-TWO

Cori felt the usual stab of jealousy that she got whenever Sigrid mentioned Rowan. She kept her head down, and pretended she hadn't heard. Samyla on the other hand, turned towards Sigrid with a frown.

"That woman..." she began.

"Just ignore it," Cori suggested, but Samyla stood. Sigrid was still talking and didn't notice the noble woman stalking towards her until she was right before her. Cori trailed half-heartedly behind her in case she had to step in.

"Excuse me," Samyla said to Sigrid. The Dijem woman looked up in surprise. "I don't know if it has come to your attention, but I feel it's my duty to inform you that you're neglecting social etiquette."

"What?" Sigrid said in surprise. Cori choked back laughter.

"You mean 'pardon', don't you?" Samyla continued. "But I digress. Your blatant disregard for respect by using the Karalis' true name is appalling."

"He's my friend," Sigrid defended herself weakly. Shaan and Melita watched on with dual expressions of bewilderment.

"That is irrelevant. In public, unless he informs you otherwise, you should address him as Karalis, or sir, or my lord. It's only the first rule of decorum, I'm surprised you don't know this. Now, I must meet my husband. Excuse me." Samyla waved to her ladies, who stood and gathered behind her. As a group, and with infinite poise, they left the dining room.

Cori followed them into the hallway, her bread roll in hand, only so she could grin without the Dijem women seeing her.

Throne room now, please. Rowan's voice came to her mind, but it sounded louder than usual. She heard the three Dijem in the dining room exclaim in surprise, and she realised that he'd called everyone at once. Taking a quick bite from her bread roll, she headed to meet him.

***

Rowan surveyed the gathered Dijem from the throne with a neutral expression. Only Cori knew how nervous he was; this was the first time he'd given his peers a directive as Karalis.

Are you completely sure we need to do this? He asked her, and not for the first time.

Yes, she responded patiently. He hesitated a moment longer before rising to his feet. The Dijem before them fell quiet.

"Some of you are already aware, but recently I've had a number of assassination attempts on my life." A murmur spread through the crowd and Rowan waited for them to fall quiet again. "I believe the assassins were being controlled by a Dijem in close proximity to Lautan." He took a deep breath. "Today, I'm going to ask each of you to submit to the healing song, so I can be sure that none of you had any involvement. If you object to this test, you're free to leave Lautan now," he paused and Cori looked carefully over the faces upturned towards the throne. They all looked nervous, "but if you chose to do so, Cori and Adro will come and find you."

Another murmur ran through the crowd. Cori glanced sideways at Adro. His expression was hard, and she wondered if she would even be needed if they had to chase down a traitor. He was certainly capable on his own; since giving up meditating, the strength of his magic had nearly tripled.

CHAPTER TWENTY-TWO

No one moved off the back of Rowan's words, and he descended the stairs. "Melita," he said. "You first, please."

Melita stepped forward and Rowan put his hand on her arm. Neither of them spoke, and the song lasted all of two minutes. When Rowan was finished, Melita nodded to an unspoken request and the two of them split to work on the rest.

The process took time and conversations broke out among the Dijem as they waited their turn. The Advisors continued to watch from the dais. Cori noticed the general direction in which Rowan was working and before he could get to her, Cori said, *Melita can do Sigrid.* Rowan abruptly turned away at the demand, and Sigrid watched him go, disappointed.

After almost two hours, it was done. Rowan wove through the Dijem to return to the dais, and when he caught Cori and Adro's eyes he shrugged.

Nothing.

Cori and Adro glanced at each other. Now what?

Rowan stopped at the throne and turned to face the crowd. "Thank you, I didn't believe any of you were involved, but I had to be sure."

"What about Cori and Adro?" Someone called. Cori couldn't see who it was, but she thought it was one of the Uaines. "Aren't you going to check if they're traitors?"

"No," Rowan responded. He gave no explanations, and his tone ended the discussion. Cori supposed the rest didn't need to know that she and Adro had both been healed by Rowan when they'd returned from their trip. "There is one more thing I would like to inform you of before you leave, however. As of today, you are all to stop meditating."

A shocked pause was followed by a cacophony of questions,

angry denials and statements of fear. Rowan let them talk themselves back to silence. "I need an effective army and that means having each of you at your full strength. I don't have enough humans to spare to boost your magic every time it runs low. If you have concerns, raise them with your elders who can bring them to me. Thank you."

* * *

Cori and Jonothan sat in Adro's office, the three of them waiting for the Karalis. Cori rocked back in her chair, her feet on the desk as she stared towards the ceiling. Jonothan was beside her, scribbling furiously on a pad of parchment as Adro dictated numbers to him. Despite the boy's parent's arrival at Lautan, Rowan had asked him to stay on as his page and to continue to attend their nightly debrief meetings. Between the demands that both Rowan and Adro placed on him, Jonothan had been run off his feet. Of his own accord, he'd enlisted the help of some servant's and soldier's children to help him run messages and errands. Cori was quietly impressed by the boy's resourcefulness.

"How many?" Adro asked. Jonothan bent over his paper, calculating the numbers there.

"Fifteen hundred," he responded. Adro looked at Cori.

"Does that sound right?"

"Including the five hundred mounted soldiers Dristan has along his borders? Yes, that sounds like a correct count of the army."

Adro nodded and marked the final figure down. "Let's start on the weapon inventory." He was interrupted by Rowan's arrival.

CHAPTER TWENTY-TWO

"I'm sure you can understand my position, Acacia," he was saying as he walked up the hallway. "I know you're concerned about Hum intoxication, but I assure you, myself, Cori and Adro have all trained in preventing it and we'll be extra diligent in listening for signs of it over the coming weeks. I have some literature on the matter, if you wish to read it." He paused at the door, and Cori saw him turn to face the elder.

"Thank you, Karalis, that would be welcome," Acacia replied. "I'll bid you goodnight then."

The elder strolled away, and Rowan frowned at her use of his formal title. Cori had to hide her smile as he turned to enter the room. It seemed word of Samyla's berating of Sigrid had spread.

"Have we all had a good day?" Rowan addressed the group. He kissed Cori's cheek as he passed her to perch on the edge of the desk by her feet.

"There are too many refugees flooding in," Adro started. He was frowning at Rowan, and Cori decided that it had been a long time since she'd seen her fellow Advisor smile. It was a shame that the stress was getting to him; normally Adro's humour was what helped carry them through the long days. "We cannot house and feed them all as well as the army."

"Can we ask Shaw to take them?"

"Shaw is already receiving their own influx along the borders."

"What about Dodici?" Rowan suggested. "What's one of their king's names?"

"Vecchio," Cori offered quietly.

"That's it. Send a letter to Vecchio. Tell him I'll pay him to take some of our people."

Adro surveyed Rowan with pursed lips. He had voiced his disapproval of Rowan's use of money a few times before. Cori didn't see the problem. They had a steady income flowing from the states who had allied with them, coupled with Rowan's seemingly endless supply of personal funds. She wondered how much money Adro had stowed away from his holdings with his frugal attitude. She really should consider getting herself some sort of income.

"Why don't we go out to the sparring ring for a while?" Rowan suggested, noticing the look on Adro's face. "We can have our meeting out there."

"I'd like that," Jonothan piped up.

"I have too much work to do." Adro moved to his desk and began shuffling papers into piles.

"It will be here tomorrow." Rowan stood. "I'm sure you'll feel much more productive after swinging a sword at my head."

Finally, Adro smiled a little. "Yes, that would make me feel better. All right, let's go."

They passed Myce and Melita in the hallway on their way to the sparring ring.

"Evening," Rowan greeted them.

"Good evening, Karalis," Melita replied. Rowan turned his head to watch them as they passed. Cori had to look away to hide her smile.

"Weird," Rowan muttered, before continuing on his way.

* * *

The following morning, Samyla departed. Cori was sad to

CHAPTER TWENTY-TWO

see her go, but the noblewoman had to return to Rikdom to prepare for her baby. Dristan remained at the palace, however, staying true to his word to lead his own army in the war.

"I hope we can see each other soon," Samyla told Cori, her guard and ladies working in a flurry around her to saddle the horses and pack the carriages. "You must come and visit once the baby is born."

"I promise I will," Cori replied. She leaned forward to kiss Samyla on the cheek before stepping back so that Dristan could farewell his wife. She waited until Samyla had climbed into her carriage and was on her way down the cliff road before heading around the side of the palace with Dristan at her side.

"So I was thinking I might rotate a few of my contingents out to the borders and recall some back here to rest," he said, and Cori could hear the way his voice trembled as he tried to contain his emotion. She sympathised with him; she'd felt much the same when she'd left Rowan for her trip north.

"That sounds like a good idea," she replied. "I might mix a few of the other soldiers in so they can get off the training ground and into the field."

Cori, Rowan called her, *have you got a moment?*

"Excuse me," she told Dristan. She headed back to the palace and found Rowan in a small receiving room with a few pieces of parchment in front of him.

"We've received a report from Kenneth with the latest group of refugees," he began without preamble. "Two dragons, who are not Daiyu, have been attacking flocks of cattle in Hearth."

"That seems strange," Cori took the sheet of parchment he

offered and read the report. "Why would they attack Hearth if Cadmus is allied with Hearth?"

"The only thing I can think of is that they're too young to understand better. He might have lost some control over them."

"Dragons are still problematic," she sighed. "Anything else?"

"Yes." He pushed the next bit of parchment towards her. "Previously separate raiding groups have joined to form contingents. They don't seem to have purpose or direction, from what Kenneth can tell, they're just forming together. Getting ready."

"I'll let Dristan know. He wants to rotate his contingents, I think I'll send Eamoyn or Ether out with them to get a fuller idea of what's happening." They sat quietly for a few moments.

"It's getting close," Cori said eventually. "I can feel the tension."

"Someone will have to make a first move soon," Rowan agreed. Cori wondered if he intended to make that move.

"Karalis?" Shaan knocked at the door and poked her head inside. "Sorry to interrupt. Acacia and I have been reading that book you loaned us last night, and we wanted to know if you'd help us with an energy release."

"Of course," Rowan grinned and Cori knew it pleased him that they had taken the front foot on dropping meditation. "Let me finish here and I'll come find you."

"Thank you, sir." Shaan closed the door and Rowan's smile slipped at the formality. Cori couldn't help herself, she snorted with laughter.

"What have you done?" He rounded on her.

CHAPTER TWENTY-TWO

"Oh, it wasn't me," Cori said through her laughter. She leaned against the table and wiped a tear from the corner of her eye. "Samyla gave Sigrid a dressing down yesterday on her uncouth use of your real name. Melita and Shaan were there to hear it and I guess the idea of Dijem using basic manners has spread."

Rowan stared at her. "Basic manners?"

"I know. Hard to believe that people who are thousands of years old don't have them."

"Says you," he muttered. "I notice you haven't bowed to the decorum rules."

"I'm the Karaliene. I make the rules." The words were out of her mouth before she could stop herself, but surprisingly she didn't regret them.

Rowan rocked back in his chair. "The Karaliene?"

"Yeah, well," she said without meeting his eye as she scratched at a grain in the wooden table top. "I suppose the title isn't as bad as it once was."

For a long moment he stared at her, then he rocked forward again and stood, rounding the table. His eyes smouldered and his lips curled deliciously as he leaned down to kiss her. "Well, my lady Karaliene," he murmured against her lips. "If you set the rules, how do you propose I break them?"

Chapter Twenty-Three

There was no announcement to declare Cori as the Karaliene, but Rowan made some small changes to reflect her elevated position. Now, when they had formal engagements, she stood directly beside the throne with Adro on her other side. Her wardrobe was updated from the light blue of an Advisor to the deep blue that Rowan wore as the Karalis. She didn't allow him any other adjustments; she didn't want a fuss made when they were so close to the war.

Of his own predicament, Cori advised him to allow the Dijem to continue to show deference to him. It can't hurt, she told him, to let them practise courtesy. This lasted all of two weeks when someone, who had obviously decided to read further into the rules of decorum, bowed before the Karalis. Rowan immediately put a stop to the civilities and once more began asking people to address him by his first name.

Cori was disappointed. She'd enjoyed watching the other Dijem fumble their way through court manners. Having grown up a servant, and then attending the School of Auksas, she was well versed in decorum, though she remembered, ironically, how she'd defied Rowan at every turn during her

CHAPTER TWENTY-THREE

youth. Insolent, he had called her.

It was these memories that were on her mind as she looked down at Sigrid, kneeling in the dirt of the sparring ring. "Again," she said, and Sigrid looked up at her, her face covered in sweat and dust. She heaved herself to her feet and held her practice sword in front of her with tired, trembling hands. Cori had to admit a begrudging admiration for the woman; no matter how many times Cori beat her down, she still came back for training every day. She hefted her own sword and swung it. The Valkoinen parried two blows before Cori slapped the side of her wooden blade against her arm.

Sigrid grunted in pain - she had days ago stopped crying out - and prepared to go again. Cori moved faster this time, feigning a blow before sliding around behind Sigrid to smack her over the back of the legs. Sigrid tried to twist with Cori but tripped over her feet, sprawling in the dirt once more.

"Why can't I beat you?" Sigrid cried, and Cori surveyed her with an expressionless gaze. The woman had reached the end of her tether for the day.

"You won't ever beat me," Cori told her. "None of my army can beat me, not even the Karalis can beat me. Why do you think you can?"

Sigrid just stared up at her, a desolate look on her face, and Cori wondered if she had misunderstood the other woman's question. She tossed her sword down to the dirt. "Enough for today, I think."

Sigrid got up and limped away. Cori walked among the other Valkoinens for a time, answering their questions and sometimes demonstrating a move. Finally, the last of them headed back to the palace, and Cori was alone. She stretched and looked towards the sky. It was late afternoon. The soldiers were finishing up their drills and were packing away their weapons. She decided she might as well head back to the palace early for a bath.

Rowan was waiting for her in their suite and she paused when she saw him, not only because it was far too early for him to be there, but also because he was dressed up.

"Have we got an official engagement I forgot about?" She wondered, eyeing his crisp white shirt and dark grey pants. He even had rings on his fingers, rubies set in gold. She hadn't seen him wear rings since they'd fled the palace half a millennium ago. He smiled at her in a rather disarming way.

"You might say that. It's your birthday."

"My…" she hadn't celebrated a birthday since she'd left Balforde.

"I thought I might take you out to dinner." He came to stand in front of her, running his hands down her arms.

"Dinner." A smile lifted her lips. "As in a date?"

"I've never taken you on one before. Will you go on a date with me, Cori?" he made the proposal with a mock bashfulness that made her laugh.

"Stop it! Yes, all right, I'll go on a date with you if I have to."

"Get ready then."

She bathed first, washing off the dirt of her day's work, then braided her hair from one side and pinned it so that the rest fell over the opposite shoulder. Rowan had organised a dress for her and she found it in the bedroom. It was a strapless dress - a fashion she'd never seen before - and the bust was decorated with glittering gold sequins before giving way to a flowing, pale gold skirt.

He watched her descend the steps with his hands in his

CHAPTER TWENTY-THREE

pockets and a smile on his face. He met her at the bottom and held out his hand for her. She took it, and he raised her hand to his lips.

"You are so beautiful," he told her, and she blushed. How did she get so lucky?

It was getting dark as they arrived in Lautan and Rowan led her to the strip of restaurants along the waterfront. Other couples and groups were out for the evening, and their heads turned as the Karalis and Karaliene passed them. Cori could see the envy in their eyes.

They stopped at a restaurant that had a single table at its front, overlooking a pier with a sleek merchant ship docked at it.

"You booked a whole restaurant?" Cori asked incredulously as Rowan gestured that she should precede him to the table. He merely smiled at her question. Music played from within the restaurant and the sound floated gently out to them and as they sat down, a server came over and placed two glasses and a bottle of rum on the table.

"A whole bottle? You're too kind," she joked. Rowan pulled the stopper and poured the amber liquid into their glasses.

"The less we're interrupted the better, I think."

"You know," she mused as they looked out over the water. The ship creaked against the pier and water slapped softly against the stone embankment. "The last time I went on a date was when Quart took me on one." She wrinkled her nose at the memory. "All he ever wanted to do was kiss."

"Ah well," Rowan gave her a sideways smile, "I better cross that one off the list then." Then to contradict himself, he leaned towards her, cupping her face with his hand and kissing her gently. "What do you feel like eating?" He asked as he sat back in his seat.

"Cake." She felt a pang of sadness as she remembered how her mother had always made her a cake for her birthday. Saasha had continued the tradition in the years they'd lived together in Balforde.

"Cake it is." Rowan waved the server over and placed his order. The server went into the restaurant and returned shortly with an entire cake. He handed Rowan two spoons with a wry smile.

"Seriously?" Cori laughed. She accepted the spoon he handed her and scrapped it across the white icing.

"My grandmother was the cook in the family," Rowan dug his spoon through the soft sponge and cream within. "She was the House elder, so there wasn't a huge amount of time for her to cook, but once a month she'd have a family dinner, spending all day in the kitchen cooking everything you could think of from canapes to dessert and then we'd sit outside under these huge canopies strung with lights and some of my cousins would play music and we'd eat every single plate clean."

"Which was your favourite dish?" Cori watched him across the top of the cake. His eyes held a glow that spoke of both warmth and sadness.

"It was hard to choose. I always liked the meat dishes. She made them so deliciously tender, it would just fall apart on your fork. And the sauces she made to go with them were smokey and hot. No one was ever able to copy them."

"Saasha's husband was a good meat cook like that," she reached over the cake for the bottle of rum to pour herself another drink. "Had no clue what to do with a vegetable, but on his days off would stand for hours beside his smoker, cooking slabs of meat and drying flavoured jerky that would last the month."

She put the bottle back and accidentally slid the side of her hand across the edge of the cake. Before she could wipe the icing off with a napkin, Rowan caught her wrist and pulled her hand to his mouth.

With a shiver of heat that curled down her spine and pooled low in her abdomen, she watched his lips close over the edge of her hand, felt the flick of his tongue as he licked the icing away.

"I bet your cooking puts both of them to shame," he decided, lowering her hand slightly.

She let out a huff of laughter, one eyebrow arching at the hungry look in his eyes. "You've never tasted my best cooking. For years it's been campfires and rations, or having staff cook for me. But," she shrugged, a blush creeping up her neck. "Maybe when this war is good and done I'll cook something special, just for you."

He lifted her hand once more, this time pressing his lips to her palm. "I would love that."

They ate cake and drank rum well into the evening. They laughed, and they talked and they didn't once mention the army, or supplies, or noblemen, and as they finally left the carriage at the top of the cliff road, Cori decided it had been one of the best nights of her life.

They strolled arm in arm along the drive towards the throne room. When they were before the arches, Rowan turned and led her towards the gardens and the cliffs instead. The water rushed below them, swirling and crashing over the rocks as it had forever.

"Dance with me?" He requested. She placed her hand in

his and he twirled her once before pulling her in. Cheek laid against his chest, they turned in gentle circles, with only the music in their heads to guide them. Cori tentatively wove a song, the first she had ever learned, and the one she called the Dragon's Song.

Rowan took it and flung it out around them, spreading the magic, throwing it towards the universe. They moved faster, the lights of the palace creating a golden blur that fused with the stars spiralling above them. The magic of all the Dijem within the palace and barracks reached curiously towards the Dragon's Song. Still they moved faster, their Hums more powerful than those nearby, yet strangely soft beneath the song they wove.

Cori was aware the Dijem had come to the throne room. They were silhouettes beneath the arches as they watched their Karalis and his Karaliene, drawn by their magical presence.

Then the spell shattered like glass as a roar ripped through the night, bringing their dance to a halt. A burst of flame scorched the sky above, and they tilted their heads back to watch the black dragon swoop overhead. Cori instinctively reached out, finding a bare flicker of a Hum within the dragon's mind. She heard the shouting of the Dijem nearby, and that of the army further away in their barracks, but she and Rowan stood where they were and watched as Daiyu looped back and let forth another great gout of flames towards the stars.

She surprisingly felt no fear and, as the dragon tilted a wing towards them in a salute before vanishing into the night sky, she met Rowan's eye and wondered if Daiyu was their enemy at all.

Chapter Twenty-Four

"Cadmus sent her to warn us!"

"She won't be far away, what if she comes back while we're sleeping and attacks?"

"She's going to kill us all! How did we even think we were a match for Cadmus and Daiyu?"

Cori listened to the clamour in the throne room and said nothing. She sat on Arasy, looking over the heads of the Dijem to the army that had assembled before the arches. She was pleased at how quickly her soldiers had spilled out of the barracks and formed rank. The Dijem, on the other hand, were working themselves into an embarrassing panic.

Rowan perched on the arm of the throne and he stared down at his shoes. His back was to her, but she could still feel the faint residue of magic emitting from him after their dance above the cliffs.

I don't think Daiyu meant us harm, she told him.

Nor do I, he replied, *but I don't know what to make of it.*

Could she have been drawn by the song? I felt her Hum, only faintly.

Rowan turned slightly to look at her. *Perhaps she remembered the way you used to sing it to her.* He continued to stare, and she had a feeling he was forming some sort of conclusion about her. She didn't want to know what it was.

Could that be it? That Daiyu remembered the way Cori had used the song as a child to lull the dragons in her dreams?

"Quiet!" Adro roared. "QUIET!"

Silence fell over the hall and the captains who stood before their soldiers outside moved closer to listen.

"Daiyu didn't mean us harm," Adro explained in a calm, carrying voice. "She has no magic - Rowan and Cori saw to that."

"She still has teeth!" Someone called out.

"And fire!" Said another.

"But she didn't use them. If she attacks in the future, then we'll fight her as best we can. We're at war now, we can hardly expect to sit around the palace forever. You all need to pull yourselves together."

The Dijem seemed to straighten at his words. The protesting stopped and was replaced with contemplative conversation.

Adro could be the Karalis, Cori told Rowan.

I was just thinking that, he replied.

She allowed herself a moment to fantasise about walking out of Lautan with only Rowan at her side and never coming back. Of going south to the beaches with their turquoise waters and endless summers. The thought was fleeting, and she pushed it away; they had a war to fight and the dragon's presence, friendly or not, made it seem even more imminent.

Adro ordered the Dijem from the hall and the captains took the army back to the barracks, leaving Cori and Rowan alone in the silent throne room.

Rowan turned on the arm of the throne to face her more fully. "There's still a few hours left of your birthday," he said

CHAPTER TWENTY-FOUR

with a dashing smile. She laughed and took the hand he offered. He led her down the steps of the dais and twirled her into his arms. They resumed their dancing, this time without the audience.

* * *

The content and purposeful atmosphere that Cori had felt over the past few weeks evaporated the following night with the arrival of news about Samyla.

It was late when Rowan called her to the throne room. She could hear yelling before she'd even arrived.

Dristan and Rowan were there, and Rowan held a creased letter in front of him while Dristan, looking panicked, was saying "I have to go to her. I have to get her back!"

"Calm down, Dristan," Rowan told him, "let's think this through." He handed the letter to Cori as she reached them, and she moved towards the lamplight near an arch to read it.

Dristan, the looping cursive began, *I have reclaimed my niece from you. If you wish to have her back, you will bring your army to Tengah and you will join sides with the rightful Karalis. Our states could do great things together. Warm regards, Brentyn.*

Cori felt a chill at the words she read. The Head of Hearth had taken Samyla captive. Kind, gentle Samyla. How had he gotten to her? To be in Tengah already, she must have been abducted on her trip home.

"-Of course I will do what he says!" Dristan was ranting. "He's taken my wife! I'm sorry, Karalis, but I need to give my men to him to get her back. This war doesn't matter if she's not at my side."

"Dristan," Rowan began as the Head of Hale turned away

from him and moved towards the arches. "Let's talk about it. There are other ways we can get Samyla back."

Cori moved to block Dristan's exit through the arches. "Move, Karaliene," he said angrily.

"You signed a contract," she warned him. "I protected you in exchange for your army. We cannot let you go." And they really couldn't. Dristan's soldiers made up almost half their army.

"I don't care about contracts - they took my wife! Get out of my way!" Before his raised hands could even make contact to push her aside, she'd pulled the dagger from her belt and plunged it into his chest.

It was a quick death; his eyes only having a moment to look surprised before he slumped to the ground. Cori let the letter flutter down beside him, exhaling sharply, before looking up.

Rowan hadn't reacted at all to the killing and he watched her with an expressionless gaze. Their eyes met for a long, hard moment and she felt the silent struggle for power between them. Although she'd reclaimed the role of Karaliene, she still deferred to Rowan as the ruler of the realm. She didn't need to. If he looked away first, she could claim that title from him. All he had to do was look away...

What was she doing! She didn't want this. Quickly, she dragged her gaze down to the body at her feet, feeling both relieved and ashamed that she'd backed down from the challenge. When she looked up again, Rowan was walking away.

Dristan's body was heavy as she dragged it across the garden towards the cliffs. Thankfully there was no blood left on the throne room floor, stoppered by the dagger still

CHAPTER TWENTY-FOUR

in his heart. He probably deserved a burial, she thought as she heaved him closer to the cliffs, but a fresh mound of dirt in the gardens would raise questions with the gardeners in the morning.

She rolled him close to the edge, then pulled the dagger from his chest. A small amount of blood spilled out with it, covering her hands. She straightened, putting her foot to his side and rolling him over the edge. He fell into darkness, body devoured by the sea. She held up her bloody hands, almost black in the darkness, and started to tremble. She'd just killed the Head of Hale.

Blood splattered from her hands when she shook them, and she turned away from the cliffs, trudging back to the palace. She passed no one as she returned to her suite and, careful not to drip blood on the light-coloured carpet, she headed straight to the bathroom.

She turned on the tap and put her hands under the running water, watching the blood wash from her hands and swirl down the drain. Dristan's blood. She'd killed Dristan. Ally to the throne and husband to her friend. She'd killed him. Samyla's baby no longer had a father.

Her hands shook beneath the water. What had she done? She should have tried to talk sense into him, as Rowan had. He'd been distraught about his wife's abduction, of course he would make rash decisions. Now he was dead. Gone. And she couldn't bring him back. A hard lump formed in her throat and her stomach churned as she was thoroughly sick into the sink.

Each breath she tried to draw was ragged and tight as she turned away and slid down the cabinet to the floor. She'd just killed a man who didn't need to die. She was disgusting, a heartless monster. She drew her knees up and wrapped her arms around them. Sobs wracked her body so hard it hurt.

She had always assumed that when her violent ways caught up with her, she'd have a mental blow out like Rowan did. She hadn't expected to be crippled by regret and guilt.

Minutes or hours could have passed before Rowan found her there on the bathroom floor. He moved into the room and turned off the running tap before sliding down the cabinet to sit beside her, head back against the bench.

"Sometimes I wonder what we're doing here," he said in a low voice. Then he opened his arms to her. She fell across his lap, her sobs renewed. She didn't deserve this; to hug the man she loved when Samyla would never see her husband again.

* * *

They didn't mention Dristan again after that night, though he was all Cori could think about. Every time she spoke to one of his soldiers, she saw him. Each time she went into the throne room, her eyes strayed to the place beneath the arches where he'd fallen. In her dreams, she tried to stop herself stabbing him, but she did it, over and over. Samyla was present too, in her nightmares, crying for her husband and screaming at Cori, calling her a monster.

And she felt like a monster. Her stomach churned nervously every time she thought of him. She couldn't eat - she didn't deserve to - and she barely slept. Rowan was kind to her, but she could feel a distance between them that she didn't want to bridge. She didn't deserve him either.

CHAPTER TWENTY-FOUR

None of the soldiers from Hale asked after their Head. Cori thought Rowan must have planted some memories in the heads of the Hiram - rumours to spread through the rest - for they seemed sombre, but they never asked or wondered why Dristan wasn't there.

Cori's turmoil was also affecting her performance in the sparring ring. Where she'd once been swift and decisive in her actions, she was now hesitant, defending more than she attacked. She worried, after killing Dristan with no forethought, that she might do it to someone else.

In the back of her mind, she knew her logic was convoluted - she'd always been so sure with a blade, never drawing blood on an opponent unless the rules of the spar stated it - but as the days wore on, she withdrew more and more into herself.

The first person to beat her at first blood was a regular human soldier. She didn't know his name, but he worked well with his blade, as if it were an extension of his arm. She almost had him beat, but faltered at the last minute. Instead of darting forward under the blow he dealt her, she took half a step back, letting her sword drop slightly. He moved with her, reversing his swing and slashing her across the arm.

It was deeper than any cut she'd ever dealt in the game. Perhaps the soldier had expected her to move out of range - she certainly could have - for his eyes widened in surprise and his mouth dropped open a little.

A hush fell over those who stood around the ring, watching. Cori watched blood well from the cut and drip down her arm. The pain was slow to come, but she could feel the beginning of a burning sensation deep in the muscle. She tossed her sword down into the dirt.

"Good match," she said to the soldier.

"I-" he began, still looking shocked, and a little horrified, at what he'd done. "Do you need assistance?"

"I'm fine," she told him and turned away. She saw Adro watching from the fence, but she didn't want to talk to him. She walked in another direction, towards the palace. He moved to intercept her.

She was sure Rowan would have told Adro what had happened. The other Dijem didn't have an interest in the noblemen at the palace, but Adro would notice that Dristan was missing. "You need to go to Rowan and get that healed," he told her shortly.

"I will," she lied.

"And then you need to stay away from the sparring ring until you get your shit together. You cannot lose like that again."

"Why not?" She couldn't even muster anger at his words. "It's good for them to know they've trained so well that they can beat me."

"They won't see it that way. All they'll see is one of their leaders failing. You're supposed to lead this war and win and they lose confidence if you start losing at home."

Cori just stared at him, waiting to see if he had anything further to say. He shook his head and turned away. She went back to the palace, entering through the kitchens. She glanced at the floor as she passed. The spot where her mother had died. She'd been to the kitchens a lot over the last week and a half, usually late at night when all the servants were asleep. She would sit on the floor and stare at the wall. This is where it had all started, where she'd killed her first man without even realising it, and without remorse.

She wondered how different life would be if that riot had

never happened. Would she and Rowan still be here, both their hands clean of blood, and ruling the realm? Probably not. She had, only moments before the riot, tried to kill Quart, and she would have succeeded if Rowan hadn't intervened. No matter what way she looked at it, it seemed she'd always been destined to be a murderer.

She went to her suite and to the bathroom. The cut truly throbbed now, and she held her arm tight to her side while she rummaged with her other hand through the draws for a bandage. With clumsy fingers, she wiped the blood away and wrapped the bandage around her arm. She didn't look in the mirror, didn't want to see the monster staring back at her.

She returned to the receiving room and sat down on the couch. She knew she should go back to her soldiers, but she wasn't ready to plaster on a smile and face them yet. Instead, she stared at the ceiling and willed a numbness to take her.

The door opened, and Rowan slipped into the room. She should have known Adro would tell him.

"I'm fine," she told him before he could say anything. "It's just a cut."

"It doesn't look like just a cut." He looked pointedly at her arm and when she followed his gaze, she saw that blood was already seeping through the bandage.

"Let me heal you."

"No," she said harshly, rising and moving towards the door. "I don't want to be healed. I don't deserve to be healed."

He caught her good arm as she tried to brush past and turned her to face him. He forced her to meet his eyes. "I need you to fight in this war," he told her. "I can't have you get cold feet, not now."

"Don't worry, I'll fight," she finally dropped her gaze and hoped that her actions would match her words when the time came.

"Please let me heal you," he said softly. "I don't like seeing you in pain."

She wanted to deny his words, but couldn't. The cut really hurt. A lump formed in her throat as she once more felt undeserving of his kindness. She let him lead her back to the couch and sat beside him. He put his arm around her and pulled her closer before placing his hand on her arm and starting the healing song. It hurt more than she expected, and she realised that the soldier had cut through to the muscle.

"I think I need to go to Tengah," she told him hesitantly. She didn't need to tell him that she had to find and save Samyla, then admit to the other woman that she'd killed her husband, he could read it from her mind. He didn't disagree with her, as she had expected him to. In fact, he didn't respond to her at all.

"I mean it when I said I need you to fight," he said instead, as the pain eased from the healing and the song became comfortable. "I need you to kill without hesitation."

"Look at where that got me," she muttered.

"One regretted kill of the many you've dealt was bound to happen. It's a shame that your confidence is shaken by it right at this moment."

She pulled away from him slightly, and he stopped the song. "Why do you say 'right at this moment'?"

He smiled knowingly. "In a few moments, one of Jonothan's messengers is going to burst into the room to tell us that there are five hundred Hearthians a day's march from Lautan."

CHAPTER TWENTY-FOUR

Before she could react, the door was flung open, and a child stumbled into the room, his hair wild and cheeks red from running.

"Karalis!" He gasped, belatedly remembering to bow. "A scout has come in and told us that there are five hundred Hearthians only a day's march from Lautan!" Cori looked at Rowan. He was still smiling.

The war was about to begin.

Chapter Twenty-Five

They left their suite to find the palace, understandably, in an uproar.

"We should get the army outside the gates," Cori said, her reservations momentarily set aside as she strode alongside Rowan towards the throne room.

"No," he replied. Adro, with the captains and Jonothan close behind, met them at the door.

"We should march the army to the gates," Adro said as they all entered the hall together. Servants were already there, setting up a large square table for them all to gather around.

"No," Rowan said again. "Where's the scout?"

Jonothan ran to get the scout while Han and Ether unrolled maps onto the table. One was of Lautan, the other of the entire realm. Rowan moved past them all to sit on the throne. Cori watched him and wondered what his game was. He was too calm. Jonothan returned with the scout.

"Report please," Rowan said.

"Five hundred on foot, Karalis," the scout began. "Most swordsmen, perhaps a hundred archers. They have siege equipment and supplies. I believe this is an advance contingent sent to lock us in the town and set up camp for when the main army arrives."

CHAPTER TWENTY-FIVE

"Thank you." Rowan nodded, as if he already knew all of what the scout had reported. Maybe he did, Cori realised. He'd preempted the boy coming to find them after all.

How long have you known? She wondered.

Four days.

And you didn't think to tell anyone?

There was no need.

He's gone mad, she decided.

"We really need to get the army outside the gates if they plan to start a siege," Adro warned again.

"No," Rowan said for a third time.

"The city is indefensible from the inside. Too many streets, the army cannot form up properly," Han explained, running his finger over the map of Lautan. "We can defend for a time from the cliff road, but if they overwhelm us, they will have us trapped in the palace. There is no way off this rock." He looked up at Rowan. "No offence, Karalis, but how did you ever intend to defend this place when you built it?"

Rowan gave him a strange look. "I am the defence."

They were all quiet for a moment, then Ether spread her palms wide. "So how do you plan to defend us?"

Rowan grinned. "I thought you'd never ask."

* * *

Under Rowan's direction, they worked through the night to prepare. The townspeople gathered in the public garden, as did the army and the Dijem. Rowan ordered all the horses and their tack be taken from the town to the paddocks at the south of the cliffs, as well as all their supply carts.

"We're going to march on Tengah," he explained as he

watched everyone move about him, carrying out his orders.

"To save Samyla?" Cori asked.

"To take the whole city." A bold move. Their army was large, but it seemed reckless to waste soldiers to take such a well-fortified city such as Tengah.

"You think Cadmus is there?"

"No."

She asked nothing further on the matter; it was useless trying to pry information from him when he began responding in one-word answers. He would either keep his plans close to his chest, or tell her when he needed to. She didn't begrudge him that. She turned the conversation back to the matter at hand.

"Are we going to abandon Lautan?" She didn't think so; they'd spent too long renovating the palace and injecting money into the town to let their enemies take it.

Once more his response was one syllable. "No."

"If we're marching on Tengah," Adro said from nearby where he worked with Ailey to lock all their important documents into wooden chests, "should we not get outside the gate before the Hearthians arrive?"

"You will," Rowan said. Adro glanced at him. The Karalis pointed to the chests. "Are those ready? The Hearthians marched through the night. They'll be here by morning."

They took the chests, along with other valuables that they didn't intend to take with them, to the Karalis' suite. Rowan locked the door so no one could interrupt them, then he, Cori and Adro loaded their cargo into the secret chamber beneath the floor.

By the time they were done, the sun was rising. They packed clothes into saddle bags and Adro took them when

CHAPTER TWENTY-FIVE

he left. Finally, they changed into their armour.

Their uniforms matched those of their soldiers, leather pants and a vest dyed a deep blue worn over a white shirt, or tunic, in Cori's case. Only their vests set them apart from the others, with brilliant gold thread stitched in elaborate swirls across the front of the leather.

They returned to the throne room where everyone had gathered. Rowan moved to the dais, running his hand over the dragon's head on the arm of the throne, but not sitting down.

"We're going to march on Tengah," he announced to the waiting crowd. "The Head of Hearth, Brentyn, has openly declared himself our enemy, so it's time we showed him that he chose the wrong side." The soldiers outside cheered and stamped their feet. Rowan made a sweeping motion with his hand. "Will everyone please make space?"

Those within the hall shuffled back, leaving the floor bare before the dais. "Arasy," Rowan addressed the throne aloud for the benefit of those watching. "Will you please do the honours."

A deep rumbling vibrated up from beneath their feet and the crowd moved even further back, looking around nervously. A large square of stone shifted, throwing up a puff of dust, then sank into the floor and slid into a long compartment, much the way Rowan's vault opened. The opening revealed a wide stairwell that spiralled down into the darkness.

"These stairs lead to the southern cliffs and the lower paddocks where the horses are. Adro will lead those who are coming with us towards the west. We'll clear Shaw's border as we go, then turn north and approach Tengah from the south."

"And the army at the gates?" Someone queried.

"Cori and I will deal with the Hearthians."

Cori was still - her years of training stopping her from physically reacting to his words - but inside, she felt as if she'd jumped into a cold pool of water.

I know the stories about me are amazing, she told Rowan, *but five hundred soldiers could be out of my league.*

We'll be fine.

"Time to go," he said aloud, ignoring the worrying looks Adro was giving him. "The Hearthians are almost here."

The Dijem and soldiers collected their things and filed into the stairwell. Adro came to the dais.

"Are you sure about this?" He asked. "Five hundred is far too many for the two of you, and Cori hasn't been feeling herself lately." He glanced at her and she kept her gaze studiously away, lest he see the panic she felt in her eyes.

"We'll be fine," Rowan assured him. "Like I said earlier, if I didn't think I could defend this palace against an army, I would never have put it here. Start along the border, Adro, we'll catch up to you in a few hours."

The army finally dwindled away into the darkness of the underground, leaving only the townspeople, one hundred soldiers and four Dijem.

"You're in charge while we're gone," Rowan said to Jonothan, his hand on his shoulder. The boy's chest puffed importantly, yet his eyes looked sad. "If any enemies come, ask Arasy to open the stairwell and get out. Don't fight them."

"Yes sir," Jonothan said.

Rowan straightened and faced the other three Dijem -

CHAPTER TWENTY-FIVE

Jonothan's father, one other Uaine and a Valkoinen. "Keep everyone up here until all the Hearthian's are dead. Unfortunately, you will have to clean up after us, we won't have time to stay and dig the grave." Finally, he turned to Cori. "Let's go."

The town was eerily silent as they walked through it towards the gate. They could hear the Hearthians marching down the road on the other side, and Cori shoved her hands in her pockets to keep them from trembling. Rowan was absolutely calm, and she wondered if that was making her even more nervous. They stopped at the gate, and Rowan gestured towards them. "Will you do the honours?"

Normally the gate would take at least four men to heave open. Cori put her hands together, back-to-back, and pried them apart with her magic. The Hearthian's waited beyond, their numbers sprawled in even rows, divided into units of fifty. Those at the fore seemed surprised that the gates had opened, but they held their ground.

Rowan strode forward with Cori a step behind. She expected him to address them. Instead, his Hum reached out across the waiting force. Row by row, the eyes of their soldiers glazed over, like an epidemic. Cori's eyes widened at the impossible number that Rowan took hold of. It didn't even seem to strain him. Defender of Lautan indeed.

The soldiers stood to attention, then bowed down to one knee before the Karalis. Such a fluid and controlled movement. She didn't know how he did it - she could barely bring a handful of men to a halt, and he controlled an army like they were puppets. Some hundred and fifty were left standing - the humans - and they looked around at their peers, first in confusion and then, as realisation dawned, sheer terror. Cori glanced at Rowan. He watched those who were standing, waiting.

The ones at the back turned and ran first. Within moments the lot of them were fleeing back up the road. The archers stood under Rowan's silent command and let loose a volley of arrows. Each one flew true, each slaying a soldier who ran. A second volley finished them, all save two.

Cori watched the survivors stagger up the road and knew why Rowan had let them go. They would go back and tell the others what had happened, how their own men had turned on them at the whims of the Karalis.

"There's a Dijem among them," Rowan said, bringing her attention back to those who still knelt before them. "He's kneeling, but pretending. I don't have control of him, but I can feel his Hum along with the blankness." His eyes scanned the rows, then he pointed to their left. "Somewhere on this side."

They moved forward, walking slowly through the ranks of still soldiers, looking for signs of someone who had control of themselves. They were two rows away when Cori saw a man's shoulder quiver. Before she could point him out, he jumped up and tried to run, but not before he flung an attack at her mind. She slammed her barriers up, cursing, and stepped forward to give chase. Rowan grabbed her arm to stop her.

"Let your barriers down," he told her. "You're strong enough to withstand a one-on-one attack." His voice was calm. Ever the teacher, she thought, even as an enemy tries to escape. Nonetheless, she did as he said, making a grasping motion and yanking the Dijem back. He hit the heads of the still soldiers as he flew through the air, landing hard at

CHAPTER TWENTY-FIVE

Rowan's feet. Rowan grabbed his arms and yanked him up to face him. The moment Rowan touched him, the Dijem's eyes lost their colour. Cori could feel Rowan's Hum probing the mind of the other, not seeking to take control, but just listening.

The Dijem jerked and exhaled a final breath. Rowan let the body slump to the ground.

"Weak," Rowan said. "Like there's barely enough magic for there to be a Hum." He shook his head and walked away from the body. Cori followed him, glancing back once and feeling the unease that she always did when she saw a Dijem die. When would she get over that?

"Should we try the song?" He wondered, pausing before a swordsman. "Make sure it works?"

Cori nodded. She had the song ready in her mind so that Rowan could be the vessel. He put his hand on the swordsman's shoulder. Cori felt as if the song had been yanked from her mind, it was so fast. Before she could react, the swordsman keeled over. Rowan shuddered.

"What was it like?" She asked, though she didn't really want to know.

"Like a bad aftertaste." He turned away and met her eye. "Can you kill them? I could pit them against each other, but…" His hand trailed to his chest and Cori remembered when she had killed Raiyn the innkeeper while Rowan had been controlling her and how he'd felt the blow as if it had been inflicted on him instead. He'd do it if he had to, but she got the feeling he was testing her. Not only because of her reluctance since Dristan's death, but to gauge her strength. He hadn't seen her fight at full power before. Not that killing stationary men and women was fighting.

She turned to the soldiers around her, hands suddenly clammy. Families. Mothers and fathers. They have children. Dristan.

The thoughts rolled around her mind, over and over. Still, she made a scooping motion and flung about fifty of them high into the air. They were heavy, and more than she had ever managed before, but they went high enough that when they returned to earth, the impact was enough to kill them. Rowan let go of them just before they hit the ground. They wouldn't have known a thing.

Brothers, sisters, sons and daughters. Dristan.

She dispatched another unit, her palms still sweating. She had to force herself to watch, to keep her eyes open, to not shudder as their bones cracked and their limbs turned to pulp on impact.

They should have been given a chance to fight her. Her stomach churned as unit after unit was flung into the air to fall to a silent death. She felt none of the fierce joy that she normally experienced when fighting.

Not that this was fighting. This is slaughter. She'd once loved slaughtering too. What was wrong with her? If this was empathy, she didn't like it.

Dristan.

Finally they were all dead. She stood among the broken bodies, breathing hard, arms aching from the exertion. A numbness settled over her, pushing her guilt away for later. She saw those who had stayed behind watching from the top of the cliff road. Thank goodness she didn't have to go back and face them. She didn't think she could stand their judgement right now.

Rowan approached, and she met his eye. She had done as

CHAPTER TWENTY-FIVE

he'd asked, and she hadn't hesitated. She realised, as he put his arm across her shoulder and turned her towards the west, that this is how he must feel every time he killed someone. And he'd feel as if he'd killed these soldiers, too. She may have dealt the blow, but he had held them down.

Well, he'd gotten good at hiding his feelings. She would keep hers contained too, and just do as she was told. She was the weapon, after all.

Chapter Twenty-Six

Not for the first time in the two weeks that it had taken them to storm along the border between Shaw and Hearth, did Cori decide that the people of Tauta were lucky that during his thousand-year reign, Rowan had preferred peace and diplomacy.

All the misgivings he'd had about the war, and himself, seemed to have evaporated and what was left proved to be a ruthless warlord that even Cori would have had second thoughts about engaging had she come across him in a battle.

Of the ten Hearthian contingents that they came across on the border, Rowan dealt with most himself, leaving in the cover of darkness and returning by morning to order some of their soldiers to bury the dead. Cori sometimes saw the aftermath and knew that he had forced the Hearthians against each other. She didn't know how he could withstand the echoes of pain that the blows would have left on his own body.

Sometimes he took Cori with him, and she would tear them apart with her magic. With each kill, the voice of her conscience that told her this was wrong faded. Her enjoyment in the sport didn't return, but she settled into a sort of numbing routine with what she had to do.

CHAPTER TWENTY-SIX

Killing field after killing field, they left behind them. Cori couldn't bring herself to call it a battlefield - there was no battle to speak of, just a silent massacre of men and women who had no opportunity to fight for their lives. Even their own soldiers were spooked by the way their Karalis and Karaliene went to war.

"What are you thinking about?" Rowan's fingers traced over the bare skin of her back, small spirals and swirls. She turned her head, pillowed on her folded arms, to face him. Above them, rain fell in torrential waves against the canvas of their tent, as it had for almost a week.

He wasn't a warlord now, she decided as she looked at him. Candlelight bathed his skin in a golden glow and his features were soft in the semi-darkness, his eyes warm as he waited for her to answer.

"I think we need to give the soldiers an opportunity to fight," she told him. "They fear us and think they have no purpose."

His hand moved to her hair, tucking a few stray strands behind her ear before fingering the braid that held her blue and gold bead. "All right," he said eventually. "The next force is moving towards us from Tengah - probably the army that was supposed to come to us in Lautan once the siege was established. There's about a thousand of them, two days away."

"You were going to let them fight, anyway?"

"A thousand is a few too many for me."

Somehow, Cori doubted that. She pushed herself up onto all fours and made to climb over Rowan. "Speaking of soldiers, I better get them out for their afternoon training, and give them the good news that they finally get to fight someone."

He put his hands on her hips, stilling her as she straddled him to get off the bed. "Harsh of you to get them out in this weather," he teased, pulling her down so he could kiss her.

"You know me," she said when she broke free of him, "their misery is my pleasure."

"That is starting to sound like the old you." He was reluctant to let her go, but she wiggled from his grasp and gathered her clothes from where they had been unceremoniously dumped on the ground.

"Besides," she added as she pulled on her pants. "We stopped to make camp so early today, you know I hate that. I can't let them slack off for the rest of the day."

Rowan tucked his arms behind his head and watched her with a smile on his face. "Do you want me to come with you?"

"No, you stay." She leaned across the bed to kiss him, trailing soft fingers across the muscles of his chest, promising more fun for the two of them later.

"Seems unfair that the Karalis gets to stay warm while his soldiers are out being flogged in the rain."

"My soldiers," she corrected as she strapped her sword to her belt. "And you're the Karalis, you can do what you want."

He laughed. "Have fun then."

She pushed back the tent flap and stepped into the rain. Within seconds she was drenched, her hair plastered to her head. She strode through the deserted camp, making towards one of the larger spaces between the soldier's tents.

There were no campfires - it was too wet - but some of the larger tents had smoke rising from netting in their ceilings. Cori imagined them all within, warm and dry, and she smiled at the thought of them having to drag themselves out into the mud. She took a deep breath.

"Guess what?" She bellowed at the top of her lungs, pleased to hear startled cries from within the tents closest to her. "The enemy is two days away and this time, you're going to fight them!" Heads poked out of tents to watch her. Han, Ether, Eamoyn and Alastar emerged from the command tent, fully dressed and swords at their belts. Cori smiled at them, feeling proud, as she often did, at how quickly they responded. "If you haven't come to the right conclusion yet," she continued to yell. Soldiers were appearing around her, waiting quietly, "I'll lay it out for you. Get out here and start training! That means you too, Dijem! You aren't getting out of this one!"

Within ten minutes, her army, including the Dijem, had assembled before her. Even Rowan appeared, dressed in his gold-stitched leathers. She should have known he wouldn't stay in bed while she had everyone else out in the mud.

Instead of the usual one-on-one sparring, she had them break into large groups, pitting humans and Hiram against Dijem. Cori paired herself with Sigrid, as usual, though this time they were on the same team. Rowan faced his group alone, a nervous bunch who kept glancing Cori's way as if she might protect them.

"Shouldn't the Karalis have a handicap?" One of them asked nervously.

"And what if you were to come up against Cadmus?" Cori shot back. "Do you think he'll go easy on you?"

The soldier looked down. "No, my lady." Rowan held up his hands in surrender, anyway.

"I won't use magic to stop you, is that handicap enough?"

Cori shook her head with a smile and faced her own group. Rowan's group looked pleased, but then, they hadn't seen the double meaning behind his words.

"Off we go," she said. She waited for the Hiram and humans to attack first, her sword held loosely at her side. Sigrid threw nervous glances at her, the woman's sword held before her in defence.

Cori had switched the Valkoinens to steel swords some weeks ago, but they were still learning, and this was the first time many of them had faced a group of enemies instead of one partner.

The Hiram and humans rushed forward in a group and Cori raised her hand and pushed at them. She didn't apply a strengthening song, so they merely stumbled back. It reminded the Hiram in the group, however, to use their own magic. They pushed back at her, and she dodged aside. Sigrid was too slow and was pushed back into the mud. Cori pushed again and made some of them fall back. But many of the humans had darted forward under the cover of the Hiram's magic. "Up," she said to Sigrid and raised her own sword to meet them.

She'd gotten over her hesitation when sparring. Since killing so many enemies in the past two weeks, she had realised that she would not accidentally kill her own soldiers - she was too good a swordswoman for that. Even so, having been beaten once, the soldiers now knew she was fallible, and they took up her challenges with renewed earnest.

Swords clashed, and people yelled in both exertion and humour. The ground beneath their feet turned to slush, which proved to be a barrier in itself, and groups merged so that no one really knew who was fighting who.

CHAPTER TWENTY-SIX

Cori moved as fast as she could in the mud, occasionally blocking a blow with her sword but mostly pushing soldiers to their backsides with her magic. She laughed, as she hadn't in a while, and knew that it was because she was finally fighting people who could return the blow, not killing Hearthians who knelt immobilised at her feet.

Sigrid stuck to her like a stain, barely managing to defend herself and being pushed down into the mud more times than Cori could count.

"Use your magic," she told her eventually.

"You told me not to," Sigrid gasped. Cori shoved a handful of people away and turned to face her.

"I said don't use it on me. It's your strongest skill, you're going to have to use it when we fight for real."

Sigrid hesitated a moment, then Cori felt the woman's Hum flare out. Six or seven Hiram stopped, their eyes glazing over. They sheathed their swords and sat down, cross-legged in the mud. Cori couldn't help the smile that tugged at her lips.

"That's pretty good," she said to Sigrid. The Valkoinen looked startled at the compliment.

"Thank you," she replied slowly, her voice rising as if she didn't quite believe Cori's words.

Cori turned back to the fight. She could appreciate Sigrid's skills - she certainly didn't have the same finesse when it came to using her Hum - but she wasn't about to sit down and swap friendly stories with the woman. While Sigrid said nothing in front of her anymore, Cori still heard her talk about Rowan, still saw the way she looked at him with a sad sort of longing.

Speaking of Rowan. She darted through the fray to where

she could see a particularly large skirmish. In their midst was the Karalis. True to his word, he didn't use his Hum to immobilise the Hiram, but he was in their heads. He ghosted around those who tried to attack him, slapping the flat of his sword across their backs as he passed, and Cori knew he was reading their thoughts and anticipating their attacks. He only engaged for any significant period of time with the humans immune to his magic.

"I'm sending my uniform to you to clean, Cori," Adro said as he passed her. He had five Hiram on his trail, trying to push him over with their magic. Adro's large body mass kept him standing. Cori grinned and stuck out her own hand, slamming the Advisor down into the mud. He spluttered and cursed at her, but she'd already moved on.

She intercepted Rowan this time, thrusting her sword before his and forcing it up into an arc.

You traitor, he teased, jumping back a few steps to place some distance between them.

Someone has to save these poor soldiers from your tyranny. She moved with him, not giving him the relief he sought, and swung her sword at him. He blocked her and retaliated.

Harsh. he ducked under one of her swings and made a kick for her legs. She sidestepped. *I would have preferred we stayed in bed, you know.*

Ah, but this is so much fun!

The soldiers around stopped to watch the Karalis and Karaliene spar. A strong gust of wind blew the rain sideways at them. Cori moved so it was at her back. Rowan used his forearm to wipe the water from his face. She darted forward within the swing of his sword and grabbed him around the chest. She tucked her leg around the back of his. One push and he would be on the ground. For a moment they teetered there.

"We could always finish this in a draw," he said with a smile. He knew he was beaten.

"When I've clearly won?" Still, she released him, much to the disappointment of those watching. "That's enough," she told them. "Go and get warm."

The army trudged back to their tents, laughing and joking about the skirmish. Cori watched them go, feeling good about the afternoon.

"Hey!" she heard Adro behind her, and she glanced back to see the murderous look on his face.

"Oh no," she whispered and tried to dart away, but Adro grabbed her around the waist and wrestled her to the ground.

"Take that!" He yelled and rubbed a handful of mud in her hair.

"Ack, get off!" She twisted beneath him, jerking a knee into his back. He fell to the side with an oomph and she tossed a handful of mud at him before scrabbling to her feet.

Rowan stood by and watched the scene, shaking his head. "Shall I just leave you two to it?"

Adro flung mud at him from the ground. It hit the Karalis right on his otherwise clean vest. Rowan stared at the clump of mud as it slowly slid down his front. "That's it," he growled and dove at Adro.

Cori shook the mud from her hands and left them at it. "I'll get the beer," she called over her shoulder.

* * *

They sat in the command tent, dried, mostly clean of mud -

Adro still seemed to be picking it from his teeth - and drinks in hand.

"So will you tell us about this army that is coming, Karalis?" Han asked as he pressed his smoking herbs into the bowl of his pipe. The captains had long ago stopped asking how Rowan knew an enemy force was nearby and had accepted the fact that it was just another of the Karalis' tricks.

"About a thousand of them. Almost an equal split of humans and Hiram." He paused, looking at the fire crackling in the middle of the tent. "If there are Dijem with them, they have their barriers in place."

"And where are they? Where will we meet them?" Alastar asked. Rowan stood and went to the map table. The captains, Cori and Adro followed him. He pointed to where they were currently camped then followed the Pale River that marked Shaw's border.

"We'll leave the camp here," Rowan explained. "They're tracking due south. They know we're following the border, but they don't know where we are exactly. We'll let them get to the river then meet them from the side, so we don't have the water at our backs."

"All right," Adro said, taking up the pen and parchment that had become an extension of him. "If we're going to them, let's talk about what supplies we need to take."

Cori went back to her seat and settled into it with her beer. She listened to the preparations around her as she watched the fire. She felt calmer after the afternoon's skirmish. She hoped it would carry her into the upcoming battle. She needed a proper fight, she decided, to clear the last of the doubts that Dristan's death had left in her mind. No more silent massacres.

Chapter Twenty-Seven

The roar of the flooding river on their left obscured the sound of the approaching army. The rain still hadn't abated and water pooled on the ground at their feet, soaking through their boots.

Cori's soldiers were at her back, waiting solemnly for her command. The tradition of having humans march at the front of an army was one Cori had broken during the Advisor's war. Hiram stood at the front now, followed by the humans, then the Dijem, save a few who had broken rank.

During the night, the Dijem they suspected were travelling with the Hearthians had raised their barriers. There were five of them; three unknown - though they sounded as if they were from the Tauta region - and two Sarkans.

Myce and Melita were the two who'd left their stations at the back of the army. They were behind Cori now, and Melita was pleading with Rowan and Adro.

"Adro, tell him! They're our friends! Please spare them, Rowan!"

Cori didn't need to look back to know that Rowan would have a troubled look on his face.

"They went to Cadmus, Melita," Rowan tried to explain. "They chose their side. We knew we would face them, eventually."

"Please," she said again, "just give them the opportunity to come over to us."

What do you think, Cori? He asked her.

You know how I feel about Sarkans. The words were harsher than they needed to be, but she could see the enemy materialising through the rain, could feel her blood lust rising. She let it take her as she flexed her fingers at her sides. *Give them one opportunity only to change sides, otherwise kill them.*

She looked at Adro. "Ten paces behind," she reminded him, "until I'm through the front line."

It was a lesson she'd learned early in her days as Karaliene. Her magic was most effective in those first few moments of a battle, when chaos reigned. Once her allies joined the fray, she risked killing them.

The enemy stopped their march, and for a long moment, the two armies faced each other through the rain. Cori took a step, then another. Her strengthening song flared, and her pace increased, water splashing around her legs with each pounding step. Magic surged within, pumping like the blood that rushed through her veins. She was strength, she was power. Her fingers flexed, and she lifted her hand. Time was undefined and the space between the two armies flanked her. Then she could see the faces of those on the front line, could see their eyes glazed in submission. She unleashed her magic.

Those directly before her shot backwards into their peers. The soldiers under the control of the Dijem didn't cry out as they died, but the others did. She pushed again, this time scattering almost fifty of them up in the air to rain back down on those in the back. The screams of the dying and the shouts of their commanders became louder than the rain. She drew her sword. Her own soldiers roared behind her and surged forward. Rowan's Hum reached over her, blanketing the enemy and capturing Hiram uncontrolled by the five rival Dijem. They turned on their brothers and sisters, and small pockets of fighting broke out within the ranks of the Hearthians. Her own army reached her and swallowed her before colliding with the enemy front line.

Chaos like she hadn't seen in a long time ensued. Spells filled her mind as her Dijem both attacked the other Hiram and defended their own from being controlled. The Hiram fought with magic, and as the human ranks met, more swords were drawn. Bodies fell around her, and she saw red. Screams of pain and the roars of battle fury was all she could hear. It calmed her. She could do this. She was the weapon, and these were her targets.

She forced herself deep into the enemy ranks, plunging her sword into chests with one hand and ripping limbs from bodies with the other. She was peripherally aware of Rowan nearby, his Hum drowning out the sound of the others in its strength as he pitted soldiers against each other. She could feel the Hums of the three enemy Dijem attacking him. He didn't even bother with barriers; they had no effect on him. Cori whirled, taking off a head with her sword and driving it through the torso of another man with the same momentum.

Blood splattered across her chest and she pushed hard with her magic, sending those closest to her flying backwards into the men and women behind them. They fell in a heap over each other and she plunged her sword into the ground so she could use both hands to fling the lot of them high in the air. She ripped her sword from the dirt and spun to kill a man behind her before they'd even fallen back to earth.

"Get the Karaliene!" She heard them shouting. "Kill her first!" she smiled. It was always the way. They thought if they could kill her first, it would end the fighting. All it did was draw their attention to her, which meant her own soldiers could attack from behind. She raised her sword, ready.

Four Hums slammed into her mind and she physically reeled under the onslaught. Rowan had told her she could withstand an attack, and she had so far against the weaker Dijem they had been encountering, but these were full, battle trained Dijem, and they hadn't been meditating.

She put her barriers up to block out the daggers that speared at her mind. She found relief and lunged at those closest to her with her sword. She had half expected the Dijem who attacked her to withdraw and go back to attacking Rowan, but they continued to pester her, ramming against her barriers, trying to break through.

Two of the Hiram nearby pushed her with their magic. She dodged aside, ramming her shoulder into a man then stabbing him in the gut as he fell off balance. The Hiram continued to push - more than two now - and she used the momentum to move forward through the soldiers towards the edge of the battlefield.

She found who she was looking for there; one of the enemy Dijem, a Sarkans woman. Cori recognised her, though she didn't know her name. Cori barreled into her, the Hiram still at her back, and forced the woman to her knees.

"One opportunity to change sides," she said through clenched teeth, planting her feet against the insistent attacks from behind. "Say yes and I'll let you live."

CHAPTER TWENTY-SEVEN

"No," the Sarkans woman glowered at her. "You're an abomination that goes against everything the Dijem community stands for."

Cori's eyes widened. She hadn't expected a push back from the woman. "I'm the abomination? You're the one who sided with Cadmus! He's been your enemy... You know what? Forget it." She rammed her sword into the woman's neck at an angle that crossed over to her heart. One of the Hums attacking her abruptly stopped. The other three persisted.

She tried to pull her blade out of the corpse but the Hiram behind had gotten too close; they pushed her and she stumbled over the body to her hands and knees, barely getting upright before they shoved her again. She staggered forward, remaining standing, but without a weapon and unable to use her Hum. She pushed back with little effect.

They closed in a semi-circle around her, and in horror she realised that they were pushing her towards the swollen river. They forced her back step after staggering step, as she looked over their heads to see if any of her own soldiers were nearby. She'd been close to Rowan before, but she couldn't see him now. She didn't even know how long ago that had been - it could have been hours. Her blood lust gave way to sheer panic as she felt the soft bank of the river underfoot, felt its roaring in her soul. She was running out of options.

She dropped her barriers as she was forced back another step, arms windmilling to keep her balance. The three Hums speared into her mind, and she was blinded by their attack. She pushed with as much force as she could manage and heard the Hiram blast away from her. It was too late though; her foot slipped, and she plunged into the raging waters.

Rowan! She flung out with her Hum. She didn't know

if it got past the three that still attacked her. She forced her barriers up again as she submerged under the water. Her back slammed against a rock and the current threw her around like a child's toy. She couldn't tell which way was up in the murky, frothing waters and she was running out of breath. One of the Hums attacking her vanished, then the other two. Her face broke the surface, and she gasped in air and water. She couldn't tell where she was, and the roaring of the water was deafening. She dropped her barriers again as she tried to swim towards the side, but the current dragged her back down.

Rowan was trying to talk to her, but she was so focused on survival that she couldn't comprehend what he was saying, let alone respond. Panic bloomed in her chest as she floundered in the water. The current wasn't taking her back to the surface, and her vision was blackening. Dragon scales flashed through her mind, bluish-black. She tried to keep her mouth clamped shut, but her instincts were urging otherwise, demanding she draw breath.

I was supposed to die on a battlefield, she thought hysterically, *not in a cursed river!*

Something snagged on the back of her shirt. A branch had her. She was definitely going to die. She could no longer hold her mouth closed, she drew in water... and then she drew in air. She gasped it in as if she'd tasted nothing sweeter. She heard Rowan swear, felt his hand leave the back of her shirt and come around her chest.

Her vision was still dark at the edges, but she could see that he was chest deep in the water. Behind him, and holding onto the back of his vest, was Adro. There were more men again behind the Advisor, and now that they had her, they

CHAPTER TWENTY-SEVEN

backed out of the roaring water. The current tugged at them, but eventually they got to land. Rowan let her go, and she doubled over, vomiting water.

"I thought you could swim!" He said in exasperation, though she could hear the panic behind his tone.

"I'd like to see you try and swim in that," she retorted. The battle was still going, but it was muted to her waterlogged ears.

"Can you fight?" He asked, collecting his sword from where it had been unceremoniously dumped on the ground in his haste to get her from the river.

"Yes." Her knees buckled, and she hit the ground. "Just give me a minute." She blacked out.

She came to with Rowan's mouth over hers and lungs full of air. Her stomach heaved, and he rolled her to her side, so she could vomit up more water. She rolled to her back with a groan. He looked down at her, worried.

The fighting had moved close to them, the enemy were trying to get to the Karalis and Karaliene. She turned her head to the side, looking past Rowan to where Adro and the others who had helped pull her from the river were holding the Hearthians back.

The noise of the fighting was still muted, but the stench of blood and spilled guts burned in her nostrils. The scene before her was too much to take in - she'd fallen out of the red haze of battle fury, and the screaming and dying hit her with a sharp clarity.

"Can you fight?" Rowan asked again. She lifted her palm towards an enemy who broke through the line of defence. He shot so high in the air that he vanished momentarily through the clouds before coming back to earth.

Rowan stood, pulling her up with him. "Do you need a sword?"

"Are the Dijem dead?" She tried to ignore the shaking of her limbs. She couldn't succumb to exhaustion yet.

"Yes, save one of the Sarkans who surrendered."

"Then I don't need a sword."

She moved forward. She may have fallen from her blood lust, but she was still angry. Angry that she hadn't been able to fight off her attackers. Angry that she'd almost died.

She passed their defenders and grabbed the first Hearthian she came across. She ripped his head from his body and flung it hard at another, smashing both skulls. She didn't stop there.

She stormed through the ranks of their enemies and tore them apart. Rowan moved with her, his Hum whirling around them, dragging Hiram into her path for her to destroy. With his sword, he cut down any who tried to flank them.

None were given the opportunity to fight back, and she imagined that even the ground rumbled in response to her fury. Before long, the Hearthians were fleeing. She pursued them, ripping them down as they ran.

Rowan stopped her eventually. A touch on her arm and she slowed to a standstill. She pressed her hands to her chest, lungs searing. The last of the Hearthians - perhaps only one hundred - vanished into the rain.

"I want to lie down," she gasped, her voice hoarse. Her whole body shook with the exertion of the day. Was it afternoon already? It felt like only moments had passed since she'd taken that first brutal swing at the enemy.

"No," Rowan said, his voice sounding as exhausted as hers.

CHAPTER TWENTY-SEVEN

He put pressure on her arm, and she turned. Her army was there, and she was relieved to see a great number of them. Spread around them was a horrific mix of blood, mud and bodies. When she faced them, however, they erupted into resounding cheers of victory. Smiling, she forced herself towards them on heavy legs. Rowan trudged alongside her, his dragon head sword hanging at his side and dripping with blood. The soldiers enveloped them into their midst, chanting for the Karalis and Karaliene.

Chapter Twenty Eight

"There were four of them attacking you, Cori, of course you had to put your barriers up," Adro told her.

They were sitting in the command tent, Cori with her knees drawn up to her chest and a blanket tucked around her. In her hand was a steaming cup of… something. Harmony had concocted it from her supply of herbs and other strange things. It was to help with the pain in Cori's chest, but it wasn't working.

"I should be able to fight them," she insisted. "I'm still stronger, even if they have stopped meditating. If I had fought back, I wouldn't have been thrown into the river by the Hiram."

Adro frowned at her. He held a cup too, but his was filled with hot coffee. Cori wanted to swap. "I'm telling you, four is too many, even if you had used an attack song, you would have only been able to fight one at a time. The other three would have still attacked, probably pushing you to an even worse situation."

"But Rowan can -"

"Rowan is not natural," Adro scoffed. "And he's an idiot. Letting them attack him the way he did cost him more magic than he's letting on, I'm sure."

Cori craned her head back to look at the man of whom they spoke about. Rowan was standing behind her chair and didn't seem to be paying any attention to their conversation at all. Rather, he looked deep in thought. His hand was on her shoulder, her neck cuffed between his thumb and forefinger. For the past hour she'd felt hints of the healing song he was weaving around her. Not healing anything in particular, but more as if he were checking her temperature.

He'd earlier healed the bruise on her back that she'd gained when she'd hit the rock in the river, but he couldn't seem to find the cause of the pain in her chest that was making her short of breath. They'd asked Melita, who was appointed head of the healers, and she'd offered to use the healing song on Cori herself. Both Cori and Rowan had responded with a resounding no.

"Probably water in her lungs," Melita had said curtly before returning to the soldier she'd been bandaging. Cori knew it wasn't just the denial of healing that had Melita acting coldly towards her. They'd also found the Sarkan woman who had still had Cori's sword stuck through her body. Melita assumed Cori hadn't offered the woman a chance at all to change sides.

Water in her lungs was worrying. There was no magical way to remove objects from the body that shouldn't be there, and Harmony had told her when she'd delivered her brew that sometimes people could drown on dry land because they had water in their lungs. She put the thought aside as she reached up and poked Rowan.

"Are you going to defend yourself?"

"It didn't cost more than I could give," he replied automatically, his eyes still trained on the far side of the tent. "It did give me quite the headache though." He blinked and looked down at her. "Adro's right, you couldn't have fought four of them, even if you are stronger. The fact that you have to use your strengthening song almost constantly to fight the soldiers leaves little room to focus on fighting Dijem."

"But you can fend them off as well as attack their Hiram *and* protect ours." She coughed and his hand tightened briefly on her shoulder before he pulled up a chair to sit down beside her.

"Like Adro said," he muttered. "I'm an idiot."

Adro raised his mug in a salute to Rowan's words. "Doesn't fix our problem, though. How is Cori going to fight when there's such a big target on her back?"

"I should be able to attack on multiple fronts, like Rowan."

"You could try," Rowan shrugged. "You know the songs, but I think the lapse in concentration could be debilitating. A wiser course of action would be for us to be able to protect you better, so you don't have to choose."

"If you're so bent on fighting Dijem instead of Hiram, we could always put you at the back of our ranks," Adro chortled. Cori imagined herself standing among the other Dijem behind the army while her soldiers fought to the death. She couldn't think of anything worse.

Their conversation was paused by the arrival of Han, Alastar and Eamoyn into the tent. Cori glanced at the three wet - and in Alastar's case, bloody - captains then looked away. Ether, their captain from Balforde, had been killed during the battle. It saddened Cori that she had lost one of her leaders. She hadn't realised until she'd heard the news of Ether's death how fond of them she'd become.

CHAPTER TWENTY EIGHT

Following behind the captains was Ailey and Evdox. Neither had been in the battle, rather remaining at camp and coordinating the servants and other support staff to prepare for the return of the army.

"How many?" Rowan asked as the captains settled into chairs around the fire. Ailey pulled a rough piece of parchment from her coat where she'd been keeping it dry from the rain.

"Three hundred dead," she read from the paper. "Ninety two injured. On the other side, nine hundred dead, none injured."

Not bad odds, Cori thought. That there were none injured on the other side didn't surprise her; she rarely left people alive, and she'd swept across the battlefield after the fight to kill as many living Hearthians as she could.

"Tomorrow we'll rest and bury the dead," Rowan said as he stood. "Then we'll start north for Tengah."

He held out his hand for Cori's and she took it, shrugging off the blanket as she rose. They left the command tent together as those they left behind settled in to celebrate their victory. The camp beyond the tent was celebrating too, with soldiers braving the drizzling rain to share drinks and smoking herbs with their fellows. The conversations were still quiet as they mourned the ones they'd lost, but Cori knew as they drank more, they would revel with earnestness.

She and Rowan made their way through the camp, stopping occasionally to talk to soldiers. When they finally reached the privacy of their tent, they stripped off their wet clothes, changed into dry ones in relative silence and climbed into bed. Rowan kissed her on the temple, but he was quick to fall asleep. She watched him for a time. He'd healed away most of her aches while he had been searching for the source of her chest pain, but she knew he would have been beyond fatigued, both mentally and physically, from the battle that day.

When he was sleeping deeply, she rose to stoke the fire. She hadn't wanted to alarm him by waking him, but laying on her back made it even more difficult for her to breathe. She pulled a chair closer and sat down, staring into the flames.

Adro and Rowan were just being kind by saying that it was all right that she couldn't fight Dijem while she was using the strengthening song to fuel her Hiram magic. Whether or not it was true, that she couldn't fight both was a serious flaw. If she kept using her barriers to defend herself, she would be utterly useless. Not to mention, the Hiram and Dijem targeting her that day had also drawn the Karalis and the Advisor from the heat of the battle to save her. That couldn't happen again.

She looked from the fire to Rowan. His hair fell over his face, and his features were peaceful. She had, for a time, been the most powerful being in Tauta. No one had even come close to matching her. Now that Rowan, Cadmus and the other Dijem had returned to the realm, she felt as if she'd been playing in a pond while they crashed over the land like waves of the ocean.

No. She looked back to the fire, her hands tapping the arm of the chair. She needed to be better. She needed to get back to the top of the pack and stop falling toward mediocrity.

The noise outside the tent was rising as the soldiers filled themselves with drink, their revelry becoming steadily more chaotic as they found an outlet for the violence and destruction they'd witnessed that day. She shifted in her

CHAPTER TWENTY EIGHT

chair and pushed her hand to her ribs. The pain in her chest was worsening. Water in the lungs. She just didn't want to think about it.

The tent flap shifted, and a woman with golden eyes and black hair stepped inside. For a moment Cori was still, wondering if this was an Uaine or Valkoinen that she didn't recognise. The woman didn't even notice Cori, her eyes instead falling unerringly to the bed where Rowan slept. The woman freed a dagger from her belt and darted forward. Cori lunged from her chair to intercept her.

She grabbed the woman's dagger arm and forced it aside. The momentum took them both to the ground, and the assassin finally seemed to notice her. The woman attacked her mind, and Cori let her. This was one of Cadmus' strange, weaker Dijem. This one, Cori could withstand. She grappled with the woman's arm, trying to free the dagger from her grip before she got stabbed. Her hand slipped, and the dagger sliced across her forearm.

"Bitch!" Cori gasped, grabbing for the arm again. The woman hissed at her. The colour of her eyes was dulling but still she continued to attack Cori's mind. Cori wove an attack song and flung it back against the woman, only to have the assassin's eyes darken all the quicker. Rowan shifted in the bed behind them, swore, then was in the fray, grabbing the woman's dagger arm as well. Cori let go and grasped the woman's head, slamming it back against the ground and knocking her out cold.

"Don't kill this one," Cori warned Rowan, climbing away from the woman and wiping the blood from her arm. "I want to talk to her." The cut was shallow, but that wasn't what bothered Cori. Her lungs were searing, and she was struggling to breathe. She watched Rowan toss the woman's dagger towards the fire, then step towards her. She looked up at his eyes, still a bit fogged with sleep, and tried to keep her fear from showing in her own as she said "I think I'm drowning."

* * *

"Lift your shirt up," Melita instructed, her voice still as curt as it had been earlier. Cori did as she was told, and the redhead pressed her ear to Cori's back. "Yes," she said eventually. "I can hear the fluid."

"What can you do?" Rowan asked. Cori pulled down her shirt and turned in time to see Melita give Rowan a baleful look. "Melita," he warned. She sighed and looked around the healer's tent, waving Harmony over from where the herbalist had been administering a poultice to a gash on a soldier's leg.

"Have you ever drained fluid from lungs before?" Melita asked her. Harmony looked at Cori and Rowan nervously.

"I've seen the procedure once," she said. "But the patient didn't survive."

"Good enough," Melita responded. It certainly wasn't, but Cori didn't object as she watched Melita and Harmony collect various utensils, until she saw the long thin knife.

"She's going to kill me."

"She won't," Rowan responded, though he didn't sound confident. His hand fell protectively to her shoulder. "try to think of something else."

"Like how I'm going to find that damn Sarkan after we're done here and beat him until he admits to sending that

CHAPTER TWENTY EIGHT

assassin?"

"You'll do no such thing!" Melita said shrilly. "Keite didn't send any assassins!"

"No?" Cori glared at her. She wanted to yell, but even drawing breath to speak normally was difficult. "Seems like too much of a coincidence that he gets spared and then an assassin shows up in our tent!"

"Cori," Rowan warned, his hand tightening on her shoulder. Melita dumped the knife and two long glass tubes on the table beside Cori's cot with a clatter. Harmony placed her ointments and cloths down beside them, looking between the two Dijem women nervously.

"Take your shirt off," Melita ordered. "He was spared because he's a good man! He didn't want to go to Cadmus. Frew didn't want to go to Cadmus either. She was forced to march with that army and you killed her!"

Cori yanked her shirt off and tossed it aside. She didn't care that she wasn't wearing a brassiere, or that she was in a tent full of soldiers. "I gave that woman a chance to surrender. She didn't take it so yes, I killed her."

"Cori, Melita!" Rowan sounded bewildered.

Melita pushed Cori roughly to her side and crouched down in front of her, pressing her fingers along Cori's ribs. Cori couldn't suppress the groan that escaped her lips from the pressure on her lungs that lying down caused. "You should have given her another chance," Melita hissed. "You should have given her every chance, or dragged her back alive! You shouldn't have killed her! Hold this." She shoved a tube at Harmony, who crouched, frightened beside the angry red head. Melita took up the long, thin knife and positioned it in a space between two of Cori's ribs.

"If you kill me," Cori warned, and she felt Rowan's hand tighten on her arm, "I will find a way back and haunt you for eternity."

"I won't kill you," Melita replied bitterly, "but I hope it hurts." Then she plunged the knife into Cori's lung.

Chapter Twenty-Nine

Having fluid drained from one's lungs was not a pleasant experience. In fact, the pressure on Cori's chest when Melita had made the incision had been downright painful. Not that she would ever tell the redhead that. Cori had continued to swear at the Sarkan woman with the little breath she had available until Rowan had clamped his hand over her mouth.

This, of course, had left Melita free to continue ranting at her without objection. "You are a bully, Cori, do you know that?" She took the tube from Harmony and inserted it into the incision. "If anyone objects to what you want, you kill them! How is that fair? Why did Frew deserve to die?"

"It's a war, and she chose the wrong side," Cori tried to respond through Rowan's hand. It came through as a muffled garble of words. Melita's words stung somewhat, and Dristan's death came to the fore of her mind. Her stomach twisted at the memory.

"I won't let you do the same to Keite," the redhead had continued. "He has come over to us and I know he would never send an assassin. Heal her Rowan." Rowan did as he was told, healing up the incision Melita had made. Cori rolled to her other side and once more endured Melita's knife, this time into her other lung.

"I'll speak to Keite," Rowan reasoned with Melita, "and perform the healing song on him as I did everyone else. As for Frew, you knew she wouldn't come over to us. You tried to contact her yourself, I felt you. You're being too hard on Cori, she was only doing her job."

"Heal her," was all Melita responded with. Rowan did so, and as Cori felt the second incision close up, she took a deep breath.

"Thank you," she said to Melita. Fight aside, Cori knew to be grateful for the healer's help. The red head merely glowered at her, though her anger had dissipated somewhat. She'd seen the truth in Rowan's words.

"I was just doing my job," she responded eventually. She collected her tools and moved away. Harmony handed Cori her shirt.

"That was quite something, wasn't it?" the herbalist said with a weak laugh before taking up her ointments and following Melita to the next patient.

"Let's go see the assassin," Cori said, pulling her shirt back on and leading Rowan from the tent. "She should be awake now."

"Don't you need to rest?" He countered as they strode through the revelries still going on in the camp. She turned to face him. He looked exhausted.

"Are you all right?"

"I'm not the one who almost drowned then killed half an army, fought off an assassin and had holes jabbed into her lungs." He shook his head with a weary smile. "The luck you attract is perplexing."

She eyed him. He'd dodged her question, but she didn't

think he was hiding anything more than fatigue. She stepped close and kissed him. Nearby soldiers whistled and cheered. "Let's see the assassin, then we'll go to bed, I promise." She turned from him and pointed to the soldiers, still watching with drunken grins. "You lot are on grave digging duty first up." Their smiles slipped, and Cori headed towards the tent where the assassin was.

"That wasn't very nice," Rowan fell in beside her.

"Serves them right for not minding their own business." She pushed back the tent flap and stepped into the dim interior. The assassin was tied to a chair and Adro sat in another, watching her with a tired expression. He glanced up when Cori moved to stand behind him, then did a double take when he noticed Rowan.

"Is it wise for him to be here?" The Advisor asked wearily.

"He won't kill this one," Cori assured him.

"I am standing right here," Rowan scowled at the both of them. Cori ignored him and crouched down before the woman, searching her face.

"How much grybas did you give her?" she asked Adro.

"Not as much as the last one, but still too much for her to be intelligible, I think."

The tent flap shifted, and Shaan stepped in with two mugs of coffee. "Oh," she paused when she saw Cori and Rowan. She glanced nervously at Adro, then set one of the mugs on the table. "I was just dropping this off, I'll -"

"Stay," Rowan told her and pulled out another chair for her. Shaan set her own mug on the table and sat down hesitantly. Cori hid a smile. She knew Shaan and Adro were still sleeping together, though both of them seemed to go to great pains to keep their arrangement private. It reminded her of the early days in her own relationship with Rowan when she had feared retribution from the likes of Jarrah.

"What's your name?" Cori asked the woman. The assassin hissed at her, her eyes darting wildly to each side. Cori rocked back on her heels. "Charming," she muttered. "Who sent you?"

At the question, the woman's eyes fell unerringly on Rowan. She jerked against her bindings, as if she might lunge at him. "Cadmus sends his regards."

"Doesn't he always," Rowan replied bitterly. He moved forward to crouch beside Cori. With her target so close, the woman struggled all the harder to get to him. Rowan reached out with his Hum. Cori wasn't sure why; someone who'd been indulging in grybas shouldn't have a magical presence. She said nothing however, if anyone were to find something, it would be Rowan.

Shaan whispered something to Adro, and with a sinking feeling, Cori heard her name. She pretended not to hear them. She hadn't really spoken to Shaan since she had overheard her conversation with Melita and Sigrid and her ostracization by the other Dijem women was beginning to sting a little.

Rowan, however, had no reservations about confronting Shaan. His search of the woman's mind abruptly stopped, and he turned his head sharply to look at the Uaine woman. "What did you say?"

"Nothing!" Shaan said quickly, shrinking back into her chair under the Karalis' hard gaze.

"Tell them," Adro said. Cori didn't miss the way he shifted to put himself between Shaan and Rowan. She would have

CHAPTER TWENTY-NINE

thought the gesture to be sweet if she hadn't been dreading Shaan's words.

"All I asked Adro," Shaan whispered, "is why don't these assassins attempt to flatten our army the way Cori would... or could, I should say," she added hastily. Rowan stared at her for a long, uncomfortable moment, perhaps trying to find malice in her words. Cori glanced down. Shaan's question wasn't as bad as she'd expected it to be. Maybe her run in with Melita earlier had made her skittish.

It had been a point of discussion before between Cori, Rowan and Adro as they'd mused over the strange Dijem. They had the same duel magics as Cori, but they never used them in conjunction with one another.

"We don't think they know how," Rowan said eventually. "Though that is only one theory. Cori learned to use her magic instinctively. It seems strange that not one of them has done the same. The other is that they're too weak to combine them. Their magic just doesn't feel fully formed. I don't know if it's because they've only very recently turned, or if Cadmus, or some other Dijem, is holding them back somehow... something akin to meditation, but that doesn't eliminate one magic or the other." He looked back to the assassin and sighed. "I just don't know. It's all foreign to me."

Cori could see his self doubt creeping through. She stood, nudging him as she did. "Why don't you all go to bed? I'll stay with this one for a while longer."

"Aren't you tired as well?" Adro asked, though he stood and stretched, anyway.

"No," she said truthfully. "I can stay up a little longer."

Adro and Shaan left and Cori moved to sit on the ground, her back resting against one of the tent poles. Rowan sat down beside her.

"You should go to bed," she said. "I know you're tired."

"I'll keep you company for a while," he replied, leaning against her. Within moments, however, he was asleep. Cori smiled and shifted so that his head was pillowed in her lap. Then she took up her vigil of staring at the woman. The woman stared right back, her lips curled in an angry snarl.

* * *

"I'll go," Cori said. Rowan gave her a searching look.

"There are two Dijem among them," he warned.

"All the more reason for me to go."

They were halfway to Tengah now. The rain had finally stopped, and the soldiers rejoiced at not having to slog through mud all day. Rowan slowed their pace as well. Tengah knew they were coming, so he wanted their army to be rested when they arrived. The assassin, even with a lowered dose of grybas, was refusing to say anything except 'Cadmus sends his regards'. Some days, Cori wanted to just kill her and be done with it, but she persisted in the hopes of finding out who'd sent the woman.

Despite their easier pace, they had also just come across their first Heathian contingent since leaving Shaw's border and Cori was determined to fight them and prove that she was as capable as Rowan.

He continued to watch her. It was only the two of them left in the command tent after their usual evening meeting, and he'd been giving her prior warning of the close-by contingent. He had planned to go himself that night. "I feel like this is something I should pull rank on," he said

CHAPTER TWENTY-NINE

carefully.

"If you pull rank, I'll have to topple you from your throne." She was joking, of course. She had no desire to trade places with him.

"We could go together," he suggested, but she shook her head.

"No, I need to do this."

He watched her with his bottom lip caught between his teeth. "It goes against every instinct I have to let you go alone."

"You do realise that I spent five hundred years fighting these people?"

"I know," he moved closer, his arms circling her waist. "But I still don't like it."

"What if you come and watch?" she offered. "That way, you can help if I need you too, but I can still fight on my own."

He still looked hesitant, and she used his pause to insist "I need to learn to fight them, you know that."

"Fine," he sighed. "Fine. But if you even so much as look like you're going to be overwhelmed, I'm coming to save you."

"Always the hero," she grinned, patting his arms where they still hugged her. "Let's go then."

* * *

Cori stood in the darkness, her fingers flexing at her sides. There were perhaps fifty of them in the camp. A number that would seem impossible to many, but was simply a challenge for her.

I wanted to do this, she told herself, thinking briefly of Dristan. How quickly I fall back into old habits. She was aware of Rowan some distance behind her, his Hum touching nervously on her mind, like an annoying fly that she wanted to swat away.

The Hearthian's in the camp were alert as they sat about their fires and tents. They would be aware of the Karalis' army nearby. Cori wondered if they were a scouting group, or if they had been on the border and were trying to return to Tengah. It didn't matter. They'd all shortly be dead.

She moved towards the camp, trying to pick out the two Dijem. She didn't search them out with her Hum. Being this close, they would sense her immediately if she touched their minds. She hadn't perfected subtlety the way Rowan had. She reached the edge of the camp and the circle of firelight.

She drew her sword and, with a deep breath, she lunged forward. Two men were sitting outside a tent, facing the perimeter of the camp but not her. She slammed her sword into the back of one and snapped the neck of the other with her free hand. She whirled, grasping a woman who appeared at the edge of the tent and flinging her up and back into the darkness. She surged forward, killing two more with her sword before the rest became aware of her.

Shouts of warning met her ears as she jumped around the edge of a fire, kicking hot embers up into the face of a woman. The Hearthians formed up and came to meet her. Soldiers had a tendency to group together for protection, but this only made it easier for her to push them away with her magic. Tents collapsed around them and some canvases caught alight in the fires. Cori danced through them all, slashing and pushing in equal measures.

CHAPTER TWENTY-NINE

The first Hum hit her mind, then the second. Two Hums, albeit weak, were distracting. She attempted to push them aside as she forced her way through three soldiers before her. When she'd dispatched them, she flung an immobilising song at the first Hum. The barriers of that Dijem fell into place, blocking her attack. Barriers meant that the Dijem couldn't attack her either, and it gave her some relief. She slammed the hilt of her sword into the gut of a man, then decapitated another.

She wove another immobilising song, but realised belatedly that the notes were off, and were meant for a Hiram mind, rather than a Dijem. She swore, pushed it aside and drew on her strengthening song again, forcing those before her away. They smashed across the ground like rag dolls.

She spotted a lone figure huddled by a fallen tent and she darted forward. The Dijem jumped and tried to run, but Cori drove her sword into his back and felt the second Hum cease its attack on her barriers. She whirled again, clashing swords with the Hearthians who'd approached from behind. She withdrew a little from them, trying to find the space she needed to push them away. She felt the first Hum resume its attack, and then another Hum appeared.

She reeled under the onslaught of this new Hum. It was foreign, like those from the Tundra, but even more wild. It was strong, too, as if its user hadn't been meditating for quite some time.

Ah, the Karaliene, the user greeted with amusement. Even his accent was so heavy it was hard to understand him. *Finally, we come face-to-face on the battlefield.*

Kalle? What was The Captain doing all the way down here? She momentarily dropped her sword so she could grasp those in front of her with both hands and fling them sideways into their fellows. She scooped up her sword again and jumped through the gap she'd created in the soldiers. One of them slashed at her, and she threw herself on the ground to avoid it.

She could still feel the strange Hum at the edge of her mind, as well as the weaker Hum that still attacked her. Kalle made her nervous, and as she rolled to her feet she glanced around, looking for him.

I've dreamed of this day, Karaliene, he mused. *Of meeting you face to face and destroying you.* She parried a few blows with a woman, then darted away between a row of tents that were still standing. The Hearthian's gave chase, and the first Hum still battered against her mind. It was giving her a headache. She wove a quick attacking song. She had missed a few notes, but when she directed it to the weaker Dijem, it hit its mark. The Dijem withdrew just as Cori changed direction and found him. She charged forward to kill him, but he dropped to the ground before she reached him. Burned out.

She wheeled back and shoved her hand at those who followed her. They blasted away, into the air and into the surrounding tents. She was suddenly aware that Rowan's Hum had gone silent against her mind, as if he were hiding. He was coming to the camp, she realised.

Just me left, Karaliene, said Kalle. She braced herself as she continued to fight through the Hearthians, but he didn't attack right away. She veered through the tents, back towards the centre of the camp. She wove an immobilising song as she ran. If she were quick enough, maybe she could attack him first.

CHAPTER TWENTY-NINE

He was waiting for her, among the tents she'd already destroyed. He was just as she remembered from their brief meeting at Cadmus' palace with icy blond hair cropped close to his head and a clean-shaven face. His golden eyes glittered with amusement, and he crossed his arms over his chest. *There you are.*

She flung the song at him. His barriers snapped up, deflecting it, and she had to duck aside under the blade of a soldier. She switched quickly to her strengthening song to push the soldier away from her. Kalle struck.

His attacking song was like a dagger against her mind. She staggered to her knees, but she couldn't put her barriers up; the Hearthians were too close. She dropped her sword, gathered what she could of her Hum and slammed her hands out to the side with a hoarse yell. Everything froze.

She felt the attack on her mind abruptly stop and she jerked back to her feet, her sword in her hand. No one attacked her; they were all frozen where they stood. The only movement was Rowan, weaving through the Hearthians towards her.

"I was handling that," she told him.

"I know," he paused beside a soldier, looking closely at her face. Then his eyes met Cori's. "This wasn't me, it was you."

She turned towards where Kalle had been, but he'd vanished. She whirled, searching for him, but his barriers were up, and he'd fled. She swore, but returned her attention to the soldiers. Their eyes weren't glazed in submission, rather they were frozen like statues.

"Have I killed them?" She whispered, advancing wearily on a soldier with hands raised, ready to attack her. Rowan crouched beside a fire. Even the flames had stilled. He waved his hands through them, and they suddenly started flickering again.

Cori reached out to touch the soldier. "No!" Rowan said suddenly, but it was too late. The moment Cori touched him, the soldier jerked back to life and his shove of magic hit her squarely in the chest. She reeled back several steps with a cry of shock. She heard the rest of the Hearthians unfreeze and there was a sudden clamour of noise.

Rowan did several things at once. His Hum reached to cover the Hiram soldiers, who turned to kill the humans among them, and his hand grasped Cori's - the one that still held her sword - and jerked it forward so that the blade went through the chest of the soldier closest to her.

The soldier choked, blood spurting from the wound as Rowan and Cori pulled the sword free. His hands grappled at the hole in his chest, then he fell, dead to the ground. The rest of the Hearthians swiftly finished each other off until there were only two Hiram left. They straightened and stood side by side, covered in the gore of their fellows, and waited for the Karalis' next orders. Cori knew Rowan would pick their minds to find out more about their purpose there before sending them back to Tengah. All she could think about, though, was how she had frozen them all in place, rather than blasting them away.

She didn't know how she had done it. The only thing she could think of was that she had accidentally used the botched immobilising song that had been at the back of her mind, rather than her strengthening song. She breathed heavily, feeling her body return to the present, feeling the aches that came with battle, and the blood sticky on her skin.

She looked at Rowan, and he met her eye. She knew they were both thinking the same thing; she had discovered a new

CHAPTER TWENTY-NINE

way to use her magic.

* * *

"He knew who you were," Rowan observed as they walked in the darkness back to their own camp.

"Yes," Cori frowned. "He's The Captain."

Rowan's eyebrows rose, and he slowed, turning to face her. "The Captain that sends all the other captains? How do you know?"

Cori's frown deepened, and she kept her gaze on the dark landscape. "I met him in Cadmus' palace. But I'd forgotten." She pressed her palms to her temples, applying pressure. "Why would I forget something like that?"

And she had. She hadn't forgotten that The Captain existed, but her meeting with him, and knowing his identity had completely slipped her mind until he'd spoken to her. Now the memory was back as clear as day.

Finally she looked at Rowan. She couldn't put into words the embarrassment she felt at not reporting on her meeting with Kalle and Cadmus, nor the worry that knotted in her stomach at such an obvious oversight. She could vividly recall battles from five hundred years ago, but not an encounter with Cadmus' second in command?

Rowan looked reserved, as he often did if she mentioned their captivity in the mountain palace, and he continued to walk.

Cori followed along behind him, her bloodied sword hanging at her side. They reached the perimeter of their own camp, but Rowan stopped again before stepping into the light of the fires.

"He erased your memory," he told her bluntly, and a chill crawled down her spine, making the hairs on her arms stand on end.

"Who, Kalle?"

"No, Cadmus."

A horse whinnied and the sound of soldiers laughing floated towards them. Cori didn't know what to say.

"He can do that?" She finally whispered. Rowan didn't meet her eye, rather he stared at the camp, his fingers twisting in the hem of his shirt.

"It would seem so." His voice was tight. "Do you remember anything else from his palace?"

"Of course," Cori said immediately. "I remember breakfast every day, standing beside his throne for hours on end, the two women in my bedroom…" she trailed off, frowning. She remembered conversations too, but some of them were foggy.

"Well," Rowan conceded with a sigh. He reached back and took her hand, and they stepped into the light of the camp together. "You remember him now. You can add him to your hunt and kill list."

Chapter Thirty

Tengah was one of the most heavily fortified cities in Tauta, perhaps made even more so by Cori in her earlier reign as Karaliene. The citizens then had seemed to take her frequent storming of the city and execution of their Heads of State as a challenge. It had once been a sprawling, colourful city, backed by a crescent moon lake. Now, its front was rimmed with thick stone walls and an arched timber gate, reinforced with steel. Cori was confident that she could knock the gate down, but Rowan declined her offer.

"They'll open the gates for us," he'd told her as their army set up camp at one of the points of the lake. From where they settled, they could see the soldiers who manned the walls, plus all the others who had climbed up there to watch the approaching army.

Already, Cori could hear Hums at work within the city, covering the Hiram soldiers to protect them from falling prey to Rowan. She didn't know what he planned to do to get the gate open, and it disappointed her that she couldn't explode it with brute force, but she didn't question his decision.

He returned to the same infuriating calmness that had taken him when they'd been preparing to leave Lautan.

This time, however, instead of fearing for his sanity, Cori embraced his quiet confidence and knew that, true to form, he would unveil something spectacular when they went to take the city.

They did nothing on the day they arrived outside of Tengah, and they ordered the army to rest, though maintain their alertness in case Hearth attacked. Cori, with no soldiers to train, found herself in the prison tent where the assassin was still being held. The woman still hadn't said much, even though her dose of grybas was as low as they thought they could allow it without her burning out.

Cori had given up on trying to talk to her some time ago, but she had another reason for visiting the woman alone; she'd been practising her newly discovered song on her. She sat down across from the woman, who gave her a baleful look and jerked against her bindings. Cori didn't bother to speak. Instead, she held up her hands, applied the immobilising song she had ready, and pushed it towards the assassin.

The woman froze, but only for a brief moment. Slowly, as if coming unstuck from mud, she resumed pulling against her bindings as if nothing had happened. Cori sat back with a frown. In the Hearthian camp, she'd frozen her attackers until she'd touched one of them. She knew the song she'd used then had been incorrectly woven, and Rowan seemed to think it may have melded with her strengthening song somehow, but no matter the variations she tried, she couldn't replicate the strength of that first push.

"Where are we?" The assassin asked suddenly and Cori started. She so far hadn't heard the woman say anything other than 'Cadmus sends his regards.'

"We're at Tengah," Cori said carefully. To Rowan, she

CHAPTER THIRTY

reached out and said, *the assassin is talking.*

Coming, he replied.

A wistful look flashed over the woman's face.

"Tengah is your home?" Cori guessed. The woman seemed to hesitate before nodding.

"Will you tell me how you turned into a Dijem?" She queried.

"You don't want to know who sent me?"

"I know who sent you, in the larger sense of things."

The woman was quiet for a time and she rocked in her chair, her hands twisting in their bindings. "I don't know how I turned. I don't know who I was before that. I only knew my name."

"And that is?"

Once more, the woman hesitated. "Gretchyn," she whispered eventually, as if she couldn't bear to let go the last piece she had of herself. The tent flap lifted and Rowan slipped inside. Gretchyn hissed and shrank into her chair.

"What's wrong?" Cori asked her. Gretchyn seemed to have come out of the spell that had made her an assassin, but her reaction to seeing Rowan hadn't changed.

"He feels like Cadmus."

Rowan jerked to a halt. Cori didn't need to look at him to know he would be trying to school his expression. She leaned towards Gretchyn, trying to get the woman's attention back.

"What do you mean?"

"The way he tries to get in my head. It's so..." she struggled with the word, her eyes darting between Cori and Rowan. "Invasive," she finally finished.

Cori glanced up at Rowan. His expression was flat and his eyes hard as he watched the assassin. She reached out to give him a mental nudge. *Softer,* she cautioned, *you're frightening her.*

The words were probably not the right choice. Rowan shoved her Hum away, and she winced. He struggled to keep his expression straight, but eventually his eyes softened a little. He crouched down beside Cori's chair so he wasn't so imposing.

"So Cadmus was the one who told you to assassinate the Karalis?" Cori continued, resisting the urge to rub her temple in the aftermath of Rowan's mental push.

"Yes. No. I don't know." Gretchyn yanked against her bindings. "I've never seen him. No one's ever seen him, but I've heard his voice in my head before, talking through the dragon."

"Daiyu?" Rowan queried. Gretchyn stared at him, then nodded. "Was it Daiyu who sent you?"

"No," she seemed more firm in this answer. "I haven't heard her in months."

Not surprising, Cori thought. She and Rowan had damaged Daiyu's mind beyond usability. Cadmus must be speaking to his minions some other way now.

"Other dragons?" Cori asked. "Do they talk to you?"

"I - I don't know. Everything has been so hazy lately. The last orders I received were feminine, I think."

The assassin seemed unsure, but Cori sighed. Was it a female dragon or woman? It narrowed the search a little, but the only ones they knew who'd had a direct link to Cadmus was Kalle and the dragons. A woman associated with him could literally be anyone.

"Who taught you to use the Hum?" Rowan changed the topic. "You know how to attack with it. Someone must have

CHAPTER THIRTY

shown you how."

"Daiyu did."

Cori and Rowan glanced at each other. Gretchyn's responses had only created more questions for them.

"What will happen to me?" Gretchyn whispered. Cori looked at her. It was hard to imagine this woman had been the assassin who'd walked into their tent all those weeks ago.

"I don't know," she said.

"Will you kill me?"

Cori's hands twitched in her lap. Gretchyn's words tugged at her. "I don't know," she admitted quietly.

Rowan rose slowly. "We'll unbind you and post guards. You'll be more comfortable with the tent to yourself until we've come to a firmer decision."

Gretchyn didn't thank him, but she didn't snarl at him either. He gestured that Cori should undo the ropes that bound the assassin's hands. She did as he asked, then stepped warily between Gretchyn and Rowan. The other woman may have no weapons handy, but she could still use Hiram magic if she so chose to. Gretchyn stayed seated, however, until the Karalis and Karaliene left the tent.

Rowan started to speak, but Cori held up her hand to stop him. "Don't push me like that again," she told him, "I don't appreciate it." Then she walked away, leaving him staring open-mouthed after her.

* * *

Faster, Cori said to Dijem who were with her. They raced across the realm until the stars blurred above them. She could feel the presence of one of the other teams to her right.

Up, she instructed her own. As a group, they flung their Hums as high as they could, before free falling back towards the earth, catching the other team unaware. Hums tangled in mock battle, and Cori sought their leader.

Adro was faster than she was, and he zipped away from her into the night. She gave chase, knowing that her reach was greater than his and she would catch him eventually. He stopped before that, though, and Cori slammed into him. It was like hitting a stone wall. Adro tried to grab her, but she danced away.

Can't catch me, she teased, just as the third team swooped around them. She lost Adro in the fray. Rowan's team formed a ring around her, preventing her escape. She let herself drop into an uncontrolled free fall, knowing the others wouldn't follow her. Such an unrestrained dive pushed one close to intoxication. She was willing to risk it to avoid capture. She should have, however, expected Rowan to be waiting for her.

His Hum winked into existence below her, and it was all she could do to pull herself out of the fall to avoid him. Without hesitating, she shot off across the realm again. She went west. Over Tengah, over the Western Range and into the unknown lands beyond. If she could get far enough, she would be out of Rowan's reach.

He appeared suddenly before her. She didn't know how he had outpaced her without her realising, but it didn't matter. He enveloped her Hum in his and dragged her back into the free fall. She felt the inevitable laughter of near-madness bubble within her, and then he forced her back into her body.

Her head jerked up from her knees and the firelight danced overly bright before her. "Dammit," she muttered and

CHAPTER THIRTY

lurched to her feet. She'd lost.

She could still feel the Hums of the others flowing about her in the mass energy release as she left her tent and made her way through the camp towards the gate of Tengah. It had been Rowan's idea for them all to partake in an energy release together. Firstly, so they could get a better sense of each other, but also to stir confusion among the Dijem waiting behind the walls of Tengah.

She found Rowan sitting alone on the grass between their camp and the gate. He turned his head slightly as she dropped down beside him. She could feel his Hum whirring in a flurry of notes and songs. At once anchoring his Dijem to keep them from falling into a Hum intoxication and simultaneously reaching towards Tengah, intimidating those beyond. Far more than one mind should be capable of.

"Any luck?" She asked, plucking idly at the blades of grass between her feet.

"I have eight more."

They'd been camped outside Tengah for four days, and Rowan had finally confided in her his plan to get the gate open. He was, one-by-one, taking hold of the minds of the Hiram who guarded the gate. It was not an easy feat; she'd discovered. Those particular Hiram were already being controlled by their own Dijem. Rowan had, through stealth and trickery, managed to take a couple of minds during patrol change over, and in times of stress, such as their energy release was putting on the enemy Dijem now.

Holding the minds - he had twenty now - meant that he'd not slept the past two nights. He looked haggard, but he refused to let Cori or Adro hold the minds in his stead while he rested. He was concerned that their presences would be more detectable than his, and that they wouldn't be able to hold all the Hiram at once for an extended period.

She sat with him for a while, the water in the lake to their left lapping gently against its shore. Cori tried out her new song while she waited. In the fight against the Hearthians, she had frozen the flames of the fire, but so far her ability to replicate that hold over nature had been reduced to naught. The water of the lake was probably too ambitious, considering she had yet to freeze another flame, but she tried merely to pass the time. She could hear Rowan counting under his breath as he slowly captured more minds.

"Smother the eastern side of the city with your Hum," he told her. She obliged, reaching out and blanketing everyone she felt there with magic. The Hiram minds she touched seemed confused. The Dijem, however, knew several moments of panic before they tried to attack her. She withstood the sharp pain as long as she could before withdrawing to herself, briefly raising her barriers so they couldn't find her.

"I have them all," Rowan said hoarsely, and she knew he meant all one hundred Hiram who were stationed at the gates that night. She stood quickly, already anticipating his next words; "Get the army, we're going in now."

She jogged back to the camp, slapping tent canvases as she passed. She didn't yell; she didn't want her soldiers in a flurry, but they came to attention quickly and efficiently. The Dijem were also quick to join the ranks, having already been awake and alert from the energy release.

While the army gathered, she went to her tent and strapped on her sword and collected Rowan's to take to him. She then went to the edge of the camp and waited. In the dark space

CHAPTER THIRTY

between the city and the camp, Rowan rose slowly to his feet.

There was a flurry of motion on the wall above the gate as the Hiram under his control turned and killed their human counterparts. Cori took this as her cue to wave her army forward. The soldiers moved carefully and deliberately, making little noise for so many people.

As they reached Rowan, he turned to look at them all. "No pillaging," he stated, and those closest relayed the message back in whispers, "and no killing unarmed townsfolk or those who surrender. We are not brutes, and we will prove that we are better than they." He held out his hand, and Cori placed his sword in it. He met her eye for a long, knowing moment.

We'll go to the keep, he told her. She nodded, and he turned back to the city. Together they stepped forward with their army at their back. The gate opened.

Chapter Thirty-One

They flowed through the gate and into the market square to the dismay of the Hearthians who could do nothing except watch them come.

The hundred soldiers who'd been on the gate were pushed ahead of them by Rowan and they cut down their own who flooded into the square to rally against the invading force.

Attacking at night meant that most townspeople were abed in their houses. Cori hoped they had the good sense to stay there.

She moved with Rowan at the head of the army towards the main thoroughfare that led to the keep. They wouldn't go that way - she'd discovered a far quicker route in the many times she had stormed this city before - but the enemy soldiers were coming from this direction as they spilled from their barracks near the keep.

Cori signalled to Adro. He nodded and raised his sword above his head. The soldiers behind them rallied to him and, with a ground-shaking roar, he led the charge against the enemy.

Battle cracked through the quiet of the night with jarring clarity. Those first deaths always hit like a cold shock of water. The blood was vivid, the screams intense.

CHAPTER THIRTY-ONE

Cori let her men and women flow around her, allowing the ringing of steel against steel, and the cries of the dying to exhilarate her before she moved across the market square with Rowan behind her.

They found many of the enemy Dijem in the side streets, trying to influence the battle from afar. Cori called on her strengthening song and slammed a handful of them against the stone wall of a building. They slumped, dead, to the ground. Five Hums struck Cori's mind at once, driving her to her knees. The Dijem attacking her fled.

"Ouch." She pressed a hand to her forehead as she put her barriers in place. Rowan pulled her back to her feet with a sigh.

"Come on, Little One," he said and she glanced at him. He looked so tired, yet she'd wager any sum of gold that he was letting the enemy Dijem attack his mind. As if to prove her right, two of the fleeing Dijem suddenly stumbled to their hands and knees, gasping as if they were being choked. Cori knew they could breathe fine - it was all a trick of the mind. Rowan gave her a small push, and she darted forward, plunging her sword into the back of one, then the other. He released their minds and grabbed hold of two more.

They moved up the street like this, with Rowan immobilising and Cori killing. In the brief moments of respite she got, she would lift her barriers and use her magic to cause chaos.

The street Cori had chosen was winding, with many offshoots. It appeared, at first, to lead away from the keep, so they got halfway up the street before normal soldiers were sent to intercept them.

The sound of the main battle in the market square echoed in the night. Cori moved as if in a dream. She used her barriers almost automatically, raising and lowering as she needed. Rowan's Hum wove in and around hers, at once complimenting and urging her on. Together they were invincible.

The houses that lined the street became progressively larger. Gardens sprouted around them, providing a lush green contrast to the stone dwellings. As they fought their way along the street, Cori saw glimpses of the frightened occupants watching the battle through their windows.

"Hello, Karaliene!" The shout came from above, and Cori craned her head back. Holding onto a flagpole and leaning precariously over the edge of a rooftop was Kalle. He waved to her, and she flung her magic at him. The top corner of the house exploded, showering rubble down in the garden. Kalle threw himself back, vanishing momentarily.

"Did I get him?" Cori kept her hands raised. Rowan shook his head, his gaze also on the roof.

"No. His barriers are up."

"I just want to talk, Karaliene!" Kalle poked his head over the edge of the roof again, grinning. Cori aimed her hands at him, but held off. "Funny how we keep meeting like this, isn't it?"

"Come down and fight me!" She demanded. He shook his head.

"Oh no. Not while your Karalis is here. I want the fight to be just you and I, Karaliene. A battle for the ages."

"What do you want?"

He sat up, leaning further over the lip of the roof. "I wanted to let you know that I'm leaving. Our battle will come, but it's not in the taking of Tengah. Watch for me, and I'll watch for you."

CHAPTER THIRTY-ONE

Cori unleashed her magic again, blowing up more of the roof, but Kalle was gone.

"Bastard," Cori muttered. Rowan said nothing, but looked thoughtful. They waited a few more moments to see if Kalle would return, but when he didn't they continued along the road.

They reached a sharp turn where the street wound towards the back of the keep. They dispatched a final smattering of enemies. Then Cori pointed at the wall that lined the road.

"Give me a leg up?"

"Anything for you, my lady Karaliene," Rowan obliged. He cupped his hands and stirruped them beneath her foot, hoisting her up against the wall. She caught hold of the lip with her fingertips and heaved herself up. Laying flat across the top, she reached down and, with inhuman strength, pulled Rowan up beside her.

They both stood, balancing atop the stone wall, and looked back across the city. Fires had started in the buildings around the market square, and their flames lit the night. They could see the main battle as well, still moving steadily up the main thoroughfare. Cori took it all in as she drew deep breaths of the chill night air. It was always lulls like this that reminded her how arduous fighting could be. It was also in this quiet moment that she realised that Rowan was weaving a strengthening song.

She could use her strengthening songs externally with her Hiram magic, but typical Dijem used the song to bolster their own strength and stave off fatigue. She felt a moment of alarm as she turned precariously on the wall to face him.

"Are you all right?"

"Fine," he turned his head to look at her, and his expression demanded no argument. Not that she would have said anything further; the Karalis couldn't exactly abandon the claiming of Tengah because he was exhausted. Still, she worried that he'd pushed himself too far. He must have seen something in her face because his expression softened slightly and he turned away from the city to instead face the keep's dark gardens. "I am looking forward to a long, uninterrupted sleep once this is done," he admitted.

Cori remained facing the city. For a few quiet moments she scanned the rooftops. "What do you think Kalle wanted?" She wondered aloud. Rowan shrugged, and she thought it out of character for him not to care.

"I think he's a coward who's looking for excuses not to face you head on," he offered eventually. Cori breathed out a huff of laughter, then turned to the keep. Rowan gestured to the ground below them. "After you."

Cori jumped, her arms windmilling in the air. She hit the ground hard and rolled. A moment later Rowan landed beside her on light feet. He held out his hand to her, and she cursed his agility as she rose. He merely smiled and gestured once more that she should lead the way.

There were none of the usual guards in the garden, and Cori assumed that they'd all been called away to defend the keep from the army that was advancing on it. None of the keep's inhabitants realised that their two most dangerous enemies were about to walk unopposed through the back door.

The kitchen was empty, though only just. The next day's bread had just been put in the oven and a large pot of stew sat, steaming, on a stovetop. Cori heard shuffling mixed with whispered voices and whimpers of fear coming from the pantry. She ignored them as she led Rowan through to the corridors of the keep. Servants were always smarter than their masters; they knew when to stay out of the way.

The lower corridors were just as empty, but as they gained the main receiving rooms, they could hear frantic voices conversing within. Still, they ignored them and moved to the upper levels. Here were the residential suites.

"Brentyn would already be in the throne room," Cori warned. "He could escape when he hears the noise."

"He won't escape," Rowan assured her. She shrugged, then slammed her fist against the first door. It blasted off its hinges, revealing an older couple cowering within.

Cori didn't go into the room, instead she moved to the next door, yelling all the while at the top of her voice, "Up, up, up! The Karalis has come, as he said he would. Do you want your lives? Then get up!"

She smashed down each door as they moved along the corridors. Some rooms were empty, but most were occupied with noblemen and women dressed in their night-robes and looking like rabbits stuck before a fox. As Cori hollered down the hallway, Rowan following with amusement, the nobles ran from their rooms, fleeing towards the lower levels.

"To the throne room!" Cori yelled at them. "If you're not there when we return, I will find you and rip your legs off!"

"Cori?"

Cori faltered at the soft voice that emitted from the room of which she had just knocked the door down. She backtracked a few steps; her stomach twisting and her breath faltering. She knew this moment was coming, but now that it was here, she wasn't sure she was ready for it.

"Samyla?"

"Oh Cori!" Samyla flung herself at Cori, paying no heed to the blood splashed across the Karaliene's front. "I knew you'd come! They haven't been cruel to me, of course, but I've missed Dristan so much." Samyla pulled back and Cori saw the small swell of her stomach protruding beneath her nightgown. "Where is he?"

Cori's chest was so tight she thought her heart might stop. She wished she could go back to the Pale River and throw herself into it. But she had to tell her. She owed her that much. She opened her mouth.

"He died, fighting to get to you," Rowan said softly. Cori snapped her mouth shut. Samyla looked between the two of them, for a long moment not comprehending. Then her face crumpled, and she threw herself back against Cori.

The guilt was a crushing weight. She glanced sideways at Rowan as she wrapped her arms around her friend. The motion felt traitorous. She knew why Rowan had spared her. He thought it kinder that Samyla believed her husband had died trying to save her from his enemies, not at the hands of his own allies.

Tears tracked down her own cheeks as the gentle Samyla sobbed against her chest. She had killed this woman's father and husband, and she was about to punish her uncle. She was not someone Samyla should have as a friend. Rowan leaned against the wall, then slid down to the floor. He rested his head back against the stone and closed his eyes. Cori could hear the intensity of his strengthening song increase. She looked up and down the hallway. All the nobles were gone, and they needed to keep this raid moving. If Rowan passed out, she wouldn't be able to rouse him.

CHAPTER THIRTY-ONE

"Samyla." Cori peeled the other woman off her. "I need you to go back into your room. Stay there until the fighting is done and one of us comes for you. Can you do that?"

"Yes, Cori." Cori's heart broke a little more at Samyla's resolve. Cori pushed her gently back into the room, then held out her hand for Rowan. His eyes flickered open again as he took it and allowed her to pull him to his feet.

Without speaking, they moved back the way they'd come and down to the lower levels of the keep. They found all the nobles in the throne room and, on the throne itself, was Brentyn. Guards moved to intercept them, but Cori swatted them away as if they were flies. Rowan strode ahead of her now. The exhaustion he'd succumbed to only moments before was all but gone.

"Courtesy dictates," Rowan began, his voice ringing across the stone hall, "that the throne be vacated for the Karalis when he is in residence." The nobles cowered back against the walls, some screaming, as Cori moved through them, dispatching those who sought to oppose them. She felt a trio of Hums - all Sarkans - slam into her mind. She put her barriers up and unsheathed her sword, seeking them out in the crowd.

She spotted them to the right of the throne and was surprised to see four of them. One hadn't attacked. Only a moment later their attack ceased as Rowan countered it, forcing all of them to their knees.

"Or," Rowan continued as if there had been no interruption at all, "perhaps the Karaliene would like to claim the seat. She has more experience with the renegade Heads of Hearth, as I'm sure you're aware."

Brentyn glanced Cori's way as she grabbed a guard by the

throat and slammed him against the ground, shattering his bones. Rowan stopped before the throne and Cori moved to stand beside him, grinning. Brentyn gripped the arms of the chair, and Cori could tell by the resolved look on his face that he was prepared to die there. Well, he was in for a rude shock.

"I will only defer to the true and rightful Karalis," Brentyn said loudly. "Not to one who storms my city, kills my people and presumes to take my throne."

"Very well." Rowan crossed his arms over his chest. Cori let her sword clatter to the floor as she darted forward. Brentyn reeled back in his chair, but Cori grasped his wrist and yanked him bodily from it. She threw him down on the floor and pressed her boot to his back to keep him from rising.

Rowan moved to a window and pulled the binding from one of the curtains free. As he returned, he passed the four Sarkans and let them rise from their torturous, breathless bind. "Melita has asked that we give all the Sarkans in the city one opportunity to surrender. Take it or I will kill you."

"We surrender," one of them blurted and Cori realised that it was the older woman that had often been close by Daniyl's side. She wondered where the false elder was. Rowan merely nodded, then moved onto Cori and handed her the strip of material from the curtain. She used it to tie Brentyn's hands behind his back, then she pulled him to his feet.

"I may have missed a few generations," she said conversationally as she shoved the Head forward towards the door, "but I am somewhat a traditionalist."

Brentyn jerked against his bindings, panting, as he grasped the meaning of her words. She ignored his terror and pressed

CHAPTER THIRTY-ONE

him forward.

"All of you, to the market square," Rowan directed the noblemen and women.

"But they're fighting out there!" One man yelled, his wife clutching his arm. "They'll attack us!"

"Then you better hope you can fight back. GO!"

They scurried forward, the four Sarkans among them, and preceded the Karalis, Karaliene and Head of State out the door.

Outside the keep, the noises of the battle were sharp and Cori could smell the tang of blood in the night air, blending with the thick smoke pluming from the nearby buildings. She pushed her reluctant charge forward with one hand, keeping her other free to defend herself if she needed.

The nobles led the way down the main thoroughfare, screaming and crying as Cori and Rowan forced them through their own troops. Some were cut down by accident, but as the soldiers realised that their lords were passing through, they backed away in confusion.

The fighting paused briefly as they crossed the line between one army and the other. Cori glimpsed Adro, his ringlets dripping with blood and his eyes wild with battle fury.

Retreat to the market square, she told him as her own troops enveloped her. Adro didn't respond, but the army backed down the road with the nobles, the Karalis and Karaliene, and Brentyn in their midst.

The two armies spilled into the market square, the fighting unabated. There were townspeople there too, perhaps trying to escape the city. Mixed with the glow that the burning buildings threw across the square, the scene was chaos.

Cori dragged Brentyn through the battle towards the far side of the square. When he saw that she was taking him to the stone dais usually reserved for theatre shows and musical performances, he dug in his heels.

"I'll tell you where Cadmus is," he begged when Cori shoved him forward again, side stepping to avoid the urine now puddling beneath him. Rowan moved ahead of them, creating a path with both sword and mind.

"You don't know where he is," Cori replied, forcing him up the steps of the dais. "Cadmus isn't stupid enough to reveal his location to the likes of you."

They gained the dais and faced the surging mayhem of the battle below. The soldiers fought, and the nobles and townspeople found themselves trapped in the fray, pushing and scrabbling to escape. Rowan stood at the front of dais, the firelight flickering off the blade at his side and blood dripping from its tip. He surveyed the war below him for a moment, his golden eyes flashing dangerously.

"*Watch.*" The word hissed through his teeth, and yet it carried across the square like a rumble in the earth. Heads turned, and the fighting slowed. Cori pushed Brentyn to his knees.

"Last words?" Cori offered.

"Karaliene, please!" He begged. They always begged. She brought her hands together and his head exploded, spraying blood and gore over the noblemen and women closest to the dais. They screamed, and the fighting erupted again around them.

The dynamics were different this time; the Hearthians fought for their lives, rather than their lord, and they surged towards the edges of the square as if they might escape up

CHAPTER THIRTY-ONE

the streets. They were blocked, however, by the arrival of many of Cadmus' Dijem. The golden-eyed soldiers joined the fray, pushing and shoving with their Hiram magic.

Rowan jumped from the dais and joined the battle. Cori did the same, kicking Brentyn's body away before drawing her sword and slamming it through the back of the closest Hearthian soldier. She moved through the battle, feeling the Hums of the Dijem flowing through the air around her and the heat of the bodies pressing against her. She kept her own Hum small and less of a target. The battle was in too close quarters for her to use her magic. She was content with her sword.

Something's happening, Rowan said suddenly. She looked towards the other side of the square, trying to see above the heads of those fighting around her. There was a disturbance that her soldiers were trying to get away from. She stabbed the man in front of her, then pushed through the battle towards whatever everyone was running from.

The ground was slick with blood and she had to scramble over the bodies of the fallen. A break in the fighting ahead showed her Rowan pushing his way to the disturbance too. She paused to fight off one of the enemy Dijem who was trying to shove her from the side. She bore the brunt of the magic head on, reached with her free hand to grasp the Dijem's arm and tear it from his body. He screamed and fell. She turned away - he would die quickly enough - and tripped over a mangled corpse.

She righted herself but stared down at the woman who'd once been one of her own soldiers. The woman's chest was wide open, her ribs peeled back, revealing her lungs and heart. Cori's breath hitched in her throat. It had been a long time since she had seen a wound like that.

She sought the disturbance again. Rowan was almost there. She used her magic now to push through the fight, not caring whether she hit her own or the enemy. She saw one of the enemy Dijem ahead, a large space around him as people tried to get away. His hands were out in front of him and he slammed people away from him with more force than a regular Hiram had the strength to do. Cori had only ever known one person to possess stronger than average Hiram magic. Rowan whirled in from the side, his sword raised, ready to take off the man's head.

"*No!*" Cori screamed, both aloud and mentally. Rowan stopped, his blade mere inches from the man's neck. The Dijem turned, shoving as he did so. Rowan flew back through the air, hitting the ground hard, sword skittering across the cobblestones. The man's hands came together, back to back, and he made a prying motion. Rowan cried out, his own hands going to his chest. Cori finally broke through the crowd, slamming bodily into the Dijem and forcing him to the ground. She scrabbled with him for a moment, then took hold of his head and smacked it against the cobblestones, knocking him out.

"What was that?" Rowan spat, pushing himself to his feet and stumbling towards her, one hand still over his heart. Cori sat on the man's chest, staring down at his face in disbelief. He was almost unrecognisable with his clean-shaven face and gold eyes. If it weren't for his signature magic, she wouldn't have even known him. "Cori!" Rowan demanded, his hand landing on her shoulder to give her a shake. She finally found her voice.

"It's Orin."

Chapter Thirty-Two

"Who is he?"

"He was the Head of Resso when Cori was first the Karaliene."

There was a long pause, then Adro asked, "so Cadmus is turning Hiram into Dijem?"

"It would seem so."

Cori listened to Adro and Rowan talk behind her, and the greater noise of those who moved in and out of the throne room of the Tengah keep. She didn't join the conversation, rather she crouched before Orin, her arms wrapped around her legs and her chin resting on her knees.

As she watched his grybas affected eyes dart about the room, a sick feeling welled in the pit of her stomach. Orin had been alive all this time, and she hadn't known. She'd assumed he'd died a natural death and that his eldest son had taken the reins of the state. Though once she'd left Tauta, she'd never checked back.

She reached out and touched his arm. He jolted away from her, gold eyes meeting hers for only a moment before they resumed their roaming of the room. Those eyes had been brown and warm the last time she'd seen him.

"It would explain why all his new Dijem are so weak. They

don't have the capacity for our magic so they burn out when they try to use it." Rowan's voice was wooden. Cori could feel the strengthening song that he still wove for himself. Anyone else would be comatose after the effort of the past few days, yet he was still on his feet.

"But how is he turning them? Normally a young Dijem would have to use the magic for years to get to the point of turning."

"He knows the old magic," Rowan replied. "And even if he cannot use much of it himself anymore, Daiyu still could. I bet she has been the one forcing them to turn."

They were quiet for a moment, and in the silence, Cori burst into tears. She could almost feel the look that the two men gave each other.

"Get them out," Rowan requested. Adro moved away, ushering those who waited to speak to the Karalis and Karaliene in the aftermath of the battle from the room. Rowan waited until they were alone before he crouched down beside Cori.

"Why Orin?" She sobbed. "He doesn't deserve this."

Rowan put his arm across her shoulder but said nothing.

"I should have checked in more," Cori continued. "I should have attended his funeral instead of assuming that he'd died. Instead, I ran away and left him and Cadmus got him."

"I don't think you can blame yourself for this, Cori. I think Cadmus' choice of which Hiram to turn into Dijem was probably random. That Orin was among them is just a coincidence."

"A coincidence that he chooses the strongest Hiram of that century? Orin was two hundred years old when I left, and he doesn't look a day over forty. And he was the Head of

CHAPTER THIRTY-TWO

Resso and friend of the Karaliene. I think Cadmus targeted him." Cadmus had once admitted that he was turning young Dijem. Had he also accessed a latent magic in the Hiram?

"If he was targeted for those reasons, then why would Cadmus send him to fight in Tengah? Why wouldn't he have him hold Resso…" Rowan trailed off. Cori turned to look at him. "I think I know where Cadmus is," he whispered.

The words were barely out of his mouth when Cadmus attacked. Cori felt his Hum as it speared into Rowan's mind. Rowan fell back, crying out. Cori scrabbled towards him, even as she heard Adro re enter the room with a shout. She didn't know what to do, so she flung her own Hum back at Cadmus.

It was a mere immobilising song - not even meant for a Dijem mind - but Cadmus ceased his attack as soon as he felt it.

Hello, Cori, he said as conversationally as if they were having breakfast on the balcony of his mountain-carved palace. She didn't reply, merely letting her mind hang between his and Rowan's.

Please tell Rowan that he is welcome to Tengah. It was but a means to an end for me. I look forward to receiving you soon.

Cadmus withdrew after that, but Cori stayed where she was for a long time, tense and waiting.

Come back, Rowan whispered eventually, and she obliged.

Although her mind had been elsewhere, Cori had pulled Rowan to his feet. Her fingers gripped his wrist, and she noticed immediately how pale his skin was, the tight pinch of his lips, the fear in his eyes.

Why she'd made him stand, she didn't know. Self preservation perhaps, so that no one saw a weakness in the Karalis.

Dijem were spilling into the throne room. They'd felt Cadmus' attack, had they seen Rowan fall prey to it? No, she decided. Adro may have seen, for he was watching Rowan with worry, but the rest looked merely frightened.

Cori expected them to panic, to cry that they couldn't defeat someone as strong as Cadmus, but they stopped in a semi-circle around the Karalis and Karaliene, waiting. Their Hums buzzed and Cori realised that they were prepared for Cadmus to attack again.

She watched them; Acacia and Shaan, Sigrid and Bjarte, Myce and many more, prepared to defend their leaders against their enemy. She felt a touch of pride at how far they'd come from the panicked mess they had once been.

She couldn't address that now though, she had a feeling that her grip on his wrist was the only thing keeping Rowan upright.

"He's gone," she told them. "It was a bluff. You should all get what sleep you can until dawn. We have a big job cleaning up Tengah tomorrow."

"Are you sure?" Adro asked, his concerned eyes moving from Rowan to Cori. They must have been quite a sight, the pair of them. Cori, with blood dried across her leather vest and tear tracks down her cheeks and Rowan, almost dead on his feet.

"I'm sure." She affirmed. "In any case, you don't have to be in the room to fight Cadmus if he returns."

Adro gave her a long, searching look before he turned and ushered the other Dijem from the room. As the last of them left, Rowan let out a low sigh.

"You should sleep too," she told him.

"Will you come?" He asked. She turned to look at Orin,

still sitting against the wall, gaze floating across the room as if he hadn't noticed the disturbance at all.

"No," she said. "I'll stay with Orin."

"I'll stay too, then."

She didn't argue with him. He desperately needed sleep, but she knew that after Cadmus' attack he was reluctant to leave her side. She finally let go of his wrist and he took several steps to slide down the wall beside Orin. The former Head of Resso turned to look at the Karalis.

"You complicate things," Rowan told him. Orin raised an eyebrow before looking away. Rowan rested his head back against the wall and let go of his strengthening song. Within moments he was asleep.

Cori resumed her crouched position before them. The two most important men in her life and both of them were so defeated. Orin's eyes came to meet hers and her breath caught in her throat, but his gaze slid away again, coming to rest on his own feet. She felt tears prick her eyes again. He didn't know her. He probably would never know her. Cadmus' method of turning the Hiram into Dijem had so far left all those they'd talked to with no recollection of their former lives. She abruptly stood and began pacing.

The throne room of Tengah was bare of decorations. There were no tapestries on the walls, nor carpets on the floor. There wasn't even any seating bar for the throne itself, which was little more than a tall-backed stone chair. It seemed, Cori decided as she walked, that despite Tengah's pretence of wealth and stability, that Brentyn had sold his own household items for money.

She reached the door and turned on her heels, pacing back towards the throne. Cadmus, she seethed, glancing at Rowan and Orin as she passed them. How could one man cause so much personal destruction? What did he really hope to gain from this? Why was control of Tauta so much more important to him than his family?

Her pacing turned to storming. She reached the head of the room and flung her hands up. The throne exploded, throwing shards of stone across the room. Both Rowan and Orin jumped. Rowan glanced, bleary-eyed, at Orin before heaving himself to his feet. He said nothing as he approached Cori, he simply took her in his arms and held her.

Orin watched on, not knowing them at all.

* * *

They spent a little over a week organising the restoration of Tengah and putting a new Head in place. Brentyn had a son, but he'd been killed in the battle, which left Samyla as his heir. The woman was too distraught to take control of Hearth, and she admitted to wanting to return to Hale so that her baby could be born in the same state its father had run.

"Your baby is the heir to both states," Rowan had told her. "I think when he or she comes of age, that perhaps a realignment of borders will be warranted. Until then, the throne will hold control of both states and I'll appoint guardians to help run them."

"Thank you, Karalis," she had replied quietly with a bow of her head and one hand on her stomach. "Your support is appreciated and I know that Dristan would have been glad to have it too."

Cori had turned away after that. She couldn't bear to be

in Samyla's presence while she was riddled with so much guilt. She still wanted to tell the other woman that she was responsible for her husband's death, but Rowan forbade it.

Guilt at Dristan's death wasn't the only thing that plagued her in that week. She also couldn't stop thinking about Cadmus' attack. Now that her anger had subsided, she wondered why he'd done it. It seemed strange to her that he would so suddenly attack Rowan, but pause to talk to her. He could have effectively attacked her as well; she was nowhere near as strong as he was. She wondered if it were a reminder of his power, that Rowan could take his cities, but he could not defeat his father. Or perhaps Cadmus simply enjoyed the game.

Rowan had finally gotten enough sleep to recover from his exhaustion. On that first morning, Adro had returned at dawn and, after promising that he would see that no harm came to Orin, he insisted that both Rowan and Cori go to bed. Cori had slept a few hours, Rowan had slept the whole day.

He didn't spiral back into his black mood after Cadmus' attack the way he had when the assassin had stabbed him, but he was more reserved and on edge. He kept Cori close, and if she happened to be in another room to him, it wouldn't be long until he found her. She tried not to worry that he'd lost confidence in himself - Cadmus had attacked him in a very vulnerable moment. She hoped he'd recover it in time for their march to Resso.

Finally, the day that their army was due to depart arrived. Alastar was going east with Samyla and a contingent of Hale soldiers to ensure she arrived safely and to take charge of the state. Acacia and a few of her Uaines were to remain as guardians of Hearth.

Rowan had released the assassin, Gretchyn, free in Tengah. Surprisingly, Gretchyn had asked to join Rowan's army, but he'd declined, unsure of whether she might suddenly snap again and attack him.

Orin was coming with them, however. His dose of Grybas had been lowered, and he'd been released from his bindings. He didn't attack anyone, in fact it didn't seem to phase him at all that his allegiance was forced from one side to the other. His nonchalance put Cori in memory of Cat, who'd always been carefree and untroubled. She supposed forgetting one's history might have that effect. As with the other Dijem they'd met who'd been created by Cadmus, Orin only knew his name and that he was from Resso. He didn't remember his wife or children, or that he had lived for two hundred long years as the Head of State. He didn't remember Cori.

When they departed Tengah, Rowan rode at the head of the army with Adro beside him. Cori rode a way back with her soldiers and Orin at her side. The day was fair, and they made good time. Orin told Cori stories about living in Tengah with the other Dijem who, like himself, didn't remember their pasts. She listened to them, feeling sad at how different her friend was now. He was almost another man with features she recognised.

When they stopped in the late afternoon to make camp, however, Orin dismounted and moved to her horse to untie her saddle pack and hand it to her. "Thank you," she said in surprise as he turned back to his own horse. It had always been a habit of his to help her with her pack first.

"Ladies first," he'd replied, but hope flared. Perhaps if the old quirks were there, the rest of him was too.

CHAPTER THIRTY-TWO

She led Orin to the centre of the camp where her own tent that she shared with Rowan was pitched. She saw the Karalis not far off, talking to some men about the water barrels strapped to a nearby cart. He waved to her as she opened the tent flap to toss her pack inside. Then she turned to point out a row of tents to Orin. "You can pitch yours here," she told him. The tents belonged to Adro, Han, Eamoyn, Ailey and Evdox. Orin obliged, not questioning why he was to camp among the inner circle. Perhaps a ghost memory of his previous status? More likely he just didn't care.

She left Orin to his own devices and made her rounds through the camp, talking to soldiers and helping where she could. By the time she got back to her tent, it was dark, and a fire had been lit outside. Inside, food was laid out, but Rowan hadn't returned. She sat at the edge of the cot with a sigh and rubbed her eyes. It was always this moment of quiet at the end of the day when she realised how tired she was. Her tasks weren't done yet, however. She still had to attend the nightly meeting in the command tent, go over the numbers in the army and appoint another captain. If she could, she'd like to get in some sword work. Maybe Sigrid would be up for a bout...

Gleaming blue-black scales swam across her vision. Warm light flickered across them, as if they reflected the flame of a candle. The dragon turned its head towards her and a growl rumbled deep in its chest. She could feel the presence of the dragon's mind - male, she thought - but she could also feel another presence, trying to conceal itself behind the greater mind of the dragon. She tore herself away from them, forcing her eyes open.

She was standing by the entrance of the tent, one hand

raised to push back the flap. In the other was her dagger with its pink gemstone. She stared at it for a long moment, her mind fogged. The dragon returned, flashing into her mind, blinding her vision, forcing its presence against hers. She pushed back and found herself outside, striding through the camp. The dragon swooped back in, once more blocking out the world. This time she could definitely feel Cadmus bearing down behind the dragon's strength.

kill him, the dragon hissed.

No! Cori screamed and shoved at their presence with everything she had. They vanished, and she snapped her barriers down around her mind. The foggy feeling cleared instantly. She was on her hands and knees on the grass, her shirt drenched with sweat, the dagger still clasped tightly in her fist. Horror crashed over her like buckets of ice cold water. Her limbs trembled with the realisation of what had just happened.

Had Cadmus not told her he'd experimentally accessed her mind when she had first been coming into her magic? Did she not now have the greatest reach in Tauta? How simple would it be for him to plant a thought in her mind through his dragons and have her pass it onto the assassins? If he could make Orin forget two hundred years of his life, he could make her forget a simple dream. A pair of boots stepped into her line of sight.

"Cori?" Rowan said. "What's wrong?"

"It's me," she gasped. Rowan crouched down, pushing her back so she sat on her knees. She searched his eyes, begging his forgiveness. "Cadmus has been using me as the controller. I sent the assassins."

The colour drained from his face and his lips moved as

if he might say something but didn't know what. His gaze dropped to her hand. She followed it and found the dagger still tight in her fingers. She flung it away as hard as she could. Tears welled in her eyes and she pressed trembling hands to her head, fingers knotting in her hair.

"Rowan," she pleaded. "I'm so sorry."

But his expression was shutting down, shutting her out. She knew, just by looking at him, that they'd just lost the war.

Chapter Thirty-Three

Cori watched Rowan, who stared down at the table. In the command tent around them, the Dijem gathered there discussed their predicament.

After her admittance to Rowan, he'd finally uttered the words, "what do we do?"

They'd gone to Adro then, and, with bile in her throat, Cori had haltingly told him the same thing she'd told Rowan. Adro had stared between them. "How?" He'd asked.

"Cadmus used to access my mind when I was a child, through his dragons. He's been doing it again, though this time using me to plant the orders in the minds of the assassins."

Adro had continued to stare. His expression turned to one of grave concern as he processed what she'd said. "How long have you known?" Was his next question. Cori cringed.

"I only just realised," she responded in barely more than a whisper. "He tried to take control of me. I came to with a dagger in my hand." Rowan blanched. Cori continued. "His attack last week must have been to test his reach, but I think he overestimated his ability to hold me at a distance and I was able to pull away."

"We need to talk to the others about this," Adro said finally.

CHAPTER THIRTY-THREE

"I don't know what to do."

He'd gathered a handful of other Dijem; Myce and Melita, Shaan, Bjarte and Sigrid, and had explained the situation to them.

"We could send her back to Lautan," Melita said frankly. Of all those gathered, the healer seemed the least surprised that Cori had in fact turned out to be Cadmus' tool. Sigrid nodded along with the redhead and Cori reflected bitterly that the Valkoinen woman would be happy to see the back of her.

"And have her at our back?" Bjarte had countered. "What if Cadmus gets hold of her again? We'd be trapped between the two of them."

"What about going back to Tengah?" Myce suggested. "It's only a day away. Acacia could confine her?"

"A prison wouldn't hold her."

"What if we chain her up? She couldn't use her magic if her hands were bound."

"And what's to stop Cadmus sending his other Dijem to free her? There's still a lot of them in Tengah."

"We can't send her away," Adro said, cutting through the arguing of the others. "We need her strength for the battle against Cadmus."

"And when she turns around and uses it against us?" Melita retorted. "What then?"

Cori stared at Rowan. His eyes remained downcast, and he wouldn't meet hers. She could feel everything silently falling apart between them, the chasm widening with every breaking heartbeat. This, it seemed, was truly the final straw. She said nothing to the others, but she knew there was only one way that she could be removed as a threat to them and that was for them to kill her, or for her to kill herself. One of her hands shifted to her other arm, feeling the twin scars beneath her shirt. The wound that had started it all.

"What if Rowan took control of Cori instead?" Shaan suggested quietly.

"No," Rowan responded immediately. It seemed he had already come to that conclusion and dismissed it. Why, Cori didn't know. Was it because he was loath to do the thing that his father had already set in motion, or because he didn't want to see what was in her mind? "Someone else should…"

"Rowan," Adro cut him off. "You know that none of us could protect her against Cadmus. I wouldn't even be surprised if Cori herself could shuck us off. It has to be you."

Rowan finally glanced at her, haunted. The others slowly filed out of the tent, perhaps at the order of Adro, Cori wasn't sure. Her chest was tight, as if she might cry, but no tears fell down her cheeks.

"We might as well get it over with," she said with more bravado than she felt. "How different could it be to the healing song?"

Very, his expression told her, and who was she kidding? She remembered what it was like to have Cadmus in her head. It wasn't just her thoughts he could read; he'd been able to *see* everything. She tried to quell her fears about what Rowan would think of her memories. They had talked about her past before, but seeing it was very different.

"Just do it," she whispered. She let down her barriers, which she had in place from the moment she'd put them up against Cadmus. Rowan's mind touched hers, slid hesitantly towards the side of her that held her Hiram magic. She felt him taking hold, felt the memories she wanted to keep

CHAPTER THIRTY-THREE

hidden surfacing. As she lost control of herself, she baulked. Rowan immediately withdrew.

"I can't," he said in a broken voice, his hand atop the table curling into a tense fist. "I can't do it."

"You have to," Cori replied harshly. "Because do you know what the alternative is? I have to-"

"Don't say it." It seemed he'd come to that conclusion as well. He pushed back his chair and came around the table towards her. He gripped her arms, and she had only a moment to register the hard look in his eyes before his mind slammed into hers, taking control.

Panic welled within her as her own mind instinctively struggled for freedom. He held firm, a vice-like grip, and moments later the memories that she so desperately didn't want him to see came to the fore.

He saw all of them, some flashing past, others drawn out to torturous lengths. He saw all the people she'd killed, the ones she'd slain in her duty to the realm and the others she had murdered for fun. He felt the furious joy she got from destroying people weaker than she.

He saw all her desolate memories, the ones where she'd said goodbye to all her friends as they'd died and left her, the moment she'd turned into a full Dijem, how afraid and alone she'd been. He saw all the times she'd stood at the edge of the Hen Goeden forest and willed him to walk back out, all the times she'd cursed him and hated him for leaving her.

He watched her conversations with Cadmus, the ones she should have told him about, but didn't because of his petty jealousy at the fact she had spoken to him at all. Hindsight was a lovely thing. Perhaps if he'd known about Cadmus' early experiments, he may have seen this coming.

He felt the depression that had taken her during the creation of the Deathsong, the many cliffs she'd stood upon, trying to drag herself back while the song had urged her on. The spirals of madness she'd fallen into and the violent mental blowouts she'd experienced when she'd neglected to feed it.

He saw all the men too, the ones she'd willingly gone to bed with and crept away from in the middle of the night. He saw the eventual downfall of her promiscuity at the hands of Amante who'd taken her captive and imprisoned her. He saw the many more men who had tried to claim her and abuse her, her near escapes from drugging and rapes. He saw Daniyl and the way he'd grabbed her that night at the tavern. He felt Cori's fear as she'd forced the Sarkans off and the fear that had resurfaced every time she'd crossed his path after that.

"Daniyl?" Rowan said angrily, and Cori was ripped from her memories. He gave her a shake. "I was right inside! Why didn't you call out to me?"

Nothing happened, Cori wanted to say. She'd fought him off herself, hadn't she? But she couldn't find her voice. Rowan let go of her with a jerk and stormed from the tent.

Cori stayed where she was, numb. She could feel Rowan's presence in her mind, more prominent than she'd felt Cadmus' when he'd taken hold of her. In fact, Rowan's hold was so tight that she couldn't move at all. No sooner had the thought crossed her mind, however, then he gave her back control of her body. She shuddered and wrapped her arms across her middle. Pressing a hand over the hole that bloomed in her chest, growing, spreading, suffocating. She could still feel him, he wasn't going away. She couldn't stop

CHAPTER THIRTY-THREE

the bad memories from replaying in her mind, all the things she didn't want him to know about her. She wondered if he could shut them out, or if they played endlessly in his mind too.

Eventually she forced herself from the tent. Han, Eamoyn, Evdox and Ailey would arrive soon for the nightly meeting and she didn't want to be there when they did. She didn't go back to her own tent, instead she moved through the camp, avoiding the fires around which her soldiers sat and had their dinner. She didn't stop when she reached the perimeter of the camp either. She kept walking until she crested a small rise that overlooked the road to Resso. Once more she wrapped her arms across her middle, this time letting a sob escape. She dragged the cool night air into her lungs and tried to clear her mind. She could still feel him. He was still there.

She didn't know where he was, and he said nothing to her nor acknowledged any of her thoughts. This is the only way, she told herself. It's better than the alternative. A hand touched her arm, and she jumped.

"Orin," she gasped. "You startled me."

"You don't seem like an easy person to startle," he replied. "I hope you don't mind, I followed you because you seem upset."

"Still looking out for me," she murmured, feeling another stab of angst that he didn't remember her.

"Sorry?"

"Nothing," she said dully. She remembered when she'd first met Orin and enlisted his father's army to her aid, what a bitch she'd been to him. He'd remained as courteous to her then as he was being now. She wished she could apologise for how she'd treated him.

"I wish you could remember your past," she told him. He smiled at her.

"Oh, I'm sure it wasn't very eventful."

"Probably not," she conceded with a heavy sigh. At that moment she wished very much that she could trade places with him and forgot her life as easily as he had forgotten his.

* * *

Cori didn't sleep that night, nor did she return to her tent. She was afraid of seeing Rowan, of seeing the accusations in his eyes. She didn't blame him for rejecting her. She would probably do the same thing if their situations had been reversed, and she'd had to see her memories. No matter how hard she might try now, she had not been a decent person back then.

The following day she rode among the army, and when they stopped for the evening, she kept herself busy in the camp. It wasn't long before she noticed the soldiers giving her sideways looks and whispering to each other as she passed. With a twist of her gut, she knew that they knew. They didn't understand the intricacies of the Hum, all they needed to know to fuel their rumours was that she had been working for Cadmus. She tried to ignore them as best she could, but the tears she was holding back burned in her throat. Once more she was on the outside and it hurt.

She was keenly aware of Rowan's movements through the camp, though he seemed to avoid her as much as she was avoiding him. Late on that second night, she'd gone in search of Orin and had spotted Rowan sitting at the fire outside his tent, Sigrid so close beside him that their thighs touched. He was staring at the flames while Sigrid talked earnestly to him. Cori watched them and felt as if she'd been punched in the stomach. All her fears and insecurities about Sigrid were coming true. And the worst part was that she knew Rowan was aware of her presence - how could he not be when he was so deeply embedded in her mind - and yet he didn't move away, nor acknowledge Cori. She turned her back on them and felt the last of her heart breaking apart.

By the third day, she was being positively ostracised by the army. The soldiers spoke openly about her, and the Dijem ignored her completely. The only people who would speak to her were Adro, though he still seemed troubled by the situation, and Orin, who acted utterly oblivious to what was happening.

She was with Orin when one of her soldiers finally confronted her. They were walking past a group of them - she was almost used to the whispers now - when she heard the word "traitor" uttered. She stopped dead, then turned back to face the group.

"Say that again," she demanded. Most of the soldiers looked nervous, but one woman stepped forward - a soldier from Hale.

"You're a traitor," she told Cori clearly. "Why are you even here now that your ruse is up?"

"You shouldn't speak about things you don't understand," Cori responded through gritted teeth. The soldier laughed harshly.

"It's pretty easy to understand. You sent assassins against your own Karalis. You should be ashamed enough to go hang yourself."

Fury ripped through Cori. She brought her hands together, intending to behead the woman in true Karaliene fashion, only to have Orin yank one of her arms down at the last second.

"Not this time," he told her steadily. She breathed heavily, and her vision swam red. The soldier seemed to have realised that she'd narrowly escaped death, for she took two hasty steps back to stand among her group. Cori let Orin turn and guide her to the outer edges of the camp.

"This whole situation is shit," Cori whispered furiously. Not that Orin would know what the situation was. Tears spilled down her cheeks once more. She'd lost count of how many times she had cried since Rowan had taken control of her. It hurt. Every part of her hurt. Breathing was hard, speaking was hard and the hole in her chest was gaping and raw. "That soldier is right, I should just hang myself."

Orin surveyed her with sad, gold eyes. She noticed that he had stopped shaving and dark stubble now lined his chin. "He's treating you horribly," he said.

"What?" Cori asked, wiping her cheeks with her sleeves.

"The Karalis, he's treating you horribly again."

"Again?" Cori queried, looking up. "What do you mean, again?"

"I-" Orin looked confused. "Has he treated you badly before? I feel like he has..." He trailed off, but Cori stood straighter, heart thumping unevenly.

"Orin, are you remembering?"

Chapter Thirty-Four

Orin struggled for a moment, his mouth working. Finally, he shook his head. "I'm sorry, Cori. I can't remember anything. I spoke out of turn."

"There's nothing to apologise for," she sighed, looking away so he wouldn't see her disappointment.

"Cori," Adro appeared from among the tents. She quickly wiped her face once more to ensure her eyes were dry before she turned to face the Advisor. "I heard about what happened with the soldiers before."

"Did you?" News certainly travelled fast. Or had Rowan told him what had happened? She wondered what the Karalis must think of her outburst, then tried to push the thought from her mind. No point dwelling on what Rowan thought. It would probably just bring her to tears again. "Don't worry," she said before Adro could speak again. "It won't happen again, and if my men want to take me on, I'll let them, without a fight. No point decimating my own army."

Adro frowned, "I'd rather none of you died. I came to see if you were all right, that was all."

She let her eyes fall to the ground. "I'm fine."

"Do you want something to eat?"

"No."

"Cori…"

"No, Adro." She glanced between Adro and Orin. "I'd actually prefer to be alone now." She walked away before either of them could say anything further. She left the camp, as she had the previous two nights, and just walked. While she did, she practised weaving immobilising songs to keep her mind occupied. She could feel Rowan there, as she constantly could. She just wished she could escape.

* * *

On the fourth day, and another four days from Resso, the Karalis stopped the army partway through the day to set up camp and have half a day's rest. Cori didn't know why - she had attended none of the command meetings in days - but she could only assume that Rowan wanted the soldiers as fresh as possible before they tried to take the next city.

Cori unsaddled her grey mare and brushed her down before heading towards the edge of camp as she often did. She had a worrying feeling that her soldiers might try to gang up on her if she remained in their midst, and despite her words to Adro the previous day, she knew she would have to fight them off and she didn't relish the fallout if she killed anyone.

She walked the perimeter of the camp, watching scouts set up outposts and servants unpacking supply carts. It surprised her when Sigrid sought her out, a sword in hand.

"Do you want to spar?"

Cori stared at her, trying to sense if there was a trap. Sigrid's silvery blonde hair was tied back in a tail, and her expression was resolute. Cori slowly pulled her sword from its sheath at her waist and backed away to give herself space. Sigrid moved with her, prowling forward with her blade before her.

"I wanted to tell you," Sigrid said, darting forward and slicing at Cori's left. Cori deftly stepped aside, letting the other woman's momentum carry her past. Nearby, scouts at their post watched curiously. "That you have officially won." She swung her sword angrily, but Cori once more moved out of reach. Sigrid may have improved significantly with her blade under Cori's tutelage, but she was still no match for the Karaliene.

"What are you talking about?" Cori asked, sliding out of range of another blow. That she hadn't yet raised her own sword seemed to infuriate Sigrid.

"Rowan," Sigrid seethed. "I had a fair idea that nothing would happen between us again, but the fact he never said so left me wondering." Sigrid whirled and sliced. This time Cori raised her sword. The two blades met with a resounding clang. "He told me the other night, that even what we had was nothing. That he made a mistake, that there has only ever been you."

So Rowan had finally warned Sigrid off. Cori couldn't help but think it was too little too late. He was there in her mind, he would be aware of her spar with Sigrid, of what the other woman was saying, and still he said nothing to her.

"What do you want from me?" Cori asked, deflecting another blow with her sword. She didn't attack Sigrid, she only defended herself. Sigrid laughed bitterly.

"It seems we've both been scorned."

Sigrid wasn't mad at her, Cori realised. She was mad at Rowan for dismissing her feelings. She really had sought

Cori out to spar with her, to relieve her anger. Sigrid swung once more and Cori let her sword arm drop. The Valkoinen's eyes widened as she realised what Cori was doing. She staggered as she tried to reverse her swing, but the blade still bit into Cori's side, sinking through leather, cotton then flesh. The wound burned as the blade was wrenched away.

Sigrid cried out and dropped her sword. "What are you doing!"

"It's not deep," Cori said as Sigrid scrambled to her side. She twisted away so the Valkoinen couldn't see the blood bloom on her shirt.

The cut wouldn't be deep; Cori still wore her leather vest, which lessened the blow. Still, it stung.

"Why did you do that!" Sigrid said angrily. Cori shrugged.

"He would have felt it through me. That's all I can give you."

"That's..." Sigrid struggled for words, her breathing heavy. "You're mad! I could have killed you!"

Cori gave her a wry smile and sheathed her sword. "I doubt it. Not with a swing like that."

Cori backed away, leaving Sigrid to collect her sword and stare after her. She wondered why Rowan had told Sigrid that he had no feelings for her now. It seemed like a strange time to do so, when he didn't want to be with her either. She found a tree and sat down beneath it, wincing as the new cut on her side pinched. She inspected it more closely. The blood was thick but slow, and it might need a stitch or two, but for the moment it would be fine with her shirt against it to staunch the bleeding.

She rested her head back against the tree and closed her eyes briefly. She hadn't slept in the four days that she'd had

CHAPTER THIRTY-FOUR

Rowan in her mind. Not that she'd been avoiding it, but sleep seemed to elude her. She wondered if he'd slept. Probably not.

She suddenly found herself standing on the cliffs over Lautan. The waves rushed against the rocks below and the wind whipped her hair back. In the distance, she could see a black dragon circling. She could feel the presence of the dragon too, a mere shadow of its former self, but it pressed insistently against her mind. Daiyu suddenly wheeled and shot towards her, letting out a mighty roar that Cori felt in her chest. As the dragon passed overhead, she let forth a great gout of flame that enveloped Cori in a searing brightness. Cori's eyes snapped open.

What was that? Rowan. Speaking to her for the first time in four days. She didn't have time to deliberate on that, though.

A warning, she replied, lurching to her feet. *Tell everyone to run!*

She'd barely got the words out when a roar ripped through the air, then another, and another. She ran back towards the camp just as a dragon swooped down over it. It was a deep blue, almost black, and it was less than half the size of Daiyu, but that didn't make it any less dangerous as it spewed flame across the left side of the camp. People screamed, and the tents were suddenly alight.

Cori ripped her sword from her sheath and slashed the rope fencing of one of the horse paddocks. The beasts screamed in fear, the whites of their eyes showing. The moment Cori freed them, they thundered away.

A second dragon appeared, a blue so bright it was almost invisible against the sky. It swooped down low, grasping a handful of soldiers in its claws and dragging them back into the air before dropping them to their deaths.

Soldiers ran - there was nothing they could do against the dragons - and Cori could feel the Hums of the Dijem attacking the minds of the dragons with little effect. Even Rowan's Hum, stronger by far than the rest, seemed to do nothing to sway the beasts from their decimation of the camp.

A roar sounded from behind Cori and she looked back over her shoulder to see a steel grey dragon soaring towards her. It opened its maw and spewed fire at her. She turned and *pushed.* The flames swirled back on themselves, exploding in a fiery ball around their maker's head. The grey roared furiously as it swept over Cori's head and set the nearby tents on fire.

This isn't going to work, Cori thought desperately as she watched the two blue dragons snap playfully at each other before the darker one swept down and grasped a horse in its jaw. They would all be killed at this rate.

She turned in a circle, watching the dragons dance overhead. They seemed to have untrained minds and cavorted around as if they'd been sent out to play.

She renewed her strengthening song then reached up, grasping hold of the wing of the light blue dragon with her magic. The first beat of its wing almost lifted Cori from the ground. She gritted her teeth, dug in her heels and pulled. The dragon roared angrily, but its wing dipped towards her. She wove a second strengthening song, threading it through the first that was already almost spent, and then almost as quickly, she was weaving a third. The dragon tipped further to its side.

Cori, Rowan said in warning. She ignored him, threw all

CHAPTER THIRTY-FOUR

her strength into her magic and pulled harder. The dragon roared furiously. Just a bit further...

Cori, STOP!

The command jolted her, and her hands uncurled from their hold on the dragon against her will. But it had been enough. Just as Rowan's order sounded in her mind, she'd heard the snap of the dragon's wing. The creature screamed as it plummeted to the ground, its one good wing flapping uselessly without the other. It hit the earth hard, flailing recklessly among the tents.

As she'd released the dragon, Cori had fallen back against the ground. Now that she'd stopped using her magic, she realised how little of it she had left. She experienced a sudden yank on her mind and for a dreadful moment she thought someone was draining the last of her magic with a Deathsong, then the dragon abruptly stopped thrashing and instead glowed a bright blue and gold colour.

When the light subsided, the dragon carcass had vanished and left standing in its place was the Karalis. His golden eyes pulsed with power and his clothes and hair whipped about him, as if there was a harsh wind that only he could feel. Rowan had used the energy draining song stored perpetually in the back of her mind to kill the dragon and take its magic.

The two other dragons, alarmed at the quick death of their sibling, retreated, roaring and keening, towards the north. The camp fell quiet, save for the moans of the dying and the crackling of the flames that kept the tents alight. Rowan and Cori stared at each other for a long moment, then Rowan swore at her.

"What were you thinking!" He raged, storming towards her. "You almost burned out!"

"If you didn't notice," she retorted angrily, letting him yank her to her feet, "I just pulled a dragon out of the sky."

"I noticed," he hissed, his face close to hers. His eyes were so bright they were hard to look at. "It was stupid." He grasped her upper arm, turning her roughly towards the middle of the camp. "You need a human to give you energy."

"No." She yanked free. Soldiers and Dijem were gathering around.

"Don't be stubborn!"

"I'm not. I felt how much magic the rest expended. They can get energy first, then the injured can be tended to."

"Cori -"

"I am the Karaliene," she hissed. "I will not go before them!" She stormed away from him, through the soldiers who stood back to let her pass and the Dijem who stared at her in awe. Rowan may have killed the dragon with the song, but they'd all seen her pull it down to earth with her magic. She flung her hands out to her sides, using magic that she really shouldn't expend, and froze the flames that ate the tents either side of her. She didn't stop to admire that she'd finally made the immobilising song work, she was too frustrated for that.

The traitorous whispers had stopped, and as she stalked through the camp with no goal in mind except to release her anger, only a respectful silence followed her.

Chapter Thirty-Five

Cori's heart beat faster than normal, a sign her body wasn't coping with the toll almost burning out had taken on it. Still, she didn't seek Ailey to ask for energy. She would stick to her word and ensure every other man and woman had been tended to before herself.

The dragons had killed almost two hundred people, though there weren't many bodies to bury considering most of them had burned to ash. With an air of desolation, they packed up what hadn't been damaged and moved the camp several hours away from its original place.

Melita set up an infirmary tent, and those with burn injuries were flowing through it. The air around the tent was thick with the stench of comfrey as Melita set servants to cooking big pots of salve to put over the burns.

After their argument, Rowan returned to his silent vigil at the back of her mind and Cori, after her anger had been spent, returned to her misery at how they had ended up in this situation to begin with. She thought a lot about Rowan as she helped capture escaped horses, set up new tents and moved supplies from broken carts to fresh ones. His anger at her downing of the dragon was perplexing. She could admit that she'd pushed herself too far, but had he not benefited by being able to take the dragon's energy?

As darkness fell, small fires were lit, and stews were made for dinner. Finding nothing left that she could help with, Cori sought Adro. She found him on a rise outside the camp, looking south.

"Hey there," he said when she sat down beside him. "Where's your tail tonight?"

"Orin's in the infirmary," she explained. "He got burned pulling someone from a tent."

"Quite the hero." Adro looked at her, and she noticed that his eyes were quite dark and not their usual golden hue. It seemed he'd held off on replenishing his energy, too. "How are you?" he asked.

She stared straight ahead. She didn't want to lie and say that she was fine - he knew it to be otherwise - but she didn't know how else to describe how she was feeling. "I don't understand why he was so angry about the dragon today," she finally said.

"I think he was afraid for you, Cori."

"Well, he has a horrible way of showing it," she muttered. Adro gave a small huff of laughter.

"He's never been the most astute man when it comes to emotions and dealing with them."

Cori turned her head to look at the Advisor. He was smiling slightly. "You know he can hear you through me, don't you?"

"That's why I said it."

She turned back to face the dark landscape before them. Smoke still rose from their old camp, blocking part of the sky. She pulled her knees up to her chest and rested her chin on them. "I don't know what to do, Adro," she admitted quietly. "We've fought before, but it never felt this final. One person shouldn't know so much about another."

"Love or duty?" He asked her, reverting to the game they had often played on their journey through Hale together. His voice was heavy, and she wondered why.

"Love," she whispered. "If I could go back and do it again, I would get on Akane with him and go north to the Tundra."

Soft footfalls sounded behind them. "If I could do it again," Rowan said, "I would go back even further and take you south with your sister. We would never have gone north at all."

Adro stood, brushing off his pants. "I better see how Shaan is," he muttered and took his leave. Rowan sat down in his place, drawing his knees up to mimic Cori.

"Isn't it funny that we both say we'd choose love, and yet duty is all we seem to know?"

Cori stared straight ahead and didn't respond. He was right. They both talked about love, about how they chose each other above all else, and yet when a choice truly presented itself, their actions spoke otherwise. Cadmus had tried to take hold of Cori's mind, but really, he'd been controlling them both since the beginning. They'd both chosen Cadmus over each other.

"He's taken everything from me," Rowan said hoarsely. "Everything."

His words were a slap across the face. "He hasn't taken me," she said, a tightness settling across her chest. "I'm still here."

He struggled to respond, jaw working, eyes darting left and right across the horizon. "I know that," he said eventually, but she could tell he didn't believe his own words.

Cori grappled with her emotions. Fury and misery warred within at how he'd so easily rejected her. She could feel him in her mind, as clear as his body was sitting beside her and she wanted to push him away.

"You resent me," he said, and there was a sadness in his voice that pulled that gaping hole in her chest even wider.

"Yes." She tried to find words to describe what she was feeling. "Your rejection hurts and your indifference hurts. You've acknowledged none of my thoughts and yet the decision to end this relationship seems to be all yours. You said forever…" Her voice wavered, and she couldn't force anymore words out. Tears rolled down her cheeks and the lump in her throat was so hard that she thought it might choke her.

"Please don't cry," he begged, and tears streaked his face too. She couldn't stop herself. She let her forehead drop to her knees, and she sobbed.

"I don't know how we get past this, Cori," he said when her tears had stopped. "But I want to try. I don't want duty to win."

She nodded numbly, staring towards the stars on the horizon. He put his hand on her back and she briefly closed her eyes, willing away another wave of tears. "I'm sorry for being indifferent. All I can feel is how miserable you are at having me control you. I was trying to give you as much space as I could so your thoughts could be your own. I can see now that I was making things worse. I'll acknowledge your thoughts if it will help."

She turned her head to look at him. His eyes glowed in the night, eerie and barely human with the excess power they held.

CHAPTER THIRTY-FIVE

"I'm sorry about yelling at you earlier too," he added, "Adro was right. I was afraid that I wouldn't get to you in time to stop you from burning out."

"You have control of my mind," she reminded him dully.

"I'd forgotten that I could give you commands until I did," he paused. "I'll also admit, pulling that dragon from the sky was an impressive feat."

She looked away from him, but a smile tugged at the edge of her lips at his words. It only lasted a moment before her anguish settled back in. "What do we do now?"

Rowan's jaw worked, and the look in his eyes matched the sadness she felt. "Will you come to bed?" He asked. "I know I'm finally ready to sleep."

Yes, sleep was something she could probably submit to. She pushed herself to her feet and felt a wave of lethargy sweep over her. Rowan's hand twitched, but he made no move to help her; he had already read from her mind that she would push him away.

"I'm surprised you aren't demanding I find Ailey to replenish my energy," she muttered as they walked side-by-side back towards the camp.

"I wouldn't dare," he shoved his hands into his pockets, nodding to the men sitting at the outpost as they passed. "At least not until morning."

They reached their tent and Rowan pushed back the flap to allow Cori to enter before him. The interior was dimly lit with only a few candles on the table. Most items were still in their cases from the quick move from the other camp. Rowan moved through their things, looking for their saddle packs that held their clothes. Cori watched him. He seemed different, and it wasn't just his over-bright eyes. Was he moving faster than normal, or was it just a trick of the light? His hair moved softly about his face too, as though there was a slight breeze in the tent that Cori couldn't feel. She cocked her head to the side and narrowed her eyes. He would hear all these thoughts in her head, yet he studiously ignored her, even despite his earlier promise to acknowledge them.

"How did you know that song would work on the dragon?" She asked. He found her pack and tossed it to her.

"A lucky guess."

"What does it feel like?"

He found his own pack and turned to face her. "Heavy."

"It looks light."

He struggled for a moment, then the breeze that touched him faded and his eyes didn't glow so brightly.

"The dragon's name is Seika, and he's difficult to contain."

"You can feel him," Cori whispered. She felt ill at what Rowan was implying.

"His presence, yes. The way I could Akane's. Though hers was given, and this one was taken."

Cori remembered feeling Akane's presence through Rowan when he'd helped her unleash her Deathsong on Daiyu. She glanced away from him and down at her pack. She didn't know what to say - he was dabbling in magic that she didn't understand. One that didn't feel right.

She turned away and pulled a shirt free from her pack - one of Rowan's shirts that she liked to sleep in - and changed into it. She got into bed and faced the tent wall. She listened to Rowan change, then move through the tent to extinguish the candles before climbing in behind her. He lay on his back. The only sound in the tent was their breathing.

Cori felt as if the distance between them was greater now

CHAPTER THIRTY-FIVE

than it had been in their days of not speaking to one another. Memories began surfacing again, ones that had often flashed through her mind the past few days. Was it because she hadn't told him about Daniyl that he was angry? Or that she'd held seemingly amicable conversations with Cadmus while he'd been chained in a cell? Or was it simply how wretched her past had been as a whole? He suddenly rolled towards her, looping his arm over her side, his chest pressed to her back.

"It's none of those things," he said haltingly. "Though I wish you had told me about some of them, I understand why you didn't. It's just..." He paused, trying to find the right words. "Your emotions are so overwhelming. I can barely distinguish my own feelings from yours. I don't know how to separate myself from you."

"I wish I could have a glimpse into your head," she said. "So I didn't have to wonder what you're thinking all the time."

He hesitated for a moment, then opened his mind to her. It wasn't the same as taking control of someone's mind. She couldn't see everything, the way he could her, nor even read his thoughts the way she would be able to if she took hold of a Hiram's mind. But she could feel his emotions.

There was sadness there - a strange echo of hers - and anger, but overwhelmingly, she felt fear. She hadn't been expecting that.

"I'm scared I won't be strong enough when the time comes," he admitted quietly. "That I won't be able to protect you from him. That if he takes hold of you, I'll have to fight you too. I'm scared of how like him I am. I can see it in your mind, the comparisons, though you don't intentionally make them. Why am I any more deserving of being the Karalis than he?

We've both ripped this realm apart, and for what?" he took a deep, shaking breath, burying his face in her hair. "I'm scared that when the time comes to kill him, I won't be able to, because he's my father and at one point in my life, I loved him."

His words hung in the darkness between them. She could still feel the fear in his mind, and his words had given it context. They were very different fears to her own, and she'd never considered that he might be carrying them around because he was afraid of what she would think of him... Just like she had been when she'd let him take control of her mind.

She had no words of comfort to offer him, they were legitimate concerns that she had no explanation for. They could only keep moving forward and hope for the best. They'd come too far to do otherwise. She took his hand and squeezed it.

"Hope for the best," he echoed her thoughts. His fingers found the sapphire ring on her hand, and he fiddled with it. She remembered the day he'd given it to her. Her seventeenth birthday. A time before she'd loved him, but he'd been her closest friend. It had just been the two of them against the world.

Rowan relaxed against her. "That's a nicer memory," he said. She could hear relief in his voice and she finally grasped just how her misery and constant recalling of bad memories had been affecting him until now. She returned to the memory. It had been winter, and he'd been using his sword. She remembered, with a wry amusement, how she'd not understood why he was training with it. She'd never even touched such a weapon. That was also the day she'd gone on

CHAPTER THIRTY-FIVE

her first date with Quart. Rowan had been so jealous of him.

I was not, he said haughtily in her mind. *Jealous of a rat like him? Come on...*

She breathed out a huff of laughter and let the memory play through. Quart had died many centuries ago - she no longer felt anything for him, other than that he had been a part of her childhood. Rowan watched the memory too, cringing along with her when Quart kissed her in the coffee shop, laughing at her excitement when she had later told Saasha about Quart over her birthday cake.

They eventually fell asleep watching the happier memories of her childhood, their shared days when they had been the only two Dijem in the realm and the world had been theirs.

Chapter Thirty-Six

When Cori woke, it was light. Outside the tent, she could hear voices in conversation, though not the usual hustle of the morning camp. She was instantly aware of Rowan in her mind, even as she felt the weight of his arm still draped over her.

A spur of confused emotions stirred within her. Despite their physical closeness, she could still feel a distance between them that she couldn't find a reason for. He wanted to try and work things out, so why did she just want to push him away?

He stirred with a groan. "Do you always think so hard in the morning?"

She shrugged his arm off and he obliged her, rolling over onto his back and rubbing his face. Cori rolled over as well and became acutely aware of how much pain her body was in. She'd put off renewing her energy for long enough. Her organs were failing, she needed a human.

"Rowan," she began, "can you get-"

He was already rolling out of bed, having read the thought from her mind. She scowled as she tried to sit up. "I wasn't finished talking."

He jerked to a stop in the middle of the tent and turned

CHAPTER THIRTY-SIX

back to face her. "Last night you wanted me to acknowledge what you were thinking, and now you don't?" He lifted his hands, palms up, fingers spread wide. "What do you want me to do?"

"Just get Ailey," she groaned, falling back against her pillow as a wave of dizziness engulfed her. He returned to her instead, climbing across the bed towards her.

"Adro will get Ailey," he said in response to her baleful look. He put his hand on her, but hesitated. "Can I heal you?"

"It's not like you'll see anything more than you already have."

"Cori," he sighed, looking down as he started the healing song. "I hate this too, don't you understand that?"

She closed her eyes, struggling to control her frustration. It wasn't his fault. This was the only way. "Sorry," she said. She kept her eyes closed and listened to the healing song. It was slow going, and she wasn't feeling less pain because of it.

"You have no energy to sustain yourself," Rowan murmured. "Start weaving the song, Ailey will be here in a moment."

The tent flap opened, and Adro and Ailey entered.

"It's past noon," Rowan said irritably as Ailey moved to the bed to sit beside Cori. She uttered the words of offering and Cori felt herself filling with a glowing light.

"You needed to sleep," Adro replied. "Both of you."

"We don't," Rowan retorted. The healing song abruptly stopped as Cori felt her energy levels rising. Rowan stood, and she immediately sat up and climbed towards the edge of the bed.

"Tell everyone to pack up," she told Adro. "We'll get as far as we can today."

Adro surveyed them both with a stony expression, then sighed. "You're impossible," he muttered and turned and left the tent. He promptly began bellowing orders, and Cori heard the soldiers outside hurry to attention.

"Thank you," she said to Ailey.

"I think you might need someone else," Ailey told her. "Your eyes are still a bit dark."

"I'll be fine," she responded at the same time that Rowan said, "send Evdox."

The two of them stared at each other, while Ailey shifted nervously towards the door. Wind whipped around Rowan and his eyes pulsed with power as he let some of the dragon's presence show. No, the Dragon's Fury, Cori decided. This beast did not want to be contained.

As she watched, she had the sudden urge to fight him. Not because she was angry, but simply because she wanted to see if she could take him on. Her fingers flexed at her side and he bared his teeth in a feral grin, goading her on. She felt a hard smile curl her own lips, but she shifted her hands behind her back. "Ailey," she said, stopping the woman as she was sliding through the doorway. "Send Evdox."

She wouldn't fight Rowan today, though she was very curious to see what would happen.

* * *

The mood of the army over the next few days was confusing and tumultuous. On one hand, they were deathly afraid of being attacked again; Cori saw many of them glancing furtively towards the sky and confiding in each other of

CHAPTER THIRTY-SIX

experiencing nightmares drenched in flames and screams. Some of them looked as if they hadn't been sleeping at all.

On the other hand, she could see hope in their eyes when she passed them, and hear it in their voices when they addressed her. Their Karaliene had achieved an impossible feat and pulled a dragon from the sky.

Cori had not forgotten that only days earlier they'd been calling her a traitor to her face. She didn't raise the matter with any of them, nor respond bitterly to their renewed adoration. She'd been the Karaliene once before; she knew how the popularity of a leader could change as quickly as the wind, though in the face of the turnabout, she wondered how Rowan had always maintained a constant confidence with the people he ruled over.

You have to be consistent, he responded to her thoughts. She was becoming accustomed to him being in the back of her mind, sometimes going through brief periods where she forgot he was there at all. In those times he didn't respond to her thoughts, perhaps sensing the time to herself was helping mend their relationship. Otherwise, he often intruded on her contemplation, responding to her musings in such an offhand way that she wondered if he realised he was doing it.

In the following three days of travel, and after their stand off in the tent, Rowan had ridden at the head of the army, whilst Cori had ridden among the troops. They'd needed the space from each other; Cori's feelings towards him had been nothing short of bipolar. She went through stages of resenting him, her mind pushing against his in an attempt to expel him as if he were a foreign matter. Other times she felt sad for the both of them. She had to remind herself that there was no other way, that Rowan disliked having to control her as much as she did.

In the evenings, they forced themselves into each other's company. Being physically close to him, and having him in her head, was suffocating, and she knew he was being affected by her thoughts too. If she were feeling moody, he would be the one who would suddenly snap at passersby.

He was trying his best to make things work though, so Cori did too. At night, as they lay down in bed together, Cori would try to recall some happier memories. Some of them were from her childhood, growing up in the palace with the other servants, and later under his tutelage. She recalled the years, though tainted with sadness, when she had lived with Saasha, and later Orin. She showed him memories of Shanti, the old Hiram woman from Dodici who had trained her to use a sword properly, and of the colourful and exotic parties hosted by the Twelve Kings. She had many recent memories too; her latest birthday, and the rare, quiet moments they had spent together in Lautan while they had rebuilt their kingdom. Even the invincibility she felt when fighting alongside him; she showed them all to him.

And in turn, Rowan would open his mind to her. Sometimes his fears were so heavy that she wondered how he was not paralysed beneath them, other times she could sense the joy and contentment that he felt when she showed him her more pleasant recollections. Slowly they healed.

I am consistent, Cori replied, returning to her current thought. *It's the rumours that aren't.*

Perhaps. He withdrew, and she turned to Orin, who was at her side. There was no trace of the burns that had marred his arms after the battle with the dragons. Now that he was Dijem, he could be healed with the healing song.

After Melita had healed the former Head of Resso, Cori had sought her out to ask her if she had seen anything in Orin's mind that might help them unlock his lost memory.

"I won't betray my patient's trust," Melita had responded, giving Cori a haughty look. Though most of the Dijem were now treating Cori with a strange kind of reverence, Melita still openly maintained her dislike and disapproval of her. Cori had to admit a healthy respect for the redhead; Melita was the definition of consistency.

Cori hadn't backed down at Melita's statement, however, and had stared the woman down. She'd wished in that moment that she possessed Rowan's power of presence. He'd appeared in her mind then, as if she'd summoned him, and had woven a small song.

It was a strange feeling, having her own magic used without her input. The song was short, with similar notes to a strengthening song. She felt a quick flare of heat within her, but nothing else happened... except that Melita suddenly looked a bit disconcerted and broke eye contact with her. Had Rowan made her eyes flash the way his sometimes did?

"There was nothing strange about his mind," Melita had finally conceded. "Mostly his thoughts were occupied with the pain of the burns." She hesitated, then added, "he seemed like a very selfless person. More so than anyone else I've healed. He was very concerned with the wellbeing of others around him. I don't know if that's a product of losing many of his memories."

"No," Cori had said. "He's always been that way. Thank you."

Now she listened to Orin telling her an inconsequential story about a brawl he'd once broken up in a tavern in Bandar Utara, and she wondered if there was any hope of bringing his history back to him.

"... And the second man claimed that the first had slept with his wife. Ugly bloke, the first, so I didn't really believe - oh, hello." Cori glanced back to see Sigrid moving her horse up beside Orin's. She'd seen Sigrid a few times since the bout that Cori had conceded to her; they'd even sparred twice more. Despite Rowan's rejection of her, Sigrid seemed to have made her peace with Cori.

"The sun is getting low," Sigrid said, once she had returned Orin's greeting.

"We'll stop for camp soon," Cori replied. "There's a good forested area up ahead that will provide us cover for the night."

Sigrid nodded, but at the same time she said "trees are a fire hazard."

Cori knew that Sigrid - like everyone else - was afraid that the other two dragons would return to finish the job. She herself didn't know how to feel. If the dragons came back, she would just have to try to take down another one and hope that she could survive once more.

You've defeated three dragons now, Rowan said. *That's quite a feat.*

She didn't agree. Rowan had killed the green dragon, and the blue from a few days before. Even in the downfall of Daiyu, he'd been the driving force behind releasing the Deathsong from Cori's mind.

You underestimate yourself. None of those things would have been possible without your actions first.

CHAPTER THIRTY-SIX

"The trees won't burn as fast as being hit directly with the flame from the dragon's maw," Cori replied to Sigrid, ignoring Rowan. "At least under the cover of trees, the soldiers have some chance of escape."

She didn't voice her concerns of what would happen after that. Eventually they'd have to face the dragons, and men always came off second best to the beasts.

"Will we spar this evening?" Sigrid asked, drawing Cori back to their conversation. She smiled at the Valkoinen.

"Yes, I think so. Being so close to Resso, I think I might get all the soldiers out for a bout."

"You're good with a sword?" Orin asked Sigrid. Both women laughed.

"I'm dismal," she admitted, with a glance at Cori, "but I find it a good outlet for stress. What about you, Orin? What's your preferred weapon?"

"My magic," he said, holding his hands up. "I can use a sword, but using my hands feels much more natural."

"My magic is my strongest point too," Sigrid replied, though she tapped her head. "I -" she suddenly looked before them, scowling. Cori followed her gaze to see Rowan cantering down the column towards them.

"I'll go meet him," Cori said before Sigrid could turn her horse and escape. She pushed her grey mare into a trot to cover the distance to the Karalis.

"Hello," he said when they reached each other. He wheeled Mischief around and urged him alongside the mare. He said nothing further, rather just rode at her side.

"Were you looking for me for something?" Cori asked eventually. That stifling feeling she got when she was in close proximity to him was rising.

"I wanted to ride with you, that's all," he told her and she could sense discomfort from him, a product of the hostile emotions he was feeling from her. She closed her eyes and took a deep breath, then another. It's not his fault, she told herself. Not his fault.

"It's not your fault either," he said quietly, then changed the subject. "The head of the army is stopping now. They've reached the wooded area. Adro wants to speak to us too."

"He wasn't up there with you?"

"No, he's been riding with Shaan lately."

They crested a hill and saw the forest sprawled out before them, covering the next few valleys. The head of the army was already spreading out, dispersing among the trees. They rode past the tents being erected beneath the canopy and found Adro a few hundred metres from the treeline.

He was watching them approach, shifting his weight nervously from one foot to the other. He'd been withdrawn lately, and Cori wondered suddenly if, despite her and Rowan's problems, that perhaps they should have been paying more attention to their friend.

"Adro," Rowan greeted as they dismounted before the Advisor. A servant came by to lead their horses away.

"There's something I need to tell you before we get to Bandar Utara," Adro said without preamble. Cori and Rowan glanced at each other.

This sounds bad, Cori said. Rowan gestured that Adro should continue. The Advisor pressed a trembling hand over his wild hair, then waved to them to follow him. They moved further from the camp, completely out of earshot. He glanced around again, checking no one was about.

"Shaan is pregnant."

CHAPTER THIRTY-SIX

The words tumbling from his mouth were almost unintelligible, yet Cori couldn't stop the sharp pang of jealousy that stabbed her in the gut. She simultaneously felt herself flush with horror as she remembered that Rowan could feel everything she did. She pushed the emotions away so forcefully that she was sure she almost expelled Rowan from her mind. But it was too late, the damage was done.

Rowan's eyebrows had risen at Adro's news, but at the revelation of Cori's feelings, all the colour drained from his face. *Why didn't you tell me?* He whispered in her mind. *Why wouldn't you tell me something like that?*

"This is bad, isn't it?" Adro said, misreading their twin expressions of horror. "I mean, we all know how babies are made, but Dijem women usually take hundreds, if not thousands of years to fall pregnant. Will either of you say something?"

"It's not bad," Rowan replied woodenly. "Well, perhaps the timing is, but..." He struggled for a moment then added, "congratulations."

"What do we do?" Adro asked, and Cori could hear the fear in his voice. It wasn't dissimilar to the way she and Rowan had gone to Adro for help when she'd discovered that Cadmus had been using her.

"Shaan should leave," she said, and Adro's shoulders slumped in relief.

"She could go back to Acacia," he said. "I told her that. She's resistant."

"No. She needs to leave Tauta altogether," Cori responded, almost harshly. "Send her south, to your homeland. If Cadmus wins..." She trailed off as the fear returned to Adro's expression.

"Cori's right," Rowan's voice was still stiff. "Shaan and the baby will be safest outside of this realm. And you should go with them."

"What?" Adro looked as if the thought had never even crossed his mind. "I won't leave you. I helped start this war, I'll help finish it."

Love or duty, Cori thought. Duty had trapped Adro, too.

"Adro," Rowan tried to reason. "You should be with your family. We will cope."

The look Adro gave them both clearly said that he didn't think they would cope at all. He was probably right. The army would most likely still be in Lautan without Adro keeping things moving. Rowan must have agreed with Adro's look because he said nothing further. Adro sighed.

"I should find Shaan and tell her." As Adro turned away from them, his hand once more nervously playing with his hair, Cori did the same.

"Cori." Rowan followed her as she walked away towards the treeline again. She didn't want to talk to him. Her feelings should be her own, shared when she wanted to share them. "Cori, please talk to me!"

She halted at the treeline, and Rowan stepped up beside her. For a moment they watched the back of the army moving down the hill to the forest.

"I understand why there are some things you don't want to tell me," he said eventually, "but why this? Why hide something you so desperately want?"

"Because," Cori kept her eyes on the soldiers so she could avoid his gaze, "desperately wanting something doesn't mean that it will ever happen."

"Why wouldn't you talk to me about it? It's a decision that

involves us both, isn't it?"

Was it? She hadn't truly considered children since she'd been with Dahl. They'd never intended to parent together. He had offered; she had accepted. That's how human relationships worked. Only one parent needed to want the children because human relationships weren't always monogamous. The relationship dynamics didn't really matter, anyway. She had other reasons for not raising it with Rowan.

"I never told you," she said, finally turning to look at him, "because I never intended to act on it. Maybe once I could have been a mother, but not anymore. I'm a killer, Rowan, and killers shouldn't raise children."

He said nothing, and she took his silence for agreement.

"I don't agree with you," he responded softly to her thoughts. "I... just don't know what to say."

She snorted derisively. "Do *you* even want to have children?"

"I..." He trailed off, looking confused. "Don't know," he finished. He let his head fall in defeat. "More and more I can't help thinking how different things could have been for us if we'd never gone north when the Advisor had seized control of the palace. Who would we be if we had simply run away?"

It was something Cori had often thought about too. Would they have even been together at all? Rowan had only admitted his feelings for her in an angry outburst. She had only realised hers when she thought she might lose him. Would they have tried as hard as they were now to make their relationship work if they hadn't been through the hardships they had? She didn't have an answer to that.

Rowan's fingers on her wrist brought her back to her surroundings with a jolt. He gave her hand a tentative tug and when she didn't resist; he pulled her into his arms. "I wish I could give you everything you deserve."

She laughed bitterly against his shirt. "I think I've gotten everything I deserve, actually."

He laughed with her, then sighed. "Thank goodness we have Adro looking out for us. I don't pay him nearly enough."

Cori nodded, then pulled back to look at him. "Wait… Adro gets paid? Why don't I get paid?"

Rowan grinned and opened his mouth to respond. Someone hollered a warning, and then all the soldiers still out in the open were running towards the trees. Cori jerked away from Rowan and started forward, even though she was unsure what the threat was.

A roar ripped through the air and made her heart skip a beat. The army flowing past her into the trees started screaming, "dragon!"

Chapter Thirty-Seven

A shadow passed over the land as the massive beast shot from the horizon to momentarily blot out the sun. Cori shaded her eyes and tilted her head back, feeling a moment's relief.

Soldiers still flowed past her like the current of the Pale River. "Do something, Karaliene!" some yelled as they passed.

"I will," she whispered, though instead of moving forward, she took several steps back to stand beneath the shade of the trees. Rowan was still beside her, his head cocked thoughtfully.

Daiyu swooped low over the forest, letting forth another mighty roar and drowning out the renewed screams of the people beneath the canopy. Cori reached out with her Hum, but Rowan put his hand on her arm, stilling her.

"Are you sure she's on our side?" He asked. She knew what he was thinking. Daiyu had been Cadmus' dragon for a long time. Just because she didn't outright attack them, didn't mean the two of them didn't have a bigger plan in play. In any case, she had to try.

She reached out again, feeling Rowan tense in the back of her mind. She didn't think he needed to worry about losing his hold over her; even now the presence she could feel from Daiyu was very weak. She touched the dragon's mind, feeling the vastness of it; almost otherworldly. Then Daiyu pushed her away. It wasn't a forceful shove, rather a gentle separation, and Cori got the sense that she simply didn't want to speak to her.

She withdrew to her body and let her eyes rove the sky for the dragon. Daiyu, after announcing her presence, had lifted herself high into the air, and was now circling the valleys below. The camp behind them had fallen silent and a glance over her shoulder showed Cori that they were all watching her, waiting. She looked briefly back to Daiyu, then turned bodily to face her army.

"She won't hurt us," she told them. Muttering began among those closest to her. She watched the soldiers wearily as their voices became louder. She picked out words such as 'Cadmus', 'enemy' and 'traitor'.

"Calm down," Cori tried to say in the face of their renewed accusations, but her voice was lost among the many. She could have yelled, she could have pushed them, but frankly, she was exhausted by their constantly shifting loyalties. Why couldn't they just trust her word and stop trying to draw parallels between herself and Cadmus?

Rowan's Hum suddenly exploded across them. More than half the soldiers were forced to their knees with shouts of dismay. Even the Dijem recoiled as they experienced the rippling effects of Rowan's immobilising song. The dragon's fury flared around him, whipping through his hair and clothes. His eyes blazed.

"Your Karaliene has told you that Daiyu is not a threat to us. *LISTEN TO HER!*" His voice thundered across the army,

CHAPTER THIRTY-SEVEN

and the humans who could still move stumbled back several steps. Everyone fell silent, and Rowan immediately reined in the dragon's presence. Daiyu roared overhead, as if to remind them she was still there. Still, no one made a sound.

Cori turned from the army to face the open valley behind her. Her eyes found the dragon, and she watched the black beast turn large circles in the sky. Behind her, she heard the soldiers disperse with quiet conversation to continue setting up camp. She could still feel a nervousness from them at Daiyu's presence, but that was to be expected. She herself didn't even know if the dragon above them was a good or bad omen. She just had to trust her instincts.

Rowan remained at her side and she could still feel anger burning from him. His outburst at the army was out of character. He generally let her fight her own battles unless she asked him to intervene. That was how it had always been.

I won't let them break you, he said, though she hadn't asked for an explanation. Her shoulders slumped at words, the band that was a near constant vice around her chest these days loosened. She didn't think the continued accusations would break her, but she was tired. So damn tired of trying so hard to get people to understand her that she welcomed his defence. For just a moment she allowed her vulnerabilities to consume her thoughts and she didn't care that he saw. The iron-hard reflexes of her mind that were near constantly raging about his presence weakened.

He didn't say anything, but she could feel his relief that, for a moment anyway, she was not fighting him.

Daiyu circled into view, barely a speck in the sky, and Cori trained her gaze on the dragon. She felt oddly comforted by

Daiyu's presence, though she didn't know why. The beast had hounded her all her life and had ripped holes through her from the inside out before Cori and Rowan had defeated her. She briefly wondered if somehow Daiyu had gotten into her head and was manipulating her emotions, the way Cadmus had when he had had control of her. At her thought, Rowan reflexively tightened his hold on her mind. She groaned, restricted to the point of claustrophobia.

What's that? He asked.

What's what? She could barely think straight. He loosened his hold a little, though not enough for her to feel comfortable.

That memory. It was Daiyu.

She tried to recall what she'd just been thinking about. Cadmus holding her in captivity, not Daiyu, though Daiyu had held her afterwards.

There it is again.

What? Cori said angrily. *I don't know what you're talking about.*

She felt Rowan reach further into her mind, rummaging about as if he were searching through a cupboard. She winced, recalling that Cadmus had been much smoother when looking for things in her head. Rowan ignored her comparison and pulled a memory to the fore of her mind. *This one.*

Even right in front of her, Cori barely remembered the recollection. It was one of Daiyu, when the dragon had held control of her mind in lieu of Cadmus. She'd sung to Cori, though Cori didn't understand the notes. Rowan let out a low breath beside her.

I think she was teaching you the Old Magic. His tone was

one of disbelief. He dragged the memory back and watched it again. It was clearer for Cori this time, and she thought some notes sounded like her strengthening song.

Why would she teach me Old Magic? Cori sensed a trap. Cadmus was possibly the last living Dijem who knew the Old Magic. Why would his dragon give away his secrets, even before Cori and Rowan had defeated her?

Does it matter? Rowan asked. He had pulled forth another recollection, another song. In his excitement at discovering a new magic, he seemed to have forgotten that it was Cori's mind that he was rifling through.

She gritted her teeth against the headache that was forming and lifted her eyes back to the dragon. She couldn't understand why Daiyu would teach her the ancient magic when she was supposed to be their enemy. She reached out with her Hum once more, but the dragon still ignored her.

* * *

Throughout that night Rowan watched her memories of Daiyu. When they finally fell asleep, Cori dreamed about the dragon, though it was the moment they used the Deathsong on her, rather than when Daiyu had been singing to her. Cori had thought she would die in that moment, and the dream felt just as real.

She was awoken the following morning by Rowan already shifting through her mind. He was still looking at her memories when they said goodbye to Shaan, who was embarking on her trip south, and when the army got back on the road towards Resso.

Daiyu was nowhere to be seen, but Cori could sense that

she was close. She rode with Rowan at the head of the army that day, though she could barely see where she was going through the constant replay of thoughts in her mind. Her head throbbed, yet Rowan was unrelenting. It wasn't until they reached the southern side of Bandar Utara that she snapped.

They saw the arched stone bridge first, followed by the impenetrable walls that separated the capital of Resso and the glistening river. The gate was - as expected - down, and soldiers lined the walls, watching the approaching army.

Bandar Utara was a difficult city to lay siege to. The river was the border marker between Resso and Hearth, and Bandar Utara could access all its resources in the north. Rowan told the soldiers to go through the motions anyway and make it look like they were setting up camp for the long haul.

He and Cori then walked to the southern base of the bridge, looking up towards its high arch. Cori had been to Bandar Utara many times before, and had even lived there with Orin for several years after his wife Yasana had died, but she also remembered the first time she'd seen this city, when she and Rowan had galloped over the bridge with a Hearthian army on their tail. The gate had been closed then too, and Cori was sure they would die against it, only to be saved by Orin's father, Tobin, at the very last moment as he'd let them in.

They stood now, looking at the bridge and the water beneath, while listening to the camp assemble behind them. Flashes of song and visions of Daiyu clouded her mind as Rowan sifted through the spells he had discovered. Finally, she couldn't take it anymore. She swung her arm, hitting him in the abdomen with the back of her hand.

CHAPTER THIRTY-SEVEN

"Will you stop?" She demanded as he doubled over, the breath whooshing out of him. The recollections finally ceased.

"If we can work out what they are, we might be able to use them," he wheezed. He straightened, rubbing his stomach with his hand.

"Why don't we just try them?" Before he could dissuade her, she wove one of the songs. For a moment she thought nothing was happening. Then she felt a strange power fill her. Her Hum, usually a discordant mash of notes, suddenly blended to create a fluid, harmonious sound. By instinct, she lifted her hands, palms facing down. The ground beneath their feet trembled.

Rowan swore under his breath, holding his arms out for balance. Behind them, their soldiers exclaimed in alarm. Even those who lined the walls of Bandar Utara seemed to be looking at their feet in confusion. Cori abruptly stopped the song, and they stood in stillness, only the lapping of water against the riverbank providing any movement.

"Wow." Cori let the word hiss through her teeth. "We should try another one."

"No, we should not," Rowan said emphatically. His expression showed a strange combination of fear and curiosity. She gave him a sideways smile.

"Admit it, you're impressed."

He returned her look. "Of course I am, but we need to be careful. We could kill someone. We could kill ourselves."

Cori didn't miss that he spoke in plurals. Was he becoming so entrenching in her mind that the lines between them were beginning to blur? The uncomfortable look that suddenly crossed his face was confirmation enough that her theory was correct.

"Are we going to take the city tomorrow?" She asked, though, like the other times they had prepared to fight, she expected him to be vague.

"Yes," he said.

"Will you let me take the gate this time?"

He turned his head to give her a long, searching look. "Yes."

* * *

"The rest of the Sarkans are in there," Melita said urgently, "you must have felt them."

"I have," Rowan responded. They gathered in the command tent, and it was a few hours before dawn. He was standing between Han and Eamoyn and the three of them were pouring over maps of the city.

This was the first time Cori had been in the command tent since Rowan had taken control of her mind, but she knew this wasn't the first time they'd looked at this map. The way they pointed and spoke about it showed that they were only rehearsing plans that had already been decided.

Adro was there, too. Cori had expected him to be miserable at the fact that Shaan had left, but his spirits were surprisingly high.

"Will you let them surrender?" Melita asked, as she had each time they had come across someone from her House. Rowan sighed and turned to face the redhead fully.

"You've been talking to them," he told her. "I've felt you. You tell me if they're going to surrender."

Melita looked worried. "Maybe they'll change their minds once they see you."

CHAPTER THIRTY-SEVEN

Rowan shook his head. "Not this time, Melita. We don't know if Cadmus is in Bandar Utara, we don't know if his dragons lie in wait. We don't have time to deal with Sarkans who change their mind at the sight of blood. They've made their bed, now they need to lie in it." He paused, turning back to the map and tapping his fingers against it. Melita remained where she stood in the doorway of the tent. She stood tall, but Cori could see her jaw working and tears glistening in the corners of her eyes.

"I will let you try to convince them again," Rowan said quietly, his eyes still on the map. "Tell them to be at the gate at dawn and we will let them through. That's the only chance they get."

"Thank you," Melita whispered. She turned to leave, but Rowan stopped her.

"Do not contact Daniyl. He doesn't get an opportunity to surrender."

Melita looked as if she might say something, but at the look on Rowan's face, she nodded quickly and left the tent.

"She might tell him to run," Adro warned. He rocked back in his chair, kicking his feet up on the table and locking his hands behind his head. Rowan shrugged, returning to the maps.

"He can run, I'll find him eventually."

Cori knew Rowan hated Daniyl, and that loathing had been compounded after he'd found out that Daniyl had tried to assault her. She herself had once promised to kill the new elder of the Sarkans. She wondered if she'd be able to beat Rowan to him.

No, Rowan said firmly. *Daniyl is mine.*

Cori slouched in her seat a little as Rowan returned to

his conversation with the captains. At least he was letting her blow up the gate. She supposed that would have to be enough.

The men talked for a few hours more, pointing out routes for the army. Adro himself put up his hand to take control of the keep. "You two got to take the last one," he reasoned. Cori and Rowan had exchanged a glance. Cori had shrugged.

"Take Orin with you," she said. He'll know best how to get in. Adro frowned.

"How would he know? He remembers nothing."

"He remembers instinctual things," she said with a quick look at Rowan. "And going back to the keep may refresh his memory."

"He won't turn on me, will he?"

"No, he's still taking daily grybas doses. He has no magic, but he's strong with a sword or axe."

Adro shrugged. "Alrighty then, Orin's onboard."

Rowan suddenly straightened and looked towards the tent flaps. "Something's happening," he said. Cori couldn't hear anything out of the ordinary. Still, she stood warily. She felt his Hum reach out, then he smiled. "You might want to check this out," he said to Adro.

Adro frowned and reached out with his own Hum. Cori followed him with hers and found Rowan's target. Starch. Ardo jumped to his feet with a whoop and led the other two out of the tent. Han and Eamoyn followed the Dijem with confused looks on their faces.

Outside, the camp was peaceful as their soldiers got the last rest they could before the next battle. The five of them wove through the tents towards the river. At the edge of the camp, the sentries had left their posts to stand by the water,

CHAPTER THIRTY-SEVEN

pointing and muttering.

It must have been their restlessness that had alerted Rowan. Cori didn't know how he could possibly have the capacity to sweep through the minds of his own men, and those in Bandar Utara, as well as hold hers. The cacophony of thoughts in his head must be terribly confusing. The sentries saw them coming and stepped back so the Dijem and the captains could stand on the riverbanks.

They heard him before they saw him, a tuneless whistle in the dark, the thwack, thwack, thwack of a paddle against water. Then a canoe glided into view with Starch in its belly. Adro roared with laughter, causing the soldiers on the wall opposite them to jump to attention. Cori heard the shouts for archers, but Starch had already steered his boat towards the shore and out of their range.

Adro and Han waded into the water to pull the bow of the boat up onto the bank. "What are you doing here?" Adro exclaimed, grabbing Starch into a bear hug as the elder made land.

"Thought I better pull my head out of my arse and give you a hand," Starch said gruffly, slapping Adro on the back. The two men released each other and Starch moved to shake the other men's hands. He gave Cori a fond, but strange, pat on the shoulder. He stretched, arms above his head, then looked from the dark camp to the lit city. "You're not trying to siege this city, are you?"

"Of course not," Rowan said. Behind them in the camp, soldiers were stirring. Cori could see the horizon beginning to lighten. "Cori will break us in, we're just waiting for daylight so that everyone can see the show."

Starch scratched his bearded chin and nodded. "Not far

off then. Tell me, what else has happened?"

"You'll never guess," Adro said with a wide grin, before Rowan could respond. "I'm going to be a pa!"

"You?" Starch said incredulously. "What woman in her right mind would sleep with you, let alone have a baby?"

It seemed to be congratulations enough for Adro. He laughed once more and grasped his elder in a headlock. Cori moved away from them, looking towards the bridge. Rowan followed her, his hand briefly touching the small of her back. "Time to go," she said, taking a deep breath of night air. Time to kill.

Chapter Thirty-Eight

Pink and gold ribbons streaked the dawn sky in the moments before the sun broke over the horizon, kissing the highest points of the land with light.

The arch of the bridge that led from Hearth into Resso was the first place to be touched by the sun. Cori stepped into it, looking down the incline to the gate. The Resso soldiers watched her anxiously from the walls, and Cori felt a twinge of sadness for them. Resso had always been her ally. Now she was going to tear them apart.

Rowan stepped into the golden dawn light beside her. For once, she didn't feel restricted by having him close. She was focussed on the task ahead, and even Rowan couldn't disturb the calm that was settling over her.

As the path of the sun flowed down the bridge, she surveyed the gate ahead of her. Gates were her favourite type of infrastructure. They were designed to protect as much as they were to keep people out. None had ever kept her out, which is why she enjoyed them so much, but sometimes they gave her a challenge.

This one would, she knew, because she'd watched Orin himself order it reinforced multiple times over. It had been an unconscious thing on his part. He never intended to keep her out, but after fighting alongside her for so many years against the Hearthians, he'd developed a healthy fear of her powers which drove him to protect his people any way he could in case one day she turned on them. Like today.

From the top of the bridge, she could see that the thickness of the wall might hold five gates beneath it, stacked horizontally one after the other.

"When I came back through a few years ago," Rowan said, "they didn't have all the gates closed, but one of them was made of steel."

Cori chewed on the inside of her lip. Steel was difficult to explode. No harm in trying, she supposed. The sun was almost at the gate. She closed her eyes, taking a deep breath and reaching out with her Hum. She could feel her own army assembled behind her. She could feel the soldiers on the wall before her, feel their fear as they waited for her to act. She could feel more enemy soldiers beyond, along with the Sarkans and a mixture of other Dijem. Waiting. Waiting. Waiting.

The Sun touched the gate. Cori lifted her hands and pushed. The wood exploded, throwing shards through the air and back towards her. The soldiers on the wall murmured but held their ground.

The next layer was steel and when Cori pushed again, nothing happened. She wasn't dissuaded though. She curled her fingers into fists and shoved again. Dents appeared in the gate, but it held firm. She looked down at her hands. Her abilities felt suddenly mediocre compared to the power she had felt the afternoon before when she had used the Old Magic. Dragon's Magic.

She searched through the songs Rowan had been listening

to over and over in her head and found one that sounded like her strengthening song. She started weaving it, and Rowan didn't stop her. She decided that he was far too curious about the Old Magic to take the precautions he'd enforced the afternoon before.

As she had when she'd tried the last song, she felt the notes of her Hum meld together in synchrony. She felt the power move beyond her mind to fill her entire being. She lifted her hands once more and *pushed.* The gates and the walls immediately surrounding them exploded upwards. Massive chunks of stone, wood and steel rained down on the gaping hole left in Bandar Utara's main defence. The morning stillness was punctuated with screams of terror as the soldiers on the wall above the blast were flung into the air. Others, who lined the walls that were still intact, fled for the stairs to get onto the streets.

Cori whooped, and beside her, Rowan smiled. He gestured back to their army, and the group started forward up the bridge. Cori and Rowan went ahead of them, down the incline towards the devastation she'd just wrought. Soldiers inside the city were shouting and scrabbling to formation. Some wore Resso uniforms, but Cori noted that most seemed to be Hearthians.

She didn't allow them time to form together. The moment she reached the end of the bridge, she darted forward through the rubble that had once been the gates. She could hear cries and painful moans coming from the fallen chunks of stone, wood and steel around her; the soldiers who'd been atop the wall lay there, dying.

Cori jumped, landing atop a long slab of stone. She slammed her hands out, the old magic song still whirling through her mind. The first wave of soldiers flew back through the air, slamming into the walls of the buildings that surrounded the small square that was the entrance into Bandar Utara. Cori heard their bones snap and the stone walls crack. The bodies fell and dust and stone followed them. She turned to the right, and this time pulled a guard tower down over the right flank, blocking access to the square from soldiers who were trying to come that way.

Her own army came from behind her, surging around the block she stood upon to engage the soldiers who were still standing. Cori could feel the Hums of other Dijem flashing around her, attacking one another and protecting their own Hiram. For once, she felt unaffected by them. She didn't know if it was the Old Magic, or maybe Rowan's influence on her mind.

Rowan climbed up on the slab of stone beside her. He rested his hand on the gold dragon head pommel of his sword and surveyed the fighting before them. Adro heaved himself up to stand on Cori's other side.

"There's the Sarkans," he said, pointing towards their left and the main streets that led to the keep.

"Are they fighting?" Rowan asked.

"Doesn't look like it." Adro shielded his eyes with his hands, squinting towards the group of Dijem who were struggling through the battle towards the gate. Cori watched them come, noting the fear upon their faces. They were clearly trying to surrender, but she wondered if Rowan would let them. Their soldiers were parting, allowing the Dijem through. Near the front of the group, Cori saw a flash of blonde hair and realised that Daniyl was among them.

She didn't need to say anything; Rowan saw Daniyl coming

CHAPTER THIRTY-EIGHT

through her eyes and she felt him tense beside her. "Let's go," he said, jumping down from the slab. Cori followed, with Adro behind her. The soldiers parted further when they saw their Karalis coming. The Uaines and Valkoinens fell in behind them, and the two Dijem parties crossed the already bloodied cobblestones to meet.

Cori could feel the dragon's fury pulsating from Rowan. Wind that belonged only to him whipped about him, flapping his clothes and his hair. Daniyl came to the fore of the group of Sarkans. "Rowan!" He started, eyes wide.

Rowan didn't allow him anymore words. With a speed no man should possess, he crossed the final distance between them and grabbed Daniyl by the front of the shirt. For a moment both men's eyes met; Daniyl's frightened, and Rowan's loathing. Then Rowan swung Daniyl to the side and shoved him away. Daniyl shot through the air, hitting a wall with a crack and slumping to the street.

A ripple of surprise went through the Dijem watching. Even Cori was taken aback at Rowan's strength. Had he gained that from the dragon's presence? Had he known he could do it? Rowan stalked towards Daniyl as the Sarkans elder struggled to sit up.

"Rowan," he gasped, frothy blood dribbling from his lips. "Please." Rowan grasped him by the throat and choked him. Daniyl's face became a mottled red colour and his eyes bulged. Hands rose to fruitlessly scratch at his captor. Rowan's grip tightened. The Dijem watched in silence while the Hiram and Humans fought around them.

Myce had moved to stand between Cori and Adro. His sister was back in the camp, waiting in the infirmary tent, but Cori could imagine that she'd sent Myce to plead on behalf of the Sarkans once more. The redhead looked uncomfortable as he watched Daniyl's slow asphyxiation under Rowan's hands, but he said nothing.

Finally, Daniyl died. Rowan stepped back from his body and surveyed it with a look of disgust. Then he turned to face the other Sarkans. Those closest took a few steps back. "Out," he said dangerously. "Get out of the city and surrender at the camp. If you do anything else, I will kill all of you."

They didn't need telling twice. Cori, Myce and Adro, as well as the Uaines and Valkoinens behind them, stepped aside to let the Sarkans file past them towards the ruined gates. Rowan watched them go, and Cori watched him. Finally, his eyes drifted to hers and the dragon's fury slowly faded from around him.

Was he happy with his kill? She wondered. She herself was relieved he was dead, but also weary. In her experience, no matter how many she killed, there were always more men like Daniyl.

"Ready?" Rowan asked the group at large. Cori and Adro nodded, then Adro put his thumb and forefinger to his lips and whistled. The soldiers who could, moved from the fighting to group around him.

"Hey!" He called. "You lot with me to the keep! Cori, can you give us a start?"

"Certainly," she said. She moved forward towards the main street where the Sarkans had come from. Marching towards was a large contingent of Hearthian soldiers. Cori pushed, slamming half of them into a building that toppled over the top of them, then she pushed again, forcing more of them into the air and back up the street.

Adro patted her shoulder as he started past her. "Thanks,

CHAPTER THIRTY-EIGHT

Little One." The Advisor moved off to engage the next lot of soldiers coming behind the first. Rowan came to her side. They watched Adro and his contingent move off.

"Which side of the city do you want?" Rowan asked.

"The riverside," Cori replied. "It's nice down that way."

Rowan gave her a sideways look. "Probably best you stay away from large bodies of water. I'll take the riverside. You go north."

"Yessir." She gave him a mock salute, then called to the last of her soldiers to follow her. Rowan headed in the opposite direction, leading the rest of the Dijem.

The streets in the city's north were not as busy as the main roads would be, but a few enemy contingents tried to come this way to flank the main army. Cori and her soldiers wiped through them with ease.

"This city is not as challenging as Tengah, Karaliene," Han observed at one point as they sliced down a handful of soldiers side-by-side. Cori had to agree with the captain. There were not as many Dijem in Bandar Utara as there had been in Tengah, and the occasional one that they came across were Cadmus' strange creations. The Sarkans had all been here, of course, but Cori doubted that Cadmus would have trusted them enough to rely on them to defend the city. She glanced towards a nearby rooftop, half expecting to find Kalle watching her, but The Captain was also suspiciously absent.

Cadmus himself hadn't made an appearance, and Cori doubted that he was in Bandar Utara, though she had no idea where else he could be. Had he gone back to the Tundra and was leading them on a wild chase?

A fresh contingent flooded into the street that Cori and

her soldiers were fighting on, just as she heard others coming from the opposite direction. She called to Han to engage the second group, then moved forward to the first. Her new strength was unparalleled, and she found no challenge in keeping the soldiers away from her. The way the song flowed perfectly through her mind made her wonder how Jarrah could have ever forced the Dijem race to give this magic up.

She thought about the other songs Daiyu had sung to her. There was another one that had a few notes similar to the strengthening song she was using now. What harm was there in trying it to see what happened?

She wove the song, and almost instantly a white light seared across her vision, as if the sun had suddenly exploded. She cried out, blinded, and flung her hands out. In her panic, she forgot that the strengthening song was still weaving, and she felt her hands connect with the ghost of a wall. The building to her right exploded. She stopped the blinding song and tried to get away as the building toppled down towards her. She forced some of the stone away, stopping it from falling on her head, but a large slab hit her arm, dragging her down to the street.

Pain ripped up her arm as she felt the bone snap. She screamed. Rowan cursed in the back of her mind. She tried to get back on her feet, but Rowan gave her a command and she blacked out.

* * *

When she came to, she was lying on her back on the cobblestones, surrounded by the rubble of the building she had pulled down on herself. She could still hear fighting, but

CHAPTER THIRTY-EIGHT

it had moved away.

Sorry, Rowan said. *I was in the middle of a battle, and your pain almost made me sick. I had to take you out.*

It's all right, she replied. She tried to sit up and felt pain lancing through her arm. She looked down at it and saw the bone had split through the skin. Her stomach turned.

Don't look at it, Rowan suggested, sounding queasy. *Go somewhere safe, I'll come and find you.*

She sat there for a moment longer, then used her good arm to get unsteadily to her feet. She trudged along the empty, blood splattered street, fighting back dizzying nausea and feeling like a fool. Rowan had warned her about using the Old Magic without understanding it better. She'd almost killed herself, and by extension of that, had almost killed Rowan.

She came across the public library and slowly climbed the steps. The double front doors were open, but the entrance hall was empty. Her footsteps echoed on the marble floor and she passed three doors before finally selecting a room to enter. The walls were lined with bookshelves, and she sat down against one with a groan. She tried not to look at her arm, but she was acutely aware of how wrecked it was.

She didn't know how long it was before Rowan found her. She listened to the sound of battle outside, sometimes close, sometimes from the main road to the keep. She eventually heard his soft footfalls on the marble in the entrance hall, then he turned unerringly into the room she'd chosen. He crouched down before her. First meeting her eye, then looking unwillingly at her arm.

He reached out and took her limp wrist. A wave of nausea hit her as pain bloomed at the break point. "I have to pull it straight to get the bone back into place," he told her, swallowing hard. She nodded.

"Just do it."

He put his other hand near her elbow, and in one sure movement, yanked her arm. She blacked out again.

* * *

When she roused from unconsciousness for a second time that day, she was slumped against the bookshelf and Rowan was sitting in front of her, his bottom lip between his teeth as he watched her.

"How long was I out?" She asked groggily, examining her now healed arm. She flexed her fingers and felt only a small stiffness.

"An hour or more," he responded. "Bone is difficult to knit back together. I'm not sure if I did it correctly."

"It feels all right." She flexed her fingers again, then tried to rise. Rowan stood before her and held his hand out to help her.

"Thanks," she said, meeting his eye. For a long moment they stared at each other, and for once she was glad he was there. After her near-death experience, she wanted to be close to him, needed him to protect her. His eyes were flicking curiously between hers as he listened to her mind.

Kiss me, she thought. And, for the first time since taking control of her mind, he did. His lips crashed down on hers hard enough to bruise, and he lifted her, pinning her back against the shelves. Books rained down around them as she wrapped her legs around his waist, pulling him closer so their bodies were flush. Her hands went to his hair, and he

CHAPTER THIRTY-EIGHT

opened his mind to her so she could feel his hunger, how badly he wanted her.

She groaned under the onslaught of his desire, and he used the moment to pull her shirt over her head. His hands slid across her skin, leaving trails of fire in their wake. His fingers rose, tracing across her face, cupping her cheeks. For a moment their eyes met and in his, she could see hope. Hope that they could fix this, that things might just turn out all right.

"I need you," she whispered. And not just his body. She needed him everyday and always. Her life would be meaningless without him in it.

"Forever, I promise."

He kissed her again, a gentle caress of his lips before he set her down and pulled off his own shirt. Together they raced to unbuckle their pants and kick off their boots.

When they stood naked before one another, Rowan closed back in, cupping the back of her neck. The thumb of his other hand stroked down the column of her throat, down over her breast, down, down to the wet heat between her legs.

She groaned as his fingers slid inside her and his thumb circled her clit. His breath hitched in his throat as he shared that pulsing want through their connected minds, and for a moment his forehead touched hers, their breaths mingling. Then he went to his knees before her and his tongue replaced his fingers.

"Oh, shit," Cori's head thunked back against the wall and she grasped the bookshelf above her head to steady herself as Rowan hooked her leg over his shoulder. Every stroke of his tongue was perfectly placed, each lick and suck driving her quickly towards the precipice.

And then he slowed his pace, edging her closer but not letting her find the pleasure she desperately sought. He teased her until her back arched and her muscles clenched, until more books fell from the shelves around them and she was begging him to finish her.

Hands gripping her thighs, he swirled his tongue around her clit then sucked hard, making her cry out as the pressure exploded into wild waves of hot pleasure. Every part of her body throbbed and weightlessness replaced the hunger. As quivering muscles gave out, she slid down the wall into his arms.

Rowan held her, and he was smirking, but his gaze was fire and before she could catch a breath he turned her over to her stomach.

"Hold on," he growled, hitching her hips upwards and filling her with a single thrust. Twin groans escaped them. A heavy hand pressed against her lower back and the other fisted in her hair as he took her hard and fast, finally finding his own release with a roar.

When he pulled away, he flopped to the ground beside her, utterly spent.

"Fuck," the word fell from his lips on a heavy exhale. Cori laughed and he grinned at her before pulling her into his arms, two sweat-drenched bodies pressed together in total bliss.

In the city beyond, the battle still raged.

Chapter Thirty-Nine

Rowan lay on his back, head rested in Cori's lap while she leaned back against a bookshelf. Her fingers raked idly through his hair.

They'd redressed in their underwear and pants, but their shirts and vests still lay discarded where they'd dropped them. The garments were covered in blood; they didn't need that between them right now.

"How do you feel about Daniyl?" Cori asked, her voice echoing softly in the empty room.

"I don't know," Rowan admitted. "Relieved, I think. But that could be your relief I'm feeling instead." His eyes met hers, and he smiled gently. His gaze was warm, and not even talking about Daniyl took that away. "I'm sorry I took your kill away from you. I know you loathed him."

Cori shrugged. "I think you hated him more. Watching was enough. You were pretty impressive with your new dragon powers."

His eyes narrowed and a smirk curled his lips. "You think so?"

She bent her head to kiss him. "Very much so."

"You know your Dragon Magic is fairly impressive too."

Once more she shrugged, though this time awkwardly.

"Except that I almost killed myself."

"Try it again," he suggested. "The song you tried before." She raised her eyebrows.

"It didn't feel very nice. Why would I do it again?"

"Close your eyes and try it. Trust me."

So she did. She closed her eyes and wove the song again. There was no flash of light, but she could suddenly see the small blood vessels in her eyelids and the layers of tissue in the skin. She could almost see the library room beyond. The song ended, and she slowly opened her eyes. Rowan was looking up at her.

"It strengthens eyesight?" She guessed. This time Rowan shrugged, but his smile was confident.

"Seems like it. I'd imagine you'd be able to see in the dark. Like a dragon."

"That's pretty amazing," she rested her head back against the bookshelf, lapsing into silence for a time, thinking about the song, and the other songs Daiyu had taught her. She once more wondered why the dragon had sung to her.

As she contemplated the Old Magic, her left hand stroked Rowan's hair, while her right rested on his bare chest. His barriers were around both their minds, making them invisible to the outside world.

They could still hear occasional sounds of battle in the distance, but they were becoming infrequent. Adro should have the keep by now. He was probably wondering where they were, wondering if they were dead.

"We could be," Rowan said to her thought. He turned his head to kiss her stomach.

"What do you mean?"

"We could die and they'd never find us."

CHAPTER THIRTY-NINE

Cori laughed, tugging his hair to pull him away. "Commit suicide like some love-struck youths with a blood pact? Not how I envisaged us going out, Rowan."

He looked at her, eyes twinkling, then he rolled over to his hands and knees. "That's not what I mean. We could let them think we're dead and run away." He kissed her. "We could go to Dodici and live by the beach." He kissed her again, his hand rising to curl around the back of her neck. "We could get married and have babies."

Cori burst out laughing and pushed him back so she could look him in the eye. "Get married and have babies? Have you lost your mind?"

He resisted her hand on his chest, leaning in to kiss her once more. She could feel him smiling. "I want to do everything with you. I want to marry you a hundred times and have a hundred babies with you."

"Ouch," she muttered, though she couldn't help but smile at his exuberance, a flutter spinning in her stomach.

"What's stopping us?" He whispered. He trailed kisses along her jaw, his breath tickling her ear.

"Adro, for one," she mused. "Do you really expect him to believe that we just died like that, with no trace of our bodies? And we can't leave him. He's going to be a father soon; if anyone survives this war, it has to be Adro."

"That's a good point," he murmured against her neck. "What if we took Adro with us? He could pretend to die too."

"Tempting," she looped her arm around his neck and pulled his face back to hers. She kissed him deeply and he sat back, lifting her into his lap in the same movement.

"I would do anything for you. Just say it."

"First," she said with a smile, smoothing her hands over his stubble, pushing back the tendrils of dark hair that had fallen loose over his face. "You can kill Cadmus so you can have your peace and I can have my mind back."

His emotions twinged with a hint of fear, but he pushed it away. "All right, but then we're going to Dodici?"

"If you insist." Her words were nonchalant, but only so they didn't reveal the deep ache she felt at his words. They were so close. So close to capturing their own freedom. She kissed him again, then pushed herself to her feet. Rowan didn't acknowledge her most recent thoughts, though his smile slipped a little. She tossed him his shirt, and pulled her own back on. It was stiff with dried blood, but she had nothing else to wear.

"Come one then, Little One," Rowan said once they were dressed. He draped his arm over her shoulder. "Let's go find our dear Advisor."

They meandered through the near-empty streets of Bandar Utara as if they were nothing more than a noble couple out for a stroll. As if they weren't covered in blood. As if they weren't the Karalis and Karaliene of Tauta.

Some people scurried about in empty streets and alleyways. Looters, most likely, looking to break into stores while their owners had abandoned them. They slunk back into the shadows as Cori and Rowan passed. They may look like a couple out on an afternoon walk, but they still exuded an air of danger.

Others watched them pass from their windows. Cori could see them whisper to one another. Did they hate them for invading their city? Were they thankful that they'd dispelled the Hearthians? Did they know what this war was for at all?

CHAPTER THIRTY-NINE

"Stop thinking so much," Rowan said, turning his head to press his lips to her temple. His barriers still encased her mind, sealing them both in their own private bubble. The emotions that she could feel from his mind were both warm and amused.

They turned onto the main road and finally found the carnage of the battle. Bodies littered the street. Some alive and moaning, but most were dead. Melita and her team of healers were moving between the injured and assigning soldiers to take them to the infirmary tent.

Other soldiers - both those that belonged to their army, as well as some Resso men - were already shifting the dead from the street.

"Looks like Orin's grybas wore off," Cori pointed to a Hearthian whose chest had been torn open. Rowan grunted.

"I'm quite glad he can't use his Dijem magic," he responded. "I think he would be even stronger than you."

Now that was concerning. Just because Orin couldn't use his Dijem magic without committing suicide, didn't mean that Cadmus couldn't get in his head and perhaps force him. Orin's time would be short, but the devastation he could cause would be irrevocable.

"We better find him and drug him again," she muttered.

They made their way to the keep, their boots slipping and skidding on the bloody cobblestones. They climbed the stairs into the throne room.

Many of the other Dijem were there, taking orders from Adro to secure parts of the city and to stop any Hearthians who might still be alive from escaping. Rowan finally let his barriers down and the Advisor glanced up at them. Rather than looking annoyed by their absence, however,

Adro looked amused. As if he knew exactly what they'd been up to.

Orin was there too, standing alone and facing the throne. As Cori and Rowan moved towards him, he turned.

Cori had only a moment to register the anger in his expression before he balled his fingers and punched Rowan in the face.

"You left her!" Orin roared as Rowan staggered back, hitting the stone floor hard. Scowling, he righted himself and lunged at Orin, the dragon's fury whirling around him. His fist slammed into Orin's stomach at the same time that Orin raised his hands and pushed Rowan away with his Hiram magic. Both men flew back from each other. Rowan landed flat on his back, the air whooshing from his lungs, and Orin hit the stairs of the dais, grunting. Neither conceded, and both lurched back to their feet to attack again.

"Whoa!" Cori jumped between, arms outstretched, stopping them at the end of her reach, a hand pressed against each of their chests. "Either you can fight without magic, or you can fight me. And I guarantee that I will flog both of you." She turned her head, looking between them. The two men glowered at each other.

"He left you," Orin said testily and Cori had to smile.

"You're remembering?"

"I remember when you came back covered in blood and almost dead on your feet because you had no magic. I remember that you couldn't even say his name, or barely step foot in any room he had been in. I remember how you used to press your hand against your chest like he'd ripped out your heart and you couldn't put yourself back together."

As Orin ranted, the anger slid from Rowan's face to be

CHAPTER THIRTY-NINE

replaced with dismay. Of course, Cori remembered the pain and abandonment she had felt when she'd put Rowan on the back of Akane to go north, while she'd returned to the south and Rowan re-lived it now through her memories. Behind them, she was aware the Dijem had paused their conversations to listen.

"You can see in her head, can't you?" Orin said directly to Rowan as he took note of the way the fight went out of the other man. "Why don't you get in my head and watch? Watch her thrash when she had nightmares. Feel hopeless when she's covered in her own blood because she pushed too hard with magic that gave her nose bleeds. Follow her across the damned realm to keep her from self sabotaging and wondering what would happen to her when you're dead because the asshole who made her immortal abandoned her!"

A pin could have dropped and the whole room would have heard it. Rowan was white, his eyes wide, and during Orin's tirade, he'd raised his hands to grip Cori's wrist, as if afraid she might vanish if he didn't hold on. Beneath her palm, she could feel how fast his heart raced.

"Orin," Cori commanded and his eyes darted to hers. "Do you remember when I told you why he left?" Orin seemed to struggle with the memory.

"You killed a dragon," he said eventually.

"*We* killed a dragon," she corrected. "And Rowan took the brunt of it so I could live. He's here now. He came back." Orin's eyes shifted to Rowan. Cori continued. "I'm happy now, Orin, can't you see that?" his eyes moved back to hers.

"You look happy now, but you haven't been. He's been treating you horribly."

She shrugged. "Perhaps. But we're working through that.

He's trying. We're both trying."

Orin said nothing more, but he took a step back, out of her reach. She lowered her arms and Rowan, fingers still around her wrist, moved closer to her, almost protectively. She could see that one of his cheeks was swelling from Orin's attack. She looked at Orin and couldn't help the grin of relief that broke on her lips.

"Orin, you remember!"

He glanced around at all the Dijem, eyes wild as if he wasn't sure how he'd ended up in their company. Then he flung his arms up. "Cori, you blew up my gate! Do you know how long that will take to rebuild?"

She laughed and gave him a one-armed hug. "One thing us Dijem aren't short on is time. I'm so happy you're here and that you remember."

"It's... I need to think about this." He pulled away from her and turned to once more contemplate his throne. Adro resumed his conversations with the other Dijem, and Cori finally turned to Rowan. She could see the sadness in his eyes. He'd had access to her mind for some time now, but perhaps hadn't realised the extent of her torment until Orin had put it into words.

Come with me, she told him. He followed her to the balcony that overlooked a now empty marketplace. They leaned side-by-side on the balustrade Rowan with his head in his hands. Cori watched him.

"He got you pretty good," she teased lightly, pulling one of his hands away to reveal the bruise Orin had dealt.

"You're telling me," he muttered, his fingers straying to the swelling that was forming on his face. "It feels like I've been hit by a rock. It makes me very glad that you've never

CHAPTER THIRTY-NINE

punched me."

She laughed, putting her arm over his shoulder and kissing his cheek. "I'm sure your retaliation hurt him just as much." He turned to her, snaking his arms about her waist and pulling her close.

"Are you truly happy?" He asked hesitantly.

"You know I am. You're in my head, remember?"

"I want to hear you say it."

Her hands went to the back of his neck and she pulled him down so she could kiss him. She didn't care that Adro, and the others were just inside, or that they should have been out on the streets, helping to clean up. All she wanted was to be with Rowan. She wondered briefly if maybe he was giving her subtle commands to make her want him. He reeled back, horrified.

I'm not, he assured her immediately. *I would never do that.*

"Speaking of subtle commands," she said, turning back to the balustrade to look over Bandar Utara. "Where do you think Cadmus could be? You don't think he's gone back to the Tundra, do you?"

"I don't know," Rowan admitted. "He could be at the Great Library? He may not be in the north at all. He may have gone back to his mountain palace."

"We could ask him."

Before Rowan could stop her, she flung her Hum out to the universe. *Where are you, Cadmus? Are you afraid?*

Hardly, Little One, he responded with amusement. His Hum, as always, was spread wide so she couldn't quite tell which direction he was contacting her from. His voice sounded clearer than it ever had before. Perhaps he wasn't far away at all.

Can we have a hint, or do you expect us to chase you across the realm? Surely you want this over with as much as we do.

I do, he admitted. He paused for a time, though she could still feel him there. Was he trying to get into her head? She didn't think so, Rowan was holding onto her pretty tightly. *Let's go back to where this all started.*

Rowan's barriers suddenly slammed up around her mind, shutting Cadmus out.

"He was just about to tell us something!" She exclaimed.

"He did." Rowan looked livid. "Back to where it all started? He's at my mother's farm."

Chapter Forty

Cori had seen Rowan on the edge of losing his mind a few times before, but this time was different. This time he looked as if he may kill someone, and it wouldn't matter if that person were a friend or foe.

They were at the cabin that had once belonged to his mother. The place where Rowan had once spent his spare time as a child. Only the cabin wasn't there anymore. It had been burned to the ground.

Rowan was staring at the place it had been, where there was a black patch of ground with part of the tin roof already growing over with vines. He'd been there for almost twenty minutes.

Cori, ten feet behind him, could see that he was shaking with fury. She'd told Adro to move the army away, to give their Karalis some space. She didn't know if she should approach him. His hold on her mind was tight, and she was resisting him again. Getting closer to him would only compound the problem, and she didn't want him to feel more rejected than he probably already was.

She finally decided to get closer, moving alongside him to look at the ruined building. They'd once spent a night together in that cabin, and later, in the intervening years, she'd sometimes lived here when she needed to escape the catastrophic state of the realm. She'd loved this place too for its quiet solace when being the Karaliene had become too hard.

She understood why Cadmus had done this; he knew the cabin had been a memory of Rowan's mother and a link to happier times for his son. He'd burned it down for no other reason than to try and shake Rowan's focus in the face of the impending battle. It was an effective move, but a low blow nonetheless.

Cori's eyes drifted to the horizon where she could see smoke rising. Cadmus' camp was not far away. They were almost at the end. She was sure she would have been able to feel his Hum if Rowan hadn't put his barriers around both their minds to keep his internal turmoils private from the other Dijem.

Speaking of... Cori turned her head to look at Rowan. She could see that his eyes were glazing and she could feel his Hum spiralling in on itself, ready to explode. It wasn't a good time for him to fall into a Hum intoxication. She didn't want to give him rum to quell it either. He needed his head about him and he couldn't go into battle against Cadmus while he was drunk. Of course, she could let him go. He might contain the unleash within his barriers the way she could, but she was within his barriers too. She would be a casualty.

His eyes closed briefly as he tried to collect himself. "I don't think I can do this," he said, hoarsely. "I don't think I can kill him."

And before she could respond, he sank to a crouch, his face buried in his hands. His whole body quivered with the sobs that wracked it. Cori kneeled beside him, pulling him into her arms. He cried like she'd never seen before. Grief, stress, fear. It all rolled down his cheeks with his tears. His fingers clutched her shirt like she was the last one left. And she was, she supposed. The last person left to keep his heart intact and he was afraid to lose her too. She smoothed his hair back from his face and cupped his cheek.

"You can do it," Cori assured him. "You are stronger than he is. Trust yourself."

"And if I can't?" He whispered. "What if I get face to face with him and freeze?"

"Then I will kill him. Or Adro will kill him. Or some damned soldier will get a lucky blow with their sword. We've come too far, Rowan. Cadmus is going to die today and I don't care whose hand it's by." She took a deep breath and wiped his tears away with her thumb. Then she lifted her own face to the sun, allowing its warmth to bathe her. Eyes closed, she imagined what it would be like when the battle was done. She pictured herself on a beach, a sea breeze in her hair. It was a beach she knew; one in Dodici, a small bay sheltered by great rocky bluffs. It was a perfect harbour, with turquoise waters, yet no one had ever settled at it. She imagined small waves lapping at her feet, then reaching behind her to find Rowan. Smiling, they danced in slow circles in the sand. No more wars, no more realm. Just the two of them.

She opened her eyes again. Rowan's face was pressed against her chest. He no longer wept, and he watched the imagined memory in her mind with a wistful expression.

"How do I do this?" He confided. "How do I get up and lead them out there? I'm tired, Cori. I can't find the strength anymore."

Her fingers smoothed over his face again, and he looked up at her. "I'll be your strength," she whispered. "So you can be theirs."

His eyes closed briefly, and his hands tightened on her shirt, then he pushed himself away from her and stood. She rose with him, waiting. He stared at the remains of the cabin a moment longer then, swallowing hard, he nodded.

Cori reached out and squeezed his arm, then turned to seek the army. Rowan finally let his barriers down, and she reached out to Adro. *Let's go.*

As Rowan's barriers came down, she was instantly aware of Cadmus' Hum in close proximity. They ignored each other for the time being, though Cadmus felt smug and that worried Cori a little. She and Rowan went to meet Adro and the army. As they headed across Rowan's farmland towards the smoky horizon, no one spoke; everyone knew this was it and they were as resolved as Cori did to finish it.

They crested a grassy hill to look across a valley. On the opposite ridge was the makings of a stone keep. It still looked under construction, with one side being held up with scaffolding, but two of its towers were complete. On the balcony of the nearest tower, Cori could make out the figure of a man leaning on the balustrade, watching them. Cadmus.

Ranged out before the keep was his army. Thousands upon thousands of them, and many of them Dijem. Cori could feel their weaker Hums thrumming together like a hive. She could instantly see that her own army was at a disadvantage. They would have to travel down into the valley, then up the rocky slope on the other side to get to Cadmus' keep. They would be easily picked off.

As they stood facing the other army across the way, a

CHAPTER FORTY

cacophony of roars ripped the air apart and two dragons shot into the sky from behind the keep, then another three. All were various shades of blue, all fairly young, though still large enough to take an army down. They rose, circling above the keep and shooting jets of flame across the sky.

Cori's heart sank. Her words to Rowan before had just been a fantasy. There was no way they would even get close to that keep, let alone inside of it. Another roar sounded, louder than all the others put together, and Daiyu rose like a black omen of death from Cadmus' side of the valley.

Cori felt all her hope wink out. Daiyu was still on Cadmus' side, and there was no way she'd be able to pull a beast that large from the sky. They were done for. Behind her, the army shifted nervously, and she knew that in a moment they would turn and flee. She was so stupid. She should have listened to Rowan to begin with and just let Cadmus have the realm.

No, a small part of her said, you wouldn't have been safe then either. He still would have come for you. He still would have used you.

You were brave to come here, Cori, Cadmus told her, *and I regret that I have to kill you. I wished you'd joined me instead.*

Daiyu beat her wings and shot towards them.

"Cori," Rowan said weakly. "Do something."

Do what? She wondered.

Her army fell back, leaving her alone atop the ridge. Daiyu's shadow fell over her, and she reached out to the dragon with her Hum.

Daiyu opened her maw and spewed forth a great gout of fire. Cori felt its heat, but behind her, she only heard screams of fear and none of pain. Daiyu had aimed high.

Heart pounding, Cori felt Daiyu's mind finally respond to hers.

Only you know our magic, the dragon told her. Then she spiralled high into the air. Across the valley, Cori saw Cadmus straighten, felt his Hum reach out for his dragon's.

Daiyu went higher and higher until she was a mere speck against the sun, then she turned and dived earthward again. Cori heard her army shouting behind her. She didn't know if they fled or not; she didn't even know where Rowan was; her eyes were on the dragon.

Daiyu pushed a few notes of a song against her mind and Cori obliged, weaving the spell the dragon suggested. Beneath her, the ground rumbled.

Now she could hear the army on the other side of the valley shouting. She saw Cadmus brace his hands on the balustrade, his head turned towards her again. She crouched and pressed her hands against the ground. The earth responded to her touch and the rumbling intensified. Tendrils of her magic seeped into it like roots, a ghostly sensation. Her eyes closed briefly as she surrendered herself to the magic, to the pulsing life that was the earth beneath her feet, then she dug her fingers into the dirt and pulled.

There was a ripping noise, and the ground beneath their feet jolted. She saw many in the army across the way lose their footing and saw Cadmus back away from the edge of the balcony. The earth was moving. The depression of the valley was rising to meet the two ridges, and she was the one pulling it up. Her Hum whirled about her in a controlled tempest. She was strength and power. She was remaking the land. She was levelling the battlefield.

Everyone's attention was on Cori when Daiyu slammed

into one of the other dragons from above. The beast screamed as Daiyu grasped it in her talons, her teeth closing over its neck as her momentum drove the other dragon to the ground that Cori was lifting to meet them. The two dragons struggled in a ferocious, screaming tangle before Daiyu broke the neck of her quarry then used its body as a springboard to launch herself back into the sky.

The dragon's body glowed blue and gold. Cori could feel its life force seeping into the earth beneath her fingers. She finally let go of the ground and the rumbling stopped. She straightened, surveying the now flat battlefield.

Perfect, Cadmus complimented her work, then he attacked her.

She was driven back to her knees under his onslaught, but Rowan was ready. He met Cadmus' attack with his own and their two Hums tangled in a furious battle in her head, Cadmus seeking to control her and Rowan fighting to retain it. She grasped her head, groaning.

Assholes, she managed a thought. She felt dual feelings of amusement from them, then Cadmus withdrew. There was a rumbling beneath her knees again. Had she woven another song? She couldn't hear it in her mind. She opened her eyes and found her army surging around her, running to meet that of Cadmus'.

Rowan grasped the back of her shirt and hauled her to her feet. His lips met hers for a brief moment, then he pushed her forward. "Go," he said hoarsely.

She joined her soldiers as they met the other army in a crash of metal and a spray of blood. Above them, the dragons were locked in battle, their roars and screams overshadowing those of the men below. Cori watched them as she ran. Four against one.

She wove her strengthening song - the one that Daiyu had taught her in the Old Magic - and reached up to take hold of a blue dragon wing. She yanked, twisting as she did to pull the beast away from Daiyu. She underestimated the strength of the Old Magic and ripped the dragon from the sky, slamming it down among the enemy ranks, crushing a contingent of soldiers.

The dragon struggled on the ground, roaring and spewing flames. She saw both Rowan and Adro make a beeline for it. She was ready for the sensation this time as Adro reached the dragon first and touched it. He pulled the energy draining song from Cori's mind as he absorbed the dragon's presence.

Cori immediately wove the song again. They would need it for Cadmus. At the thought of him, she sought the elder on the balcony above them. He wasn't watching the battle, rather his eyes were on the dragons above. Daiyu's betrayal must have come as a shock to him. Was he trying to sway her back to him now? Was he trying to control her?

His attention diverted, Cori wondered if she could pull the balcony down with him on it and kill him that way. She reached up, but the moment he felt her Hum, he countered with his own magic.

The Hiram soldiers around her - her own men and women - turned and attacked. She scrambled back, but they had her surrounded. She was loath to kill her own soldiers, but she couldn't see a way out. More and more of them were turning towards her as Cadmus took control of their minds.

Do something! She told Rowan. He reached out and slammed his mind against Cadmus'. The Hiram around her staggered and cried out, many of them dropping their

CHAPTER FORTY

weapons to clutch their heads as they experienced the furious battle of the two Karalises within them.

Cori pushed through their ranks, trying to get closer to the front line. Daiyu roared overhead and Cori looked up, intending to pull another dragon off of her, but Cadmus attacked.

Cori went to the ground under the agony of the two other Hums in her head. She forced herself up and forward; she couldn't be still in the middle of a battle or she'd be killed. Other Hums hit her mind - more than she could count - and she realised with a flash of dread that Cadmus had directed his Dijem to attack her too.

Once more she hit the ground, skidding along the dirt and curling into a foetal position. She tried to get her barriers up, but there were too many people in her head. Then she felt Adro join in, and Sigrid and Melita. More and more of her own Dijem joined the fray in her mind until she could barely retain her own sense of self.

Get out, she groaned. *Get out, get out, get out.*

Beneath them all she could feel Cadmus forcing Rowan away, almost seizing control... Then she was floating in a black vastness and there was no one else there.

Dead, she thought. I've died. They've killed me.

But the blackness was familiar, and it was confined only to her head. Her body was still connected to the hard earth, and she could still feel the surge of people moving around her. Daiyu, Cori realised, had saturated them all with her Hum to separate them.

Hurry, Daiyu said to her. *Finish it.*

And then she was released. The world returned with a violent clarity. Blood sprayed across her, and soldiers roared. For a moment she couldn't move as she reeled in the aftershock of so many attacking her, then Rowan's Hum slammed into hers, taking control once more.

Too close, he said wildly. *We need to finish this.*

Cori rolled to her hands and knees, realising that there was space around her as someone fought off any who tried to get close. She looked up in time to see Orin bury his axe to the shaft in one of Cadmus' Dijem. He whirled to attack another, then noticed that she was trying to get up. He held out a gore coated hand.

"I have to get to the keep," she told him, looking up to the balcony. She couldn't see Cadmus. One of the blue dragons swooped low over the battle, letting loose a jet of flames. Cori covered her eyes with her arm, feeling the warmth of the fire lick her skin. As the dragon turned skyward again, she opened her eyes to see only a few Dijem in her immediate area; the soldiers who had surrounded them had been reduced to ash and bones, and those on the peripherals of the dragon's attack had been badly burned.

The smell of cooked flesh filled her nostrils, and her stomach heaved. "Come on," she said to Orin, who looked as sickened as she did. She lurched forward, wrenching one of the Dijem before her into the air. With the space made around them by the dragon's attack, Cori could see Rowan and Adro fighting ahead of her.

Both men were surrounded by their dragon's fury and moved at inhuman speeds between opponents. Cori gasped for breath as she tried to move towards them.

Any chance of throwing a dragon down to me so I can move a bit faster too? She asked Daiyu. The black dragon didn't oblige, rather she pushed the notes of another song on Cori's mind. Cori laughed. *Of course there's a song for that.*

She wove it, suddenly feeling a lightness spread through her limbs. She surged forward and away from Orin, her feet barely touching the ground and everyone passing in a blur. It was a sickening feeling to move so fast, as if she'd left her stomach behind. She jerked to a stop before a contingent of Hearthians and slammed them away from her with her strengthening song. Cadmus attacked again.

Stop! She roared at him. *Come and fight us, you coward!*

I'll fight you, another voice said. She whirled to find Kalle approaching. His uniform was free of blood, and he grinned. Cori raised a hand towards him, but someone grasped her wrist, jerking it away. Alarmed, Cori swung and found glazed-eyed Hiram clamouring to get to her, Kalle's Hum spread over them.

"That would not be a fair fight, now would it, Karaliene?" Kalle said, close enough now that she could hear him over the fighting. She ignored him, raising her other hand to blast away the Hiram that held her. More replaced them, grabbing both arms this time, pinning her in place.

"This isn't any sort of fight at all," she growled. Kalle got close enough to grasp her chin. He was still smiling.

"Let's see if I can get your Karalis out of your head. Imagine, me controlling the Karaliene. Ha!"

And to Cori's horror, he snaked into her mind beneath Rowan's awareness.

Rowan! She called, panicked. He'd been preoccupied with fighting, but he returned to her now, dangerous and cold.

Get out, he hissed, slamming the other man from her mind. Before her, Kalle physically reeled. He let go of her chin to rub his head. Cori yanked against her captors, but they held her firm.

"It was worth a try," Kalle conceded, and instead unsheathed his sword. An ungodly roar came from behind her and Cori sighed in relief. Kalle's eyes narrowed. "Ah yes, I remember this bodyguard. I'll be back, Karaliene. Don't die before I can kill you."

And he vanished into the fray as Orin appeared. He hacked at the Hiram who held her, and she got an arm free to blast the rest away.

"Remind me how you survived all these years without me?" He said dryly. She could only shrug as together they threw themselves at the next approaching contingent.

They were close to some of their own Dijem now. She could see Myce fighting with a sword, and Starch further away, wrestling a weapon away from a Hearthian. Sigrid was there too, fighting with a frightened expression alongside her fellow Valkoinens. As Cori watched, a Hearthian broke through their ranks and, with a clean stroke, beheaded Bjarte, the Valkoinen elder.

Cori felt the immediate anguish in the Hums of the Valkoinens, saw a handful of them drop their weapons to race to their elder's body. She forced herself forward to get between the suddenly unarmed Dijem and the Hearthians who were still attacking. They cut down three more Valkoinens before Cori barrelled into Sigrid, pushing her out of the way. She turned, flinging the Hearthians back with her magic.

"He's dead!" she roared at the Valkoinens. "Get up and fight!"

Many seemed comatose with grief, but some, including Sigrid, retrieved their weapons. "With me!" Cori demanded, and they fell in behind her as she forced herself into the

CHAPTER FORTY

enemy ranks. There were so many Hearthians and so few on their side that Cori struggled for a long moment to keep the remaining Valkoinens from being killed.

Finally she got a clear shot to push the closest of their enemies away. Soldiers flew through the air, some landing on their fellows, others hitting the ground and not getting up. She saw Rowan not far away, and when she met his eye, he made a hurrying motion.

When she reached his side, he pointed to the keep. "We need to get up there. You need to make a path."

Cori nodded and raised her hands. The soldiers before them were flung away, creating a gap for them to move into. She pushed again, and again, and slowly, they forced their way towards the keep.

The dragons swooped overhead; Daiyu and her three attackers. One of the blues broke away from the black dragon to shoot flames at the soldiers below. The beast was so wild that it didn't seem to care whether the soldiers were on its side or not. Cori adjusted her aim and pushed the flames back at their maker, engulfing the dragon's head with fire. It roared furiously and with gritted teeth, Cori reached up and grasped its lower jaw with her magic. With a tremendous pull, and a resounding crack, Cori both broke the dragon's jaw and dragged it to the ground.

No one reached it this time - though Rowan tried to push through their enemies - to steal its presence. The dragon slammed into the ground, and with a second crack, its neck broke.

The glow of the dragon returning to the earth threw a strange light across the fighting, giving the whites of people's eyes an eerie cast.

The other three dragons flew by again, and once more, a blue dragon was seized and pulled away from the black. But this time it wasn't Cori.

She looked around wildly to see that several contingents of her own Hiram had banded together to pool their strength and take on the dragon.

"Yes!" She laughed before returning to the enemy before her. Her enthusiasm at her soldier's win was short-lived. Cadmus' army seemed endless; for every contingent that Cori destroyed, two more replaced it. The constant pushing was exhausting her, both physically and mentally.

Rowan grasped her arm and turned her to face him. Blood was sprayed across his vest and his eyes were hard, but she could see he was fatigued too. "Can you make the ground go down?" He demanded. She stared at him and decided he'd gone mad. He gave her a small shake. "With your magic, can you take the ground from under their feet?"

It was worth a try. She cut off her strengthening song and wove the land sculpting song, as Cadmus had once referred to it. Immediately, the ground beneath them trembled and the soldiers before them fell back in alarm and, as the rumbling intensified, many lost their footing.

Cori crouched and pressed her hands against the ground. Rowan went down to one knee beside her, unable to remain upright so close to the epicentre. As she had before, Cori let herself feel the energy of the earth beneath her, let the screams of the dying become a peripheral noise. Then she pushed.

The ground gave way with a ripping, sucking sound and the screams intensified as soldiers fell with it. Cori maintained her focus on the ground, pulling fissures beneath

CHAPTER FORTY

the ranks of the enemy soldiers.

Pull the keep into it, Rowan suggested, and Cori moved the direction of the chasm towards Cadmus' stronghold. The scaffolding shook violently, then fell into the abyss, then the cornerstones of the keep cracked. Cadmus attacked her.

It was a painful attack; one that drove like a knife through her mind. Rowan forced Cadmus back, then put his barriers up around both their minds. It ceased the song, and the soldiers who'd escaped the chasms were able to get to their feet.

Rowan pulled Cori back up and pushed her before him. Adro was nearby, as was Sigrid, Myce and Orin, and the six of them moved quickly towards the keep. Very few soldiers tried to engage them, and they cut down those that did down. They finally reached a door to the keep, and Orin took to it with his axe. Her old friend was caked in so much blood and gore that he was almost unrecognisable. It reminded Cori of their glory days together, when they'd once fought against the Hearthians as Karaliene and Head of Resso.

The door cracked and splintered and Orin kicked it inwards. Rowan let down his barriers so Cori could use her magic again. They found themselves in a spiralling stone stairwell that led both up and down. They climbed, with Cori at the fore. They met several of Cadmus' soldiers on the way and Cori flung them over the railing to hit the dark bottom below.

The room they entered was one that was being renovated, but by the look of the stone dais that had been built on the far side, it was going to be a throne room. Cadmus was there, standing atop the dais with his arms crossed over his chest. Between him and them was a contingent of soldiers, and a dozen Dijem. Their Hums felt foreign, and Cori knew they were Dijem that Cadmus had recruited from the Tundra.

Cori paused, and she felt Rowan behind her, the heaving of his chest brushing against her back. She didn't look at him; she didn't want to know if he was having reservations again at seeing his father. They just had to kill Cadmus, and at that moment, Cori was closest. She'd happily get the job done.

She jumped forward, slamming soldiers away, and the room exploded into battle. She felt the other Dijem's attacks like sharp knives in her mind, and saw Cadmus' arms unfurl as he stepped off the dais. She didn't feel the dragons crash into the roof until it was almost too late. Stone and tin cracked above them and Cori shot her hands up, taking hold of the roof before it could cave in on them all. Holding the ceiling up, though, meant she couldn't move.

The enemy Dijem continued to attack, and she gritted her teeth against it. She couldn't put her barriers up or she'd have to let go of the song that was giving her strength to hold the roof up. Sigrid, Orin, Adro and Myce moved past her to engage the soldiers. Rowan brushed past her too, pausing only to meet her eye and touch her arm. She hoped that wasn't a goodbye.

Don't give up on us, she told him. He didn't respond as he approached the battle. Both he and Cadmus moved towards each other, untouched and unchallenged by those fighting around them. They met in the middle of the room, and father and son reached out to grasp the forearm of the other. Neither drew swords, though both had them on their belts.

The wonderful thing about the energy draining song, Cadmus explained, and Cori knew he was broadcasting his thoughts to everyone in the immediate vicinity. Overhead, the battling dragons slammed into the roof again. Cori's knees almost buckled under the added pressure, but she kept her footing as the dragons took off again. Sweat trickled down her temple. Cadmus continued as if they hadn't been interrupted. *Is that anyone who knows how to use it, can take it from anyone's mind. Whose should I use? Starch, the one who betrayed the song to begin with? Or perhaps from your Advisor over there? Of course, I could always use Cori's. That would be a bittersweet ending.*

Cori let her eyes close briefly. They'd known anyone could use the song, but she had expected Cadmus to use his own Dijem as the power source, not use Rowan's friends against him. It hardly came as a shock though.

Rowan, just kill him, she thought desperately. Yet Rowan just stood there, staring at Cadmus as Cadmus was staring back at him.

Cadmus, Daiyu said, and her dragon's mind fell over them all. *You can make this right. Remember.*

For a heart-stopping moment, Cori thought the dragon had switched sides again. Her vision flickered, and suddenly she was standing over a field of golden wheat. Her peripherals were far wider than they should be, and the colours were impossibly vivid. She realised she was watching one of Daiyu's own memories.

Cadmus stepped into view, a dark-haired woman beside him. Together they watched a boy racing through the wheat, chasing a dog. Cadmus and the woman smiled at each other. The memory faded to another. Cadmus approached Daiyu holding a dark-haired baby tenderly in his arms. He was beaming. "Look Daiyu, a boy! I have a son!" The memory changed again. Cadmus reading to his son, the two of them talking to Daiyu, learning magic together. The recollections shifted through faster and faster until they were a kaleidoscopic blur. Then they slowed. Daiyu was circling high above a sprawling white farmhouse. It was close to dark. Cori could feel Daiyu's confusion; why did Cadmus want this? They loved the boy. The memory was drenched in Daiyu's sadness as she swooped down and set the house alight.

STOP! Rowan's voice. Anguished. Angry.

Cori reeled back into the present. Tears rolled unchecked down her cheeks even as she still held the roof above. Her arms shook under the weight and her head throbbed under the Dijem who still attacked her. She saw Orin take a sword slice to his side, just as he took off the head of one of Cadmus' Dijem. She saw Sigrid gut the soldier who'd cut Orin with a frightened cry. She saw Myce vanish from view under the relentless pushing of a group of Hiram and she saw Adro whirling through the soldiers with his dragon's fury, trying to reach Cadmus and Rowan to finish the fight before Rowan was the one killed.

You can make this right, Daiyu repeated. Cori searched the fray for Cadmus and Rowan. They still gripped each other, and though she couldn't see Rowan's face, she could see his father's.

"I can't do it," Cadmus said to Rowan, and Cori could only just hear his voice above the fighting. He seemed surprised by his own words. "I can't kill you. Not like this. Rowan, ple-"

Rowan's grip on Cadmus' arm tightened and Cori felt the energy draining song ripped from her mind. The gold drained from Cadmus' eyes and his face went slack. Rowan let him go and he slumped back, hitting the floor with a thud. The room fell silent as everyone took in the death of a Karalis, then Cadmus' soldiers fled. Rowan fell to his knees, the heels of his palms pressed to his eyes.

"Get out," Cori said to Adro when he started towards Rowan. "I can't hold the roof much longer."

"I'll take Rowan," Adro said.

"No. Take Myce, if he's still alive. I'll get Rowan."

Adro nodded, then turned and picked up Myce's unconscious body from the floor and heaved it over his shoulder. He motioned to Sigrid, who was supporting Orin, and the four of them left via the stairwell.

"Rowan," Cori said gently. "It's done. We've done it." He lowered his hands from his face and leaned towards Cadmus' body. With a trembling hand, he closes his father's eyes.

"He was going to beg me to let him live," Rowan whispered. Cori's heart broke for him. She wanted to go to him and take him in her arms, but she couldn't.

"I need you to go," Cori told him. Her arms were shaking and dust, and chips of stone rained down around them. Rowan finally looked up at her. "I'll be right behind you," she said to his unasked question. "You have to go."

He pushed himself to his feet and looked down at Cadmus once more. Then he turned and ran to the stairwell. He paused there, though, and looked back to Cori. She nodded at him, then let the roof collapse.

She wove the lightness song that Daiyu had taught her and ran for the balcony, dodging around falling chunks of stone. She gained the balustrade - already crumbling under the stress of the falling roof - and jumped.

The height was massive, and she windmilled her arms

as she fell. Below, she could see that the two armies were still fighting, unaware that one of the Karalises had just been defeated. She wove her strengthening song as she fell, threading it through the lightness one. The songs combined eased her landing, but it was still hard and she staggered, rolling across the dusty ground.

She jumped to her feet and, despite the fighting still before her, elation bloomed within. They'd done it. Cadmus, the bane of her entire existence, was finally dead. They were free to live their lives. Rowan still had control of her mind and, at her exuberance, he returned the feeling, albeit tinged with sadness. It didn't matter, he would heal. They had all the time in the world to heal from this.

She jerked, a ripping sensation tearing through her abdomen, and for a second she thought a dragon had attacked her from the inside. Then she looked down to see the glint of steel poking through her middle. As she stared, it was wrenched back, and blood spurted from her mouth.

A random plunging of blade into flesh, she thought. Citlali was right.

Rowan's scream of horror echoed in her mind. She couldn't feel anything except her own blood drowning her, and all she could see was the blue sky above. Had she fallen back? She didn't remember hitting the ground. Boots shifted nearby. Someone whistled as they walked away. She glimpsed a flash of ice blonde hair.

Cori, don't die! Rowan commanded. Her body seized at the order as it tried and failed to do as he asked. He let her go immediately, but he held on tight to her mind. *Where are you? I can't find you! Just roll your head to the side so I can see where you are, Cori, that's all you need to do. Please!*

CHAPTER FORTY

But she couldn't. She couldn't move her eyes from the sky above. She could hear fighting nearby, but no one passed into her vision.

You know, she said to Rowan, *I've never told you I love y-*

Don't, he begged. *Don't say it now. Not yet. Adro, find her!*

I'm trying, Adro's voice chimed in, though Cori could hear the resignation in it. *I think she's across the chasm. I can't get to her.*

Cori. Cori, stay with me. Somebody find her!

Cori didn't know what to say to him. Rowan was hysterical. She wanted to tell him to be happy, to look after himself, but she couldn't form the words. She was sad that she was dying. This wasn't how it was supposed to end. She wished she'd loved him sooner, that they'd not wasted so much time on arguments.

Back off, man, Adro said gently. *You're overwhelming her.*

Just find her! Rowan responded angrily. He didn't give her space. If anything, his hold on her mind tightened. She should be dead by now. She couldn't feel anything, not the wound through her middle, nor the blood in her lungs. Had it only been minutes that she'd been laying here? It felt like hours, just as it felt like only moments ago she was standing in the streets of Lautan as a nervous apprentice cook under the fierce eyes of the Karalis. *Who are you?* He'd said to her, and that day her life had changed forever.

She could feel tears, though she didn't know if they were hers or Rowan's, so tightly he was holding onto her, unwilling to let her go.

The sky above was fading, darkening under the shadow of the dragon that circled down towards her. Daiyu's mind fell over Cori's, gently pushing Rowan aside so she could no longer feel him.

Close your eyes, Little one, Daiyu told her. *It's time to rest.*

Cori obliged, finally letting her eyelids drift shut as she surrendered to darkness.

Epilogue

Rowan stirred and shifted under the sheets. He knew the room was empty before he opened his eyes. In fact, he'd feigned sleep until Melita and Adro had left. As the door clicked shut behind them, he stared up at the ceiling.

An echoing silence hung around him, and it had nothing to do with the vacant room. He'd become so accustomed to having Cori's thoughts in his head that their absence was jarring. As hard as they'd been to stomach to begin with, the more she accepted his presence, the less she dwelled on the bad memories that she thought he would judge her by.

Her thoughts in the moments when she forgot he was listening were the most beautiful. She saw the world so differently to him, and despite what she thought of herself, her intentions were good and her acts selfless. He would have given up on trying to defeat Cadmus long ago if it hadn't been for her unwavering belief that they would win.

And they had won, though it didn't really feel like a victory. Cadmus had tried to surrender, and Rowan hadn't given him the chance. Thinking about it made his stomach churn. He'd killed his own father when the man had tried to beg for forgiveness. Was Rowan any better than he?

The door opened, and before Rowan could close his eyes again, Adro stepped into the room.

"You're up," he said, closing the door behind him and moving towards the bed. Rowan pushed himself up against the pillows.

"How long?" Rowan asked. He felt groggy and weak.

"It's been a week."

A week. He'd been out longer than he thought. He'd fallen unconscious on the battlefield, following Cori into blackness, unwilling to let her go.

"We didn't find her," Adro whispered. He sat on the edge of the bed, the mattress dipping under his weight. "We searched the whole battlefield after it was done but we didn't find her."

Rowan looked away. He didn't want to talk about it. Thankfully, Adro seemed to understand. He patted Rowan's leg and stood. "I'll send some food up for you."

Rowan slept on and off. He ate the food that was offered and he suffered the people who came to see him. Melita visited often under her role as a healer. Rowan's extended unconsciousness perplexed her when he'd sustained no injuries to cause it. Only once she spoke of Cori.

"We never got along," she said in her usual business-like voice, "but I never wished this on her, or you."

Rowan just stared at her until she left the room. Sigrid dropped by next and Rowan could tell she'd been crying.

"I know why she was the only one for you," she said as she picked at the edge of his blanket. "I couldn't understand at first because she just seemed so plain when really, she surpassed all of us." Well, Rowan couldn't disagree with that.

He lasted twenty-four hours before he couldn't take any more messages of condolence. He had to get away from them all. Adro walked into the room as Rowan was sitting at the edge of the bed, pulling on his boots.

"You're leaving," Adro said.

"You're perceptive," Rowan responded. He pulled on his second boot and stood, shouldering his pack. Adro crossed his arms over his chest.

"Do you think it's wise to be alone right now?"

"Actually, I think that's exactly what I need."

"And the realm? You're just going to abandon the throne?"

"Adro, you knew this was only temporary. I never wanted to be the Karalis. I did my duty and look where it got me. I killed my father and Cori is… gone." He sighed, looking towards the door. "If you want the throne, take it. You'd make a far better Karalis than I, and if you don't want it, then give it to Orin. Goodness knows he kept the realm afloat for a lot of years while Cori was tearing it apart."

Adro stared at him with a hard expression, and Rowan wondered if he would have to force his way past his friend. Adro finally stepped aside. "I'll walk you out," he said.

They went side by side through the halls of the keep in Bandar Utara. Servants passed them, but thankfully Rowan saw no one he knew until they reached the throne room. Orin was there, sitting on the throne. He watched Rowan and Adro approach, then finally stood, stepping to the side of the throne as decorum dictated when the Karalis was in residence.

For a long moment none of them spoke. Orin had every reason to hate him for how he'd treated Cori, and there was nothing Rowan could say right now to change that. Instead, he held out his hand; a peace offering. Orin hesitated, then extended his own hand, completing the shake.

"It's a funny thing," Orin mused, "having forever in front of you and nothing to take you through it."

"Something will come up," Rowan responded. "It always does."

He turned away then, and with Adro at his side he left the keep. He found a stable boy waiting with Mischief, as he'd requested earlier before Adro had sprung him trying to leave. He took the reins of his stallion and thanked the boy.

"You'll reach out when Shaan has the baby?" Rowan requested as he smoothed a hand down Mischief's neck. Adro nodded.

"Where will you go?" He asked, hands in pockets as he watched Rowan tie his pack onto the back of the saddle. Rowan took a moment to decide how much to tell Adro. Finally, he turned away from the horse to face his friend.

"I thought I might go south to Dodici. Cori always wanted to go somewhere warm when all of this was done."

Adro gave him a pitying look, and Rowan was disappointed. Normally he could rely on Adro to understand his implied messages. They shook hands in farewell and Adro started back up the stairs. Rowan turned back to Mischief and checked the buckles on the saddle one last time. Behind him, he heard Adro suddenly laugh as he finally understood the true meaning behind Rowan's words. Rowan smiled and started towards the gates, Mischief at his side.

As he walked, he let his Hum span across the city. He felt the other Dijem there; the few surviving Valkoinens, half the number of Sarkans than there had been before this had all started and most of the Uaines. He also felt numerous weaker Hums, all contained to the eastern side of the city where the prisons were. It seemed Adro had contained all the Dijem Cadmus had created after the battle had ended. Rowan didn't know what his friend planned to do with them all, but if anyone would work it out, it was Adro.

He reached the gates - still a crumbled mess from Cori's attack on it - and passed through to the bridge. He waited until he was at the top of the arch before he spread his Hum further, pressing it across the realm that, less than an hour ago, had been his. He'd so easily given it away, and he didn't regret that decision at all. Even now, he struggled to muster the will to care what happened to it. All he wanted to do was leave and not return for a very long time.

He allowed himself to touch all the life around him, then he lifted his Hum as high as he could, far beyond the awareness of any Dijem in the city behind him. Few could go as high as he. His father had been one, and in the past year they'd occasionally crossed paths as they'd both reached over the realm. Neither had spoken to the other; that would require them to come closer to the earth and put themselves in the vicinity of others who may have been listening. Rowan wished they had spoken though. He wished he'd asked Cadmus why he'd killed Rowan's mother, asked if dominance was worth it.

The other Hum that soared as high as his was Daiyu's, and it was her presence that he touched now. The dragon had surprised him with her change in allegiance, as well as her extensive knowledge in the Old Magic. Her teaching methods put him in mind of the way his father had taught him as a child, and a little of the way he had taught Cori. He'd discovered the songs of the Old Magic weren't just for those who possessed both mental and physical abilities as Cadmus had led him to believe. Of course, having both skills made the magic more potent, but someone as strong as Rowan could wield the mental songs just as effectively.

The key is to hold the soul, the dragon had explained. *The body - all bodies of all creatures - are resilient vessels. When trauma is experienced, it is the soul that tries to escape, and that is when the body dies.*

And so Daiyu had held Cori's mind while Rowan had healed her body with an older, stronger variation of the healing song. It had been a difficult process, made even more evident by the time it had taken. He'd had to remain unconscious to maintain the link with Daiyu, who served as the physical link to Cori. To make the situation even stranger, Cori had been present throughout the entire process. It had helped in a way. Her dry jibes at him whilst he'd painstakingly put her back together had been a reminder that it was worth it, that he was saving her.

Daiyu acknowledged Rowan's touch, then withdrew, revealing the mind he was really seeking. Her Hum had strengthened with the use of the Old Magic, but within it he still felt the youthful freedom he'd first been drawn to, a wildness that was hers alone and that no one else could touch.

She reached back towards him and as the notes of their Hums intertwined; he smiled. For a moment there he was sure he'd lost her, and it had scared him even more than all the other things he'd been afraid of during the war. But magic had saved them once more. This time their duty was done and now all the time left in the world was for them. Cori gave him a mental nudge akin to a poke in the ribs, drawing him from his thoughts and back to her.

Come and find me, she laughed.

Bonus Chapter - The Dragon's Cove

Her feet pounded across the sand, flicking grit up behind her. Calves searing, she forced herself onwards until her hand slapped the rock at the end of the beach. She whirled, racing back the other way.

Sweat dripped down her brow and spine and her muscles screamed in protest. Overhead, Daiyu rode the currents in lazy circles.

He's coming, the dragon informed her.

Cori knew already. She could feel him approaching. It was the reason she was running herself into exhaustion, otherwise the anticipation might kill her.

It had been a month since Cadmus' defeat. A month in which Cori had been waiting on the Dodici beach with Daiyu. At first, passing the time had been suffocating. But slowly she found a calming rhythm in her own company - a space in which she could slowly recover from the trauma of the war.

Daiyu remained with her, and though at first Cori hadn't understood why, she'd eventually come to the realisation that Daiyu needed space to heal too.

But Rowan was coming now, having travelled non-stop all the way from Resso to find her, and Cori was desperate for him.

Daiyu rose higher. *I can see him,* she informed Cori, then

abandoned her circling and shot inland. Cori jerked to a stop, dragging in great lungfuls of air, stomach twisting in anticipation. She didn't follow the dragon, however. First she went to the ocean, plunging into the chill waves, clothes and all, to wash the sweat from her body.

Beneath the surface she was engulfed in silence. The gentle bay currents swirled against her and miniscule bubbles of air danced away.

She was desparate to see Rowan, and yet nerves ate at her. She hadn't seen him since he'd killed Cadmus. Since she'd been stabbed with a sword through the back. Since he'd brought her back to life.

The battle was a haze in her memory - long periods of blood and sweat, spiked with sharp moments of adrenaline and clarity. That didn't stop it from haunting her dreams every night.

When her lungs tightened, demanding air, she kicked off from the bottom and resurfaced. She tread water, allowing her body to flow with the gentle swell of the waves, turquoise against white sands. On the horizon, dark clouds brewed. Daiyu had told her it would rain today. She hadn't believed her.

Finally she turned and struck out for the shoreline. Jagged peaks and smooth bluffs of rock encircled the beach, making access difficult at the same time as providing a sturdy shelter from the elements. It was a beach Cori had visited often when she'd been weaving her Deathsong. The stillness of the cove against the ever-rushing waves had been cathartic in a time when her mind had been in a constant state of turmoil.

She trudged across the sand, each step leaving an imprint of her foot behind her. She'd sourced other clothes from a township about an hour's walk away - half that if she used the lightness song to run - and she changed into them now; dry pants and a loose shirt. For a few moments she busied herself rearranging the few things in her pack, checking the rations she had within, then she slung her wet clothes over a rock to dry.

Daiyu returned then, gliding over the beach, her shadow throwing dark ripples across the water. The dragon tilted and came to land on one of the bluffs, roaring a joyous welcome. Heart lurching, Cori took off, climbing the rugged track to the bluffs with inhuman speed. She gained the top by Daiyu's front claws and wind whipped her hair back from her face.

She watched Rowan approaching, galloping down the dirt road on Mischief, feeling just a little apprehensive.

Horse and rider got close enough that Cori could see his face, then Mischief baulked at the dragon, spinning away. As agile as a cat, Rowan dove from the saddle, running the last few feet. His gold eyes shone, and his hair was windswept. Cori couldn't help the grin that pulled the corners of her lips.

Rowan skidded to his knees before her, arms circling her waist and head pressed to her stomach. She steadied herself and brushed a hand over his hair and he sobbed, his whole body shaking.

"Hey," she whispered, tears pricking her own eyes. He held her tight, and his fingers dug into her back. "You did great," she told him. He wept harder, and from him she felt sadness, but also relief. It was over. They'd both come out the other side of the war that had consumed five hundred years of her life and even more of his. She took his hands, releasing them from her waist so she could crouch down before him. With one hand she cupped his face, tracing his stubble, soaking in his warmth, memorising every inch of his face. His eyes were rimmed red, but they held her gaze and he smiled.

"You did great," she said again, touching her forehead to his. He laughed lightly - a sound of absolute relief - then placed his hands on her face, drawing her in for a kiss.

A hot blast of air hit them and Rowan started, looking aside at Daiyu who had extended her snout towards them. Cori - used to the dragon's quirky traits now - raised a hand, pressing it to the dragon's nose. Rowan mimicked her.

"Thank you," he told Daiyu earnestly. "For saving her."

Cori felt a lump form in her throat and tears threatened to fall again. How had they gotten so lucky?

Daiyu didn't respond, instead she exhaled another hot breath - affection, Cori decided - then spread her wings and launched into the sky.

Cori shielded her eyes from the dust stirred by Daiyu's departure, and followed the dragon's rise to resume her lazy circling of the beach. Slowly, her gaze returned to Rowan. He was already watching her, and when he had her attention, he flung his arms around her again, crushing her against his chest.

"Gerroff!" She pushed at him but he merely laughed and tightened his hold.

"Never," he said. "You are staying right here until the end of eternity."

She got hold of his wrists, applying magical pressure to free herself. "I'd love that," she gasped, smoothing down her hair. "Just make sure I can breathe though." She rose, pulling him up. "Come on, I'll show you the cove."

She helped him unsaddle Mischief and they let the stallion free to roam the bluff, then they picked their way down the treacherous track to the beach. The sun slipped away behind the dark clouds that boiled closer.

They walked along the beach to the overhang Cori liked to use for shelter and they settled into it as a chill gust of wind hit them. "This," she gestured wide, taking in the calm bay, the dramatic storm building, the crescent of white sand and the jagged, rocky bluffs, "is my cove."

Rowan's arm crept around her shoulder and he pressed his lips to her hair, breathing deeply. Cori closed her eyes briefly, allowing the ebb and flow of nature to ground her, to twine her Hum through his. For a long, still moment she relished that they were no-one. Not the Karalis and Karaliene, not destroyers or warlords or saviours of Tauta.

The first drops of rain splattered down on the rocks above. Daiyu glided down, alighting on the beach with a thud that sent tremors through the ground. She settled down, head resting on her front claws, much like a cat.

Rowan watched the dragon, his expression unreadable. His arm remained around Cori, though, and his posture was calm. Cori watched him, her heart so full it hurt. She bumped his knee with hers, just as the rain began to fall in earnest, and he turned his head to look at her.

"I love you," she said, and the smile that lit up his features was beautiful. He leaned in, their breaths mingling, his lips brushing lightly over hers.

"I love you too."

About the Author

You can connect with me on:
- http://www.emilylk.com
- http://www.tiktok.com/thepagesshewrote
- http://www.instagram.com/thepagesshewrote

Also by Emily L K

The Archmage (Mages Of Might Series)
n this world, strength is noticed, strength is feared, strength is punished.

Desperate to fund a Healer for her dying mother, Illusionist Tsillah tricks her way into an apprenticeship with a visiting Archmage by pretending to be an elementalist. When she learns that the Archmage intends for her to compete on the circuit - a fierce competition for combat mages - Tsillah is desperate enough to try the unthinkable - she teaches herself to wield fire to become a dual wielder, a practice outlawed by the High Magus. Certain she'll be executed on the spot when she's found out, she discovers that her Archmage and his other apprentice have some world altering secrets of their own. If you love show stopping magic, high stakes tournaments and a heroine desperate to stay alive, you'll love this first instalment of the Mages of Might series.